To Janet

Best wishes,

Freda Bowman.

A Question of
Choice

A Question of Choice

Freda Bowman

First published in Great Britain in 2014 by

Bannister Publications Ltd
118 Saltergate
Chesterfield
Derbyshire S40 1NG

ISBN 978-1-909813-09-0

A catalogue record for this book is available from the British Library

Typeset in Palatino Linotype by Escritor Design, Chesterfield, Derbyshire

Printed and bound in Great Britain by Peppermint Press Ltd
Clay Cross, Derbyshire

Acknowledgements

My love and thanks to Bob for his unfailing support and encouragement.

To Pam for her careful study of the text.

To Anne B. for her artistic skill in the creation of the cover design.

Sometimes I stand for a while beside his grave. A simple affair, just along from the village chapel. Hidden, almost, at the end of a narrow, rough pathway. I imagine there are few who know of its existence.

He could, of course, have made arrangements for something grander, more public. But it comes as no surprise to me that he lies quietly here. It was the graves of others – lost, ancient others – that obsessed him; he would have no interest, none whatever, in his own.

Eighteen sixty-one, he died, so the words on the tomb inform me. Not that I need any words to be aware of that. Or to know that it was August. On the twenty-eighth day. Very early in the morning.

The course of my life crossed his, *collided* with his. Though it should never have been so. Would not have been so, in all probability, but for what happened to my mother.

I was nineteen, at that time......

1

Pa was blunt, as could have been predicted. He told me I could have done a great deal better for myself, and he was right. There was no doubt I could have done *better*, but it would have taken time. I was determined and impatient to leave, and believed there was good enough reason for it.

I doubt if he ever said such a thing to my sisters. Neither he nor they would have expected anything much out of the ordinary to come their way, even though, by some irony, they had all been given fancier names than mine. Especially the two closest to me in age – Alice and Edwina. Those are names that suggest good breeding, that could sit comfortably on daughters of the wealthy and privileged. Alice and Edwina were not well bred, being the offspring of an illiterate mill worker and his down-trodden wife. But they were decent girls, loyal and good-hearted, and that judgment could still be made of them now, as aging women.

Even Fanny, some years younger than the three of us, had a slightly more arresting name than mine, provided it took its proper form of *Frances*, as Ma always tried to insist on. To everyone else, in the family or outside, she has never been anything but Fanny. Frances did not suit her; it simply did not sit well.

My own name happens to be Mary Ann. Not too bad if both bits are included, but even Ma would forget to do that. So I was just plain *Mary*, one of a good few in the village. As a child, I dismissed the name as dull, and despite the assurance of a devout Sunday School teacher, remained unimpressed by its holy connection.

Later, though, it struck me that the ordinariness of being a *Mary* might be one of life's balances, a sort of strike for fairness. For by the age of twelve or so, perhaps earlier, it was becoming clear that not only was I the most attractive of the girls, but also the cleverest, and both of these things by some distance. So it seemed reasonable not to expect an appealing name into the bargain.

We do have another sister – Marguerite – much younger even than Fanny. *Marguerite* – whose name was chosen by Ma months before she was born – is also suggestive of a certain style. Our mother was convinced – rightly as it turned out – that she would bring into the world yet another girl.

For a while, I think, we put blame on Marguerite; in Fanny's case, perhaps for a long while. Understandable, in the circumstances, but we were wrong. How can anyone be held responsible for being dragged into the world? Nobody chooses it. I felt no affection for my sister at first, but even the day she was born I saw that guilt lay squarely on the shoulders of another.

Pa knew all too well that our mother was not strong, that indeed she had become frail, prone to long bouts of unwellness. So was it wise to be bearing yet another child at the age of forty-four? I should mention that we girls have two older brothers, who had taken more than they wanted from Pa by that time and left home. And there had been others – twin girls – who were born much too soon and died the same day. It is difficult for me to recall, now, just when. The two of them share a tiny, unmarked grave in the churchyard.

By the time Marguerite was about to be born, our mother – a small, delicately framed woman – was physically spent. During the long and terrible time in which her body laboured, she began to bleed; a bleeding that could not be stopped. The wretched midwife, convinced that both of them would soon be lost, used all her strength to wrench the baby out. Mrs Booth was not a young woman, nor a skilful one, so I suppose we should be grateful that she managed that, at least. But Ma she failed to save. To this day, my memory of it all remains vivid, terrible.

Aside from Ma and old Mrs Booth, there was only me in the house. During a long, agitated morning I found myself standing about, impatient to help, too overwrought to deal with other tasks.

'What can I do? Please just tell me what to *do*,' I begged of Mrs Booth, for it was an ordeal to remain useless in the face of my mother's pain.

'Nothing yet, dear, nothing yet,' the weary voice replied. 'I'll need you soon enough. Stay where you can hear me, that's all.'

And at last I did hear her; could hardly fail to catch the rough yelp of her voice.

'Get yourself downstairs now, girl! I'll need that water warmed.' I had long ago been out to the pump with a couple of buckets.

Carrying out the mundane task came as a relief, but not one that was to last long. My pan of water was barely on the fire's iron plate when the screech was for 'Rags! Be quick with them!' Her sharp tone of panic sent through me a sudden, cold spike of fear.

I rummaged through the ancient wardrobe that served as a cupboard for both clothes and cloths, throwing its contents haphazardly to the floor and seizing anything that might be used as a rag. Ma, I saw just moments later, was leeching blood, a shocking amount of it.

'You'll not want this bed fouled!' Mrs Booth announced, with touching concern for the unimportant. 'It's a decent bed. You'll not want it ruined.'

'I don't care tuppence for the bed!'

Between rag and water errands, I attempted to reassure and comfort Ma, wiping the sweat from her face, stroking her thin hands. Telling her all would be well.

But all was not well; I knew it was not. Ma was becoming weak, incapable even of sipping the water I put time and again to her colourless, dry lips. Feeble mutterings of '*please... help me*' were as good as drowned out by Mrs Booth's loud commands.

'Push! Come on, dear, now come *on*! I can *see* the child, at long last. It's there. In the name of *God*, dear – just *push*!'

Since there was no strength left to obey, the instruction was pointless. Ma's child was almost into the world, but she could do nothing more to aid it. Mrs Booth, though, now found a ferocious energy. I was dimly aware of an order screamed at me, heard her shout oaths into the air. And after a short time of nothing further occurring, I watched as she forced her blooded hands into Ma's body.

There was a strange, sickening squelch as she grasped at the baby and dragged it forth.

Clutched in Mrs Booth's fingers was a limp, wrinkled creature, as bloody as her hands. It made no sound. This lifeless thing was shaken with some violence, held upside down by its ankles, its wet body slapped almost viciously. I stood and watched, rigid.

When, at long last, there came a high, wailing cry, I doubt if Ma heard it. She was still taking shallow breaths but her eyes were closed and her face a damp, deathly grey. She was never to glimpse the child that moments later was shoved against her breast.

Just a few minutes after that, Mrs Booth told me that Ma was dead. With an expansive sigh, she squeezed me on both shoulders, slowly shaking her head as if in a state of sad disbelief. Then the head stilled and she seemed to gather herself, releasing her grip on me. She straightened up, and with disturbing briskness retrieved the complaining baby and began to wrap it in an old bit of blanket from her basket.

'It's a terrible sadness, dear, a terrible sadness for you all. The *poor* lady. But I shall try my very best to get things sorted out for this little girl, dear. That's something I think I might be able to do for you.'

I remained still, staring at her with what must have seemed utter blankness.

'There's a woman I know, dear, lives quite close to me. You might know her yourself – a Mrs Spence, it is. Well, I think she might be willing to nurse the child, you see, for just a very small payment. Along with one of her own.' I imagine she still saw nothing in my face.

'She's a very decent woman. A *Christian* woman,' Mrs Booth continued, as if the latter point might be of particular importance to me. 'And you see, the baby will stand a much better chance, dear, if I take her there straight away.' She looked quizzically at me, waiting for a response that did not come.

'Trying to force milk down its throat any other way just doesn't work, dear. Do you understand what I'm saying to you? They nearly always die, believe me.'

I did believe her, though at that moment the matter was of little concern.

'Just put that shawl round my shoulders, will you? There's a good girl.'

I obeyed, reaching for her mangy shawl, but then hesitated, my mind beginning to grope its way towards thought again. I saw she was about to walk out of our house and leave me alone.

'But are you going *now*, without laying my mother out?'

'Well, the baby's hunger must come first, now mustn't it? Your poor mother's passed away and sadly there was nothing that could be done about it. I tried my very best for her, as the good Lord knows, but it wasn't to be… though at least the child's alive and well; let's thank God and my strong hands for that!'

She beamed at me, with some pride. 'And now she needs to be fed, and that's what I shall see to.' She placed a hand back on my shoulder. 'Surely you can wash down your own mother, put a clean sheet around her? That's all there is to it. You're twenty years old, aren't you dear, or near enough? Don't tell me you and your sisters can't be left to cope with that!'

I muttered assent, for it was clear this was a task she did not want and had decided she had good enough reason to avoid. And the baby's unremitting, high-pitched cries felt like shards of glass inside my head. I felt resentment towards the tightly wrapped bundle, now clutched against a stout body that reeked of staleness and sweat, and bitterness towards the woman who had failed to keep my mother alive. All at once I wanted them both to go; a wish that was granted swiftly and without apology.

I could not allow myself to shed tears. They would delay what needed to be done; may have reduced me to not managing the task at all, and it was one that I faced alone. Edwina lived a good mile away and was not far off giving birth again herself. The scene here was not something she should be asked to witness.

Fanny had left the house before six o'clock that morning and would not be home until dusk. Poor Alice had dissolved into uselessness as soon as Ma's labour, which had grinded on from the early hours of morning, became acute. As cries of anguish filled the house, Alice had put her hands to her ears and rushed away in distress.

'Oh, *poor* Ma! I can't bear it, I just can't *bear* it!' was her tearful declaration before she rushed out of the door and disappeared down the street. I did not hold it against her. Alice's nature was a kinder, more generous one than my own, and she would find it hard to forgive herself.

I wondered where she might be, by this time. Perhaps around the area of the mill yard, on the lookout for Pa? She would be hoping that when they returned, all would be calm. That Ma would be sitting up in her bed, cradling some tiny, wrinkled thing. Exhausted but content.

That room had to be made less dreadful before Alice entered it. It seemed a pity that accomplishing this would hide the awfulness from Pa, for I had no desire whatever to protect *him*. I would have had him inhale the sharp stench of exhaustion, take in the sight of blood-soaked rags littering the floor. I wanted him to feel Ma's pain and despair. There was no reason on earth, to my mind, why he should be spared.

But such things could not be left to accost Pa's senses. My poor mother needed to be washed and cared for, to be put at her ease and into a dignified state. I braced myself to do these tasks for her.

A part of me shrank from it; I longed to escape, to rush out into the fresh air and weak sunshine. But courage would be harder to find after even a brief respite, so instead I headed downstairs, donned Ma's largest apron and added a handful of sticks and a few bits of coal to the remaining hot embers in the grate. Then I filled an iron pot with water and put it on to heat, before rooting in the back of the cupboard for yet more bits of clean cloth. They were not to be found, every last one having already been put to use. I did not dare to tear up clothes, for they would be hard to replace.

Something else came to mind. Taking an old, cumbersome pair of scissors – the ones Ma used for cutting garments into rags when not a day's more wear remained in them – I went up to the bed I shared with Alice and Fanny and started to cut out three large squares from the top of our sheet. These would have to be my washcloths. The remaining part of the sheet, which was well patched but not noticeably stained, would serve as a winding cloth. We could manage without such a thing on the bed for now. There was still a blanket, though it was likely to chafe.

Having retrieved the pot and struggled with it – yet again – up the stairs, I returned to the heavy, sour atmosphere of Ma and Pa's room. Years ago Pa had separated this space from where my sisters and I slept, fixing up a makeshift divide of rough wooden board. It provided privacy of a sort, though the board did not seal at the corners and was a poor barrier against sound. Until his throaty snores could be heard, we would talk in low voices and take great care in what we said. Pa had always seemed less concerned about anything that might be heard by us in return.

I did not begin the task of washing Ma's body quite yet. Crawling beneath that ancient bed, which sagged almost to the floor, I salvaged from the dust and fluff a small, battered, wooden box that I knew contained her few treasures, her *bits*, as she called them. As young children, we had sometimes been allowed to look inside, and I recalled that among several cheap trinkets lay a delicate bracelet made from tiny beads of black marble. Quite precious, Ma had once proudly claimed, though where it came from we never knew, and nor do I remember her ever wearing it. It seems unlikely to have been given to her by Pa. Had it been passed down from his mother, Ma would surely have told us, and would have worn it on occasions to please him.

The bracelet, I decided, would now be placed around her wrist, where it would lie hidden beneath the winding sheet. It was the only pretty thing that Ma possessed, and I had once wondered if it had been given to her by some man who perhaps thought much of her long ago. At a time before she made the ill-judged decision to marry Pa. All sorts of ideas had weaved their way round my head as to who he was and why the two of them must have parted. Silly romantic nonsense, no doubt; the sort of thoughts young girls are prone too, though I did not remain prone to such fanciful notions for long. But if nothing else, burying the thing with her would save arguments among my sisters as to who should be the one to have it.

I could have decided to save the bracelet for Marguerite; that would have been the kindest decision. If she lived, then she was destined to grow up without Ma's care and love, without a single memory of her. It might have been a comfort to possess such a thing. There was no chance of it, though, for I have to admit that the good of my newly born sister was nowhere in my mind.

I began to wash Ma's body with care, using the folded cloth in a soft, dabbing motion. It seemed important that she should be treated in this gentle way, after the wretched pain she had suffered. Twice I returned downstairs to heat more water. Progress was slow, and I hoped Alice would not return before the task was done.

The dreadful bleeding seemed to have stopped, but I was unsure whether a dead person could continue to lose blood or not, or if it might somehow start again. For safety, I cut another large piece from the sheet, folded it into a thick wodge and placed it between her thighs. Then I began to wrap the makeshift winding cloth around her; a task that did not prove as challenging as might be thought, for although slimly built I was not lacking in strength. And despite the all too recent pregnancy, Ma weighed pathetically little.

This done, and the room cleared of its unpleasant debris, I escaped outside at last, perching on the front steps and gratefully drinking in fresh air. No-one seemed to be about in the street, an unusual absence for which I was thankful, for I did not feel ready to convey the terrible news and had not yet found anything to cover our windows. Despite the distressing task of the last hour or two, Ma's death was not real to me.

I lost track of how much time went by. Could not recall, later, if others had appeared in our street and whether I must have acknowledged them in some way, if only with a nod. Certainly I talked to no-one. At some point I got up and picked a few handfuls of flowers, using the large square pockets of Ma's apron to store them. In those years, wild flowers grew in small clumps on a rough strip of grass down the middle of the street.

Slowly, I climbed back up the steep stairs to the bedroom, trying not to drop the best of the blooms, which were cupped in my hands. These were laid carefully on the sheet that covered poor Ma; the rest I scattered on the bed around her.

They would not stay nice for long, but no matter .The scene, as I looked back on it from the doorway, now struck me as fresh, colourful. Almost pretty.

2

Alice and Pa arrived back together. She looked exhausted, her plump face blotchy and her hair bedraggled. At some time during the long tramp she had gone to the old mill yard and been spotted by Pa, who had shouted out to know what was going on. Alice, I heard later, had burst into tears – a not infrequent thing. She told him things were not well, that Ma was in terrible pain, that there was no sign of the child. He must have felt he had no choice but to accompany her home. Being in charge of other packers and shifters gave him an occasional freedom they did not have.

As the two of them approached I was again sitting outside, perched on the highest of three steps leading up to the door. Alice must at once have suspected the worst, for I did not shout or wave, but merely stared towards them. As she ran from Pa's side in her haste to reach me, I stood up, my arms stretched out to her.

Tears began to rise in me at last, though nothing like the howls of anguish that came from Alice. Raw outpouring of emotion has never been a part of my nature. At times I have wished for it to be, for I think a certain relief can be had that way.

I did not so much as glance at Pa, let alone attempt to touch him. He stood quite still, looking at us, for several moments, then without speaking turned towards the door and pushed it open with his boot. It banged against the wall inside. For a moment he seemed to hesitate, unsure, and I had a strong sense of his reluctance to enter the house. But he knew he must, and even above the dreadful sounds from Alice, I heard a creaking as heavy, mud-laden boots mounted the wooden staircase. Any moment now, he would have to open the door to *that* room.

Taking Alice's hand I led her inside and closed the front door behind us, reluctant to have a group of neighbours gathering outside. It would not be long before someone noticed our strange behaviour. Very likely it had happened already.

He cannot have stayed in the room for more than a minute or so; it is possible he did not go further than the doorway. I soon heard the sound of our own bedroom floor, followed by the creak of someone sitting down heavily upon the bed. After that it seemed he did not move again for a good while, and we did nothing to disturb him. I sat Alice on an old mat near the fire and prepared her a drink of tea, sweetening it more than usual. Exhaustion had reduced her to sobs, but as yet she was quite unable to speak.

'The baby's alive,' I said, placing the cup beside her. 'It's a girl. The mid-wife's taken her away. She knows a woman who can look after her for a while.'

Alice shook her head, before burying it again in her arms.' I don't care,' was all she managed, at length.

Neither did I. I sat down with her on the mat and we leaned into each other, my arm around her slumped shoulders.

'*Drink* it,' I urged several times, but the tea could no longer have had any warmth in it by the time she tried.

When Pa finally reappeared, his face was grey and expressionless. He sat himself in his usual chair at the fire and stared morosely ahead. By then I was busying myself with bowls and spoons and said nothing whatever to him. It was a while before he turned towards me.

'Anything to eat?' The question was muttered, barely audible.

'I'm warming a bit of potato broth.'

Alice moved to crouch, in misery, beside him. She held a hand against her nose, which was dripping.

'I don't want anything', she said quietly. She leant her head against Pa's knee but he made no move to comfort her.

'You *must*,' I replied. 'You've eaten nothing all day, you've walked for miles, you're likely to faint if you don't eat. It's a wonder you haven't already. Ma would want you to eat, Alice.'

That particular encouragement proved a mistake, as her distress instantly returned to its more strident form. I put a bowl of thick broth on the stone floor beside her and lodged a hunk of dark, crusty bread in her hand.

'Now eat it,' I said.

Pa's bowl and bread I put down without a word. I had no interest in whether it was consumed or not, but he reached for the bowl at once and began to slurp his way

through the stuff with noisy enthusiasm, before demanding a refill. As always, he tore his bread into bits and
dropped them into the thick liquid. Pa's teeth had never
been good; by then several were missing and others loose.

Afterwards he sat very still once again, staring towards
the fire. Alice, who had finally been persuaded to eat – and
with surprising appetite when started – was also still, her
head resting yet again on his knee. Of us all, she had
always been closest to Pa, I the least so. The others seemed
a matter of indifference to him. It was only Alice who ever
received an occasional, brief glance of affection from those
sour, discontented features.

Looking at them, I wondered if she saw Pa as guilty in
any way. It seemed doubtful. At not quite eighteen, Alice
remained oddly innocent. It is possible she believed Ma
was carrying because she longed for one last child, as some
women – though few, I imagine – seem to as they enter *that*
time of life. Perhaps she imagined that Pa, concerned
about the danger, had complied only with reluctance.

I did not nurse such fantasies. Ma was dead because it
had never so much as crossed Pa's mind to deny himself
what was his *right*. Though it is likely that Ma believed it
to be his right as well. My wakefulness had taught me
things it would have been better not to have known, one of
them being that after a few ales he became coarser even
than usual. Alice and Fanny were fortunate in being
sounder sleepers than I was. And perhaps they were less
willing to think badly of him, readier to accept Ma's soothing reassurances.

In my mind, he may as well have seized a kitchen knife
and attacked her with it, for his responsibility seemed no

less. But this was not a death for which he could be tried or condemned. All but me, in family, village and mill, would feel for him a simple, untangled sympathy.

I did not intend to share my views with Alice; they would distress her and she would never be persuaded to share them. Nor did I want her to, for the thoughts were not comfortable ones.

Though I also saw that Alice's affection for Pa could be something of a blessing for me. Surely it would make leaving easier? Because the thought of continuing to live in that house, under *his* roof, now struck me as something I could no longer bear to do.

Such a thought must seem odd, inexcusable even, given the grief that hung over all of us. I was jolted out of it by the creaking chair and wheezy breathing occasioned by Pa slowly heaving himself to his feet. Alice, raising her head from his knee, looked at him with wide, damp eyes.

'I'll be off for a drink then. I'll need to let people know what's happened.'

The whites of Pa's eyes were bloodshot; his face struck me for the first time as startlingly old. Damp soup stains were visible down the front of his rough working clothes. For just a second I felt something dangerously close to pity, a sentiment that needed to be quickly squashed. I stared at him, without expression.

'I'll see the Reverend first thing tomorrow. I've no stomach for it now, and it's late, anyway.'

Neither of us made a reply.

'We'll do her proud enough,' he added, perhaps seeing distress break into Alice's features once again.

'Fanny will be back any time now,' I told him, aware that her imminent arrival was unlikely to delay his departure.

Fanny would be returning home from a large house on the fringe of the village, where only recently she had been taken on as scullery maid. Their usual girl had fallen ill and been packed off to her family to recover. An old neighbour, once in service there, had put in a good word and Fanny was taken on for a couple of months. Horrified at the thought of a strange bed, she pleaded to sleep at home, even though it meant leaving by five each morning. For the moment, the family had agreed.

It was plain that Fanny hated the work, but at least she was fed and earned a small wage. Not to be sneezed at, since the knitting frames in the attic were providing us with precious little in the way of income. Home knitted stockings were no longer in demand, it seemed. Nothing produced in a home was much in demand, for factories up in the North could now make all manner of things better and cheaper. Somehow, Pa managed to find an ill-tempered, perverse pleasure in this. Without him, he took pains to point out, we would be half-starved and in rags. He may have been right. Yet another reason why the arrival of a new child was unwelcome.

'You'll need to tell her what's happened, then,' he informed us. 'She'll be all right with you two. And make sure you all get yourselves off to bed early. I'll be sleeping in the chair down here, once I'm back.'

Of course he would. His own bed was occupied.

Only after Pa had closed the door behind him did I realise he had asked nothing at all about the child, and that neither of us had once thought to mention her.

3

Sometime during the hour or two before dawn, tears and exhaustion finally dragged Alice and Fanny into a restless sleep. I was spent also, but no sleep came to relieve me, for the image of Ma was vivid. Grief and anger vied for position and my only defence against them was to engage in battle with another problem. That of leaving the house.

It so happened that a means had been given to me, and only weeks ago. I had rejected this means, laughed it off as something not worthy even of the briefest consideration. But now I looked again; started to give it the thought it had not merited before.

I had been the recipient of a marriage proposal. The ungracious recipient of a tongue-tied, inarticulate offer made by Tom Mason, a Cromford man who worked on the canal. A full ten years older than me, not noticeably handsome and without the least skill in conversation, Tom was affable and good-hearted. He had been known to me, if at a distance, since childhood.

I have always been alert to character. It is something I have an immediate sense of or can, at the least, quickly judge. I am not easy to deceive, therefore, and rarely find the need to revise an opinion once formed. Tom, I *knew*, was a gentle man, devoid of nastiness or spite. Unlike me he was without guile. But easy as those qualities were to warm to, they were not enough to make the prospect of becoming his wife an enticing one. I had thanked him – with something like a fond chuckle – and declined.

Afterwards, the matter received no further thought, other than as a topic of light amusement with my sisters. Even Ma, who professed she had always had an affection for Tom, recognised that such a coupling would be absurd. 'It's not the likes of poor old Tom that's going to suit *you*,' she declared.

Now, however, I set my mind to exploring the question again. If nothing else, it was more bearable than setting free what remained a closed, unexpressed grief.

With his regular work on the canal, Tom Mason would earn a steady wage. It was never destined to be more than a modest one, but I was unlikely to go hungry and our children, as they arrived, should at least be fed and clothed – though it must be admitted I had never managed to picture myself as a mother.

A union with Tom would offer me a steady, simple, adequate existence, with a predictable future. It did not surprise me to discover that I felt no more yearning for it than before. But I saw it would be a tolerable way of life. One that could be stepped into without difficulty, without too much delay.

Might Tom decide not to have me, having once, and with little grace or tact, been turned down? I thought not. Knew not, in fact. He would forgive the humiliation, may not even see it as such. This was an unassuming, even-tempered man, who had once been a gentle, if slightly slow-witted boy. As his wife, I would be well treated. As a husband he would be loyal and affectionate; in every way a different sort of man from Pa. Was this, perhaps, good enough?

I would not, I imagined, find myself to be the object of his *passion*. It seemed unlikely that passion could find a home in one of such mild temperament. My suspicion was that Tom, whose widowed mother had died about a year ago, was lonely. He wanted someone to live with, some-one who would run his simple home and ensure he was fed and cared for. He wanted a woman to return to each night, from whom he would receive fond, undemanding companionship. Someone to belong to, to call his family. He desired, in other words, everything that was safe and good, if unenthralling. And if I could make some attempt to meet these needs, I had no doubt he would prove a grateful and kindly mate.

He would, of course, want intimacy; I was well aware that all men wanted that. But Tom, surely, was not a man to seize it in the coarse, urgent way of many? Perhaps he might be kept content with occasional goodwill, and if not encouraged – I could not think why I would encourage him – then the demands on me should not be burdensome. I could surely accept such a thing, *put up* with it, in exchange for a home of my own?

It shames me, now, to realise that Tom's happiness did not count one jot in these deliberations. I knew myself to be a wholly unsuitable match for him; in truth he should have known it also. Perhaps he did. It may be that he had never expected me to take up his offer, and so was not much pained by its rejection. Acceptance might have come as a shock. For he must have had the sense, deep down, that I was too clever either for his needs or for his good.

Perhaps too attractive, also? A simple, plainish village girl, whose desires in life matched his own, would have made a perfect coupling. There were enough of those about, and left to his own devices he would sooner or later have put his offer to a willing one. No decent man, capable of earning a living, need be on his own for long. But there was little chance he would enjoy an easy peace with me, for I outshone him in all respects.

But Tom was a good man. He offered a means of escape, and no other means were readily available. Although by far the brightest of us – there must seem a lack of modesty in this claim, but it was true and the others declared it often enough – my education consisted only of Ma's well-intentioned efforts and those of a village Sunday School teacher.

I could read, and loved to read, but knew little beyond what the mean supply of Sunday School books had taught me. Without better learning there could be no possibility of work as a children's governess. Becoming a live-in domestic servant and making myself a slave in someone else's house had always been anathema to me. I did not have the temperament for it, was not sufficiently biddable or respectful, and had no desire to be. Even contempt for Pa was not about to take me in that direction.

Instinct told me that Tom would settle into whatever domestic routine I chose to establish. He was likely to recognise my stronger will, perhaps even be glad of it. He would *go along* with things, so that even within marital ties

I would have some choice, some freedom. A great deal more, I knew, than Ma ever had.

Little more than a week after Ma's funeral, I made sure to encounter Tom on his own.

4

It seemed a good idea to find him as he walked back to his home from the canal wharf, a journey of just over two miles which I imagined he would start by the time dusk was falling. On this occasion, however, he seemed to have delayed, for I had covered almost the whole distance without seeing him and was even beginning to wonder if something could be amiss. But there he was, bending down towards the securing rope, appearing to check or recheck it, before standing up to cast his eyes over the cargo. There was no sign of the horse, which must already have been put out to graze.

Tom was unaware of my approach behind him, but started and turned sharply as I walked the final few yards, my footsteps now sounding in the gravel near the waterfront. I could see the small barge lying deep and heavy in the water, loaded at least to its capacity, and perhaps a mite beyond, with large lumps of what looked to be limestone. Tom, and the lad who worked alongside him, were likely to be setting off early tomorrow morning with this lot. Perhaps he was loth to leave things unattended, though thieves would need to be equipped and organised to seize such a cargo. In Cromford, there was respect for the boatmen and their trade and seldom any trouble. If it occurred, those suspected of theft would be hunted out and could expect some speedy form of rough justice.

Once over his shock, Tom beamed at me as I stepped across to join him, though failed to find a suitable greeting. I smiled back.

'Late out, Mary' he managed at last.' Something wrong?'

'No, Tom. Nothing wrong.'

I said no more for a moment or two, allowing him to drink in my closeness. Tom, too, remained silent, no doubt doing just that and perhaps feeling some confusion. I stared along the water towards a couple of other vessels moored there. Tom shuffled, picked up the end of the rope, looked at the thick knot.

'Your father seems to be coping alright, Mary.'

I sensed he had been desperately trying to think of what to say during the odd silence I had imposed.

'Oh, Pa will cope well enough. As long as one of us puts food in front of him and keeps the place in shape.' I was tempted to add 'until he can find some poor, needy woman to do that, and to provide other services besides.' But I held my tongue, for Tom had already raised his brows slightly at my sharp reply and I had no wish for him to see me either as driven by dislike or of coarse thought.

'Tom, I'd like to talk to you about something.' My eyes now moved to focus on his.

'Of course, yes! Is there something you want me to do, Mary? Just tell me what you need.'

His expression had changed from nervousness towards that of a hopeful, adoring dog, one that has forgiven its harsh owner for a kicking and now senses a comforting stroke might be about to come its way. This task was going to be an easy one. Contrarily, I found myself wishing that Tom would make it a little more of a challenge, for both our sakes. Surely these things should not be presented on a plate? But he was a straightforward man. There was no guile to call upon.

I cleared my throat, unnecessarily.

'I've been thinking about how I spoke to you, Tom. You know – when you said you wanted to marry me.'

He reddened. In the now deepening shadows I could sense the colour change in his cheeks without clearly seeing it.

'Well… you mustn't have any worry about that, Mary. It was, well, it was stupid of me to say it. I know that. Must have been the drink gave me a bit of courage. Didn't shock me at all when you put me straight; I'd have been… well, *thrown*, you see, if you hadn't!'

As I thought, then.

'Well, I think it took me by surprise, and I see now that I was very ungracious.'

It was doubtful if Tom knew what *ungracious* meant, but he must have gleaned that some sort of apology was being offered. As, in a way, it was.

'Well… no bones broken. And I'm very sorry indeed about your loss, Mary.'

I let a few further moments pass in silence, while we both stared out across the water.

'I'll walk you home, Mary. It's getting dark for you to be out.'

'That would be nice, Tom. But just before we go… ' He waited for me to continue, a discomfort now clear in his expression.

'I just want to say, Tom, that losing Ma has made me look at my life in a different way. I see now that it was foolish of me to turn you down the way I did. I really can't believe I spoke to you like that. But I've had some time to think about things since then… '

I allowed another silence to fall, watching his eyes widen, before making the final thrust.

'I believe you'd be a good husband, Tom, and I'd be happy to be married to you, if that's still what you would like.'

It was not a surprise to learn that Tom's affection for me, now expressed in splutters, remained just the same, as of course did his desire and readiness for us to be married. He did not find the courage to attempt to kiss me, and I neither did nor said anything that would have made such a move easier for him. Instead I suggested we should make our way back together before anyone began to worry about my safety. Though only Alice was likely to feel concern, and hardly so soon. Pa, in any case, was not at home, and could be in his usual drinking hole for some time.

We began an amble in the direction of my house. Perhaps encouraged by the descending darkness and no doubt still in a dizzying state of shock, Tom reached out after a while and took my hand in his own damply hot one, relinquishing it only when I pulled away from him as we neared the buildings. I did not want tongues wagging. I intended to be both the announcer and controller of these glad tidings.

By the time we reached my door, at which point I suggested he make his way home, it had been decided that the wedding could probably take place about six weeks from now. Only respect for my mother, we both agreed, meant it should not be even sooner. After all, Tom had a home ready to receive me, and the bans needed to be read out on only three Sundays.

Some canal men lived on the boats, but Tom did not. Most of his work came from Wheatcrofts, a thrusting and determined family set-up that by then seemed to own most of the barges and any small ferry craft on the water. Tom, I imagined, would be deemed hard-working and reliable.

He was tenant of the small cottage in which he had grown up, occupied until recently by himself and his mother, for his father had been dead a good while. I had the impression his mother fussed and cosseted him – the only one of her several children to survive early infancy. She had died around a year ago and since then Tom had managed to look after himself. I suspected my domestic skills, such as they were, would be appreciated.

The less than genial Reverend Jones would need to be called on as soon as possible. As Tom was astute enough to realise, I would be more at home than him in approaching such a person.

'I'd be glad if you'd do that for us, Mary. Very glad.' It seemed to set the tone of how I saw our life would be.

It must be clear that my future husband was not an articulate man. And like most people around me, he spoke in something of a local dialect that I have chosen not to reflect here. There are limits to what others can be expected to put up with. For some reason, my own way of speaking had always stood out as being less easily placed

29

and was often remarked upon. Just one more way in which I was *different*. And another thing that Pa resented in me.

Tom agreed that a wedding in the near future would be a very good thing for my family; it would help us all to think beyond our loss and sorrow. The event would naturally be modest and simple, but even so a celebration of some sort would be in order. It would raise everyone's spirits.

I had no intention of relying on Pa's generosity to provide such a celebration, simple or otherwise. There was a collection of coins put to one side, saved year by year and hidden away – just as Ma did with her treasures – in a small box beneath the bed. Even my sisters did not seem to know of its existence, for there were plenty of other oddments under there. Only Alice was conscientious enough to clear them out for an occasional sweep, but she had never mentioned finding it.

There had been no special plans for this modest hoard; I simply enjoyed knowing it existed and was at my disposal. Now though, it could be used for some sort of wedding party. There was enough to provide us with food and beer, and we would have an evening of enjoyment, no matter what. Even the presence of Pa could not be allowed to spoil such a thing.

I saw no reason why Pa should raise any objection to the plan, particularly when he learned that no expenditure would be required on his part. Nevertheless, the conversation we needed to have was unlikely to be warm or pleasant, for by now my dislike of him must have been palpable, and despite Alice's attempts to soften me, I made no effort these days to disguise it.

I could only believe he would be glad to be rid of me, the one sharp thorn in his side. It was a rare thing for anyone else – and especially Ma, who had sought to keep the peace at any cost – to question his self-interested stance, let alone voice a word of criticism. Even the boys, knowing a belt could be in hand within a second, had not been brave, or foolish, enough for that. As they grew older they contented themselves with being out of the house as long and as often as possible – a situation he had no problem with provided they did not disturb him by arriving back drunk and noisy. Some while back George had found work on a farm; its large barn provided makeshift accommodation that was probably no more uncomfortable than sleeping on the downstairs floor of the house. Sam worked for an inn in Matlock Bath and curled up in some corner there. No longer reliant on his good will or at the wrong end of angry moods, they were more inclined to hold Pa in some sort of gruff affection.

Nonetheless, and even given the greater height and strength the two of them had by that time, I sensed they remained wary, both by instinct and habit.

5

'So, this is it then, is it? This is what you've been up to while my back's turned. Not a lot of time wasted, I notice, since your poor mother's death.'

Pa leaned forward, spitting into the grate a lump of phlegm that must have been gathering at the back of his mouth for some time. He sniffed heavily, swallowing whatever stubbornly remained of it, watching the flame rise and sizzle.

'There's been nothing done *behind your back*, Pa. I've known Tom long enough, haven't I? And so have you. He's a good and steady man, you'd agree?'

'Good and steady enough, if that's what you're after. Surprises me you are, though. Could do a darned sight better for yourself, wouldn't you say? *Eh*? You've got the sort of face to catch something a bit brighter than Tom Mason – not that you'll need me to tell you. Know all too well what you look like. Don't you? Never been our little Miss Modesty.'

I made no response to the sourness of this observation, which was followed with a mocking half laugh.

'And the *brains*, as well,' he continued, the tone indicating an intention to insult. 'Not that I'm saying, mind, they're something any man worth the name's going to want. If you've any sense you'll take my advice for once and watch yourself – with that head of yours!' He coughed and spat again towards the fire, missing it. 'Your Ma had a good mind herself, as it happens, but she weren't like you. Never felt she had to be pushing it in my face, and not in other people's faces neither, come to that. Not a soul knew.'

' *I* knew.'

'Oh yes?' He looked at me, the eyes contemptuous.

'Yes.'

A silence fell. I was aware that if Ma was spoken of again, the anger in me was likely to tip us into an ugly scene.

He sniffed loudly and rubbed a hand across his nose. 'I take it this is something that needs to happen pretty damned quick, then? Is that it?'

'No, that isn't it, Pa, as a matter of fact. Tom and I have decided we want to be married, that's all.'

His lips pulled back to reveal stained and missing teeth. I interpreted the expression as some sort of leering amusement.

'Is that right then, as a *matter of fact*? Well… time's going to tell us, eh? But you seem to be in something of a damned, big hurry to me. Surprises me Tom Mason has it in him! So why don't you just forget all them airs and graces and come straight out with it? You're not be the first girl in the village. There's precious few, it seems to me, that go to the trouble of getting themselves wed 'til they need to. Didn't worry your sister, if I remember right. Come to that, your mother were well along the road when we got ourselves together. She'd *proved*, as they say!'

I felt myself recoil from him, crossing my arms against my belly as if trying to protect myself from a piece of information that, if hardly shocking, was somehow unwelcome. It would have been easier to hear it from Ma, but she had never mentioned any such thing. It did tell me, however, why in Heaven's name she had *chosen* him. I shuddered to think that the course of her life had been dictated by one ill-considered act.

'She'd been with me a fair while. So it were going to happen, weren't it – sooner or later?'

It was as if he had sensed my assumption and decided to trample on it. I sat still, silent, until either impatience or boredom made him turn round to look at me straight.

'Well, just get on with it then, if your mind's so made up. Don't come moaning to me, though, when you're not content with things.'

I stood up to make my way from the room, resisting the observation that he would be the last person I would ever choose to talk to, however unhappy.

'We'll make a good night of it, anyway,' I said from the doorway, making an effort to end the conversation on a pleasanter note. 'There's a few pennies I've got to one side, so I can pay for it.'

'*Have* you now? Now there's an interesting thing. Well, you can just do that then.'

I was about to turn and leave, thankful the matter was done with.

'All *I* can say is, that Tom Mason must be out of his damned mind!'

I searched for some hint in the eyes to tell me he was making an attempt at humour, but saw nothing.

'Once the looks go, girl – and it never takes long – only bloody thing he'll be left with is that sharp tongue of yours. God help the man!'

It was almost a comfort that he made no attempt to give me his blessing, for I would not have known what to do with it. I left the room with a sense of relief. The conversation, if such an unpleasant encounter could be so termed, was done with. In just a few weeks it would be not be necessary to talk to him again.

It had been hard to endure Alice in tears. She and Fanny wept at the start of each night during the couple of weeks that followed Ma's death. Lying between the two of them, I would hold a hand of each until they finally dropped off – always a long time before me. During those nights, as we all moved about naturally in our sleep, if only by the small amounts such a space allowed, I would try to ensure that some sense of bodily comfort was there for both of them; a hand on Fanny's back, a warm leg laid alongside Alice's sturdier, less shapely one.

But as time went on they cried less and slept more. Fanny, exhausted from long hours of pot washing and vegetable chopping and floor scrubbing, soon reverted to her previous habit of falling asleep the moment she lay her head down. Alice took longer and remained prone to waking during the night, rousing me from my own shallow sleep with her distress.

The news that I was soon to marry, and would no longer be tucked up beside her at night, seemed to add to the misery.

'How can you think of going? Leaving us?'

That was hardly fair. Alice, now just eighteen, was old enough to be married herself whenever she chose, or could bring herself to leave *poor Pa*. She was capable of running a house and a better cook than me.

'I'll be with you much of the time,' I reminded her, eventually with some impatience. 'We'll still work together upstairs, and I shall help with the chores.'

'It's not the *chores*,' she insisted, as if offended. 'I do most of them as it is.'

Sarcasm was not in Alice's nature; she was merely stating fact.

'Well, you often say it's easier on your own,' I added lamely, 'but the knitting frames are a different matter.'

There was little choice when it came to those. The frames were in that house; rent had been paid on the things and something, however little, had to be earned. Tom's cottage had no attic to serve as a workroom. In any case, I wanted Alice's company, if not in the heartfelt way she seemed to need mine.

'You've said you don't want to be in the same house as Pa.'

'Well, I shan't be, shall I? I shall be here when Pa is out at work. And be gone before he comes in, since he doesn't come back for dinner, thank goodness. He'll hardly remember I exist.'

It struck me that we did not even need to mention the matter to him.

'Oh do *come on*, Alice. Can't you try to be a little bit happy for me, for Heaven's sake? It's not a wicked thing, you know, wanting to be married.'

She seemed to rally a little, if in a martyred way. 'I'm trying to be happy for you, Mary, really I am. It's just that you know I rely so much on you, on just knowing you're about. Fanny's younger, it's not the same; and anyway, she's not here now in the day. By the time she comes in she's too tired to talk. And Pa's not here much either, and barely speaks when he is.'

It was true that Pa had become even more morose when in the house and was spending much of each evening absent from it. I had never bothered to ask him where he went, assuming he had become even more of a fixture in one or other of his favourite drinking houses than before. I could picture him in some dark corner, withdrawn and miserable, making a couple of mugs of ale last for hours. Or perhaps he joined in, was part of the banter, the raucous laughter. We could not know and I did not much care, finding it a relief that he seldom chose to be around until quite late.

At some point in the evening, hunger and tiredness would drive him back home and he would devour whatever had been left for him in the fireside oven before going, quite soon afterwards, upstairs to his bed. He snored heavily throughout most of the night, waking twice, and sometimes more, to relieve himself noisily into a pot. Alice would take it upon herself to dispatch the accumulated liquid each morning into the privy at the back of the yard. The rest of us had always seen fit to tidy up after ourselves in that regard.

I had to acknowledge that Pa seemed not altogether well, though it had not yet robbed him any sourness of tongue. A decent plate of food was put in front of him every evening, but he had lost weight over recent weeks; per-haps he had begun to do so even before then, without anyone noticing. Despite Alice's caring efforts, both his face and body looked scraggy and unkempt. A couple of teeth near the front had finally fallen out, and the few remaining ones were now causing him a problem in chew-ing anything slightly tough. Alice had started to stew things to an unappetising mushiness to make the process easier.

'I don't see why we must all suffer,' I complained. 'Can't we take out our own food sooner? Just let his helping boil away to destruction.' I think she thought me hard and unfeeling, which I probably was.

6

As she became used to the idea that I was to be married, Alice began, despite herself, to summon up a little excitement. This was encouraged by a late evening visit to Mrs Brown, a seamstress of no great competence, whose prices were therefore the lowest in the village. The dear lady was now attempting, with a deal of grumbling, whinging and wheezing, to put together new dresses for Alice, Fanny and for me. The coin hoard had stretched to this too, though only just. Edwina had been good enough to make do with her existing *best* dress, which could be let out an inch or two and with a bit of luck would not split on the day.

'No good having anything else while I'm in this damned state,' she informed me cheerfully. And it was a fact that her belly still looked much as it did just before the recent birth, while her breasts were alarmingly prone to leakage. I found it difficult to picture her ever making an escape from that *damned state*.

Alice and Fanny had each chosen one of the cheap and colourful pieces of material that the dressmaker had at her disposal, ensuring that neither church service nor celebration were to be dingy affairs. The new dresses would be taking pride of place as Sunday bests for a very long time to come. It was years since any of us had possessed garments worth the name and I watched as the two of them fretted over waist gatherings and chose from the cheap offcuts of lace Mrs Brown proudly laid out for view.

Though they were not the only ones to enjoy such an unaccustomed fuss. I picked out a shade of deep red for my own dress; the piece had an almost silk-like texture and had taken my eye at once. There followed an argument with dear Mrs Brown over the precise style and fit that I wanted, for it turned out the woman had a single design in her unimaginative head. One she believed more than good enough for every female in the village, be it for their Sunday bests, weddings or any other festive and jolly event.

This, she was at pains to inform me, was what enabled her to keep her prices in check.

'Silly whims, love, they take me a great deal more time and trouble. Now I've never had a complaint about any garment I've made, and I do try to keep the cost as low as I can. But you'll understand I can only do that if I know just what I'm doing. Not having to strain my eyes with this bit and that bit and then finding I'm working half the night. I can't give my time for nothing, you see – much as I'd like to do so.'

I doubted she would like to, but was determined to have not only the fashionable close fitting, sleek cut down to my waist, but a lower neckline than was usual for such an occasion. Something to show off a good and shapely form. Surely I had a right to be the focus of admiration on my wedding day? There had to be that much pleasure extracted from the event, at least. But I had neither the means nor desire to pay the woman extra for the effort she claimed required, and braced myself for a haggle.

'There are *three* dresses here,' she was briskly reminded, 'so it's hardly asking too much that you give a little more time to mine!'

It did not take too much effort before she gave in, for the poor woman had less determination than me and she could not have borne to lose the business.

'Well, you'll need to come back in the daytime,' she said sulkily, 'for another fitting. I can't be doing it late on, like this. Light's not good enough.'

The knitting machines were abandoned for the sake of a return visit a few mornings later. There was no question of Fanny joining us but at least – thanks to a carefully worded letter I had thought to send to the *big house* – she had permission to attend the morning service. We would have to trust Mrs Brown's dubious measuring skills and hope the dress would do her well enough.

Alice seemed thrilled with her own bright green affair, styled with a higher neckline and a little looser fitting than my own. The needlewoman had used her judgment there and perhaps wisely. Alice was plump, with bottom and hips amply rounded and breasts best described as *bountiful*. The position she occupied as the family's chief cook might well have been the provider of all this, for I had noticed that Alice did not always confine her eating to the table. She enjoyed scraping out bowls, licking spoons and nibbling any stray bits of pastry that might be encouraged to fall off the edges of a pie.

Though I did not miss how the new dress complimented her bright complexion and chestnut-coloured hair. It struck me, perhaps for the first time, that there could be no shortage of men in the village who found my sister desirable. For some, the attraction might be enhanced by that plentiful flesh. Not all men like a woman to be thin.

My own outfit went on and was smoothed into place by Mrs Brown. I ran my fingers through the mane of unruly dark hair to tame its wind-blown appearance, for I chose to ignore fashion in that regard and had always refused to pin it up, preferring it to fall in natural waves over my shoulders. I heard Alice gasp, and looked towards a large mirror that had been thoughtfully nailed to the wall of the parlour workroom. Despite the stained, mottled surface, it revealed a picture that was arresting, at the least. Even the irritating Mrs Brown was silenced from her usual mutterings, a couple of pins held between discoloured teeth, the points sticking out from her thin lips in an unknowingly comical way.

'Well, I think I've *excelled* myself there, young woman,' she announced, having wisely removed the said pins, drops of spittle falling to the floor as she did so. 'That dress looks grand on you, it does! I think I'll be finding myself having to do a few more on the lines of that one. Material's just right for it too, don't you think? Now I'd be glad if you could make sure that when folk tell you it looks nice – and I'm very sure they will – that you let them know who made it. You'll do that for me, won't you, love?'

Alice was gracious enough to assure her that everybody would be told, whether they asked or not.

Tom and I were to be married at ten o'clock in the morning on the first Friday of June. Despite the fact that we had barely spoken to each other over the past weeks, I assumed Pa might still feel obliged to be there, along with the rest of family. A handful of others from the street could also be expected to walk down with us to the parish church, appropriately dedicated to *Saint Mary*. Not that the saint was likely to remind anyone of me.

Tom was unusual in having very little in the way of family. He was to be accompanied by two people; his boat lad, Albert, who in any case would have nothing much to do in Tom's absence, and some distant, unmarried relative from Crich, who went by the name of Abe. Tom seemed unclear as to just how they were related.

Afterwards, most would need to return to work. Even Tom would have to do the same; a thought that did not displease me, for it was time I was happy enough to spend with my sisters. We might be hard at work ourselves, but the hours would not be without banter and easy laughter. There might, I hoped, be a lightness about the house that had not been there for a long time. Though it had never been there other than in Pa's absence.

A few of our neighbours kept a pig or two on rough patches of spare ground they owned or rented. When a beast was slaughtered it was sometimes possible to buy a piece of meat, and for less than any butcher would charge. One such chunk now sat in the scullery, its thick, fatty surface already scored and rubbed with herbs and garlic. This roast was to be the centrepiece of the table. Potatoes, with chopped onions and parsley, would provide a hearty, filling dish to accompany it.

This, it seemed to me, was plenty, but Alice seemed anxious to provide more.

'I shall make a couple of pies,' she announced. 'A carrot and turnip one and a sweet one. There's still a good few of last year's apples wrapped up in the back. I want to be sure everyone has plenty to eat... it's a *wedding*, after all!' She had acquired all the concern and worry of a housewife, of a mother. I thanked her and did not argue. Her pies were good and cost more in effort than they did in money. And if any food remained there was no chance at all it would be wasted.

We had neither space nor wherewithal to make bread, which would be got as usual from the best of the village bakers. *Best* meant only the least suspect, for I knew for a fact there were bakers who thought nothing of adding a good dose of chalk, or worse, to bulk out their flour. Most people seemed unaware of the practice or else were not concerned by it. No baker around could be trusted entirely, but I hoped my chosen one would be good enough not to cheat me on this occasion. I had already engaged him in a quiet word on the matter.

There were not enough plates, bowls or mugs for the family and neighbours likely to find their way into the house that evening, but those living alongside us – taking a warm welcome for granted – had offered use of their own.

'Well, they'll have to be washed!' Alice declared, as soon as I mentioned the offer. 'From *that* side at least... ' her arm indicated the wall in question, 'if not scraped!'

'Well, we'll do that,' I said. 'But we can't have people eating out of their hands, can we? So let's just say our thanks and get on with the scraping.'

The fare on offer promised to be tasty and ample; better than most others we knew would be able or willing to provide. I left it for Alice to decide how to deal with Pa's share in a way that might enable him to eat it.

My only hope was that he would keep himself quiet. That he would enjoy ale brought in jugs from the Bell Inn, along the road, even if he did not enjoy the company. That he would not find some way to spoil the evening.

7

At about six o'clock, on the evening before my wedding, I thought, quite unexpectedly, of Marguerite. Two or three days after Ma died, the old midwife had called round early in the morning. She must have been intent on catching Pa before he left the house, and he was visibly annoyed to see her face appear round the door while he was still hunched over the porridge that Alice had made for him. It must have been at that very moment when the possible existence of a new child at last dawned on him, for none of us had felt inclined to speak of Marguerite until then. Pa had never asked me whether his child had survived. He must have assumed, and hoped, that it had not. News coming to the contrary produced only a frown.

Despite the gruff rudeness that Pa meted out to her, the remarkably determined Mrs Booth succeeded in extracting some money from him. 'A very modest amount, as I'm sure you'll agree,' she declared, though I suspect it was enough for her to retain a sly bit for herself. She said she would call in each week at a similar time for further payments.

'Poor Mrs Spence,' she informed us, during the next such call, 'well, you know she's hardly able to leave the house, hardly at all. What with her own four young ones, and now this little one of yours. Her own youngest is still on the breast, you see, and the next one up as well, though with him it's only in the morning, and then last thing at night.'

Pa's expression on receiving this information was one of disgust, and my own reaction was not much different. Clearly Mrs Spence's daily life was reduced to that of a milking cow. The image of it sent a shudder down my spine and renewed the desire to control my own child producing capacity, one way or another. But it seemed right that we should visit our little sister and the woman who was taking on the care of her, and I suggested to Alice that we go that evening.

The two of us sauntered the mile or so to arrive at Mrs Spence's door, Alice bearing a small, straw filled box containing four eggs. A couple of old and usually less than obliging hens, that scratched and scratted their way round the back yard, had produced these during the last week. Giving them away was a sacrifice, but thanks to my treasure box there was now a rare plenty to eat in the house and I suspected that the needs of Mrs Spence's family might well be greater.

A din of young children could be heard from outside; all the louder since it was a warm evening and the downstairs window had been pushed open. I knocked once, but realised the sound was unlikely to be heard from inside, and that in any case Mrs Spence was likely to be pinned down by suckling infants, whether her own or ours. The door, however, its wood faded and heavily scratched, turned out to be unlocked and so we made our entry gingerly, finding ourselves in a space that served as both living room and kitchen. It was crowded and untidy, but appeared no less clean than most.

Two small, scruffy children shouted and wrestled on the floor, watched by a smaller one still who sat to one side, surrounded by broken wooden pegs. The rough play stopped as soon as our presence was observed and the two older children rushed towards a chair at the other side of the room, from where they turned back to stare at us with wide eyed curiosity. Only then did I realise there was someone sitting in the chair, facing away from us and towards the wall. Mrs Spence turned her head to peer over her shoulder in our direction.

'Good evening, I'm Mary and this is my sister Alice,' I began, sounding to my own ears like a prim little girl who has been carefully taught how she should introduce herself.

'Well, I can guess who you are. Come here and take a look at her, then.'

We went forward to draw level with the chair. Attached to one of Mrs Spence's extraordinarily large breasts was a baby with wispy black hair, tightly shut eyes and a rather bulbous, red face. Marguerite, our sister.

'She's doing ever so well. Always hungry – it's a day and night job with this one. Good thing it's something I never seem to run out of it, or she'd be howling her head off, wouldn't she, much of the time?'

'Is she… alright then?' Alice asked, unnecessarily.

'Very much alright, as you can surely see. Never known one get so heavy in the time. Just you have a hold of her.'

Mrs Spence pushed the baby's mouth open with her fingers and deftly removed a milk coated nipple. Then she held the shawled parcel out insistently towards Alice, who looked first at me, as if unsure what to do. Marguerite began to complain. She had lost none of her piercing tone.

'Go *on*, take her then, just feel that weight!' Alice took hold of our sister awkwardly, agreeing that she did indeed feel very heavy. She passed the squirming package with some haste on to me and I too dutifully observed that the baby appeared to be thriving.

'They always thrive with me. There's plenty for them and they take it well. Never known one that didn't. But her! Well, she's doing better than most.'

'How long will you need to keep her?' I ventured nervously, dreading to be informed that we could have her back in a week or two.

'Oh, a good while longer yet, a very good while.' The answer was unspecific, but came as a relief. Neither Alice nor I wanted responsibility for Marguerite at present; in truth I think we could hardly contemplate having it ever. I was relieved to return her to Mrs Spence, who seemed only too anxious to take possession again, stroking the baby's dark head and gazing at her proprietarily. Her own children had returned to their play, but the activity was less noisy than before and they appeared to be keeping a watchful eye on us. I now noticed that all three were boys.

'Have you got another child as well?' I enquired, faintly recalling that the midwife had spoken of four.

'Youngest one's asleep upstairs, he's not too well. Oh – it's nothing *she's* going to catch, you don't need to worry.' Mrs Spence added the reassurance quickly, though I doubt if any such concern had leapt to our minds. 'Not been too good since the day he was born. Just one of those things.

Gets very tired and needs a lot of sleep. Too much noise upsets him and all, so he's better off up there and out of it.'

Alice and I stood staring at the baby as she sucked and snuffled, stopping momentarily to produce a sound half-way between a cough and a belch. A slurp of off-white milk emerged from her mouth as she did so, but this did not deter her from putting her face back to the trough immediately after. I felt there were other questions we should be asking, other things we ought to be saying, but failed to think of anything at all. Alice fared no better.

'Well... thank you for looking after her,' I managed, bringing a long pause to an end. I suspect Mrs Spence must have found us oddly *unattached* to our new sister.

'That's no trouble. She's a fine baby. Sleeps well too, once she's good and full after a late feed.' Mrs Spence was plainly determined we should appreciate her capacity to provide nourishment. Another pause followed, while we continued to witness the miracle in action.

'It's a very sad thing, about your mother,' she said, finally looking up from the baby. 'I was sorry to hear of it, very sorry indeed.'

We both nodded in agreement and muttered our thanks.

'I didn't know her well, but she seemed a nice lady. And it's such a strange thing,' she added, 'how a woman can produce a good few children – have them as easy as shelling peas, very often – and then one time, out of the blue, it all goes wrong.'

'Well, as it happens,' I informed her, perhaps a little briskly, 'Ma was quite old to be having another child, and she wasn't at all well to start with.'

'Oh, well that was maybe a risky thing, then. I'm sure you must be missing her a great deal.'

Noticing the familiar tremor in Alice's lower lip, I expressed appreciation once again to Mrs Spence, then attempted to hasten our exit.

'And I'm grateful to you for the eggs,' she added, just before we opened the door. 'That's most kind. They'll find a good home here.'

'If you like, Mrs Spence,' – something had crossed my mind – 'one of us could bring you the money each week. Save the midwife the trouble of calling round on both of us, wouldn't it? And of course, we'd be able to see Marguerite,' I thought to add, though this was not the matter of importance. Mrs Spence, I had decided, would be given the full payment – which was hardly much, considering her admirable milk producing capabilities – without the midwife taking a crafty cut.

'Well, yes, if you would. If it's not too much trouble. I think that would be a very good thing.' No doubt she harboured the same suspicion about Mrs Booth.

Alice and I walked for a time in silence. Her thoughts probably mirrored mine in thankfulness that Marguerite appeared to be well enough cared for and that the task was not one we had to face up to ourselves. Or not yet.

'Mrs Spence seems very attached to her,' she said, after a while.

'Yes, *very* attached, in both ways. And please God it's going to stay that way for a long, long time.'

'But not forever, Mary. She'll have to come back home sometime – to someone's home. Either Pa's and mine or yours. Your new one, I mean. And then you'd have to bring her over with you in the day. I can't imagine Edwina being able to take on more than she's got at the moment.'

Nor could I imagine it. Edwina, and the man who had needed more than idle threats from our brothers before agreeing to the role of husband, struggled through a life of chaos. Their children were unkempt and had a touch of something wild about them; a state that was not set to improve as the brood increased.

Even less was I prepared to contemplate taking Marguerite on myself. The thought of a child of my own arriving was bad enough.

'Yes, well let's face it when it happens. Judging from the adoring way Mrs Spence looks at that sister of ours, I imagine she won't be at all anxious to let her go.'

I nudged Alice playfully with my elbow, as another thought entered my head. 'You never know, if Pa carries on paying her enough for a bit of extra food and a few clothes, then perhaps dear Mrs Spence might be happy enough to hold on to Marguerite for good. She could keep her as the daughter she's never had. What would you think of that?'

'Oh, but that's a wicked thought, Mary! It really is. We surely can't wish for that?'

But Alice had started to chuckle at the wicked thought, shaking her head in a mixture of amusement and shame. For my own part, I felt it would be an excellent and perhaps not wholly improbable outcome.

8

Very early the next morning – a pale grey dawn light was starting to creep round the edge of the thin piece of cloth that served as a curtain – I woke up. I lay still, staring upwards, but Alice's face was turned towards me, and I knew her eyes were open. It must have been some dreamy sense of this that had caused me to rouse.

'Do you love Tom, Mary?'

'Shush, you mustn't wake Fanny,' I hissed, not anxious to engage in any conversation with that opening enquiry.

'Fanny won't wake, you know she won't. We can just talk quietly.'

She was right about Fanny and I knew well enough there was to be no avoiding this quiet talk of hers. Sighing, I resolved to limit the damage by keeping it brief. Alice must accept that we both needed the chance of a decent night's sleep before the day ahead. The day of my wedding; a day that had indeed already begun.

'Alice, I like Tom, truly I do. He's a kind and good person.'

Both statements were true; not even arguable. Alice was acquainted with my future husband.

'Well, that would be enough for a lot of people. In fact I think it would be enough for me, at least to start with. I'm sure I could come to love a man who was good and kind. But... well, *you*, Mary?'

The rising tone sent her words into the air and they seemed to hover above us. I knew it would be churlish to ask her to explain what she meant. Tom was an odd choice for me and we were both aware of it. A perverse one, even. A choice that ran contrary to everything Alice knew about me and what she thought I would want.

For just what about Tom could enthral me? He might not be stupid, but his mind hardly compared with my own. The boundaries of his thoughts were narrow, and he showed no particular desire to widen them. What lay beyond his own life, his own family, was not of any real importance to him. Alice was right to wonder what on earth there could be for me in this marriage.

'What is it that you really like in him, Mary?'

I sighed again, but said nothing. Her face was still turned towards me; it told me, even in the dim light, that there would be no more sleep until she had an answer.

'What *is* it, then?'

It was hard to believe she did not understand, if dimly, what *it* was.

'Alice, I respect Tom. I know that he's a good, honest man.' I took a deep breath. 'And it so happens that he's something else. He's *not* Pa. So he doesn't think like Pa or act or sound like him. I like Tom for being about as different from Pa as another man can probably ever be. And that's why I've chosen to marry him and live under his roof. Because I really don't want to stay any longer here, under Pa's roof.'

There was a sharp intake of breath as Alice took in the stark words. I knew they would distress her, but she was not being asked to share my feelings. She had her own, which were different, softer, and did not seem to come under the attack that my own always had. What I had just said should not have come as too much of a surprise. I hoped that saying it now, clear and undisguised, meant we would never need to have this conversation again

'But Mary, poor Pa's suffered so much. And he must still be suffering.'

She paused and there was a suggestion of sniffing. If this progressed to full blown tears they might wake Fanny, who was already beginning to shift her position, as if starting to come round. Alice must have realised this too, for she seemed to regain control, before struggling on in a hoarse whisper.

'I know you and Pa don't always get along well,' she continued, with breath-taking understatement. 'But he, well, he does love you, Mary, I'm sure he does. It's just that he can't seem to show that sort of thing, not like Ma did. But I suppose not many fathers can.'

There was a certain childlike sweetness in it. Perhaps this was why Alice was the only one of us whom Pa found he could almost bring himself to love. It was plain she would make a devoted wife and mother, in much the same mould as Ma. Both of them forgiving, looking for the best in people and somehow, against all evidence to the contrary, believing they had found it. I prayed she would marry a decent, kind man herself. Or rather *hoped*, for it was a long time since I had prayed.

We were not spoilt for choice where decent, kind men were concerned, though my own intended husband would have fitted the bill nicely, despite being quite a lot older. Perhaps I should have had the generosity to encourage such a pairing, instead of deciding to claim him for myself and my own purposes. It was too late now.

'Alice, I loved Ma and I love you and Fanny and Edwina. Even the boys. But I don't love Pa and he's never said or done one thing in my whole life that makes me think he loves me. And so... ' I paused for breath; 'I don't choose to live in this house anymore. I don't intend to listen to him again or have to do anything he says.'

'But with *Tom*?' She did not want to let go of this.

'Why not with Tom? There's far worse.'

There was no immediate answer to a statement of such plain truth. I decided we both needed to sleep, if we were to get ourselves through the next day and enjoy any merriment it might bring. I put my hand on her arm.

'Look, we're going to have a good time, tomorrow. In fact it could be *today* now, judging by that light. It'll be a change from those damned work frames and every damned and dreary thing else.' I thought for a moment. 'And don't forget, there'll be a few men around here – one or two of them might not even be old and ugly. So why don't you get yourself back to sleep and make sure that face is worth them taking a look at?'

She snorted quietly, and I sensed a lighter mood. Or perhaps it was acceptance that the earlier conversation was going nowhere.

'You think I look nice in the new dress?'

'I think you look more than nice. And there's others going to be thinking the same, believe me.'

She touched my cheek, stroked it gently and turned over. A few minutes later, steady snores were rising to both my right and left.

I was less fortunate, for sleep would not return. I lay still, staring into the growing light, feeling ever more wide awake, but with no desire to wriggle my way out of the bed or to creep downstairs. My thoughts should surely have been tumultuous, full of doubts and uncertainty, even shadowed in guilt, but for some reason they were not. Strangely, I felt peaceful, composed. And sleep must have taken over at some point, for I was woken by Fanny, shaking my arm in a state of dishevelled anticipation.

Thankfully the morning started dry and fairly bright, even though clouds were accumulating and might threaten something worse later on. We would have found ourselves unprotected against rain, and a heavy soaking could ruin our dresses if the colours started to run. We would look no better than the proverbial drowned rats.

As it was, Alice, Fanny and I emerged from the house and went down the front steps into pleasant sunshine. A few neighbours stood out there for us, and claps and cheers greeted our appearance. A small, bony, little girl rushed towards me with a bunch of wild flowers, bound together with a narrow strip of ribbon. She must have spent time selecting them for the length of their stalks, in order to tie them together in such a way. I had had no thought of flowers until that moment and felt oddly touched.

'Would you like to carry them down to the church for me, Lizzie?' I asked, bending down towards her before thinking to glance up to her mother, who nodded back at me with a smile. She had other children to look after; losing even one for a while would be welcome.

Our motley little group headed off down the hill, moving along briskly, for I imagined the stern and humourless Reverend Jones would not be amused if we were late. I held a hand of each of my sisters, Alice on the right and Fanny to the left, just as we always lay in bed, or had done until today. That bed was the only place I had ever slept during my life – or at least from whatever day it was when Ma must have decided I no longer needed to stay tucked close to her – but tonight I would be lying in a different one. I would be in a strange house, with sounds, creaks and smells all of its own. In a bed shared, not with my sisters, but with Tom. I permitted my thoughts no further rein in that regard. There were other things to occupy them first.

Pa walked a little way behind us, along with the neighbours. He had, it seemed, made a discernible effort to look respectable, encouraged by Alice, who had wiped down his Sunday jacket and trousers – the ones he had worn when we buried Ma and possibly, in view of their faded appearance, when he married her. A year before he had struggled to squeeze himself into the outfit. Now he had lost enough weight to return roughly to the same measurements as the day the garments were acquired, though with a much changed appearance. Ma had often commented on his good looks as a young man.

'You know, your father could have married *anybody*,' she once declared. 'They were all after him, believe me, *all* of them.'

I do not recall my exact reply; I might have observed that *all of them* had had a lucky escape.

Pa had attempted to tame his hair which, although grey-ing, was still thick and unruly. Once it had been a deep brown, barely a shade from black, a mixture of dense and waves and curls, so it would seem I had him to thank for my own hair. Alice had offered this morning to pin it up for me. 'Oh, you *must*,' she declared. 'People will think it very odd, not to. And it'll show off your lovely, slim neck.' But I decided my hair would not be pulled about and restrained but stay loose around my shoulders, as always. If others found such an untamed appearance shocking on a wedding day, then so be it.

I am not sure if Pa looked at me before the four of us walked out of the door. Despite the flurry of activity that had seemed to fill the house, he and I had barely exchanged a word since waking.

As we set off I cast a glance towards Fanny and saw she was pale, her eyes red and puffy with tiredness. There were simply not enough night-time hours to sleep away the accumulated weariness. After the ceremony, Sam was to walk her back to work, since his own destination lay in the same direction and on her own she would feel conspic-uous, wearing Sunday best on an ordinary working day. Fanny was not one who liked attention. I imagined other servants might be curious to hear of the morning's event, so at least it would give her a reason to talk to them; something I suspected she rarely bothered to do. Fanny did not often make an effort in that way.

'Put the dress somewhere safe,' I reminded her, 'and make sure you don't forget to bring it home. You can change back into it for a while tonight.'

There were calls and waves from passers-by. Cart drivers shouted out to us as they prepared to whip their reluctant horses up the savage Cromford Hill. With her free hand, Alice held tight to Lizzie's. Dressed in her usual ragged smock and apron, hair matted round a grubby face, the little girl squealed in excitement much of the way down. Twice she dropped the posy of flowers, retrieving it each time with a shriek of annoyance.

Near the church, Edwina came into view. She made progress towards us as best she could, dragging along a small complaining child, a baby tucked inside her other arm. It seemed she had been able to dispose of only one elsewhere. We stopped, allowing her to reach us and I noticed that both the sleeve of her dress and the cloth wrapped around the baby were wet. Alice and Fanny must have seen it too, for none of us offered to relieve her of the burden. We could not bear the thought of our dresses being sullied quite yet.

Tom stood outside the door of the church. Beside him were two male figures, one of whom I recognised as Albert, his scrawny and gormless boat lad. The other, older and more solidly built, I presumed to be cousin Abe.

Considering he had no mother or sister to guide him, my husband-to-be had made a worthy attempt to look the part. His beard was cut close and neat, and the rest of his face red and raw enough to suggest it had been well scrubbed, unless the effect was caused by nervousness. His hair, usually something of a lank, untidy mop, had been brushed neatly back. For the first time I noticed the bulk of his upper arms and shoulders – Tom was slim, but it struck me he could not be without brawn and strength. All was squeezed into a jacket too tight for him, that might once have been a better fit on his father. The trousers were near enough the right length, however; Tom's father had been tall, like his son, though I had no recollection of him beyond that. I wondered, suddenly, if he had been as amiable a person as Tom.

'Good morning, all of you!' My voice was loud and cheerful. Tom's small group seemed to start, even visibly jump, in surprise and I wondered if I had been expected to arrive here with eyes cast down and blushing in modesty. That would hardly have been appropriate for a bride in a red, low-cut dress, one that all three of them had recovered quickly enough to be now taking in with wide-eyed appreciation. Though in any case, bashfulness was not part of my nature.

'You look very beautiful, Mary,' Tom leaned forward and whispered the words hoarsely, his mouth dry with anxiety and an even more livid blush rushing into his cheeks. 'And I'm... I'm so very glad you're here.'

I smiled and put a hand out to touch his arm. 'Why on earth wouldn't I be here, Tom?'

He gave an uncertain smile in return, but his older companion guffawed, elbowing Tom in the ribs.

'What did I say to you? Told you not to worry!'

He turned to me. 'He was so darn sure you were going to think better of it.'

'No I wasn't!' Noticing Tom's rising embarrassment I felt an odd need to protect him.

'We haven't been introduced,' I said to the teaser.

'I'm Abe.' He turned towards Tom. 'Am I an uncle, by marriage, or some sort of cousin? Never worked it out.' He turned back towards me. 'But I'm delighted to meet you, Mary. And to be here.'

For someone in middle-age, Abe was not unattractive. He had strong features and a mischievous twinkle in his clear, blue eyes..

'I hope you'll come to the house tonight? Celebrate with us?'

'I'd enjoy that. Thank-you.'

I wondered if he might feel something of a fish out of water among the likes of Pa and our neighbours. Though it would be nice for Tom to have someone around who was there for *him*. I did not know if he had asked the boat lad to come. The rest would be mine, whether by family tie or association. Whether wanted or not.

'Well, I think we should go inside and get this done.' I decided to take some sort of charge, since no-one else appeared to be. 'Otherwise there'll be *words* – the dear Reverend is not a patient man.' I linked my arm firmly through the groom's, and together we led the way inside.

Our gathering numbered about a dozen, and occupied only the front couple of pews. Despite my warning, the Reverend Jones did not deign to appear for several minutes and we sat waiting, voices lowered. I could not think of anything more to say to Tom and felt grateful for the echoing cries of Edwina's baby. The inside of the church felt chilly and sombre, not welcoming. Although it was well past Lent, there was not a flower to soften its dingy and austere interior. Perhaps I was supposed to have put some there myself.

I turned to Lizzie, who had perched herself on the edge of the pew beside me, and took possession of a now bedraggled bunch.

'Thank you for bringing these.'

'It's cold, in here. I don't like it.'

'You know, neither do I!' I giggled the words into her ear. 'But we'll not be here too long.'

Nor were we. Around fifteen minutes after the minister's tardy, unapologetic arrival, all necessary words had been said and our newly married status proclaimed. People re-emerged, thankful to be back in the now failing sunshine. The sky had clouded grey, but at least there was still no rain. The men of the group shook hands, Abe and my two brothers – whose late arrival and noisy opening of the door received the minister's stony glare – kissed me on the cheek. So did Tom, following their lead, and for a second I felt his lips brush moistly over my own. It was the first time he had attempted something so intimate.

Within moments, people were setting out in their various directions, conscious of the day's work still lying ahead of them. But unlike other days, a high-spirited gathering could be looked forward to. There would be more than usual to eat and drink that evening. Too much drink, very likely, for some.

By the time we had walked halfway up the hill on our way home, just Alice, Lizzie, Edwina with her offspring and a couple of neighbours from the street remained. Pa must have decided to call in on the landlord of The Greyhound before taking himself to work, where I hoped he would go without bothering to come home for a change of clothes. Fanny held Lizzie's hand, while Alice and I felt we must take a turn – at an awkward arm's length – to carry Edwina's odorous offspring. He seemed noticeably lighter than Marguerite.

Having waved the neighbours good-bye and dispatched Lizzie to her mother, we headed thankfully indoors. Edwina placed the baby on a mat on the floor. She had no will at present for attempting to clean him up.

'Get a good whiff of that, Mary – you may as well get yourself used to it!' There was a broad grin. 'It'll be your job, I'll bet, come less than a year! Or is it going to be something sooner? If so you've done well – getting into a dress like that.'

'No, it'll not be something sooner!' I dealt her a hearty slap on the backside. 'We're not all like you, thank the Lord.'

I felt the same as ever, relaxed in my sisters' company, quite unchanged. It seemed absurd to think that a brief morning's outing down the road had somehow trans-formed me into a different person; into one Mrs Tom Mason, wife of a canal boatman. It must have happened – *had* happened – but I could barely take it in. The notion seemed absurd.

'We'll not start on the chores yet.' Alice spoke with a housekeeper's authority. 'There's still a bit of fire left so I shall make us tea. Why don't we sit down and have it just as we are? The dresses won't come to any harm… and there's a bit of ginger cake as well.'

9

Those whose lives are relentlessly arduous are glad of any chance to celebrate. They seize it greedily. Celebration – of no matter what – promises laughter, drink, raucousness and a fuller belly than usual.

In all such things the evening did not disappoint. A fair number – bound to us in some way either through blood or familiarity – rolled up to the door and entered the house in anticipation, without bothering to knock. Some brought bits of extra food or a jug of ale and one or two arrived with small gifts they had put together themselves. Alice and Fanny presented me with what they called a *bedspread*, which was blue and had a silky texture rather like my new dress. I imagined Alice had got the material from Mrs Brown and hoped she had beaten the woman down to a low price. Whether it would be big enough to cover the bed I was not sure – never having seen Tom's bed. But it would look pretty placed on the top.

Even Pa surprised me with a gift of sorts. He told me I could have the old upright chair that sat in a corner of his bedroom, one Ma sat on to tidy her hair or to clip it up on her head. '*I've* no use for it,' he muttered, in explanation. I gave him an equally muttered thanks and said Tom would collect it sometime. The chair would be squeezed into my new bedroom, and I could tell myself it was a gift from Ma.

Apart from this brief exchange, I have no recollection of speaking to Pa that evening. For most of the time he stayed out of sight, perhaps huddled amongst a group of noisy ale drinkers who had drifted into the back yard. Perhaps they found it convenient to be near the privy, though there were some who judged that a wall and a turned back was delicacy enough.

Not too far in the evening, Abe came to bid me goodnight.

'An excellent table of food, Mary,' he said. 'You've done us all proud.' He fixed his eyes on mine and smiled. 'And young Tom's a fortunate man. I would have to say, in fact, that he's fortunate in a manner that quite amazes me.'

The compliment seemed gallant, but it was not difficult to pick up an undertone of puzzled enquiry. Perhaps it sprang from curiosity, perhaps from a perceptive concern for his naïve, younger relative.

'Well, I *hope* Tom feels fortunate. And I hope it turns out that I am also!' I kissed Abe's cheek and bade him farewell. I imagined he might find it something of a relief to leave the house, noisy and stale as it now was.

Later, when plates were scraped and jugs emptied of their last drops, my brother banged on the table and shouted for quiet – though it was a while before he managed to achieve it. By then most guests were merry and some had broken out into song, but George lifted his mug and raised his voice to a shout to wish me and Tom good luck. More shouts, whistles and cheers came in response, along with a few crudely expressed encouragements for our night's pleasures.

It signalled a close, for soon afterwards people started to drift away. I turned my attention to Fanny and urged her to get herself upstairs, but met with resistance.

'I won't be able to sleep until it all gets quiet.'

'Yes you will. You fall asleep and stay asleep through anything, so do go to bed.'

'I'll not be able to sleep on my own.' The look was turning to a sullen one.

'Alice won't be long.'

I was stabbed, suddenly, by the thought of not being with them.

'I'll wait here tomorrow, 'til you get back,' I felt impelled to say. 'To say goodnight.' If Pa should arrive home first, then I would hang about in the street.

'Will you?'

'Yes, I will. And Alice is here – you'll both have a lot more room in that bed!'

I smiled encouragement and hugged her, though did not feel it being returned with any warmth.

Saying any sort of good-bye to Alice could have been a risky, tear-inducing manoeuvre, had her giggling attention not been engaged with a young male of the next door family. Her scorn concerning dirty plates seemed forgotten; she must have blamed his mother for such sloppiness rather than hold it against young Harry.

I had not seen him pay Alice attention before, and wondered if his interest had been awakened by the sight of her in the green dress or by liberal helpings from the ale jugs. It seemed wise to keep my farewell as short as possible, and I tapped her lightly on the shoulder.

'Alice, we'll be leaving in a moment. Promise me you won't clean or tidy up. I'll be round early tomorrow and we'll have it done between us in no time.'

'You'll not be let out of bed too early tomorrow!'

Alice's admirer delivered the line with a leery grin. His arm had slipped round her waist and he pulled her in towards him, a manoeuvre she had no objection to.

'*I* decide when to get out of bed!' I cast him a hard look. It was tempting to tell him it was time he moved off, but for Alice's sake I refrained. There was no harm in him, beyond a bit to drink, but I was no longer in a mood for lewd observations. There had been enough of those all evening. But Pa would be telling this lad to disappear soon enough, and would be blunt enough about it. In the meantime, Alice's clear pleasure at being the focus of his inebriated attention might be best used for making a departure, if a less than joyful one. Catching Tom's eye – an easy thing as he had stayed as close to my side as was physically possible during the entire evening – I nodded towards the door.

Moments later we were out in the welcome cool and quiet of the night air, walking in the direction of his cottage. It was now mine too, of course, but having stepped inside only once, and briefly, I struggled to think of it as anything to do with me, let alone as somewhere to be called *home*.

Once we had decided to get married, Tom must have felt he needed to show me the place on offer, so just a few evenings later I had gone to meet him on the quayside, as before, and we walked back there together. He had made sure the room was tidy, though I noticed a stale odour as soon as we were inside and decided my first task after moving in would be to open a window. It puzzles me why people believe that keeping everything tightly closed will prevent chills, coughs or any other complaint, and live in a fug you can almost choke upon. Tom's mother must have been one such woman, and even after she died it would not have crossed her son's mind to deviate from the habits he was familiar with. I hoped this accepting nature would lead him to take on my ways of doing things with as little question.

During that visit to his home, Tom made no attempt to bed me, although it could have been seen as reasonable enough, since we were soon to marry. Perhaps the fear of being rebuffed was why he did not even suggest showing me the upstairs. Lying in my own bed that night, I wondered what would have happened had he made such an attempt. I would have been unlikely to refuse him. What would have been the point? But such an occasion did not present itself, and I felt no urge to make any encouraging moves of my own.

I was not ignorant about such matters. A large family living together in a small house meant privacy was rarely on offer. Despite Ma's well-meaning attempts to encourage what she liked to call *gentle manners*, my brothers were less than discreet in their conversation and habits, and Pa often grossly coarse in his.

It was common knowledge that many girls in the village set out to hook their men early on. They used the simplest means at their disposal and then cajoled an occasionally reluctant mate off to the church. I was familiar, too, with the carping and grumbling of older women, who had borne more children than they wanted or could provide food for and were desperate not to produce more. Some blamed their plight on the selfishness of men in general and of their own husband in particular. Others saw it as Nature's cruel dictatorship over their lives, and maintained a spirit of virtuous resignation.

In such a setting it would be a challenge to remain innocent, and I was not. Nor did I have any fear about what was likely to happen within an hour or two at most – for surely even Tom could not be expected to show restraint for ever? But I did lack any personal experience. Nothing more than the odd wandering hand – fended off with a sharp word or firm push – of some young buck, and on occasions an old one.

There had never been a shortage of appreciative looks thrown in my direction. But most young men, I think, were nervous of me, intimidated even, and did not attempt to push their luck too far. My aloofness did not spring from purity, from some determination to save myself for a *chosen* one. I simply felt no interest in the men who happened to have crossed my path.

Though I was aware, too, that a careless pregnancy – and there seemed little evidence of any other sort – would pitch me into a life outside my control. Edwina's provided a warning, though it was probable that she had never envisaged anything different. So did Ma's, I had once thought. Though if Pa had spoken the truth, it was not a sudden moment of rashness that dictated her fate.

So, if not looking forward to the night ahead, I was at least aware of what it would bring and only slightly apprehensive; probably less so than my new husband. Tom was now chattering aimlessly about the evening we had just enjoyed, speaking too rapidly and beginning to stutter over his words. In turns he clutched my hand, put an arm around my shoulders or placed his hand against the middle of my back, nervously unsure of just what particular gesture might be appreciated.

If not afraid, it would be truthful to say that I was not in the least hopeful, for there was no reason to anticipate any skill on Tom's part. I could not imagine he had had much experience to boast of either, or none that was likely to enhance his efforts tonight. But at least he would be considerate, he would not treat me with crudeness. Though if nerves continued to get the better of him, it seemed distinctly possible he might find himself incapable of treating me in any way at all.

10

Perhaps it was fortunate – for such a thing is better not delayed – that Tom's anxiety did not get the better of him, not entirely. Though it was me who suggested, almost in desperation, that we should get ourselves up to bed. Utterly spent, I longed to be lying down, to be in darkness, and could no longer cope with listening to Tom's nervous ramblings about his parents. I found myself less than interested in how the two of them had once cared for the small strip of land outside that served as a useful vegetable plot. Nor did I want to be shown the contents of the kitchen cupboard or informed about anything stored in the shed. I did try, perhaps without success, not to sound curt or unappreciative. Tom had never talked so much before, and as it turned out he was rarely to do so again. It may be that he, too, was relieved to have his wearying list of information brought to a halt.

'Tom, I'm so tired,' I was driven to say at last. 'And you must be too, surely?'

'Well, yes… yes, I suppose I am.' Though he appeared overwrought, rather than tired.

'Then perhaps we should go to bed?' I suggested.

'Yes, perhaps we should. If you think that would be the best thing, Mary.' It was hard not to smile, though I did not want Tom to feel I was mocking him.

'But I'll need to go outside first,' I added. The need had become pressing, as I had avoided our shared privy all evening, with its drinkers hanging about outside. The back yard here had its own privy in a small makeshift shed, as well as what looked like some sort of water pump – unusual luxuries. It should not be too treacherous to get across in good moonlight.

'Do you want me to guide you there, Mary?'

'No I don't, Tom, thank you. There's no need at all. And please don't feel you must hover outside the scullery door, either. I can manage on my own.'

'Well, you must take a candle with you.'

I accepted the candle in its holder, one of a couple he had lit on our arrival. It would have been unwise to risk taking a tumble and ruining my one and only nice dress, in addition to looking undignified. But at least this nuisance could be got out of the way. I had not drunk a great deal during the evening – at least compared to many of the guests – so the need should not afflict me again between now and morning. I presumed there would be a pot of some sort under Tom's bed but did not much fancy having to climb out of bed to crouch over it; not this first night, at least.

A few minutes later, while Tom was making his own visit across the yard, I sat staring around the room, trying to absorb the fact that this was now *home*. It was smaller than the room I was used to and appeared crowded with only a small table, its three chairs, and two low cupboards against a wall, pushed together and topped with a piece of faded, embroidered cloth. Along another wall was of course the fire, with a simple, open cooking range above it that had accumulated a great deal of grime and soot. A door led to the tiny scullery at the back, in which I had noticed a large shelf and a stone sink.

The place felt dreary and lifeless, but for the two of us – a situation that with good fortune and a little care I hoped might remain the case for a while – there was more than space enough and many would consider me fortunate. There might even be times when I would have this room to myself. Being alone had always been a rare luxury.

What the place needed was a good scrub and a thorough airing. It could then be brightened up with a few colourful cloths and the odd jug of wild flowers. Even such simple efforts would make it look more cheerful, though I still struggled to imagine it as somewhere that in time would come to be as familiar and natural to me as the other house.

Home, I still felt, lay a distance away, and was where two of my sisters lived. I wondered if they were now both asleep, or if Alice had ignored instructions and thrown herself into clearing and tidying. I suspected the latter and longed, all of a sudden, to be with her; discussing the evening and everyone there, teasing her about young Harry of the grubby plates.

Exhaustion can give thoughts too much poignancy. I drew a deep breath and reminded myself that the place where I sat – strange and unappealing as it seemed at that moment – was my very own domain. A place where *I* could decide things. One over which Pa held no sway whatever, any more than he now did over me.

Excursions to the privy completed, Tom led the way up narrow, creaking stairs, both of us clutching our candle holders and Tom carrying my cloth bag. His bed, I soon saw, was not large but I was well used to having only a narrow strip for myself. However, the sensation of Tom's body in tight proximity to mine was going to be very different from the careless closeness of my sisters' limbs. I wondered suddenly if his legs were hairy and whether the feel of them might be unpleasantly tickling or bristly.

The bedroom itself was very small, but I suspected the space at the other side of the wooden partition, once occupied by Tom's parents and later by his mother alone, might well be a little bigger. Tom would never have thought to move into this after his mother's death, but I decided we could soon do so, once I had had chance to sort it out. No doubt his mother's clothes and oddments were still there. Probably his father's too. And like the rest of the house, it would need vigorous treatment with washcloths and broom, as well as the inevitable blast of outside air.

An old but freshly laundered nightgown lay somewhere in my cloth bag, but I decided not to go to the trouble of rummaging for it. This now faintly absurd situation might be better faced up to directly, avoiding awkward delay and without pretence at some silly shyness. I could in truth be described as a maiden, but did not feel any inclination to act out the coy role that tradition expected of one. That could perhaps be left more easily to Tom.

Briskly blowing out my own candle, so that only the muted light of the other one remained, I began to undress. I did so without ceremony, simply roving the various layers of clothing and placing them on the wooden floor where I stood, at the side of the bed. Tom, who had moved round to the other side, followed my lead and started to do likewise. With touching modesty he turned his back to me, so any attempt to be coquettish and alluring on my part would have had no effect in any case. I wondered again about the nightgown, but decided against it.

And then we were in his bed, lying quite still on our backs beneath the thin cover, our shoulders and arms touching only through lack of sufficient space for them to do otherwise. The sensation felt strange, unreal, if not comical. At this point Alice and I would have been chattering, and pushing at one another for a bit more room. But I was aware of being exhausted, also. Had it not been for the remaining candle, still throwing odd, flickering images against the wall, I might have experienced the rare pleasure of falling to sleep within moments.

That would hardly seem appropriate, though, for a wedding night. As it was, it began to dawn on me that there might be some necessity for me to take a lead once more. Otherwise it seemed we would remain lying side by side, as motionless as marble effigies on a grave, until it was time to be up for work in the morning.

'Tom – it's *alright*, you know.'

He turned quickly towards me.

'Is it, Mary? Are you sure, I mean, are you truly sure… that it's *alright*?'

Had I related this to Edwina, who fell for her first whilst pinned against a rough outside wall of the church following a merry harvest celebration, she would have laughed in disbelief. So, of course, would Pa, though with greater scorn. I, however, although a mite exasperated, was not altogether unhappy with such diffidence.

Nonetheless, when finally reassured that what he might possibly like to do was *alright*, Tom began to pursue the matter with a surprising degree of enthusiasm. He even did so, if not with what could be perceived as skill, then with rather less cack-handedness than I had assumed might be the case. At the very least he seemed well enough aware of what he had to do, and proceeded to conduct himself in what struck me as a fairly competent, if raspingly breathless sort of way.

To my relief, I found the experience to be only slightly painful, and even this did not last for more than a few seconds. From then on the sensation seemed merely disconcerting; not unpleasant or uncomfortable, but perhaps slightly ridiculous. I remember wondering why men were so driven by the need for such a thing.

It was all over quite soon, a point signalled by hearing Tom gasp and groan more loudly still, then feeling the weight of his body as it seemed almost to collapse, heavy and perspiring, on mine. He remained in that position for a minute or so, muttering in a barely coherent way about it having been *wonderful*. My own thought soon afterwards was that I must have bled, for once I had asked him to roll away and enable me to resume breathing, I could feel a sticky and uncomfortable wetness between the top of my legs.

Tom proceeded to thank me several times, and may well have been still doing so as I turned onto my side and determinedly sought to go to sleep. For once, this state was easily achieved and I suspect neither of us knew any more for the next few hours. Not until the room started to fill with early morning light, signalling the need for us to be up and readying for another day's work.

I awoke first and decided to slip out of bed to find the working dress I had packed in the cloth bag, before going downstairs to seek out what was needed to make porridge. It would save me having to refuse, I decided, if Tom should wake up wanting an early repeat of last night's pleasures.

Apprehensively I checked the sheet, but although it still showed a clear damp patch there seemed to be only a small stain of blood. A good wash and the stain would look no worse than the many other faded ones already there. Moreover, I knew enough to realise that neither pain nor bleeding was likely to be a problem to me on the next occasion.

The first act of our marriage had been brief enough and I could hardly have described it as thrilling in any way. But neither had it turned out to be as unpleasant, even slightly repugnant, as I had prepared myself for. The experience was not something to be dreaded and this was probably just as well, since I now had an inkling that Tom might be politely requesting it more often than anticipated.

All in all, living alongside my good-natured husband, making sure he had a decent meal inside him each day and showing some willingness in bed, struck me as a very reasonable exchange for the precious sense of freedom that was mine. I could now pass my days without having sight of Pa, could sleep under a roof of which he was not the grudging provider. There would be no need any more to endure his scorn or criticism. Nor indeed rise to them with angry words of my own, which had more often than not been the case.

I wondered whether Pa might arrive before too long at our door, if only to satisfy his curiosity. If so, he was likely to come at a time when my husband would be here also, knowing that Tom would extend a welcome. Beyond such an exploratory visit, I imagined Pa would have little desire to see me again, and I felt no urge to disappoint him in that.

11

So, as the weeks rolled on and domestic routines, of a sort, became established, was I happy, living with Tom? Happiness was not something I chose to reflect on a great deal at the time, though I have given it more thought since. In the months following the wedding, it seemed enough to be mistress of my space.

I do believe I felt something that could be described as contentment. Our home was easy enough to care for and, in any case, my husband proved as uncritical in matters of housekeeping as in so many other things The place was quiet; since my only companion was a man who felt little need to talk, it was easier than before to sit and read the small but treasured collection of books. I even scribbled a bit of verse, here and there, having no fear that it might be found and poured scorn upon. And when I chose to, I could walk. Wander.

I knew that few men were so tolerant. Perhaps Tom had not yet overcome his astonishment that I had agreed to become his wife. More than agreed, of course, since I had gone against my first – and kinder – decision and set about persuading him we should be married. But despite the ceremony, despite my public vows, I sensed he never saw either my care of the home, or my willingness in bed, as his by absolute right. Though they were, of course. I was well aware that they were.

But my husband's lenient good nature may well have been simply that; his nature. The character he was born with, which had never hardened and nobody had tried to *knock out* of him. The one I had been well aware of before deciding we must marry. I was thankful for his easy-going ways and did not despise him for them, though I suspected other men might, and perhaps some women too. But sadly they did not cause me to love him, either.

At least the place looked brighter than when I had first entered it, an improvement Tom seemed to appreciate.

'Nice and cheerful you've got it, Mary,' he said, just a few weeks after my arrival. 'Mother would've liked it, I think.' This was praise indeed, for Tom had always been his mother's devoted boy. *Mother's* ancient table, chairs and cupboard still had pride of place, of course, for they remained serviceable and would do for our lifetimes, and possibly several more. However, and without bothering to discuss the matter, I had rid us of a large, rotting mat covering most of the floor, into which muck had been well trodden over many years.

Then there was the question of his mother's dusty and useless old *treasures*, littered everywhere and even occupying part of the table from which we had to eat. I have always had an aversion to arrays of cheap ornaments and trinkets. Her bits of chipped, faded pottery held no charm for me, and neither did the collection of odd wood carvings, perhaps picked up at a market stall many years ago, much broken and ineptly patched up.

Wild flowers and herbs seemed a preferable way to make the room more attractive, as well as giving it a wholesome smell. But I sensed care was needed to avoid upsetting Tom.

'I've wrapped up all those bits of things,' I told him one evening, 'and put them in a couple of boxes in the other room upstairs.' The *other* room being, of course, the small, boarded off patch we did not sleep in. The patch that everyone supposed would at some time be slept in by our children.

'They'll be much safer there,' I added, in reassurance, 'because you know I can really be so clumsy when I'm cleaning. Just ask Alice!'

Tom had not often seen me cleaning but he accepted this reasoning, and did not think to check with Alice, as far as I am aware. Perhaps he disliked the silly things himself. After a decent time had passed, I imagined they could be safely got rid of without his even noticing.

Our home, if not kept to Alice's high standards, was somewhere I knew Tom felt comfortable, somewhere he wanted to be. And I felt comfortable enough also, provided the periods of time spent inside its walls were not too long and I was free to come and go at will.

Regrettably, my skill as a cook still left much to be desired – Alice had always been so much abler in that regard. But I did make sure there was enough on the plate, or at least on Tom's plate. My husband possessed a hearty appetite, though fortunately it was an undiscerning, uncritical one. An amply heaped plateful of potatoes, with cabbage or carrot from his small vegetable plot, was the sort of meal that seemed to satisfy him perfectly well, the more so when it could be accompanied with a slice of bacon or even a few lumps of crisp bacon fat. If he noticed anything put in front of him was burnt or over boiled, he was kind enough never to make a comment.

When there was no meat, I would make the effort to produce a plain suet pudding – though I ate none of this myself, finding it lay far too heavy and would cause discomfort half the night. But any pudding – be it of the simplest or stodgiest variety – was a cause of delight to Tom.

That's filled me up well, Mary, thank-you!' was the almost daily praise I received. It was tempting to spoon out a little less on occasions, to see if gratitude for fullness might be varied with a diffident 'is there... perhaps... a bit more?' But I resisted this small, foolish unkindness, and instead tried to divert attention from his appreciative belly by relating the odd bit of news and gossip heard from Alice or around the village. I had never been one to take a great deal of interest in gossip, but efforts in other directions had revealed that not many types of conversation were available to us. Tom seemed happy to listen, nodding here and there or raising his eyebrows, until I ran out of fodder. He did not often state an opinion, and it was rarer still for him to supply any anecdotes of his own.

Alice was always glad to see me, as I pushed open the scullery door each morning, though only after noting that Pa's work boots had disappeared from the step. We would hug, then she would brew tea and usually we allowed ourselves a few minutes before climbing upstairs to the workroom. The knitting machines were noisy in action.

Further chat involved shouting and was better left until we came down to take a bite of bread and cheese at dinner time.

How much work we had would vary from week to week, from day to day. But I remember there was even less, around that time, than before and reason for us to be thankful that both Pa and Tom were earning a wage that could feed us, if only with plain fare. By the end of the afternoon I could leave if I chose to, and often earlier than that.

It was rare for me to rush straight back to the cottage. I felt no pressing need to do so, preferring to meander off in another direction altogether, or at least to take a longer, more circuitous route.

Occasionally I might call on Edwina, stopping at a nearby inn for a small jug of ale, though we would be lucky to get more than a few sips of it if the *good for nothing* happened to be about. Sometimes he would be outside with the two little boys, barely distinguishable from them with his silly noises and mud-pie throwing games.

'Evening, girl!' I would hear him shout in my direction, however stealthy my approach. 'Tell Ed I'll be in!'

He was jovial enough, especially if some drink was on offer at no cost to himself. Easy enough to rub along with much of the time, perhaps, and probably fond enough of Edwina in a rough, careless sort of way. But he was no sort of provider, other than of offspring, for when work was found, here and there, he was never kept on for long. Heaven knows how they would have survived had Edwina not taken in mending, washing, and anything else she could lure her way. I dreaded to think just what she was prepared to do, at times, and did not enquire.

The wonder of it all was that she seemed quite content.

'He's *alright* with them, you know, is Jo,' she once claimed, with some sharpness, peeved at what she sensed was my low opinion of her husband. 'Plays about with them, all the time. Built them a den, he did, the other day. Loved doing it as much as they did – more!' I had no difficulty believing it. She shifted the latest born from one shoulder to the other. He burped and some odd-coloured liquid was spattered over her shoulder. 'And he teases them, makes them laugh. You know, all the time. They think the world of him, them lads do.' She seemed to think for a moment. 'Not like Pa.'

'You'd be hard put to it,' I said, 'to find another like Pa.'

'Well *you* should think better of Jo,' she went on, resuming the peevish tone. 'Better than you do. Because I know you don't think too damned much of him, Mary, do you? And you ought to.'

I failed to see why, but decided not to argue just for the sake of it, an activity that Edwina had always enjoyed.

'I don't dislike Jo,' I said, telling her the truth.

'No, but you think he's a waste of time, don't you? Just because there's the odd day he don't work.' I did not comment on the understatement, merely shrugged. 'It's just as well he don't *know* the nasty things you think,' she went on, determined to draw me in. 'If he did, he'd be hurt.'

I could not hold back a laugh at the thought of a deeply offended Jo. 'Not too hurt to drink my ale, I'll bet! Oh come on, Edwina, Jo's as thick-skinned as an elephant. And what does it matter what I think? It's you that's married to the man. And if you're happy… '

'Oh God, what's happy? I get by, the children get by – we're alive, aren't we?' The mood seemed to have changed again. She took a last swig, straight from the jug. 'And you *know*,' she added, as if a thought had just struck, 'he makes *me* laugh too, Jo does. We laugh all the time, the pair of us. It's every damned day – we just see the funny side of things. Makes all the difference, that does. Makes a lot of it not so bad.'

I nodded, thinking she may well be right. That perhaps she and Jo shared something many pairs did not. Something it was easy to think too little of.

'And do you know something else?' It seemed my knowledge was about to be tested further. There was a mischievous grin.

'He's as good as he ever was in bed! He still wants us to… *do* things. Wants it as much as he ever did and that's every night. More than once, often as not. Well, it's both of us wants to, as it happens, and there's the good thing. It's me just as much. So thank God we're the same when it comes to *that*, an' all!'

Once again, I laughed. It was for laughter, I realised, that I came to see my oldest sister.

'Well, you're lucky then, the pair of you,' was all I could think of to say. 'Let's just hope you don't end up with more mouths than you can feed.'

'Oh, what comes, comes,' was Edwina's pearl of wisdom in reply. 'Too many already. But if you carry on feeding each one – from yourself, I mean – then did you know it stops the next one coming too quick?'

I did not know, but the thought made me shudder slightly. I changed the subject and chatted with her for a few minutes more, which was as long as I could bear to remain amongst the chaos of complaining children and days' old mess.

It would be easy, I thought on my return walk, to despair of Edwina, to dismiss her, even. To see only the rough-spoken girl struggling through life with a less than useful mate and an unkempt brood. But I saw a primitive strength there; an ability to get by on the few good things she could grasp at, and do so without bitterness. It aroused in me an odd sort of admiration.

So I did not speak, earlier, of a thrilling type of excursion and nor was it every evening of the week. Sometimes Tom and I would eat our meal and then, if the weather was good and he was not overly tired, take a short stroll together before going to bed. But quite often he declared himself exhausted and in need of a doze; unsurprising since he worked almost from first light, had many heavy loads to heave on and off the boat and was brutally exposed to all weathers.

His dozing did not bother me, for by that time any conversation I had summoned up would have run its course. Though it did strike me that this habit could be responsible for the renewed energy he seemed able to muster later on. Jo was not alone in that, though my own enthusiasm for it did not match Edwina's.

If there was a bit of candle to spare I would often choose to stay down and read for a while after Tom had gone upstairs. This was not a ploy to avoid what Edwina professed she so enjoyed, for more often than not Tom would reawaken the moment I got into bed, however careful the manoeuvre. It was for the simple enjoyment of reading, and sometimes aloud. I had discovered that poems, in particular, were best *heard*, rather than experienced only inside one's head.

Of course it was a constant frustration to me that so few books were available. What I longed for was to peer into something new; into books that offered facts I did not yet know, that explained things I could not yet understand.

12

Alice had more on her shoulders than I did, and in the early days I would offer a hand with the chores. The offer was almost always declined.

'You mustn't worry,' she soon said. 'I *can* manage things here, really I can. And you've got your own home to care for now, haven't you?'

'Well, it takes less caring for than this one,' I said. 'And Tom can get by on less attention than Pa does. He just never complains, you know, never demands. It's odd – worrying, almost.' I chuckled. It did not in the least worry me, I have to confess.

'So just be grateful. And be *good* to him, Mary!' She put on one of her stern and disapproving looks, a habit that was becoming more frequent .

'I'm not *bad* to him, Alice, if that's what you think!' I felt irritated. 'Tom's not an unhappy man, if that's the idea you've got.' Edwina's words came back to me and I decided to see if a smile could be summoned to Alice's rather self-righteous face. 'He's a very happy man indeed, I'm sure it'll please you to know, just as long as he's got me in bed!'

She choked on a laugh, putting a hand to her mouth in surprise, for I seldom alluded to such matters with Alice, in humour or otherwise. Edwina was the more natural recipient.

'Well… that's good then, isn't it?' The chuckling continued a moment, followed by a sudden return of the more serious look. 'But nothing's – I mean, you're not *expecting*, are you, yet? You'd have told me?'

'Good Heavens, no. I'm not.' I hesitated for a moment. 'I certainly hope not, anyway.'

'Do you? *Really* hope not, Mary?'

'Yes, I do hope not, but I'd be bound to know… wouldn't I? I mean, something would feel different.' I realised I had no idea just what would feel different, but assumed something would have to.

'You know, I don't even want to think about it,' I said, without waiting for her reply. My own humour had now gone. 'The longer it takes the better, as far as I'm concerned. For*ever* might be best of all.'

A puzzled, perhaps sad, look came across Alice's face. But she must have thought better of pressing the matter further, and we hugged goodbye.

Walking home that day, by a circuitous route that took me along the river and past the old mill, the thought of being a mother occupied my mind. I wondered why I had failed to give the matter much consideration before. Why, in fact, I had barely considered it at all since the day Tom and I were married. That was more than a year ago now.

I knew I had no longing to have a child. Not even a vague sort of desire. It must, I decided, be something lacking in me, for that essential part of being a woman was simply not there. Perhaps I was by nature too selfish, too independent of mind, to experience what for most women is an unthinking urge. For there could be no doubt that the arrival of children would confine and limit me.

I knew I could never be the devoted, caring mother Ma had been, the sort that Alice was destined to be also. I simply could not be as selfless as they were, nor even as helplessly resigned to motherhood as Edwina. If and when a child appeared then I would do my best by it, but the thought did not sit easily in my mind. It made me fearful.

Tom and I were not impoverished. My existence might be monotonous, but it was not too grinding a one in comparison with many. Days, nights and weeks now passed in much the way I had known they would, and other women might find it difficult to see what it was I so dreaded the loss of.

But I did have one precious possession – I was mistress of at least some of my time. After leaving Alice each day, I would sense a real freedom. As long as I made sure to be home in time to provide Tom with his meal, I could take myself off wherever I chose. Or after the meal, if he was content to rest at home, it was possible to do the same. On good, Summer evenings I would take one of my books and sit leaning against a tree, perhaps perched on some high spot with a clear view. The light for reading was better outside.

Tom never questioned where or precisely how my time was spent and seemed happy for me to come and go as I pleased. Though it may be, of course, that he *understood* rather than was happy. Understood that freedom was essential to me and attempts to curtail it would be a mistake. And perhaps there were times when he felt better able to relax in the house, without the sense of my restlessness or of his own inadequate conversation.

But it is more likely that he was merely tolerant and kind. At all events, he knew I would unfailingly be back with him well before nightfall.

Tom had put up a sturdy shelf where I could keep the precious books, for these no longer needed to be hidden away and there was a great pleasure in having them always visible and to hand. The selection might be small – four volumes including the poetry book and a handful of religious pamphlets, but it was a miniature library of sorts; the first one that cottage had ever boasted. I think he was gratified to be able to provide it; unlike Pa, Tom did not feel diminished by the presence of books or by other people's ability to read them.

It was Alice who had insisted I brought the books with me.

'No-one but you will ever want these,' she had said, dragging out the box that had long been kept under our bed, 'so you must take all of them. Ma would've wanted you to. You're the only one of us who's ever managed to read properly. She was so proud of you, Mary, do you know that?'

I longed to have them, even the devout and tedious pamphlets, but felt obliged to argue.

'What about Fanny? She tries to read things sometimes. She could practise with these. I could try to help her.'

'She *won't* practise, you know she won't. She hasn't time, and she's not interested, in any case.' I knew this was true. 'And nor am I,' Alice continued in a firm tone. 'I can read a good few words – ones I need, or most of them – and some numbers as well. I think Fanny can too. More or less.' There was less conviction regarding the latter point. '*Anyway*' came the final declaration, 'it's more than a lot of people can do!'

As so often, she was right. Within the family I had been alone in my determination to read and in discovering the task was not beyond me to achieve. Ma wanted all her children to have the skill; one that she did not possess. She had tried her best to get us to Sunday School and managed to persuade the girls, at least, down to the church most weeks.

Learning came with no thanks to the old crow of a woman whose task it was to instruct, but despite her pessimistic approach – she remained unconvinced that children of poor families were ever likely to learn very much – I looked forward to those weekly sessions. Perhaps she saw a spark of light in me for often I was allowed to bring home some old, tattered volume, with a faithful promise to return it the following week.

Any such thing needed to be kept from Pa's attention, of course, for he scorned the idea that anything of value could come from books. '*Waste of time.* Nothing in one of them that's any damned use I can see. Reading that stuff won't put food on the table. So don't you go putting stupid ideas in their heads!'

Ma did not contradict him, but quietly and surreptitiously – for it would incense him to be openly defied – she did attempt to put a few stupid ideas into our heads.

I suspect that part of what drove me to learn was a huge desire to flout Pa's dictates. And if so, perhaps I owe him an odd sort of debt.

Unlike me, Alice seemed born to run a home and to care for whoever happened to be in it. As time went by she was becoming fussier, taking more and more pride in keeping things well-ordered and clean. I suspect she found an unexpected enjoyment at finding herself to be the one *in charge* of all domestic matters. Many women do, despite their complaints.

It will be clear that being an efficient cook and housewife were never ambitions of mine. That statement is not a boast and does not spring from some misguided sense of superiority; it is simply a fact. To me, the accomplishment of domestic tasks was a necessity, never a source of pride or satisfaction. As a consequence, I spent as little time on such matters as was decently possible.

Pa's house, on the other hand, was better run than ever before. Washing, baking and cleaning out now took place on their allocated, unvarying days, replacing the more haphazard arrangements that Ma once had. Though Ma, of course, had faced greater hurdles to orderliness than Alice; a large and boisterous family, demands and carping criticism from Pa, and the physical exhaustion I realised only later had afflicted her long before she was carrying Marguerite. Alice, by contrast, was young, blessed with robust energy, and against her Pa's bite was less vicious.

Though indeed, as the months went on, it seemed the man was becoming *odd*.

'He's really no trouble anymore,' she said, 'you know, not like – if you remember – he once could be.'

'Once *was*,' I corrected, 'and yes, I do remember. I remember all too well. It's a pity he wasn't a little less *trouble* to Ma.'

'Oh, Mary, do try to forgive,' Alice said. ' He's different now, he really is. And he's getting old, remember. The work tires him out more and more, I know it does.....I think that's why he's getting... *slow*.'

I decided not to argue my case against Pa. 'Well, I'm glad he's different, if that's what you think he is, because he's got every reason to be thankful to you, Alice. So don't stand for nonsense.' I looked at her. 'You know, if he's changed, it's because it suits him in some way. Does he ever empty his own pot from under the bed, these days?'

She tutted, as if I really had no need to mention such things. 'Oh, you know it's no trouble to me at all, seeing to that. It's a job women do, isn't it?'

I shook my head. As usual, it would have been fruitless to argue further.

Soon that household would not include Fanny, who had been kept on at what we still referred to, childishly, as the *Big House*. Their scullery maid had failed to return to service and it now appeared she would not. Perhaps the girl had found better employment elsewhere, or was needed at home to look after younger children in the family. Or it may be she was simply too ill to work again; nobody seemed to know, or even much to care. But if Fanny wanted to keep her job, then it seemed things would have to change.

'They're saying she'll need to sleep in,' Alice told me one morning. 'From next week on. She's none too happy with it.'

'No, I don't suppose she is.' I considered the matter for a moment. 'But it's probably just as well, you know. No more early morning walks, in the dark. Or late night ones. It'll be a relief, in fact, as far as I'm concerned.'

'Fanny will hate it.'

'Perhaps, but there are worse places to live. She'll get used to it, won't she, before too long? At least they give her three meals a day. And probably a bed to herself.'

'She doesn't want a bed to herself. She can't bear the thought of sleeping on her own.'

'Well, she'll need to get married then, won't she, the minute she can?'

I was trying to lighten the mood, but had not succeeded for Alice looked offended.

'She's *far* too young for you to be talking like that.'

'Of course she is, I was only... it doesn't matter. The point is, Alice, we just haven't much work, have we, at the moment? Not enough for Fanny to be useful. And she hates working the machines, anyway. We can't afford for her not to be earning any money at all. And what on earth would she do with herself, anyway? So I do think she's better off in service. It won't be for ever.'

'Even though you've always said you'd die before you'd go into it yourself?'

'Yes, even *though*.' I was beginning to feel irritated. It was hardly my fault that Fanny was required to live in. Her sleeping at home had always been an odd situation, though it must have suited the family well enough until now.

'They've been getting their money's worth out of her,' Alice went on. 'She's at work before six and there till God knows what time at night.'

'Just so. And that's why it's better that she lives there. Scullery maids *do* live in, don't they? In houses like that. Sooner or later they were going to demand it.'

Nevertheless, I did feel for Fanny. She and I were quite different, for although my younger sister was not stupid, she shared none of my desire to learn. She seemed, in truth, to have precious little curiosity about the world beyond home and no desire at all to go into it. Perhaps the only thing common to us both was a proneness to discontent.

Pa, Alice told me some time later, had also taken to spending more of the evening sitting at home than before. No longer did he come in after drinking and take himself straight off to bed. The change did not affect me, of course, as we hardly set eyes on each other. I did not go to that house on Sundays, and on the rare occasions that our paths crossed in the street there was no need for me to say anything for he would hurry on by, with barely a grimace of recognition. It was a courtesy I returned.

For Alice's sake, though, I was pleased, for his presence in the house was important to her.

'Not that he talks to me much,' she said, 'because he doesn't. He just sits there, in that chair, most of the time.' She gestured towards his usual perch by the fireplace. 'More and more, he does. Even when I tell him there's food ready. I have to say it two or three times, you know, before he gets himself up and to the table. And he always used to be so famished, didn't he? First one there and yelling at the rest of us to hurry. Shouting at Ma, if she was a bit slow getting things on the table. '

At least she remembered that, then.

'But he still eats it?'

'Usually he does, yes. If I don't put too much on his plate. But sometimes he'll sit in front of it a good while. And then he'll say "What's this, Alice? What's this you've given me?" And I don't mean in an angry way, not like he once used to. You know – when he didn't like what was there. It's odd.'

It seemed odd to me, too. Pa had always been taciturn; not the sort to engage in conversation at the table or encourage it. He had rarely commented on the food other than to complain. There were occasions when a whole plateful was hurled onto the fire in temper. Once he had calmed down, Ma would make up another one, taking a little from ours, and more from her own.

'Sometimes he even *thanks* me,' Alice added, as if bewildered. The thanks struck me as odder still, for I could not recall more than the odd grunt in acknowledgment of anything at all.

I wondered if age could indeed be changing him, unless it was a realisation of his single state. An aging man whose wife has been thoughtless enough to die first has to hope one of his female offspring will be willing to care for him in his doddering years. There was no sign of another woman being tempted in, so Alice was Pa's main hope. His only hope. He would turn up his nose at living in

Edwina's hovel and Fanny was young, her life unformed. Being cared for by me he would know was out of the question.

Marguerite, as might be guessed, remained in the possession of our treasured Mrs Spence. My prediction had proved correct up till now, and I had a suspicion that if things were left well alone, it might easily remain so. Alice and I continued with weekly visits to hand over the modest payment; enough to ensure the woman would not be out of pocket, at least.

Our sister was now tottering around with a firm sense of purpose, learning admirably fast how to push her foster brothers aside and managing to get more attention than they did. Strong and thriving, she was in no need of our concern but Alice had begun to fret over the situation and refused to let it rest.

'It just doesn't seem *right*, Mary,' she said to me, as we ate a dinner time meal of slightly stale bread with some bits of cheese and her home-made onion pickle. 'Not after all this time. It can't be right, can it?'

'Why on earth not? Marguerite is settled, and she's well. Thriving, in fact. Barely two years old and more or less rules the place! She's Mrs Spence's pride and joy.' I licked some pickle from my fingers. 'And as for *Mr* Spence – well, the poor fellow looks too dim-witted to know how many there are in the house. I expect he's even forgotten by now that she's not his.'

Alice smiled but her expression suggested she was unconvinced.

'Look, this way suits everyone, Alice, so why do you feel bad about it? I don't see how she'd be any better off here, not in any way at all.'

'But we're her family, Mary, aren't we? It just seems to me she should be here. And I don't think Pa would mind. Not if I looked after her.'

'I should think not! He wouldn't have any damned right to *mind*!' My indignation at the thought took me by surprise, causing me to swallow a tough bit of crust awkwardly. There followed a few moments of red-faced coughing.

'Pa minding or not minding really isn't the point,' I managed at length. 'The thing is that Marguerite is well cared for, and barely costing any more than she would here. And we do see her often enough, don't we? She's going to know she's got sisters, we'll be here if she needs us. And brothers too, come to that – though I'll bet neither of them have made the effort to set eyes on her yet.' I reached across the table to touch Alice's hand.

'Look, you're nineteen, Alice – you've got a life to lead. That'd be harder with Marguerite to look after. This is a very good arrangement, so why... why can't you just let things be?'

I, too, had a life to lead, and dull as it might be, it was one that I intended to lead without Marguerite. Alice's life I knew to be heading with some speed in the direction of young Harry next door. The word *marriage* had already escaped her lips, followed hastily by 'perhaps – maybe – in a few months or so.' Just days later there was a further glimpse of things to come, when I learned that Harry would 'very likely – well, it would make good *sense*, wouldn't it?' – move into that house with her and Pa. I could see it might be a welcome escape for him from the more crowded space next door.

Pa, Alice assured me, *didn't mind* that arrangement either. This particular absence of minding came as less of a surprise to me. Harry – except after too much drink – was quiet and pleasant enough and could be expected to make a useful contribution. He did not boast any particular skill but managed to keep himself well employed wherever labour was needed, whether on the canal, in workshops or on farms. He might even be useful on a knitting frame, should extra hands ever again be needed.

To his credit, Harry saw work as his natural, inevitable fate and was prepared to look for it. At least Alice's choice was likely to be an improvement on Edwina's.

'Don't you close your mind to other possibilities, though,' I urged, on taking in these tentative plans.

'What do you mean – other possibilities?' I was not sure if the look of puzzlement was genuine, but quite possibly it was.

'Just don't feel you have to hurry. Because there's others around as good as him, Alice. And better.' I heard an unpleasant echo of words spat at me by Pa when I told him of my intention to marry Tom. Though unlike him, I had only her well-being at heart.

'Harry's more than good enough, to my mind.' She sounded huffy and aggrieved, already protective of her chosen mate. There followed a few moments of quiet tension between us before I saw her start to soften and then give up the struggle to hold back a smile. 'And I do *love* him, as it happens, Mary. I'd say that's not too bad a reason for wanting to get married, is it, do you think? I mean – as *reasons go*?'

I was forced to laugh, knowing I had been caught. For the time being, I decided to abandon any attempt to play the older and wiser sister. It was likely to be a waste of effort, in any case. Alice might be naïve, but like many such she possessed a stubborn core. Harry was now a *loved* man – though I was as yet unconvinced that he deserved to be – and destined for the rest of his life to be stoutly defended and have his every need catered for. I just hoped he appreciated this unmerited good fortune.

'Well, why not keep him at arm's length for a while longer yet?' I found myself urging. 'Don't be like Edwina, Alice. If things go that way, then it means you'll have no choice.'

'But it's going to be my choice in any case! Whatever happens. Why do I need to keep saying it? And it's Harry's choice too. I trust him, you see.'

I saw all too well, but accepted the information with a resigned smile and a shrug of the shoulders.

'You do *like* Harry, don't you, Mary?' Her eyes had changed in a moment from indignant to pleading. It was important to Alice that those she loved also thought well of each other.

In answer I got up and hugged her goodbye. 'I like him well enough. I just want you to be treated as you should be, that's all. I'm prepared to like anyone who's good to you.'

In truth I held no particular feelings for Harry, in either direction. He was affable enough, the best of next door's untidy bunch. Unexceptional, but Alice was not seeking the exceptional. She wanted an affectionate, reliable man to care for, and Harry was as likely to fit this not too demanding bill as well as anyone.

What I did believe was that Alice – unlike me – deserved a man who loved her. Perhaps that man, too, could be Harry.

I told her I would remember to buy fresh bread on the way there tomorrow.

13

Almost a year later, I was not in the least unhappy that there was still no sign of a child on the way. Not unhappy, but in fact a little surprised. I could remember Ma's words, when she talked of a girl in our street who had been married for around two years, and probably letting her fellow make free with her a while before that.

'I doubt she'll have any now. If it hasn't happened by this time, then it's likely not going to.' I also remember she added *'poor girl'*, for despite the drudgery involved in caring for children, Ma was unable to imagine that any woman could be happy to find herself without them.

I was fit and healthy. And Tom, as it turned out, had lost none of his initial enjoyment of night time activity. The shyness and diffidence had mellowed and I was – mercifully – *thanked* less often these days. But he remained a gentle, not a coarse, man and so there were no reasons for me to object. I did not find what we did to be a pleasure, any more than it had been that first night. It was not something I looked forward to, and had Tom not wanted it then naturally I would never have made the suggestion myself. There was a certain relief, each time, at getting it over. But after all, I had long understood that this was not regarded as a pleasure for women. It was what men desired, and unfailingly enjoyed. Something a man needed and was always hungry for.

But that part of being a wife never struck me as abhorrent. It did not repel me or cause discomfort, and those first few minutes of most nights, before he fell into an exhausted sleep, always seemed to please Tom very much. It was pleasure I was willing enough to provide for he was a hardworking man, as well as a kind one, and I felt a genuine fondness for him.

I did wonder if Tom, too, was surprised, perhaps even disappointed, that I was not yet carrying his child. We never spoke of it, but I suspected he might have been happy for such a thing to happen, if only to bind us together more closely. Motherhood would make me more reliant on him. It would also keep me in the house and discourage the wanderings he tolerated so uncomplainingly.

Though looking back, I see it could have been more than this. I believe Tom might have wanted to be the father of a child. The father of a whole family of children. And whatever his limitations, it was a role he would have been worthy of. His children could have been considered fortunate.

When I walked out alone in the evenings, I would cover a greater distance than when accompanied by Tom. One such occasion must have been an early June, by far the best time of year, I have always thought, when days are near their longest and Summer hovers in promise.

Tom had returned tired from work. He devoured a good helping of thick potato soup with a hunk of bread, sat himself down in the old armchair we had once bought for him at the market and fell resolutely asleep. I did not feel like reading that evening, and even less like busying myself with some mundane task until he came round again. In any case, our usual languid stroll was not what was needed, even supposing he might have enough energy restored for that. Despite my own early start and day of labour – admittedly less arduous than his – I felt more than normally restless and uncomfortable in the room, and even less desire than usual to spend the evening in Tom's company, undemanding as it always was. Probably for that very reason. God knows, the poor man faced an impossible task in providing me with whatever it was I needed; perhaps his frequent exhaustion was not to be wondered at.

What I wanted that evening was to walk far and to walk fast. Not with a book this time but for the sheer pleasure of movement, of freedom, space, solitude. I have always been quite different from Alice, indeed from most people, who only cared to walk for the plain purpose of arriving somewhere. With the rigours of their daily lives, that was more than sufficient for them. They would have considered it odd to wander without any particular aim, merely to feel the sun or the wind in their hair.

Ma once told me she loved to roam as a young girl. If she had lived, and as the struggle of family and motherhood lessened, perhaps she and I would have walked at times together. It could not have been at my natural pace, of course, which was a fast one; I would often find myself breaking into a run without intending or even noticing it. For a number of years before she died, Ma had been unable to move quickly and was rarely without some pain or other.

Sometimes I imagined us chatting together, free of other listeners. I would hear myself asking her questions, discovering, perhaps, the person my mother once was before harshness and exhaustion subdued her. It is sad that often we start to long for such conversations, for such understanding, only someone has slipped beyond our reach.

On that particular evening I decided to pull on my boots, open the door and set off, with no thought of returning until it started to become dark. There was no need to creep about or leave in stealth, for Tom did not disturb easily and he was not, in any case, likely to raise any objection.

It was rare for me to walk along the canal pathway, which could seem tedious in its flatness, in its sameness and regularity. But that evening I decided to do just that, simply because no further thought about the route would then be needed. I could put one foot in front of the other, fall into an easy stride and head a fair distance along the towpath. The rhythmic crunch of grit would be a steady, satisfying sound in the background. It might even help me to recite my poems.

The choice was a good one, as it turned out, for the usually grey waterway had been transformed by the beginnings of what was set to be a striking, orange sunset and had taken on the appearance of a natural river. A light breeze caused movement in the water, which was dappled with amber colours and leafy reflections from the trees that bordered it.

There was still some activity around the wharf, though it was likely to be deserted by the time I returned. Wisely or otherwise I never felt any fear in being alone. Even if I misjudged time or distance and found myself out in near darkness, I did not worry about the things that many women do, and are encouraged to. Tom, who had seemed concerned about my safety in the early days, had given in on the matter, as on much else.

Not only had I roamed the area from a young age and knew it intimately, but I moved about with the sort of sturdy, determined gait that tended to deter drunk or unsavoury men from any thought of following me, or even calling out with lewd suggestions. Though on occasions they did, of course. There will always be men who do, whether from lust, drink, or for the simple amusement of it. They expect a woman to be unnerved, and find an entertainment in that. Most are harmless enough and at the time I knew nearly all of them, in any case. A hard look and a sharp retort would prove the best ways to ensure a rather embarrassed, sulky retreat. Men with more unscrupulous intent are rare, thank God. Too rare, in my opinion, for me to sacrifice my precious freedom.

Light was just starting to fail as I completed my return along the canal path and reached the buildings of the weir once again. The sunset was now spoilt by incoming cloud and the scene was back to its familiar, almost comforting dullness. I could see two men standing near the water's edge, not far from the little warehouse. They faced one another, and the hands of the taller one were moving in what appeared to be some sort of enthusiastic, insistent explanation. The other man appeared to be listening. He seemed attentive and was quite still apart from an occasional nod of the head.

I have a well-honed ability to *take in* people, even from some distance. These two were not canal workers, may well not have been from the village, but I judged that they were no threat. It seemed more than likely they might even fail to notice me, wrapped up as they were with some matter of intense interest to themselves. Though as I drew closer and my own footsteps became audible, the listener, who was also the taller man, did look round. I was further reassured on realising that his face was somehow familiar. He peered towards me before calling out.

'Is it *Mary*? Well, good Lord!'

I moved across towards them. 'It is, Will, the very one. How are you?'

Our paths had not crossed for a long time. Will Parker had married a good while back and no longer lived in the village. I understood he had done better for himself than most but knew nothing more.

'I'm well, thank you. Yes, very well.' He hesitated, as if unsure what it was that politeness must now require. 'And this is… this is Mr *Bateman*.' The surname was not one I recognised. Mr Bateman smiled and offered his hand.

'Oh, just *Thomas*, please. I do hope we didn't frighten you, lurking around here like this. So have you walked very far, Mary?' There was an ease of manner about him that was not typical of the men I knew, including Will. He and Thomas Bateman were of different types, and I wondered what it was they had to talk about which so engaged them both.

'Some way, yes – a bit further than I intended. In fact it was quite a relief to spot Will. From a distance I had you down for a couple of boat robbers!' He laughed at that and his companion grinned, but Will seemed to be shifting his weight from one foot to the other, in the manner of someone still unsure what to do or say next.

'Nothing so exciting, I'm sorry to admit. We've been on an evening meander ourselves, and I've been talking poor old William here nearly into the ground with… well, plans for robbery *of a sort*, I suppose you'd have to say!'

'Really? I don't think you have the face of a criminal.'

'Perhaps that's an advantage. There *are* those who consider it a crime, you see. But fortunately for us it's not quite outside the law. Or not yet.'

'Well, I'm very curious. Just what sort of robbery is it that you're planning, Thomas?'

He grinned. A wide, boyish grin that invited me to share a mischievous secret.

'I'm a rather strange, eccentric type – I like to dig things out of the ground and make off with them. William, here, aids and abets me in this underhand work. Couldn't think of tackling it without him.' The face turned a little, to include his companion.

I was intrigued, as he intended. Thomas Bateman did not look in the least strange or underhand. He had a pleasing, animated face and was also young. Around my own age, as far as I could judge in the dimming light. Neither old nor odd enough to have achieved the dubious label of eccentric.

'And you dig up – what? Is it *bodies* perhaps? I know there's a great deal of money to be made doing that, provided you're in touch with the right sort of doctor, needless to say! The sort who's desperate to get his hands on the things.'

He laughed again. 'That's illegal money, though. But in fact I do manage to dig up bodies, when things go well. Very old ones. Not an ounce of flesh left on the bones.'

My eyes probably widened a little.

'Thomas is an archaeologist,' Will interjected, helpfully. 'He's interested in digging up ancient burial grounds – with great care, of course – so that he can study all the different kinds of things that… '

'I'm quite sure Mary would have worked that out, William – pity you had to butt in!' His tone was jocular but there was no mistaking who was in charge here. Despite being the elder of the two by a fair number of years, Will, I sensed, was the follower, the listener, probably the carrier out of instructions. He might well be in some awe of Thomas Bateman, who was articulate and also, I had judged in an instant, better bred than the two of us, better bred than most. There was about him the sort of intelligent and relaxed confidence that spoke of privilege.

'Perhaps I would. But at least Will's saved me time in getting there.' I sensed Will's awkwardness and felt I should say something to defend him. He had always seemed an above the run-of-the-mill type himself, a serious and thoughtful man, given his ordinary background. Though easy, sociable conversation was not a skill he had managed to acquire.

It was one possessed, however, by Thomas Bateman, and I felt more than enough interest in him and his grave robbing plans to encourage the use of it. Not to mention the pleasure in exercising my own mind, which had not become too rusted, I was relieved to find, even given the years of Tom's benign and caring neglect. The one history book I had ever managed to lay my hands on, I had devoured. But this had gone back only to the eighth King Henry and his long-suffering wives. It had not touched on the more ancient, lost times that so fascinated this Mr Thomas Bateman; times about which I knew nothing whatever. But I wanted to know. I felt an immediate desire to engage with him, to absorb just a few of the facts he had been fortunate or diligent enough to acquire.

There was a heady sort of pleasure in finding myself able to question, to discuss, to understand. Thomas did not appear to mind my insistence. He made no polite attempt to bring things to a close and to bid me a farewell, and if poor Will would like to have done so then he was unfortunate, for the man was not consulted. Thomas became all the more animated as we continued, and quite some time must have passed before I had a sudden sense of the lateness and felt compelled to bring it all to a halt.

'I really must be making my way home,' I announced, at the same time offering a hand to shake his once more. 'There might be worry about me by now.' I chose not to identify the worrier and hoped he would not ask. There did not seem any good reason to bring Tom into our conversation.

'Of course; please forgive us.' He included Will in the apology, who in fact had contributed nothing since his much earlier intervention and now bore the expression of the long suffering.

'Time's gone by, and I've been talking far too much. You must let us walk you home, Mary. It's becoming dark now.'

'No… please. There's no need at all.'

I may have replied sharply, for I did not want to be walked home. My mind rejected it. Being walked home would cause something to be spoilt; it would be broken in the act of shaking hands yet again outside the cottage and offering thanks; most of all in being obliged, in response to the inevitable polite enquiry, to define my own life in some way. I did not want to define it, or not then, for I felt it would reduce me. It would prick the bubble of Mr Thomas Bateman's curiosity, and I was well aware that his curiosity had been aroused.

For it was plain he had found it difficult to place me – this *girl from the village*, walking out alone during the middle of the evening. One who did not show embarrassment or become in the least tongue-tied when introduced, who was eager to engage in something well above an everyday type of conversation. I knew it had taken him by some surprise, that he was intrigued. He had encountered an intelligent, questioning mind where nothing of the sort could have been expected.

'Really, I assure you, I'll be quite safe.' I attempted to shed what could have been a look of panic. 'It's not far and I'm well used to all the narrow pathways round here.'

'But I'd feel much happier to… '

'No, truly, there's no need – it's very kind of you – but I'm a natural wanderer, you see, and quite used to the dark. In fact, in my own way I must be every bit as eccentric as you are!'

Thomas seemed amused at the thought, but I sensed he was torn between the feeling that as a gentleman he should insist and a reluctance to appear overbearing.

'This is one of my favourite walks,' I was shocked, even horrified, to find myself adding. 'I often come here in the evening. It's so peaceful, but very safe underfoot.'

There was a split second of silence before he gave in.

'If you're quite sure, then we'll wish you goodnight.' And I was on my way, while the pair of them remained on the weir. I knew, without turning my head, that he would be watching, keeping me in sight as far a distance as possible. Perhaps both of them were doing so.

As they made their way home – I realised they were to do the journey in poor light and by unknown means – I could guess the questions that might be put to Will. A few details would be revealed, though since he had not been about in the village for a long time, any knowledge Will had of my more recent life was likely to be vague, at best. Not that it could matter. I do not believe I had in my mind an intention to deceive, merely a desire to preserve that evening's strange experience. I wanted to *possess* it, to hold it clear and unspoilt in my memory.

I walked quickly, hoping Thomas would not suddenly think better of things and come striding up, Will dutifully alongside. But there was no sound of footsteps, and just a few minutes later I opened the door of the cottage.

14

I did not return to the canal towpath the following evening, even though a wet, dreary day had by then turned into something drier and sunnier. Tom suggested a stroll and we took a lazy one towards the home – if that grimy mess could be so called– of Edwina and Jo.

Unusually for the time of evening, Jo was there. Perhaps money was short enough to keep him from the drinking place down the road, but he was civil enough to pour us both an offering from a chipped jug of ale, kept cool on a shaded ledge with a cold, flat stone placed over the top. Edwina's raucous shouts came from the room upstairs, as she made what sounded vain attempts to get the children onto their bedding. At least they had some these days, and were not still snuggling in with their parents. A common enough habit, but one that had always caused me to shudder a little.

'I'll give her a hand,' I said, putting my mug down on the greasy floor. I had more authority about me than my sister and could often achieve things without the high-pitched, desperate tones.

'God, I never heard you come!' She had been stopped mid-shout and the two older offspring had also been surprised into bringing their jumps and leaping to a sudden halt and gawping in my direction.

'I'm not surprised.' I turned to the guilty pair, assumed an appropriate glare and pointed to the corner of the room. 'Now you get yourselves under that blanket! The pair of you, right now!'

'You'll be good at it, when you get your own,' Edwina said, shrugging her shoulders as they pouted but did as they were told.

Several evenings elapsed before I went near the canal again. Other things intervened; now that the days were stretching out and becoming warmer, Tom was less inclined to doze and on at least one other occasion was the one to suggest we take a stroll.

Another evening Fanny arrived at our door, looking anxious, red eyes and blotched cheeks announcing that she had recently been in tears. I pulled her inside and gave her a tight hug, causing more tears to emerge in the process.

'What on earth is it, Fanny?'

'I think I'm ill. There's something wrong with me. Something bad.'

I did not panic. Fanny tended to worry easily and could take her anxiety towards panic at times. There had been several occasions when she had been convinced she had some dreadful disease and would shortly die. It crossed my mind to wonder why she had not gone straight home to Alice rather than come to me. Although I was a couple of years older, it was Alice who had assumed the role of *mother* within the family, by instinct taking over that mantle from Ma. She was far more suited to the role than I was. But Fanny and I had always shared a certain bond, and perhaps that was what drew her to me now. Or it could simply have been that the distance to walk was a little less.

'Now just sit down.' I pushed her gently towards a chair. Tom, seated in the other one, looked at me, his eyebrows raised in question. I nodded, glancing towards the door, and he got to his feet with a look of relief. Like most men, Tom did not find tears a comfortable thing to deal with.

'I'll be getting on with a few jobs outside,' he muttered, touching my shoulder as he left.

'I'll make tea soon, Tom. And bring a cup out for you.' I felt grateful that he knew when to disappear and, unlike Pa, would do so without sarcasm or cruel words.

I pulled the other chair closer to where Fanny sat, hunched up in misery, and reached forward to take hold of her hands.

'Alright. So what is it, Fanny? Because you don't look ill to me, you know. Just miserable. What is it that's making you so unhappy?'

There was a loud sniff and one hand released itself from mine and went up to cover her nose. I ferreted in my sleeve for the bit of cloth always kept tucked inside – I have a horror of being caught out by a dripping nose – and passed it to her.

'I don't like it, at the house. I *hate* it!'

'Well, I know that.' She had never liked it. I did not believe she was mistreated, but the housekeeper, a Mrs Jenson, struck me as tight-faced and charmless, as well as very demanding. Nothing beyond what her job required, as she would see it.

'She can't bear it if you laugh,' Fanny had complained more than once. 'And I can't bear *her*,' she now added. 'I can't bear *any* of them!'

Perhaps Mrs Jenson set a dour tone, for none of the other three older servants had taken Fanny under her wing. Fanny believed the one who shared her small attic room resented having to do so, spending any spare moment available with the other two.

I could recognise that my sister was not a girl people might immediately warm to. She had always been the quietest of us, but as a young child possessed a sort of gentle, pretty charm that for the time being, at least, seemed to have quite deserted her. Now fourteen, she had become rather plain, any earlier attractiveness overridden by a poor complexion, lank, straight hair and an unhappy expression that was almost a fixture. She was shy, more so than ever before, and to those who did not have time or take the trouble to get to know her, this could come across as sullenness. And probably it was, of a sort. A lack of warmth, of amiability. The line between shyness and downright unfriendliness can be a fine one and it struck me that Fanny might be found on the wrong side of it.

'It won't be for ever, Fanny. And you won't always feel so miserable. It isn't always an easy thing, is it, being fourteen? You're not a child any more, but you're not a grown up person either.'

I felt sympathy for her but knew I was inadequate. The person my sister needed, the one she painfully lacked, was Ma.

'It's not just that. I do hate it there… but it's not *just* that.'
'So what is it then? Tell me.'

She took a time to wipe her nose, then looked across at me, eyes filling with tears once again.

'Something horrible's been happening to me... yesterday. And it's been happening today as well!' The tears found their way down her cheeks. I moved to the edge of my chair and put my hands on her shoulders.

'Now stop. *Whatever* it is, I'll be able to help you.' I spoke with a firm confidence but a certain sense of horror was unwrapping itself inside me. The dreadful thought had come into my head that Fanny must have been taken advantage of by some man or other. A man who worked at the house, perhaps. Or some rough delivery boy who had regular access to the kitchen or scullery and knew she was likely to be found there alone. Even a member of the family. I was aware it was not a rare occurrence in wealthy households.

Had Fanny been molested? I was ready to march over there that very minute if it turned out to be so. I would not have thought even long enough to ask Tom to come with me, for there was more than enough fury gathering for me to face the task alone.

'*What* horrible thing has been happening to you, Fanny? Tell me *exactly*.'

She hesitated, staring now at the floor, while my mind moved on. I was tempted to get up and fling on a shawl while she struggled to bring her words together.

'It's that, you see... there's blood coming out of me.' The words came in a whisper and I barely caught them. My eyes must have widened. 'A *lot* of blood – it's coming from... from down here.' She moved her hand to touch between the top of her legs.

'So something's wrong with me, isn't it? There must be something *awful*, that's wrong.' She looked at me, her red, spot-blemished face a picture of distress. 'Ma had bad bleeding, you once told me so, didn't you? And then she died. So do you think I'm going to die, Mary?'

It must have shocked Fanny when my hands went to cover my face, and I uttered a sound that was part gasp of relief, part laughter. Her own eyes widened.

'What are you laughing at?' The look of hurt mingled with angry indignation as she stood up. 'Why are you *laughing* at me?'

'I'm not. I'm not laughing at you, Fanny. It's relief, you see, just relief.'

'What do you mean?'

'Look – there's nothing *wrong* with you, that's all. Just sit down.' She remained as she was, the expression unchanged. 'Sit *down*, Fanny, for Heaven's sake! I'll try to explain it to you in a moment. First I think you need to drink something hot. And so do I!'

Though as I got to my feet it crossed my mind that a practical matter might need to be dealt with first.

'Did you find something to *use*, before you came here? You know – to soak up the blood?'

The look shifted to embarrassment. 'I got a big cloth out of the cleaning cupboard, only an old-looking one, but I didn't ask any-one, I just went upstairs and tied it… you know, tied it round me down there. But when I was com-ing back down, Mrs Jenson saw me. She asked what I was doing and I said I'd been sick and that's why I'd gone upstairs, to lie down for a couple of minutes. She said I should have told her. Her face looked like it always does.'

I nodded slowly, picturing the scene.

'And how did you manage to leave the house, to come here?'

'She said do you feel better, and I said no, Mrs Jenson, I don't. And then I said I'd been feeling bad for days, because I'd heard that Pa was ill and probably going to die soon, and I don't know why I said that because I know it's a lie but I just said it and I started crying… and then she said, look child, run off home for a couple of hours, go and see your Pa and your sisters. Just you make sure you're back here by the time it gets dark. And you'll have to do the pots then, and go to bed late.' I remembered the only time Fanny talked so much was when she was in a panic.

'Well, that was kind of her, wasn't it? Whatever you think of the woman, that was kind.'

There was another loud sniff. 'I suppose so.'

I took my time getting the drinks ready, leaving Fanny to sit quiet for a while. The fire needed to be brought back to life first in any case, for since heating up our own broth I had let it die down. The June evening did not require extra heat, though that particular day had been quite a chilly one.

Now that relief had drowned out worry, it struck me as extraordinary that she had managed to remain so ignorant. The girl had no fewer than three older sisters, and although we never spoke of such things in front of Pa or the boys – except Edwina, whose sense of modesty had never existed – they were mentioned freely enough amongst ourselves. By some strange means Fanny had managed not to hear, or else had taken nothing in. Perhaps she had not *wanted* to know, had set her mind against the knowing. Had we contrived to shield her from these inconvenient facts in some way, treating her as the child she then still seemed?

Whatever the reason, Fanny had remained unaware, and as a result for the last two days had felt a sort of lonely terror. I felt a vague but uncomfortable guilt for this, and knew Alice would too when I told her. We had not taken Ma's place; we had let our younger sister down.

I decided to make up for it as best I could. Explain to her that this messy, uncomfortable nuisance was just something women had to put up with, break the unwelcome news that from now on she could expect the same thing to happen every few weeks. Then I would search out some rags and fit her up with them before taking her back to the house.

'Here, drink this.' I put the cup straight into Fanny's hands, knowing the warmth would be comforting. 'I'd forgotten there was a little milk left, so that's what I've heated up for you; it'll do you good.' She spread her fingers around the cup and started sipping at once. There was no trace of tears now, just the tired, woebegone face that was typical of her. At least she was no longer expecting to die.

An hour or so later, the two of us set off back to the house. My efforts to chat fell on stony ground and she remained subdued, perhaps exhausted from anxiety and a sleepless night. To fill the silence and distract her from her own woes, I spoke of Marguerite and a recent chickenpox. She listened without comment.

'So she's alright now?' was all I was asked at the end.

'It seems so, yes.' I turned to glance at her. 'Perhaps you should go and see her sometime?'

'Yes – sometime.'

We walked on, more slowly than I would normally do, but Fanny was in no haste. I wondered if she had pains, to add to her general discontent.

'She doesn't remember Ma, does she?' The sudden question took me by surprise.

'Well no, of course she doesn't.'

A further silence followed.

'Would Ma be alive, do you think... if she hadn't had her?'

I sighed. 'I don't know, Fanny. Perhaps she would. But it's not Marguerite's *fault*, you know. It was just one of those things.'

I wanted to say 'if you need to blame someone, then blame Pa.' But I stopped myself, for Fanny had enough bad things in her head just now. And if the truth be known, the hatred I had for him in my own head was losing a little of its ferocity. I did not much care what happened to him, but no longer wished him harm. These days he was a dog without teeth, in every way.

It was Mrs Jenson herself who came to the servants' door, tucked away at the back of the gaunt, sprawling house, in response to Fanny's hesitant knock. I recognised her at once from my sister's comment about the poor woman's 'horrid, bulging eyes.' She was taken by surprise to see Fanny accompanied, and the severe expression modified itself in an instant to a forced half smile.

'Mrs Jenson?' My voice was confident and clear, for I suspected an assertive form of politeness was required with this woman. 'I'd like to thank you for allowing my sister to visit home for a while. It was very kind indeed.'

'Well… ' She looked a little unsure. 'Your father's ill, I believe. Gravely ill, so she's told me.'

'Yes, that's so, I'm afraid, and it was a great *comfort* for him to see Fanny,' I assured her, remaining loyal to the story. 'In fact he seems to be improved, just a little, today.'

I thought it better not to give the impression that Pa's demise was inevitable and imminent.

'It was a great help that she came,' I continued, putting a hand out to touch Fanny's arm. 'Even though we could see she's not too well herself.'

'She did say to me about that. It's nothing much, I don't expect. You know – young girls and their aches and pains. Always something.'

'Well, Fanny's never been a girl to complain,' I said, with no regard for honesty. 'And I'd be so grateful, Mrs Jenson, if you could make sure she doesn't get herself too exhausted. Especially, you know, with the *family* worry she has at the moment.'

'I'll do my best,' came the rather grudging reply. 'She's not a bad little worker, provided she's kept an eye on. Would be nice, mind you, if she didn't look so miserable most of the time.' She turned to Fanny. 'Well, are you going to get yourself inside then, my girl? There's a bit of cold supper been left for you.'

I thanked Mrs Jenson once again and kissed my sister goodbye, keeping this as brief as possible to avoid any risk of a fresh flow of tears.

The distance back of around four miles could now be covered far more quickly than it had taken the two of us earlier. But in fact I felt in no hurry to return home. It was good to be alone with my thoughts and I decided on a longer and more meandering route back to the cottage.

I hoped my doorstep conversation – for she had not invited me in – with Mrs Jenson would help Fanny a little. At least the woman was now aware of my existence, and despite the politeness I hoped she had gleaned that I was not a person to underestimate. She would now be aware that Fanny had an elder sister who was watchful for her, someone not in awe of any sour-faced housekeeper.

I also hoped my sister would pull herself together a bit; perhaps even realise her lot was not too terrible a one. She had food and a bed in a clean house. She even had money – if a tiny amount – to call her own. There were plenty of her age leading worse lives, and no shortage of girls who would be willing to take her place. Though I knew Fanny was unlikely to see things that way, and neither would I have done, at fourteen years old and in the same situation. Not at any age, in fact.

Half a mile or so on, my thoughts turned away from Fanny. Away from everyone and everything that made up the reality and routines of my daily life. They turned, with what seemed a sudden, powerful resolve of their own, towards Thomas. And their adamant, insistent message was that a way must be found of spending some time in his company again. I could not remember ever feeling so zestful, so *alive* as during that strange evening by the canal.

The heady sensation of it had to be experienced at least once more.

I could not, of course, get myself to Middleton. The return walk – even if I could find my way, would devour far too much time. In any case, what could I possibly do in that village on arrival? Loiter about in the hope that Thomas might suddenly emerge from one of the larger houses? The thought was mortifying. And this house of his may not even be in the village itself, but lie in some unknown direction beyond it.

There was no choice other than to hope Thomas might venture across to Cromford again. That he would even do so on a number of occasions in the hope of our paths crossing. A preposterous idea, if looked at coldly. Cromford was some miles from Middleton, a hard, inconvenient ride. Nevertheless, something told me my hope was not a mere flight of fancy.

Well before reaching home I had set my mind firmly on walking out alone the following evening. It was just to be hoped that neither illness, bad luck nor Fanny's woes would act in some way to prevent it, that Tom would not take it into his head to accompany me and that the weather would remain fair. The chances were not altogether in my favour, I realised, but if it were humanly possible then I would make my way back to the canal and along the towpath, at a similar time of day as had been done before. And if the excursion brought me nothing more than a hearty walk, then I would be prepared to do it again. And yet again.

15

As it was, nothing and no-one contrived to prevent my excursion. I arrived at the weir a little earlier than before and set off along the rough pathway, glad of the brisk movement and also of the evening breeze, for it had been a warm and rather humid day. I told myself that this outing must be enjoyed for its own sake, without silly expectation and the risk of disappointment. Why would Thomas make the very considerable effort to be here? And if he had already made such an effort, on a previous evening, then he was even less likely to do so again.

I turned back to make the return trip at a well-remembered point, where two branches of an unwieldy ash tree dipped right down to touch the surface of the water. The branches looked dead and in need of chopping, otherwise they would soon be broken off by passing barges and join many other bits of debris in the canal. Tom would often grumble about this, for the channel was not wide in the first place.

Perhaps I had imagined that by covering the same ground, at the same pace, events would unfold as before. As the walk neared its end I even found myself looking keenly towards the weir, in the stupid expectation of seeing two figures hanging about there in the shadows, engrossed in their conversation.

Of course no-one of the sort was anywhere to be seen, and I chided myself for the stupidity of hoping for it. It would be honest to admit that what I most hoped for was the sight of Thomas on his own, poor old Will somehow dispensed with. Just Thomas, standing there alone, reflecting, perhaps, on the latest plan to explore an ancient burial ground. This part of Derbyshire was rich in them, so he had claimed. Whole treasure troves of knowledge were waiting to be unearthed. *Plundered* as some, he said, had described it. But Thomas did not see himself as a plunderer; he had no intention of selling the goods on. The desire was to hold and to study them, to *understand*.

But if he was having any such thoughts, it was not here, on that evening. And why would it be? I pictured Thomas at home; he had barely mentioned *home* on the previous occasion and despite huge curiosity I had not probed, having no desire to be then drawn into talking of my own. All that had been gleaned on the subject was that he lived in Middleton, a tiny village near the larger one of Youlgreave, in a house that belonged to his grandfather. There was no mention either of parents or of brothers and sisters.

I did not believe for a moment that Thomas's home bore the slightest resemblance to anything I had lived in. I pictured him in a place of style and comfort, a number of servants on hand to cater for him, his grandfather and for any other as yet unmentioned person. There would be books in this house, of that I was certain; perhaps many shelves filled with books. And I saw in my mind a large table, dark oak, perhaps, and well crafted, its surface littered with Thomas's notes and sketches. His grandfather would not hurl them to the floor. He would not shout at him to 'get them damned things out of my sight, or they go on the fire!' Thomas may even have his own sitting room – or *drawing room* as he was more likely to call it. I had heard this was not unusual for a young man in a wealthy household.

A couple of evenings later I ventured to the canal again, telling myself I would walk just a little way and return home early, that it was as good a place to take exercise as any. By this time a certain logic prevailed, if only up to a point. I had no real expectation of setting eyes on Thomas; in fact it now seemed ridiculous to imagine he might make the long ride across to that particular part of Cromford, an area of no exceptional beauty, merely on the chance of crossing my path again. Whatever interest I had shown in his work, however lively and engaging our conversation, he was certain to be acquainted with plenty of others who would appreciate and entertain him just as well.

I did, of course, have an attractive face; the word *beautiful* had often enough been used. There seems no point in being coy about such things, particularly now, when the beauty has gone. From quite a young age I would turn heads whenever I walked in the street, though Ma used to claim there was more to this than appearance. 'You've got something special about you,' she used to tell me, though never, of course, in Pa's hearing. 'Some sort of power. It makes people look, makes them want to listen, as well. I don't know what it is – can't tell you. But it's not something I've ever had, and not your sisters, either.'

But it seemed likely that Thomas Bateman would be acquainted with a good number of young women with pleasant faces and *powers* all of their own. Certainly enough to deter him from hovering around Cromford canal on a damp, gloomy evening.

By the time I turned to walk back, at an earlier point than before, logic had prevailed enough for my mind even to start wandering away from the matter. Other thoughts entered, though none of any importance. Much of my attention was caught by the noisy squabbling of birds up and down the opposite bank, inspired by their perpetual quest for food, mates and territory. So it came as a confusing, almost – inexplicably – unwelcome sensation, to take in the male figure heading along the pathway towards me. A slight curve in the water course, along with the antics of the birds, had prevented me from spotting this figure earlier. But I knew immediately, despite the now poor light and fair distance that still lay between us, that it was *him*.

I debated for just a second whether to continue walking. I could do so while still staring vacantly across to the other bank as if I had noticed nothing. The alternative was to remain where I was and wait for Thomas to make his approach. This seemed a better strategy; it at least gave me a few moments to pull my thoughts together, and avoided having to decide at just what point it was appropriate to give a surprised, warm smile of recognition. Thank God for the bickering jackdaws, I thought, as I drew to a halt and turned away from the pathway, surveying them with a show of fascination. There would be no need, now, for me to speak first.

'I hoped you would be here.' He was standing behind me; close. Perhaps closer than a gentleman would normally do, for I could feel his breath on my loose hair.

'Did you?' I turned round to face him.

'I did, yes... ' He hesitated, not unsure of himself, I sensed, but merely deciding what to say next. 'It's not often,' he continued after a moment or two, 'that I've enjoyed a conversation as much as that one we had the other evening. I must admit it left me wanting to find another such occasion – in the hope of enjoying it once again.'

'Well, I'm pleased,' I made an effort to keep my voice warm but not too eager. 'And I enjoyed it very much too.' I smiled at him. 'It's a rare day in my life that I get the chance to talk of – well, such interesting things. Much rarer than in yours, I imagine!'

'Ah – now *your life*!' Thomas seized on the topic more quickly than I had anticipated. 'That's something I remember you hardly mentioned at all, that evening. And it was impolite of me not to enquire more.'

'Not at all.' It was plain enough that he intended to enquire now.

'I could tell you're someone who not only reads a great deal, but *thinks* a very great deal, also.'

'And that's surprising, is it, for a simple village girl?'

'Oh, I suspect you're far from simple, Mary.' He smiled, his eyes warm and amused, taking no offence at the sharpness in my tone, which I had immediately regretted. But it seemed no damage was done; Thomas was not a man to be easily embarrassed or cornered into apologies.

'Let me walk back with you, may I? Along this stretch, at the very least.' I was relieved there was no insistence on *walking me home*. Perhaps on this occasion he did not want that either, or else realised the suggestion was likely to unsettle me. He offered his arm, and there seemed no reason why I should not allow my own to slip into the crook of his elbow.

We started along the pathway towards the village, at a far more leisurely pace than when I had been making my way alone. But now it seemed natural to walk in this way, for I think neither of us had any desire to reach our destination quickly. Such talking as we wanted to do needed to be done here, for it would not be sensible for me to be seen loitering with him for any length of time on the weir. Tongues wagged easily in the place, and now there was – I have to say I was glad of it – no Will hanging onto his shoulder, whose presence would suggest to onlookers that things were innocent.

'I do like to read, that's true. In fact it's what I most love to do.' I could hear the enthusiasm rising in my voice. 'But it didn't come in the normal way of things, not in our family,' I had already decided on some openness, even if a limited amount. There was nothing to be gained in exposing my whole self, not so soon. Perhaps never. 'My father never had any time at all for books. In fact he's scornful of anything you could call *real* learning, resents the very idea of it – especially, for some weird, unfathomable reason, where his children are concerned. So I needed to be determined, reading was something that had to be fought for. It was never easy for me.'

'No, it can't have been. But I would say those circumstances make it all the more remarkable – the more admirable.' He spoke slowly and seemed thoughtful; genuine in the words he chose.

'It's easy enough to seem clever,' he went on, 'when you've had an education handed to you – as I did, in all honesty – on a plate. A silver plate.'

I could only agree with that. But it is something that does not always strike the recipients of such plates.

'Will must have talked about me?' I ventured, after a while.

'Well, yes he did, of course, a little. Because quite naturally I asked him! You must forgive me for that, but I'm sure it won't come as any surprise to you that I was completely intrigued! And remain so.'

My question about Will had not discomforted Thomas in the slightest. He seemed to possess the straightforward, relaxed confidence that can give honesty something of a free rein.

'But Will infuriated me by claiming not to know much at all!' he declared. 'I'm afraid I became very impatient with him. "How could you have grown up in that place and *not know*?" I kept insisting. Though to be fair, it's a good while since he lived in Cromford. He has children now, did you know that?' I did not, and recalled, a little guiltily, that after our initial greeting I had barely addressed a word to Will during that unexpected encounter. 'But he did remember you have older brothers – for all that was worth.'

'Two. And a few sisters into the bargain… ' I hesitated, wondering whether to say anything more about any one of them, but instead decided to pose a question myself. 'Do *you* have any family Thomas? Apart from your grandfather, I mean, have you brothers and sisters?' I was at least as eager for information as he was. It seemed odd that only a grandfather had been mentioned.

'No, I haven't.' The answer was short and I wondered if he, too, felt reluctant to discuss his circumstances, though it was hard to imagine why. We both fell quiet for a while, though it did not feel an uncomfortable thing.

'My mother died quite young,' he informed me at length. 'I was her first child, and she died soon after I was born, in fact. So I have no memory of her at all.'

'That's very sad for you.' I thought at once of Marguerite, and remembered I had not taken the trouble to visit my youngest sister for some time.

'It is, I suppose.' I sensed him glance towards me. 'She had the same name as you, it so happens. *Mary.* And I do often wonder what she was like. How she would have seemed to *me*, I mean, because other people's memories are exactly that, *their* memories. She would have been different for me.' He remained thoughtful for a moment. 'But I don't feel any... well, *deep* sadness, not the sort of sadness that causes you to suffer, because of course I never knew her. Never experienced any part of my life *with* her.'

'And your father?'

'Also dead, I'm afraid – about five years ago.' I was aware of a grip on my arm as he squeezed it, just for a second, against his side. 'What a tale of woe, eh? But my life is not one of sorrows and shadows, I must assure you. On the contrary! All in all, I'm very fortunate. Grandfather has been obliging enough to provide a pleasant home and to throw a useful bit of education my way. As much as I was prepared to take, anyway. I don't think I ever appreciated it as I should have. But the bad-tempered old bastard still seems to hold me in some sort of affection!' He laughed.' Albeit in his very own rigid, critical and disapproving way.'

'I'm sure your grandfather's disapproval must be well earned.'

'I make every effort to ensure it is.'

We were now only a short distance from the start of the canal. By mutual instinct our pace had slowed still further, and now ceased altogether as Thomas drew us to a gentle halt. He turned to stare towards the opposite bank, as I had done earlier. I stood at his side, silent, and gazed in the same direction, though there were no squawking birds to entertain us now. Before too long it would be dark. Well before he reached Middleton he would be relying on moonlight.

'I must go, Thomas.'

'Yes, of course, I understand. But... perhaps we could talk again? Maybe another evening?'

I knew it would be wise not to talk another evening. Not to talk at all. At the very least I should hesitate, become vague, hint I might be too busy to walk out in the evening for quite some time. My company was clearly something *different* for him. A curiosity. A fascination. Should things be made difficult, he was unlikely to persevere.

'Yes, I should enjoy that,' is what I heard myself saying.

16

It would be dishonest of me, laughable even, to claim that what persuaded me to see Thomas again was nothing more than the unusual pleasure of fascinating *conversation*. This was not so, of course, and no sane person would be made to believe otherwise. If I managed to deceive myself on the matter, it was not beyond the next meeting; perhaps not as far as that. But what I *will* claim is this. It was Thomas's lively, intelligent mind, the way my thoughts and words engaged with his, the wit and laughter that sprang from us both, that lured me to him. Without these things, nothing else could have occurred.

As it was, I found myself looking forward to our encounters in a way that I had never anticipated anything before. I felt a *need* for them, and any wise person could have predicted that one occasion in the first week would become two in the following one, more still in the next.

We would meet by the canal, on woodland pathways, in a number of places where we were felt assured of quiet. It was not too difficult to contrive such meetings. Tom was not neglected any more than usual; he was fed and cared for much as before. As must already be plain enough, I had never been unduly attentive as a wife, not one who chose to be in the home if I could find a good reason to be out of it. My habit of meandering out by myself in the evenings was already well established, even if not quite so often or for such lengths of time as now.

By some instinct, though, I did exercise a little care, claiming, for instance, that I had started to suffer with headaches and that frequent evening walks in the cool seemed to alleviate them. Occasionally Tom would accompany me – it would have seemed odd to urge him too often to stay at home – but more times than not he was content to rest himself before bedtime. Sometimes there was a thoughtful enquiry of 'are you *sure* you don't mind, Mary… you know, going out again on your own?' Naturally he was assured that I did not.

There were other thoughts too. It seemed important to return in a calm state, avoiding any appearance of being unusually animated. I would *think* myself into such calmness between leaving Thomas and arriving back at the cottage, though it was unlikely my husband would have noticed in any case, and if he had it would have been put down to the good dose of fresh air. Even had darker thoughts ever entered his mind, it is doubtful he would have voiced them, for Tom did not like to confront.

The timing of things has become a little blurred to me now. But I know that a few weeks after our first meeting, a change occurred. One evening Thomas did not offer his arm, to link with mine. In what seemed a sudden and decisive move, he took hold of my hand. I did not withdraw it; the feel of it, though it took me by surprise, seemed natural, right. I remember we fell silent for a while afterwards, absorbing, perhaps, what had happened, acknowledging with it some sort of inevitable path.

It is difficult to know just what I felt towards Tom during those weeks. It was not, I think, a sense of shame or guilt. I *should* have felt those things, but knew that I did not. What I did recognise in myself was a vague desire to protect him, and to guard us both from any vicious, wagging tongues.

Regular meeting places, and where we walked together, were chosen for their loneliness. Despite the pleasure of being with Thomas, I remained vigilant, alert to anyone coming near who might recognise me, aware that it would take only one pair of keen eyes to set a story about. And once it was about, Tom's hurt and dismay were too painful to contemplate. So, even, was Alice's.

There was, though, a simple way to make such awfulness less likely. Whenever Thomas rode across to Cromford – a distance of some seven or eight miles – his large-bodied mare would then have to trail along with us on our ramblings. Despite being only a few years old she was a docile creature; Thomas would hold the rein loosely in one hand while his other held mine. Whenever we stopped he would drop the leather strap altogether and she would graze, or snuffle about in the undergrowth. And on the rare occasions we saw someone appear in the distance, I took shelter behind her. Thomas, though, would remain in sight for he was unknown in the village and unlikely to be approached.

On one occasion he helped me to climb onto her back. I sat perched on the front of the saddle, my hands instinctively grasping her thick mane, while Thomas mounted with light ease and squeezed himself into the saddle behind me. His arms reached round to control the reins, for this, of course, was something in which I had no skill whatever. The mare took us through the trees at a steady walk, but as we reached more open land, further from the village, she was goaded by Thomas into a trot and then into a canter. It was fortunate that no-one was around to hear my excited, nervous, laughter.

'We can't go too far,' I heard Thomas announce after a while. 'This poor girl has to take me back home, don't forget!'

For me this was a new, exhilarating experience and I relished it – the height, the feel of the horse's power and speed, and the sense of Thomas behind me, his hold tight, protective. Our bodies were closer together than we had ever permitted them to be before. And I felt this as something natural and desirable, as something I *wanted*.

'Have you always owned a horse?' The question, asked as he helped me down, was unimportant. I used it to steady myself, in mind more than body.

'Oh yes, I've ridden from being very young. Can't remember not being able to. You couldn't do without a horse out there.' He turned to look at me, with some concern. 'But do we need to head down into the village now?' With reluctance I confirmed we did; knowing this evening's outing must have been longer than usual.

'Though as a matter of fact,' he continued after a while, frowning a little as if now in serious thought, 'I'm considering the possibility of living somewhere else – for a while, at least.'

'Good Heavens. Where?'

'Oh, nowhere far.' He turned his face to me. 'I've no desire at all to go far, I assure you.'

'Then where? And why? Don't be mysterious, Thomas; that's supposed to be a woman's thing, isn't it? Not that I can be bothered with it myself.'

'Grandfather and I seem to be crossing swords rather often at the moment. I think it might be a good thing to establish some ground between the two of us. You know – a proper distance.'

I understood anyone's desire for distance. I had desired *distance* from Pa for many years before I achieved it; though with more justification, I suspected, than Thomas could have.

'And what does *he* think?' I asked, just before another thought struck. 'You haven't mentioned... surely? You haven't mentioned *me*?'

'No, I haven't.' Thomas had a way of clipping an answer, quite curtly, when he did not want to proceed along a particular path. I waited for him to say something more.

'I need to feel *freer*,' he proffered at last. 'Freer to make my own decisions. As it happens I shall be twenty-one very shortly.' I may have had a quick intake of breath. We had never mentioned age up to that point, although I had my suspicions. It turned out he was younger than me by more than two years.

'So what is it you intend to do?' I looked at him. 'Because I think you've got further than *considering the possibility*, haven't you?'

Thomas laughed. 'You're too sharp for your own good, do you know that? Or for my good, anyway. But yes, that's so.'

'And?'

'When I reach twenty-one – next month – I inherit some money left to me by my father. Quite a respectable sum, it appears.' I wondered what a *respectable sum* would be, in Thomas's eyes. A large one, most likely.

'I intend to rent a place,' he continued, more blunt in his approach now. 'Nothing fancy. Just a modest house some-where.' Again, I tried to imagine Thomas's idea of *modest*. A house something like the two I had known, perhaps? The idea was quite amusing. Where would all his books go?

'We really must hurry,' was all I said. 'It's getting late.'

I did not speak again for the remaining short time we were together, and neither did he. We parted in the same place that we now so often met, a shadowy, wooded area behind the churchyard. Usually he would hold my hand tightly as he said farewell; on the last occasion he had put it, briefly, to his lips.

This time he lifted both hands to my face. I felt his fingers around my cheeks, felt myself pulled towards him – not with gentleness – until our faces were together, his mouth hard on mine. I did not resist; I did not even think to resist. I recognised only a hunger to touch him as my own hands flew to the back of his head and held it, burying them-selves in the mass of his thick, unruly hair.

It was difficult, on this occasion, to arrive home in a calm, unruffled state. I could feel a prickling energy burst-ing from every part of me, felt sure my eyes were wilder than usual and that if Tom cared to look at them he could hardly fail to notice. Some vague wisdom told me an explanation should to be put forward.

'It must be *so* late!' I exclaimed, as I pushed open the door. 'I was silly enough to go further than I'd realised, and… well, you can probably tell that I've run most of the distance back.'

This was not untrue, though I had hoped Tom might already have gone off to bed, as he sometimes did. Instead he was *there*, hovering in the room, and it was clear I had not even woken him from a sleep in the chair. His expression was now one of undisguised relief, and a picture came to my mind of him pacing anxiously about, opening the door from time to time, even walking a little distance up the rough lane. I felt a sharp, immediate guilt.

'I was worried about you,' he stated simply.

'I know. Forgive me. I promise to be more careful in the future. But you know, I was perfectly safe.' I touched his shoulder reassuringly, and then wished I had not as he turned and put his arms around me. For the second time that evening I did not resist; in this instance because it would have seemed unkind. Tom did not normally display affection in this way, not outside our bed. He was not the sort of man who could do so with any natural ease. I wondered if he had felt a particular loneliness tonight; whether it had brought with it a sudden need for reassurance. For closeness.

But I did not want closeness. My mind revolted, suddenly, at the idea of Tom's body against mine, and I shuddered inwardly at the thought he might expect this embrace to lead to something more. No such thing could be tolerated, not that night. My whole being screamed against it. Affection for Tom would not prevent a feeling of revulsion if he should press his body against mine, *inside* mine. It could not be born. Not now.

'And I've started bleeding,' I said, the words seeming to come by some power of their own and not through any thought. 'The pain's worse than usual, I don't know why. Walking's helped a little, but it's still quite bad. I do need to try and sleep, Tom.'

I saw disappointment in his face, but Tom was not one to complain. He did not express surprise that I had rarely spoken of pain before, or mention that I last bled only a couple of weeks ago. Perhaps he had forgotten.

We made our way quietly to bed and I lay, exhausted, curled up tight beneath the blanket and as near to the edge of the bed as possible. It was selfish of me, heartless even, but I wanted to be encumbered by nothing but my own thoughts. To be immersed in the memory of those powerful, intoxicating sensations.

17

I did not go out to meet Thomas for two days after that. Despite the sudden fervour of the last occasion, or perhaps because of it, we had not thought to agree a further meeting. And in view of Tom's worry, it seemed unwise to venture out again too soon.

It was impossible, though, to remain patient for long. By the third evening I was determined to take myself out no matter what, for even if I did not encounter Thomas, then at least some energy could be released through a challenging walk. But Tom frustrated this by suggesting we stroll out together. It seemed impossible to avoid without causing either suspicion or hurt, though to ensure we did not have to *stroll* for too long I did complain of some tiredness. More important, I took care to suggest a route where there was little likelihood of encountering Thomas.

Seeing Thomas should not have mattered greatly, since he was aware of Tom's existence; an existence that did not seem to cause him too much concern. Nevertheless, I felt no desire for them to be brought face to face, nor for the unpleasant feeling of not being able to acknowledge Thomas in those circumstances. It seemed better for my husband to remain as a shadowy presence in Thomas's mind, which was all he was likely to be, for I rarely spoke of him. Thomas, too, must have found it easier to remain ignorant, for he asked few questions and I had given him almost no information. He would have gleaned enough, of course, to assume that Tom and I shared little in common. Perhaps he had no interest in anything else, beyond the hope that nothing would impede the time we spent together.

The following night I did see Thomas again. Instinct had taken me towards the church, the place where we last parted, and it did not let me down for on approach I could hear the snorting, snuffling sound of a horse, coming from somewhere close by in the trees.

It turned out that Thomas had not come to seek for me for the last three nights either, though in his case the reason was different. The news was a relief, in a way, for it is a long ride merely to stand about and wait, finally to be disappointed. Despite the desire Thomas had made plain enough last time, I did not fool myself into believing that no effort was likely to prove too much, that he would find me again at any cost.

'I've been ill,' he was eager to explain, 'such a damned *nuisance*! Do say you haven't been out here too often, waiting for me. I would hate the thought of that.'

'No, I haven't,' I assured him, partly because it was true but also because I did not want him to picture me *waiting* for him. The image was a touch belittling.

'Well, thank goodness.' He did not sound altogether glad at the news, but grasped both my hands in his. 'I've had a slight fever. Nothing serious, as it's turned out, but Grandfather wouldn't hear of me going out; even dragged in my old nurse to ask her opinion – the poor woman was retired off years ago. She insisted on a couple of days in bed, and stayed at the house to make sure it happened.'

'Your old *nurse*?' I must have been smiling. Hints of Thomas's comfortable, protected childhood leaked from him quite often now.

'Well… yes. And don't you dare start with any mockery about that! Or act – how can I put it? *Superior*!' We both laughed. Thomas was superior in all matters of importance – wealth, status, learning – and we were both aware of it. I had never let him breathe too easily, however, for I knew myself to be a match for him in intelligence. He knew it also.

'Come on,' he said, taking my hand. 'Let's walk for a bit, move further away from here.' He pulled the mare from her grazing. She moved with a low snort of reluctance.

'What do you call this horse?' I asked. I had grown fond of her. She was a gentle, uncritical chaperone, who allowed her charges to do much as they pleased and minded her own business.

'Maud.'

'Maud?'

'The name of a girl I was taken with at the time – about five years ago. Just a fancy of callow youth. Quite meaningless.' He was hardly much more than a callow youth now, I found myself thinking.

'And in fact, looking back, she was rather *horsey*. Facially, that is, not in terms of riding ability. Very big teeth.'

I sensed there was nothing to fear from any warm memory he might have of the girl Maud.

We did not walk very far. Light-hearted conversation and some banter continued for a while, but I sensed they carried, for both of us, something nervous and edgy. What had happened at the end of our last meeting had somehow created a tautness between us, a feeling of anxious anticipation. No longer could our times together pose – if they ever could – merely as delightful meetings of the mind, as engaging exercises in intelligent discussion that, for me at least, were available nowhere else. They *were*, of course. But these things no longer stood alone, and perhaps never had.

I had recognised for some time a craving to be with Thomas; more importantly to be alone with him, hidden from view. Now I wanted to touch him again, wanted him to touch me, and not just with gentle affection but with an urgency, a forcefulness. These were desires I had never before experienced, not even in some far milder and more manageable form. I had never admitted their possibility in myself, never wanted them, and their sudden sway over me was disturbing. I sensed a lack of control in my life and actions, and this did not sit comfortably. There may have been a part of me that even resented it.

I doubt if Thomas was prey to such awkward, complicated emotions. What he felt towards me was a mixture of fascination and desire. Both had been born at our first meeting, but the desire had now become more insistent. I suspected it was that powerful, straightforward sort of craving that men experience, and on which they act without bothering to pose themselves too many questions.

We had not ventured a great distance – just far enough to be in a lonelier, more thickly wooded place – when Thomas chose to act on this desire. But in the same moment, as his arms gripped around me and I felt his body press itself against mine, I knew that it had become my choice, also. Thomas was stronger than I was, but he was not a man who would seek to intimidate, let alone become violent. I could have refused, resisted. He would have accepted such a rejection, if not graciously, then without rancour.

But as our mouths came together, as he lowered me into the tangle of damp grass and weeds that shrouded the base of a tree, the thought of refusal did not enter my mind. It was my own desire for him that took control, cushioned by a strange, comforting sense of inevitability.

It might be expected that guilt and unease later that evening, on returning home, would be greatly magnified from what I felt a few nights ago. After all, nothing of too serious a nature had occurred on the earlier occasion. How many women have not, at one time or another, shared an illicit kiss with a man who is not their husband? And it can be guessed that an even smaller number of married men have not done so.

But, and rather to my own surprise, I felt calmer this evening than before, more serene. It is impossible to fathom the reason for this, as plainly I was now embarked upon a dangerous course. An act had been committed that many would condemn. That almost all would condemn. I had put my married state, my safe, monotonous life at dire risk. If discovered, Tom would be in grief and I would be treated by some as an outcast. Nevertheless, my thoughts refused to darken. I felt free, unconfined.

Perhaps this unexpected mood came in part from the evening's discovery. From the strange and shocking discovery that to have one's body taken and possessed by a man is not merely something to be tolerated; that it is possible to *want* such a thing, to yearn for it. And I now knew that a woman is able to take possession also; can do so with an appetite quite as fierce as his.

I had taken care to smooth down my dress before leaving the wood, making sure there were no bits of grass or leaves still clinging. Thomas had run his fingers through my hair for the same purpose, attempting to make it behave and brushing strands away from my face.

'Don't worry too much,' I remember saying. 'It has a mind of its own in any case.'

'It's beautiful hair,' he had said.

We were not cast into seriousness, into gloom; quite the contrary. There was a palpable lightness between us, almost a joy. I knew that tonight could not be the one and only time I would experience this and the thought was a good one. It would strengthen me, I imagined, to carry on with the mundane, the every-day, the tedious. Perhaps I might even be able to do so with a little more grace than before.

'I must go,' I had said, using the familiar, unwelcome phrase that always preceded departure, though this time with my arms still about him as I did so.

'I know, I know. But soon?'

'Soon, yes.' I thought for a second or two. 'Not tomorrow, perhaps. But the day after?'

'The day after. I'll be here.' He smiled, a boyish grin. 'For talking, *as well*, of course. We must pay our dues to the first pleasure that brought us here!'

'Indeed. For talking, as well – if we must!' We were both laughing as I ran from him. I heard Maud snort loudly. She had taken no interest in anything other than foraging and munching for the duration of our woodland visit, but now felt moody and imposed upon, perhaps, by being expected to carry Thomas home.

18

I was not able to meet Thomas two evenings later, for someone rapped on the cottage door just a few minutes before I intended to leave. Tom had not yet finished his supper and I told him not to bother getting up, that I would see who the caller was. It turned out to be a Mrs Shaw, who was, she quickly explained, a neighbour of Mrs Spence. She had come out to tell me that Marguerite was ill.

'You're Mary, aren't you? I've seen you before, haven't I, dear, when you've called in on Mrs Spence? She told me to come here, not go to your sister. What's her name – Alice, isn't it? Because she said that lass has a fair bit on her plate, hasn't she? What with her children, and with your father being the way he is, you know? She's explained it to me, do you see? And you're a bit nearer, anyhow, aren't you?' It was irritating that her every statement was framed as a question, but I sensed her to be a good-hearted woman, of much the same ilk as our treasured Mrs Spence.

'Yes, I'm Mary. What's wrong with Marguerite?' My mind jangled with an uncomfortable mix of thoughts and feelings. Naturally there was worry for my little sister. The tie might be looser with her than with the others, but by then I was not without affection. Marguerite had shown an admirable will to survive and a plucky temperament. I admired her spirit, and could only hope it would see her through whatever was ailing her just now.

But the intrusion also came as a blow. All day I had been anticipating the hour and a half or so of evening that would be spent with Thomas; it had been difficult to put my mind to anything else. And now, in an instant, I knew it was not going to take place. I spoke briefly to Tom who, between hungry mouthfuls of bread and bacon, expressed his own concern, as best he could.

'Don't wait up for me,' I said to him. 'I don't know how long I'll be.'

For a few seconds, as I rummaged around for my shawl, I pictured Thomas's long ride across to Cromford – there had been a fair few showers that day and if anything they were becoming heavier and more frequent. I imagined him waiting somewhere close to the church, trees dripping and an early, mist-laden dusk coming in. I wondered how long he would be prepared to wait, and what sort of hurt, disgruntled feelings he might have during the tedious journey home. It would not be the first occasion of disappointment, but it could prove the worst one.

'So what on earth's wrong with her, Mrs Shaw?' I demanded, as soon as the door was shut behind us and we had started a brisk walk in the direction of Mrs Spence's house.

'Well, I don't know too much, dear, but poor Mrs Spence seems so worried, so upset, and she doesn't fret easily, does she? You know that, I'm sure, don't you? And she just knocks on my door, you see, and says to me "It's bad. I think someone in the family needs to be told." Because she knows that child isn't *hers*, do you see? Though she loves her like one of her own, that's for sure. In fact more than her own, don't you sometimes think? And then she says "I don't know what I'll do if anything happens to my Marg, just don't know what I'll do!" So I says "look, don't you fret, I'll go and get one of those sisters to come." You don't mind, do you dear? But she's just so upset, because it doesn't look good for that little girl, I'm sorry to say. Now I've done the right thing, haven't I?'

'Of course you have, Mrs Shaw, please don't worry.'

'Well, we're all worried now, aren't we dear? I lost one of my own, you know, quite a time back but you don't forget, do you? You don't forget what it's like… but you've no children yourself, dear, have you, not as yet?'

'Not as yet, no.'

And never likely to have. Not even though I could now boast a lover, as well as a husband. An irony, or perhaps a piece of miraculous good luck, that it seemed I was unlikely to be troubled by offspring. I wondered if the thought that he might *get me with child* had so much as crossed Thomas's mind.

'Here we are!' Mrs Shaw announced, unnecessarily, as we reached our destination.

'And please God she's no worse.'

The door led us straight into the familiar room and revealed Mrs Spence on her knees, hunched over a blanketed bundle on the floor. The air was hot and stale, almost suffocating. Two of her boys sat together in a corner and appeared to be absorbed in setting out small stones or bits of wood into rows. There was no sign of the other children or of Mr Spence.

'She's sent hubby down the road, dear,' my companion whispered, as if feeling an explanation was needed. 'He's no use, do you see, at times like this?' Mr Spence had never struck me as much use at any time. I went across and crouched on the floor by Marguerite. Her breathing sounded rasping and laboured, her face was highly flushed and looked paper dry, free of any sweat. She had her eyes closed as if in sleep, but beneath a thick blanket the small body seemed restless and twitchy. Mrs Spence looked at me, her eyes full of fear.

'It's a fever, isn't it?' she said. 'A bad one. I've never seen anything as bad; the poor mite hasn't eaten for more than two days, not managed to drink anything for a good while, either.' Her face looked stricken.

'Well, she *must* drink,' I said briskly. Have you got some clean water back there, Mrs Spence – and a clean cloth?'

'I think so, yes I can find that, I think. But you see, I did get her to take just a very little milk, yesterday morning. She threw it straight back up.'

'Not *milk*, she needs water. *Straight away.*' Mrs Spence heaved herself to her feet and hurried off. I sensed it was a relief for her to be carrying out an instruction; she was a kind woman but not a thinking one. I turned to her neighbour, of whom the same thing could be said.

'And this room's far too hot, I feel as if I'm starting a fever myself. Please open a window, or if the windows won't open, then the door. As wide as you can!'

'But we mustn't risk her catching a chill, dear. That would be even worse, wouldn't it?'

'No, it wouldn't be worse, Mrs Shaw, believe me. She *will* die if we can't cool her down – and very soon. That's what would be worse!' I was kneeling over Marguerite as I said this, pulling away the blanket in which she was tightly enveloped. At the firmness in my voice, Mrs Shaw went to the door and opened it. The damp evening was quite mild; nevertheless a welcome stream of fresh, cooler air began to flow in.

'Are you sure this won't chill her too much, dear?'

'Quite sure. In fact please push it to and fro.' I ignored her puzzled expression. 'Yes, just like that – we need to get some air wafting about.'

Mrs Spence returned from the back scullery with a jug of water and a cloth; a stained one but, I hoped, washed since its last use.

'I need a small bowl of some sort as well,' I said. She bent to place the items on the floor – though I seized the cloth before it arrived there – and scurried away once again.

Once she returned I poured a small amount of water into the bowl, tore a corner off the cloth and dipped it.

'Now lift her head up a bit,' I instructed, feeling more trepidation than my authoritative manner suggested. 'And try to bring her round. You know, keep giving her a bit of a shake.'

'But I don't want to hur… '

'You won't! Please just do it, Mrs Spence.'

It was impossible to tell if Marguerite had been roused, or was now merely more disturbed within her sleep. I put the corner of the wet cloth to her cracked lips, which hung open in a lifeless way. Unlike the rest of her they were pale, almost colourless.

The only response was a more distressed sound of breathing, but I pushed the cloth a little further into her mouth and squeezed out a drop of water. It was not enough to swallow, only to moisten. But I knew there was no choice left but to persevere with this task, drop by drop, until a point came when she *did* have to swallow. If she could not do so, then she would choke. And that would very likely be the end of her.

'Please keep trying to wake her up!' I spoke to my assistant with urgency. 'And stroke her neck – long and firm – it may help the water down. Start it right under the chin.'

We continued our labour, stopping briefly every now and then. At these intervals I used the main part of the cloth, soaked in the jug water then squeezed out hard, to wipe Marguerite's arms, legs and belly in an attempt to take some of the fire out of them. Her small body was a sturdy one, plump even, but the chest heaved in and out with what looked like painful effort. Unexpectedly, I found myself wishing I could pick her up and comfort her.

'Am I to close this now, dear? Because I think it's getting chilly, isn't it?'

'No, not yet, Mrs Shaw. It's still too warm in here. But give your arm a rest for a few moments, leave it to stay open on its own.'

Mrs Spence and I continued. It was impossible to tell if any drops of water were finding their way down Marguerite's throat in safety, or if the strange gurgling coming from that place meant I was causing my sister to choke herself horribly to death. I wished that Alice was beside me, it would have been a comfort to have her there. Though a part of me felt it better that she was not, for her distress and anxiety were likely to have been more intense than my own. And she may have questioned my methods more than the Mistresses Spence and Shaw dared to.

The person I most longed for was Ma. My mother had always had a strong, calm common sense and I believe she passed some of this on to me, though in almost all other ways we were very different. I possessed little, perhaps none, of her forbearance, her patience. Alice was the inheritor of those traits and I loved her for them, safe in the knowledge that I would never achieve, nor even want, such things for myself.

So regular was the rhythm of what we were doing – squeezing water out drop by drop, stroking Marguerite's neck, wiping her body with the damp cloth – and for such a long time had we been doing it, that the sudden and violent cough took me by surprise. Her whole face and body seemed to contort, as if in severe pain.

'Sit her up, we need to sit her up!' I shouted, unsure whether such a cough signalled the dreaded choke. Between us we raised her, and the cough came again, accompanied by a strangled sort of cry. In the next second Marguerite puked violently, her exposed belly, the old blanket, our own hands and arms, all instantly awash with a thick, sticky and foul-smelling liquid.

'Oh my goodness!' I heard Mrs Shaw exclaim from the open door, where she continued to stand guard.

'It's all right,' I assured them, remembering from early childhood Ma's usual comment on such events, albeit less impressive ones. 'It's the best thing to happen, and I think it's bringing her round a bit.' I offered the cloth to Mrs Spence to wipe herself down, and then tried to clean my own hands, at the same time longing for water to wash myself more thoroughly. There is a squirming horror in having any part of oneself puked on – but this was not a moment to move away for Marguerite was not yet safe. Her face remained creased in pain, or perhaps partly now in fright. She still looked ill and we did not know the cause or what else to do. But thank God she did, at last, appear to be awake, if not wholly so.

'If you've got another cloth,' I said to Mrs Spence, 'we'll clean her up a bit.' She nodded, and gently moved her hands away as I put my own behind Marguerite's shoulders and head. 'And we'll need something to put behind her,' I added. 'We can't hold her up for ever, but if that happens again, it's best she's not lying down.'

Mrs Spence looked doubtful. 'I can't just think I've got anything.'

'*I* have,' interjected the amiable Mrs Shaw. 'A cushion. I'll go and fetch it. But don't you think, dear, that we need to close this door now and get the room warmed up a bit? Because she mustn't get cold, must she? When you're ill, you do need to be kept warm, don't you?'

'Not always, *no*.' I spoke more shortly than intended, but I was weary now from effort and anxiety, and more irritated than I should have been.

'You see, she was so hot,' I explained, more gently. 'Burning hot. And that can be dangerous.' Mrs Shaw dutifully left the door open as she scuttled off to fetch her cushion. I noticed that the two boys were still sitting in the corner, one fiddling with their small chunks of wood and whatever else they had down there, the other curled up asleep. They had remained quiet and unmoved throughout the drama.

Some hours later, I left Mrs Spence's house. Marguerite had been washed, as best we could. She lay on an old, spare blanket that had been unearthed from somewhere, head bolstered by a lumpy but useful cushion provided by Mrs Shaw. We had continued for a further time with our drop-by-drop water feeding, and I now felt confident it was being swallowed. My sister looked ill, but the anxiety I felt about her was a little less acute than before. She drifted in and out of sleep, her breathing still rough and laboured, but her body seemed cooler, more relaxed, no longer twitching in the disturbing way it had.

'I'll be staying down here with her,' Mrs Spence assured me, 'I'll use that chair.' She had delivered the two boys upstairs earlier on, to join a brother who must have been in bed already. Mr Spence had come in not long before I left and gone straight up, with barely a word. Snores had been resonating for a while now, and I imagined he would remain oblivious to where or how his wife spent the night.

'I could stay with her, if you like. You can go up and sleep in your bed.' I felt obliged to make the offer, though longing, by then, to be out in the fresh air and moving about.

'No, no, I won't hear of it. I couldn't leave her anyway, you see.' She seized my hand. '*Thank-you.* Thank-you for coming. I know you've saved her, I know you have. But – oh goodness, what am I thinking – will you be alright, walking home so late? I can wake Alf to see you safely back, you know.'

I felt touched by her concern, if horrified at the thought. 'Oh no, I'll be quite alright, Mrs Spence, the dark doesn't concern me in the least. And as to Marguerite – well, we've *both* saved her. Or I think there's a good hope that we have.'

'I shall keep giving her water. You know, like you did it. I promise you I will. And tomorrow, who knows? She'll maybe take a sip or two of broth.'

I found my shawl, which had somehow managed to remain unsullied by the evening's events. It would be cool outside now, welcomingly so. 'I'll come and see her in the morning,' I said, thinking also I would bring something with me. Milk, perhaps, and fresh bread. Perhaps I would bring Alice, as well.

'And don't let it get too hot in here!' I made my voice sound cheerful, as I reached for the door. 'In fact, how about leaving this open again, just for a while?'

19

It was good to feel the evening air against my face. The night air, in fact, for I knew it must now be very late, perhaps around midnight. Tom should surely be in bed, and sound asleep. And Thomas, too, no doubt. It was to him that my mind now turned, the first time it had been free to do so in the last several hours. I feared just what his thoughts were likely to be, for my failure to appear would have come as a shock to him, I knew. It was possible that disappointment, on this particular occasion, might have been deep enough to make him angry.

As it was, Tom had not gone to bed. He must have been listening out for my approach and the door was open before I reached it.

'Is she alright?' He looked concerned, as well as tired, and I felt grateful.

'I think so, but she's been bad. A fever, or maybe more.' I sat myself down heavily, without discarding the shawl. There had been no fire for hours and although the night-time air was mild it felt cold in that room. I was aware, all of a sudden, of huge exhaustion.

'And of course those stupid women were doing all the usual damned things! All the wrong things!'

Tom did not bother to ask *what*; he was likely to have known no better himself. He looked as taken aback by my burst of annoyance as I was myself.

'Oh, it wasn't their fault,' I added wearily. 'They were doing their best. Poor Mrs Spence.'

'There's a bit of broth left, if you want it.'

'Yes, yes, I will.' The broth would be cold of course, but filling, and neither tiredness nor worry had quite destroyed hunger. Tom went to fetch it while I stared vacantly about me.

'I *hope* she'll live,' I said, after wolfing a couple of mouthfuls, 'but – well, we'll see how things are tomorrow. I'll go back first thing.'

'She's a strong little mite.' It was a kindly statement, though afterwards neither of us could find anything else to say and before long we got up and made our way to bed. To my relief, after a reassuring squeeze to my shoulder, Tom turned onto his side and was soon asleep. I lay awake a while longer, finding in his steady snoring, in his warm, still and solid presence, an unexpected comfort.

Very early the following morning I was on my way to Mrs Spence's house again. I had decided against calling first on Alice, for this would delay my arrival and I felt anxious to get there. Moreover, there would then be Alice's distress to cope with. If the worst had already happened – if Marguerite had died during the night – I felt it was better that I should know of it first and tell Alice afterwards. There would be more time to console her, to assure her there was nothing at all she could have done, no bit of help or advice she could have given that I had not managed to give myself.

A first sight of the house, even from some distance, came as an immediate relief. Its windows were not covered – I did not think Mrs Spence had anything much in the way of curtains but she was likely to have found something to hang up, at least in the room downstairs, had there been a death. I found myself breaking into a run and soon took in another hopeful sign; the door stood slightly ajar. It seemed the advice had been heeded, even in my absence and against what was likely to be Mrs Spence's better judgement. I pushed it further open and walked in.

This time the room felt quite cool, and if it did not smell entirely fresh then it was certainly a great deal less stuffy and fetid than before. Mrs Spence looked up at once and her weary face tried its best to break into a smile. She sat on an upright, armed chair, cradling Marguerite, who was asleep on her lap, still wrapped in a blanket. There was no sign of any other life and I assumed they were in bed, or perhaps Mr Spence had already left the house. Though it must still have been very early, for I had slept only for a while and risen soon after first light. Even Tom, always an early riser, had remained asleep as I dressed, ate a crust of bread dipped in a little bacon fat, and slipped quietly out of the house.

'I'm glad you're here. It's so good of you to come... and to come so soon.' I stepped beside her and looked closely at my sister, placing the back of my hand gently against her face.

'She's *cooler*.'

'Yes she is, she's cooler, isn't she? That's what I think.' Mrs Spence bent her head and her lips touched Marguerite's forehead. As she lifted her face again a couple of tears were making their way down the dry, rough cheeks. I felt a flush of gratitude towards this simple, kind woman, who for some reason had such affection for my motherless sister.

'I've kept giving her water, you know?' She seemed anxious to tell me this. 'Every now and then, I've done it, all night long. And I did think, it was at one of those times that I did think – she's not so hot now, not burning the way she was.' She looked at me. 'So do you think she'll be alright now?'

'I think so, Mrs Spence. I *hope* so. And I'm grateful; thank-you for being so good to her.' Grateful seemed an inadequate word. I had an urge to hug Mrs Spence but could not quite bring myself to do so. 'And Alice will be grateful too,' I added, 'for all your kindness.' I did not feel the need to mention our other brothers or sisters. None of them had much concerned themselves with Marguerite beyond feeling a relief that she was being cared for and that no part of the burden fell on them. I imagined Pa would barely be aware she existed. It was Alice who dealt with the money in that house now.

'Oh dear me, you don't need to thank me. I love her as my own, I do really. I couldn't bear to… to lose her, you see. Not now, I couldn't, I really couldn't. You do, well, understand?'

I did. 'You won't lose her, Mrs Spence. God willing, that is. But there's no need to fear losing her to anyone else.'

The following morning – and almost as early, for I found it a more difficult thing than ever to be at home – I was at Mrs Spence's door once again. She saw me through the window and beckoned me straight in.

I was thankful to see that Marguerite was awake, if drowsy. Her face was still drawn and there was no smile on seeing me – not the smallest look of curiosity or alertness – but none of this was as frightening as the scalding, crimson fever of two days ago.

'She's had a bit of broth!' Mrs Spence told me excitedly. 'Not much, mind, no more than a couple of small spoonful's, maybe not quite that. But still, eh?'

'But still, indeed!' I replied, removing from my cloth bag a few fresh eggs, wrapped carefully in straw, and trying to find room for them among the clutter on her small table.

'I'll sit with her now if you like,' I said, more in the way of an announcement than an offer, 'while you see to the others.'

'Well, I'll do that, thank-you. I'll do that.'

I lifted Marguerite onto my knee and cradled her. It was done with affection, in part at least, for I did feel something warm and genuine towards her, even if it could not quite be described as sisterly love. I also held her because I felt I *ought* to, because Ma would have done so, and because Marguerite had been deprived of Ma. The person who would have loved her most of all.

Though it seemed clear that Mrs Spence, by a miracle, was not far behind. For some reason she adored this wilful, stubborn little thing, who did not give her smiles away easily and could be put in a temper if she did not get her own way.

'You belong here, you know,' I murmured into her matted hair, before pulling my face back at the pungent smell of it. 'You do know that, don't you? Because you see, it's too late for anything else.'

Her head did not turn but the three and a half year old eyes flickered and then seemed to stare for a moment or two into mine. 'So just you make sure you get well again. I think you owe that to the woman upstairs, don't you? Because she wants to be your mother. And you know – your life could be a lot worse.'

Perhaps I imagined just the tiny vestige of a smile But I did have a sense that Marguerite, sickly and odorous as she was – her breath smelled and what emanated from the rest of her, or from the blanket, was almost causing me to retch – had somehow managed to cling on to her life.

There could be no certainty; an ill person can seem to recover a little, only for life to be snatched away. It is snatched from young children most often of all; a fact that eases any regret about not bringing them into the world.

I was determined to go out that evening. There would be no guarantee, of course, that Thomas would be there, waiting for me. Nor that he would arrive at any point during the time I was prepared to wait for *him*. He might well be offended about my absence over the last couple of days. He could, quite reasonably, have other things to do. It was not too long ago that he had mentioned plans to visit somewhere – was it in Yorkshire? Some place of archaeological interest, but I could no longer remember which one, for over the weeks we had spoken of many places. The visit was by invitation of an archaeologist whom Thomas held in high regard, and would entail a stay of several days. Usually I was receptive to any detail of this kind, but recent concerns must have dulled me.

Though it did seem unlikely he would choose to go on a visit just now. Objects unearthed from below the ground, however fascinating and informative, can hardly compete with pleasures to be had above it. With a greedy possession of someone you desire, amongst the damp roughness of weeds and acorns and leaves. I imagined he might be unwilling to forego such a pleasure just yet.

However, I waited fruitlessly, feeling chilled among the trees for a lively breeze was now cooling the early evening air. I knew I should not be out too long that night. Tom was neither perceptive nor suspicious, but he had seen my tiredness and would think it odd, at the least, if I were to be out *taking the air* for too long. My parting words had suggested it would not be so.

'I'll just take a short walk, get a little air,' I had said. 'Nothing too far.'

'Shall I come with you?'

'No, no. Have a rest, you look weary yourself.' And I had made a rapid exit before he could argue or insist.

20

I had lingered in the wooded patch as long as seemed
wise, my mood at first one of keen anticipation, later of
growing dejection. It seemed, in the end, a foolish way to
spend time, if not humiliating. I had a home, after all; a
simple one but a home nonetheless, and better than many
enjoyed. I also had a husband, of whom the same could be
said. Tom was a kind man. He was everything that my
father had never been, that very many men were not.

My actions were putting all of it at risk. And for what,
when all was said and done? Nothing would change.
Thomas's appetite for me would be satiated in the end –
even if mine for him was not. He would take himself back
into his comfortable life and seek out, at whatever time he
chose, an attractive woman to marry. Then he could take
his pleasures as others did – in a house, in a bed. And he
could use the rest of his time in more profitable ways,
instead of spending so much of it in tedious rides across to
Cromford church. How long before he grew weary of that?

And now my actions were endangering me in a more
immediate way, for I had misjudged the evening and
rushed out of the house without a shawl. I was aware of
shivering, and knew there was a risk of catching a chill. It
seemed wise to keep on the move rather than stand about
and so I paced among the trees in wide circles, my arms

crossed for warmth, listening all the time for the soft sound of Maud's hooves in the undergrowth, for her low, unmistakable snort.

I saw him approach as I emerged from the trees to cross in front of the church, my mind now set on a return home. As my eyes fell on him, I knew that nothing was any longer possible tonight, for I had already stayed out later than was reasonable. My disappointment started to mix with a touch of ill-temper as the faithful Maud turned off the lane and headed into the church ground. Thomas pulled her to a halt and dismounted, with no obvious haste.

'I feared you wouldn't be here,' he stated.

'Well, in just a moment I shan't be. I can't stay longer, Thomas.'

'I came yesterday, as well as the day before.' There was an injured tone to his voice, as there may well have been to mine.

'My youngest sister's been very ill. It wasn't possible.'

His shoulders seemed to fall; perhaps relax a little. 'I'm sorry to hear that. Is she alright?'

'Not alright, not yet. But a little better. Thomas, I can't linger here, I must… '

'I'll walk with you down the lane, there's nobody around, nobody at all. The place is as quiet as this graveyard. Oh, and in any case, why in hell's name does it *matter*? Tell me why two people shouldn't be seen walking together along a public lane!' There was a vehemence to the words, verging on anger. 'And you're *cold*,' he informed me, just as strenuously. 'I can see you're cold.'

Without discussion he removed his riding cloak and threw it around my shoulders.

'Now *you'll* be cold.'

'It doesn't matter.'

We walked for a while towards the village. In tune with Thomas's sentiments, I tried to feel less concern about being seen, quashing the desire to peer ahead in order to note who might be coming our way. As far as it concerned anyone, had I not bumped into an acquaintance? And this person and I were now walking a short distance together, chaperoned by a horse. Nothing to remark about. Like Thomas, I was growing tired of exercising so much care, though in my case there was more reason for it.

I now regretted my earlier anxiety to return home. Could Tom not have been given some sort of explanation? He had accepted strange explanations before and would have no reason to question one tonight. *Why* had I not gone with Thomas into the woodland? Why had I not taken his hand and *led* him there; given us the chance to fall upon one another? And likely with even greater hunger and wantonness than before.

Now Thomas seemed morose. Thwarted, I could only imagine; feeling he had made a great deal of effort on two occasions for nothing other than accompanying me a short distance along this road. It could hardly be what he had hoped for.

'I'm sorry.' I decided to break into the silence as we went along. 'About not being here.'

'It wasn't your fault.' The voice still sounded a mite sullen. 'This – this situation – it's bound to be fraught with problems.'

I wondered if this could be the first hint of exasperation, of discontent. Perhaps I had already overestimated the pleasure of possessing one another, at least from Thomas's point of view. There had been no doubting his delight in it the other night, but had that occasion now shaved off some sharp edge of desire? Ma once claimed that men love to chase, but that once the prey is caught they can often lose interest. But I could not believe it was so with Thomas; not yet. It was impossible to imagine he did not long, as much as I did, to experience such a thing again.

'I've taken out a lease,' he stated suddenly, 'on a house. In fact it was agreed and signed for this morning.'

This matter was not new; the possibility had been mentioned before. Nevertheless, his bald statement took me by surprise.

'Where?'

'Bakewell. A place in Matlock Street. Do you know it?' I did not, having never visited Bakewell.

'Just a small property,' he added, the tone warming a little, 'but quite nice, quite comfortable.'

'But your books, and all your, you know, *historical* things. Will you be able to move them?'

'A good few, perhaps, but there's no need to take every last one. I can go back to Middleton at any time, if there's something I want.'

I was not sure what to say. We were reaching the edge of the village, a point where I now needed to turn into the long, narrow track that would lead me to the cottage. This was where we must part company.

Thomas turned to look at me. 'Bakewell's no further away, Mary, than Middleton. In fact I would estimate it's a little closer.'

'Well, that's good.'

'I could take you there, perhaps – in a carriage. To see it for yourself. Would you like that?'

Of course I would *like* it, was my immediate, searing thought. How could I not? I would relish every single part of it – the carriage, the journey to Bakewell, our arrival in this Matlock Street, my first sight of his house. And surely there would be a *bed*? A bed offering us comfort, privacy.

But I failed to see how any such venture could ever be possible. It would need time, and time was not something at my disposal. The part of it I gave to Thomas, or to us both, was already too much and given at considerable risk. At increasing risk, very likely, for it was all too easy to put the thought of danger to one side. The temptation is always to grow more careless as time goes by, to imagine oneself as somehow beyond peril.

Thomas must have been puzzled that I had not answered his question.

'Surely you *would*?'

'Of course. Of course I would.'

'Well, then!'

'But it would be difficult, Thomas, most likely impossible. Do you not see that?'

'It *must* be possible to find a way!' There was irritation in the tone. Again I was unsure how to respond, sensing it might be easy to vex him without intending it. There was a further silence before Thomas cleared his throat.

'In any case,' he said, 'it couldn't happen quite yet. I have to be away for a while, Mary. There's a meeting, you see – a group of us getting together in London. Archaeologists. It's not something we've done before. A *conference*, they're calling it, if that's not too grandiose a word to use.'

'Well, that will be wonderful for you.'

The statement was sincere, though I recognised in myself a pang of envy. The idea that one could simply *decide* to go to London seemed astounding. It spoke of a life that belonged in a different world from my own.

'How long are you to be away?'

'Two weeks, I think, or thereabouts. Perhaps a little more. I'm invited to stay with the man who's planned the thing; one of the foremost in the field. It's quite an honour, really.' I did not doubt it, though the time involved seemed unsettlingly vague.

My ear caught the sound of voices, a couple of them, still at a distance but coming our way. They were raucous and the owners were very likely drunk, and I knew I should be making my way. Most drunks are harmless but there was an edge of something that suggested aggression to these and it always pays to take care. Even a man on his own needs to take care. Perhaps especially so.

'Get yourself on Maud's back,' I instructed with some urgency, 'and go! Use a bit of speed – they'll leave you well alone on a horse.'

'*No*, we'll both get on, I shall take you home!' His arms were already moving to lift me.

'I'm *alright*, Thomas!' I pushed him away almost violently and started to run, heading down the rough and now darkening track at what must have seemed remarkable speed, my skirts lifted and gathered in one hand. I assumed he was too shocked to follow, though had he done so I would have ordered him to leave me alone and to go straight back.

A minute or so later, I could hear the receding sound of hooves on the harder surface of the lane, moving at what must have been at least a canter. The shouting had faded, too. It seemed we were both safe, if indeed there had been the slightest danger anyway.

What sort of vexed frustrations would be coursing through Thomas's mind on his way home, of course, was another thing. And my own thoughts, too, were in turmoil as I opened the door, panting slightly, and discovered to my relief that Tom had already gone up to bed.

It was a wakeful night. I spent much of it wondering what made me act as I did; why the thought of riding up that track with Thomas, of being set down close to the cottage, had filled me with such panic. Was it merely the possibility of being seen by Tom, who might be wandering about outside, perhaps on the lookout for me? My mind toyed with what sort of explanation could have been given to him, under those circumstances. Perhaps 'There were some drunks around – this gentleman happened to be close by and heard them; he *insisted* on getting me safely home.' The picture of it was quite amusing; in a lighter frame of mind it could have made me laugh. And perhaps not unbelievable, either? Certainly there was a chance that *Tom* would have believed it.

Or did I not want Thomas to glimpse my home? Did I still, for some reason, feel a need to remain vague, not precisely identified, something of a mystery? I could not decide; could find no understanding of myself, felt just a restless and anxious discontent.

At some point in the night I must have fallen asleep. Because sometime later I was woken by the weight of Tom's body lying heavily on mine, and the feeling of my legs being pushed firmly apart. There then came an intense and even slightly painful pressure as he pushed himself inside me. It was all too evident he had decided not to seek any permission, on this occasion. He had not felt that he should wait, had not woken me and first sought some word or sign of willingness. For the first time in our marriage he was simply doing what he felt a need to do. I could feel this need, stark and raw. Sense it in the way his hands clutched at my body, almost as if in some sort of anguish. And I felt it in the unusual strength with which he entered me, in the way his breath came against my face in fast gasps. There was a fierceness about him that was alien, that was not the Tom either of us knew.

I did nothing to prevent what was happening, and not merely because it had taken me by such surprise. Had I ordered Tom to stop, I believe he would have done so, for despite the sudden ferocity, there was no part of him that was brutal. The occurrence had about it a feeling of desperation, and something within me realised that rejecting him would be cruel. Cruel and wrong. My husband was *owed* this release, he needed it, had a right to it. I felt it as something that must be allowed to happen.

When it was over, when the strength went out of him, Tom remained still for a while, his head resting on my chest. He withdrew himself from me more slowly than usual, then rolled away to lie on his back, with a deep sigh of exhaustion. I reached over to touch his hand briefly; in affection, perhaps, even in a sort of sympathy. Neither of us said anything.

He fell back to sleep within a short time. So did I, and not too long after. Mind and body had been assailed with as much as they had the capacity to take that day, and it was a relief when deep, encompassing weariness started to take control of them both. Even my dreams offered some rest, for if not entirely serene, they were less troubling and uncomfortable than I must have deserved.

21

Almost three weeks went by before I saw Thomas Bateman again. Perhaps because I accepted he was far away, knew he could not be hovering in wait for me, nor I for him, life did not become intolerable. Somehow, I settled myself down, and although he would come into my thoughts on waking each morning, I did not find myself pining for him every time an idle moment presented itself. Nor did I always fall asleep with his face as the last image in my mind.

In other words, I began to reason with myself, I was surely not *in love*? That is something I have never believed myself capable of being, and on the whole I am thankful for it. Being in love means being at someone's mercy. And it is a matter of pure good fortune, or otherwise, whether that person turns out to be worthy of such feelings of helplessness. Though from observation, I would have to say there are precious few men who could be considered worth it.

My husband was an exception, of course. He was worthy of someone's love, and it should have been mine. But it is a sad fact that we cannot choose whom to love, any more than we can choose whom to *want*. That is the cruel nature of things.

It would be a lie to say I did not feel Thomas's absence keenly, for I did. Every daily routine seemed drearier, more tedious than usual, depressingly unrelieved. A sort of lethargy began to creep over me. Even things once enjoyed in a milder way, such as passing time with Alice or calling in on Edwina to share a drink and a gossip, struck me as having a dull, wearying *sameness* about them. Everything, and most of all every*one*, now appeared predictable; the courses of their lives fixed, mapped out, inevitable. Including, I saw with a new clarity, my own.

I started to spend more of any spare time at home; not, it must be admitted, through any greater desire to be there but merely because the usual alternatives offered less distraction than before. Tom, though clearly pleased, found himself a little puzzled.

'Are you feeling unwell, Mary?' came the slightly anxious enquiry after a couple of weeks.

'No, I don't think I'm unwell. What makes you ask?'

'Well, that's good. It's just that you don't look yourself at the moment. You seem very tired.'

'Perhaps I am, yes. I think I must be tired.'

'Well, we'll make sure to get to bed early, then'.

He added no more, having suggested what must have seemed a sensible remedy. But I shuddered inwardly at the idea of this, or indeed of any *early night*, and of what was likely to happen before sleep could be allowed to take over. It had come as something of a relief during the last week or so that Tom, battling a chill and nasty cough, seemed deserted by his usual energies. That particular day, though, he appeared improved. Recovery was underway, so what could be pleasanter, he must have thought, than going early to bed? After all, only a small effort would be asked of me. And then we would both be free to sleep and I could begin my own recovery from being *tired*.

I did not want intimacy with Tom. I had never wanted it, of course, but it had always been tolerable. But at that moment, the *not* wanting rose up as a strong and insistent feeling in its own right.

However, a different thought had apparently struck Tom.

'Mary, you don't think it could be something else?'

'Such as what?'

'Well, that you're tired because you – you don't think perhaps – that you could be *carrying*?'

'No, I don't think so, Tom. I really don't.' I answered quickly, and felt a wave of guilt as his face fell a little.

I knew for certain that I could not be, for my last bleed had finished only the day before. A pity that it had fallen so, just when Tom's illness meant nothing unwanted was being asked of me. It crossed my mind that a bit of deception could postpone things for a further night or two, for he was always considerate at such times. But that thought occasioned another sting of guilt, and almost at once I decided against it. Whatever my waywardness, I still felt a need to treat him with some kindness.

In any case, I asked myself – and not for the first time – was I ever likely to set eyes again on that *other* Thomas? It could well be that he had lost all interest. No doubt the novelty of associating with a woman from a common, working family had now faded. Perhaps the surprising discovery – that as well as a pleasing face, I had a mind good enough to take on his own – no longer captivated him. He had enjoyed, taken his fill and now gone on his way. He need never bother making the trip to Cromford again, and could be confident that I had no means of seeking him out.

I felt anger towards Thomas Bateman suddenly. How dare he intrude into my simple, daily existence, then on some self-indulgent whim simply disappear from it! I told myself I owed him nothing, that he had no right whatever to hope for loyalty, any more than I could dream of expecting it of him. At this very moment he could be in the company of another woman – a more appropriate one – and very likely was. Some female relative of this *foremost in the field* character, perhaps.

Such reflection, though brief, not only sent my mind reeling in distress, but caused the next remark to emerge insistently and without warning. I found myself even reaching out to touch Tom's arm, so that its meaning would be unmistakable.

'Yes, *let's* go to bed early, Tom. Both of us. I'd like that, I really would.'

Tom was unused to such forwardness and it caused a flush of surprise and pleasure to rush into his cheeks.

'In fact why not now?' I continued brashly. 'It's not too early, and the pots can wait till morning'.

Predictably, no further persuasion was needed. Tom took hold of my hand and I was led to the staircase, from which point he was obliged to let it go on account of the awkward narrowness. Once in the bedroom, we undressed without words and got quickly beneath the blanket, for the room was chilly. But it was the first time since our wedding night that I did not bother to put on my night slip. The first time that I turned at once towards him.

Never before had I chosen to encourage Tom in such a way. But while he appeared to delight in it, there played in my mind a sad and guilty regret that what had driven me towards him was not desire, but an angry resentment against another. I saw my action for the base thing it was, and did not feel proud.

Still – and however base and shameful the reason – I felt moved that night to be more generous hearted than I had ever taken the trouble to be before. Ardour was beyond me, but at least I tried to treat my husband with a tangible warmth; to hold and touch him with something close to tenderness.

Afterwards, he held to me tightly for a while and I made no move to turn away before being released. I longed, during those moments, to feel the sort of peace I knew my husband wanted me to feel, even if he could not have put such a desire into words. But my efforts had at least provided him with a greater pleasure than usual, and I felt glad of it.

As always, Tom fell quickly asleep. I lay still, listening to his steady snores, and into my mind came the question that had posed itself so many times, and for almost as long as I could remember. 'Why can I not just be *content*?'

There came no answer. I thought of Ma, who had always, to me, seemed content. Satisfied with her lot, thankful to have her children around her, accepting Pa's rough, self-centred ways without turning to dislike.

'He's a decent man, at heart,' she once claimed, after hearing me utter some well justified criticism. 'He's always worked hard to provide for us, Mary. We've never starved, have we? Never gone hungry for long. There's far worse husbands and fathers around, believe me. Far worse.'

That appeared to me to be at the base of many women's tolerance; their belief that things could be far worse. They could have starved, been beaten by a violent husband, lost all their children to disease. They felt fortunate to have been spared all, or even some, of those things.

It must surely be a sensible way to exist. Making the best of the situation and getting on with it. There had to be, I decided, be something wrong with me that I had never learned to treat life in that way.

22

Just over two weeks into Thomas's absence there came several days of rain, much of it torrential and driven by high winds. In a way I was grateful for the bad weather, for there could be no question of him riding across in such conditions and no possibility, either, of my evening wanderings. Therefore it might be safe to conclude that he would seek me out – if it was what he still wanted to do – as soon as conditions improved. That should deal with the uncertainty of his 'two weeks or thereabouts, maybe a little more' statement. For surely by then he would be back?

That first fair evening, following a dry day, I contrived to reach our usual meeting place a little earlier than usual. It was mild and pleasant and I decided to take my poetry book with me. If Thomas did not appear then I would walk among the trees and read, occupy myself in this well-tried fashion and not allow disappointment to destroy the lovely evening.

Most important of all, I would not build up hope. I would try, in fact, not to entertain any hope at all. There was no reason to assume Thomas would arrive; his demeanour on the last occasion had suggested he could be tiring of our association, or at least of the inconvenience of it. And since then he had been in London. He had spent time with friends, had had opportunity to reflect on his life, to see a bit of *sense*.

Such was the rational state of mind I had imposed on myself, it was a shock to enter the trees and to see Thomas just a few yards away. He sat on the ground, close to a glistening Maud, a large open notebook balanced across his knees. The image of man and horse was one an artist might have enjoyed painting.

He looked up and smiled broadly. 'Do join me!'

'Isn't it muddy?'

'Not too bad just here. And I've put down the cloth from under the saddle.'

I walked across and sat down beside him. Both of us were strangely calm, it struck me. We might have been meeting after a gap of only hours.

'And with a book, no less!' He feigned a look of amazement. 'What is it?'

'A book of poems – Alfred Tennyson. My mother gave it to me years ago. Goodness knows how she came by it, I don't remember asking her.' It seemed odd to be having this type of conversation, after such an absence.

'Well, you're better educated in that respect than I am,' he said. 'I know nothing at all of poetry.'

'I know very little myself. I just like the sound of it.' I turned the book over in my hands, rubbed a thumb along its title. 'I like it almost as much as the sort of books you read. You know, books that *tell* you about things – about places, people, the past. Anything! Anything in the whole damned world that isn't Cromford!'

He laughed, and slid an arm slid around me. I turned towards him and almost at once felt the welcome pressure of his lips against mine.

'We're too close to the church here,' I warned, pulling back from him after a moment.

'That's alright.' He straightened up. 'Why don't you read a poem to me? Or just a bit of one, perhaps – if it's very long!'

I chuckled, surprised at the request but not displeased. Sharing poetry would be a new type of pleasure.

'The book's called "Poems Chiefly Lyrical," I informed him.

'Mm, doesn't fill me with hope.'

'Just close your eyes and listen. And don't dare drift off to sleep!'

I found a verse at random and began to read; it was not one of the pieces I knew by heart. The task reminded me of Sunday School, for I had often been instructed to read aloud to other children there; the only pupil who could do so with fluency.

'I like hearing your voice,' Thomas said, after a while. 'I've never bothered to read any verse. Never thought about it.'

'Perhaps there's no poetry in your soul.'

'Poetry aside, I intend to take a good collection of books to the house. The house in Bakewell. '

I closed the volume of poems and put it down on the grass. 'I expect there's plenty in Middleton for you to choose from.'

I felt dejected, suddenly. What were they to me, these precious books that would line the shelves of his new home? I was unlikely to glimpse them. I would not even be able borrow one or – better still – receive it as a gift. For how could the sudden appearance of such a thing be explained?

I must have fallen silent. After a while Thomas turned to face me, and I realised his hand was no longer touching my shoulder. The levity seemed to have passed from him, as it had from me.

'It isn't reasonable, Mary, for us to continue as we are. Wouldn't you agree that's true? Winter will make it next to impossible, if nothing else does.'

So here it was, then. The rational, awaited end to things. I felt my body stiffen.

'That's probably so.' It seemed vital to me to keep my face composed, my voice calm. A sense of humiliation would make this harder to bear.

'And so,' Thomas continued steadily, his tone conveying no emotion whatever, 'as I see it, there's only one right and proper course of action, and I would suggest we need to take it.'

'And what's *that*, Thomas? What do you suggest we do – *precisely*?' I was aware of a growing dismay, and of my attempt to disguise it with an edge of sarcasm. Thomas looked startled. He frowned.

'Well I think it's plain enough what we ought to do. Isn't it?'

I did not reply; my mind, readying itself for rejection, was confused. There was something in his direct look, in the hard focus of the grey eyes, that was suggesting a course I had not predicted. It seemed wise to wait, to remain silent, rather than make a fool of myself by putting any thought whatever into words. It would be excruciating to discover Thomas had nothing of the like in mind. I stared at him, holding his expectant gaze, aware that a sweat had broken out over my body.

'Why don't you tell me exactly what it is you're proposing, Thomas'.

He laughed; a guffaw, almost. 'Good Heavens! You make it sound as if we're about to discuss a business deal!' I said nothing and he took a longer and deeper breath than necessary, then exhaled it in a way that suggested a huge and wearying effort must now be made.

'What I'm *proposing*, Mary, is that you come and live with me at my humble abode in Matlock Street, Bakewell. That we spend all and every night together. That in fact – to put it blunt and clear – we live *as one*.' He raised his eyebrows in question, as my hand went to my mouth to cover a nervous gasp of laughter.

'That's the only sort of proposal I can make to you, isn't it? Taking into account that another man, who happens to go by the same name as I do, has beaten me to it with regard to the other kind.'

I did give voice to my instant doubt that he would have made the *other* kind. I put my face into my hands and remained still and silent for a while. Thomas said nothing more. When I raised my head again his gaze was on Maud, who had drifted further away.

'Thomas, it would be wonderful to live with you, *of course* it would! But it's nothing but a dream, a fantasy! Don't you see that? It can't happen. It can never happen. So why don't we admit that fact, acknowledge it, do what we know we must.'

'*Why* can't it happen?' he turned again to face me, looking thwarted and displeased. It struck me there was something here of the spoilt young man, the overindulged child, furious and disbelieving that his wishes are being ignored.

'Because I'm *married*!' I as good as shouted it. There followed another silence, while I tried to regain some sort of composure. 'Thomas, I wish *very much*… ' I swallowed, with awkward difficulty. 'You cannot imagine just how much – that it wasn't the case. If I could change that simple fact, then I would. Because the truth is, I find no joy, no pleasure, in being with my husband. And I did him a great wrong, a *terrible* wrong, when I walked into this church – this very church – and put us both through a miserable, dreary little wedding ceremony!'

I might have had a sense of these things before, but never had the thought been so clear, and brought such shame. Releasing the words brought an odd kind of relief, and Thomas's face began to blur as tears were fought back.

'Then why continue to be unhappy? Why continue to do him *wrong*? Why not come and live with me, enjoy *my* life – isn't that something you want?'

'Thomas, of course it's what I would *want*.'

'Then do it, Mary! Why do you not just leave him? I can hardly imagine he's a happy man – as it is now.' He hesitated, perhaps wondering if he had said too much. I made no reply and he reached out to take my hand. 'Would leaving him cause, well, a great *difficulty* for you?' His voice had taken on a gentler, less adamant tone.

Maud had meandered back to us. I held the other hand out and she put her soft, warm muzzle into it, perhaps hoping that it held a titbit. Thomas's arm slid once again around my back; he leaned towards me and I felt his lips and chin against my head.

'I could teach you to ride, and to use a horse and trap,' he said at last. 'You could use it to visit your sisters.' Warmth from his breath came through my hair. 'You'd be very good, I think, with practice. Probably quite fearless.'

'Thomas, I need to go. Forgive me!' I felt compelled to leave, even though it must still have been early and there was no necessity to return home. I had a need to be alone. That night there could be no venturing further into the trees, no deep kisses and urgent, exploring hands. My mind was taut with confusion. Ripples of excitement, of delight, fought with a sense of horror. Picking up the book, I scrambled a little clumsily to get to my feet.

'What on earth's the matter?' He looked startled.

'I'll come back here *tomorrow*,' I insisted anxiously. 'Only if something awful happens, will I not come to meet you tomorrow. So please try be here also, Thomas. Be here if you possibly can.'

He must have thought better of saying anything more. There was a slow nod, his face serious and thoughtful, but he remained seated, arms around his knees and his back slightly hunched. I turned without further farewell and made my way quickly out of the trees, through the church-yard and back onto the lane.

From there I headed in the opposite direction from the cottage, attacking the incline with determined, energetic strides. Within moments I had broken into a run, one that carried me forward for some distance, even after the body began to protest and breath was coming in rapid, pained gasps. No sound of hooves followed me but it was a while longer before I gave in and threw myself down into a patch of long, damp grass. When breath had recovered a little, I shuffled across to lean against a moss-covered rock. My skirt was now wet and muddy, but of no care.

There was a view from this spot, over the roofs and chimneys of Cromford, over the walls of the old mill, and way beyond. For a long time I stared, vacant, aware of heavy perspiration and of an uncomfortable thirst. I realised my book was lying on the damp ground and scooped it up. Already the cover had been damaged.

Only when a clouded, early dusk started to fall and I became aware that I was shivering, did I rise to my feet and make a reluctant way home.

The rest of the evening drifted by me. Tom and I ate a late meal of stew, prepared the day before from onions and a bit of ox cheek, albeit a cheap, sinewy piece the butcher had left over. It had not been stewed long enough and was still too tough, though Tom seemed to enjoy the meal as much as always and finished every bit, using a crust of bread to soak up the last drop of gravy. He also finished off what was left on my plate.

'That was very good, Mary,' he declared, before taking himself over to the big chair and loosening off his clothes a little. I guessed a nap would soon follow and was thankful for it. I had no wish to venture out anywhere with Tom, nor to make any vain attempt at conversation. Relating bits of meaningless gossip would have been beyond me that night. They would have seemed ridiculous also, when I had been invited to make my own life the most fruitful piece of gossip the village had known for some time.

We went to bed early, and I declared myself tired and a little unwell. Tom patted my hand in a gesture of understanding, and was then considerate enough to fall asleep; a heavy, purposeful sleep which no amount of restlessness from me was likely to disturb.

Though in fact I lay quite still. Lay still and stared into the darkness. I heard the familiar creeks of the house, heard Tom's snores and his occasional grunts, heard the night sounds of animals, from close and far.

Steadily, as the chilly, lonesome hours of night passed by, it became clear to me what was going to happen. It did not present itself as a decision, as such. I had not argued the case with myself, back and forth; had not weighed one side against the other. There had been no delving into the questions of right and wrong, no consideration of duty or of danger. A moment simply came when I knew what I was going to do; accepted I was going to do it even though there would be hurt and anguish. My life was to change; whatever the risk to my own safety, and whatever might be the final consequences.

I laid my hand gently on Tom's back, knowing he would not wake. I wished I could ask his forgiveness.

23

'Have you thought about what I said, Mary?'

We had barely greeted one another, but it was enough to tell me he had had no second thoughts, no sudden change of heart. I turned away and began to stroke Maud's neck and between her ears. As often, she ignored the gesture of affection and continued to nose for something tasty in the grass.

'I have thought, yes.'

'*And*?'

I took my time before turning back to look at him and tried to keep my expression solemn; something in me wanted to hold the power, to cast him down for just a moment. It did not work, however, for the suggestion of a smile must already have been escaping. Thomas's face broke into a simple, boyish grin, a mixture of joy and triumphant glee. My own smile, perhaps, remained more diffident.

Though there was a joy in it, for a life with Thomas now lay within my hands. It could be felt, tasted almost. I did not bother to remind myself, in that heady moment, that such a life could only be one of uncertainty, that any wise soul might warn of its being as short as it might well be sweet. It needed no reminder, for I knew it. Knew it better than Thomas did, I suspect. Yet the prospect remained irresistible. Neither cowardice nor goodness had proved strong enough to stop me seizing it.

'Will there be, well, *difficulty* for you?'

He had asked this before, and received no answer. Nor could I answer it now.

'I shall be able to manage things, Thomas.'

'That's good. That's so very good!' He took my hands in his. 'And it can be done soon, do you think? There's no need for us to wait?' He made no attempt to disguise his impatience. I wondered how much of it came from desire to spend his days and nights with me, how much from a weariness with the travelling, the waiting, the frequent disappointment. The proportions did not matter to me greatly.

'I think so – yes. It might be better that way. Yes, soon, I think.'

'Tomorrow?'

'Good Heavens, Thomas! Not tomorrow! No, I didn't mean *quite* so soon. But not long – I promise you it need not be long.'

'Then when?'

I thought wildly for a moment. There really seemed no good reason for delay. What benefit could there be in it? What harshness or cruelty would be avoided?

'Thursday, perhaps. Yes, I think Thursday – in the evening might be better.'

It was then Monday. For some reason I felt convinced that the days between must be needed for *something*. Surely there were matters I would have to see to? Though I could not think what.

'I'll come to meet you somewhere, Thomas. Tell me where you'll be – but I don't think here, perhaps. No, not here. It would be wise to meet somewhere more – *out of the way*.' I could hear a rush of anxiety in my voice.

It was Thomas who was now required to think quickly. He stared into space, his forehead pulled into a frown. I waited, breathing quickly, my mouth dry.

'A place called the *Old Smithy*.' He announced the name with clear relief at having thought of it. 'It's out on the other side of the village – some way out. Small place, nothing to it. Just some dump of a house inn. Can't imagine more than a handful of locals ever go inside. I've never been through the door, but I've ridden past.' He looked at me, worried, it seemed, for the first time. 'You do know where I mean, Mary, do you? On the road towards What-standwell? Far side of a ramshackle old farm, two or three muddy fields with a huge number of pigs.'

'I think I know. I'll find it.' I would make sure of the place in advance, I decided; walk in that direction very early the next morning.

'I'll be waiting for you there. On Thursday – that's where I'll be. From early evening.'

Making a reluctant way home, I forced myself into think-ing only of practical matters. These were all I had to com-bat a gnawing apprehension that had started to worm its way inside me just as soon as we made our brief, cursory farewell.

Tomorrow had seemed ridiculously soon to carry out our plan, yet now I wished I had agreed to it. Just one night, and then it would all be over – I would be gone. It struck me as I walked along, pulling my wrap closely about me for the breeze had a bite to it, that an early, even immediate, move would have proved easier. Thomas had been right, even though it was unlikely to have been my *ease* that concerned him. Because I had panicked a little, three nights and days had somehow to be got through. I could not break the news to my husband until the end of that time, for once done it would be intolerable for us both if I did not leave at once.

Two other questions posed themselves. Apart from Tom, was there anyone I needed to tell before Thursday? And beyond what I stood up in, was there anything I should take with me?

I decided it was only Alice who had to know the truth at this time. That would be a difficult enough thing, Heaven knew. I would go to see Fanny when I could. Surely there was no one else who needed to be told just yet? The lives of others would be little affected and the task could wait. They would know soon enough.

As for what to take with me, it would be very little, since there was nothing much I could lay claim to. My old canvas bag would carry the four books – for which Tom had no possible use – along with my two spare slips and perhaps the dress made by Mrs Booth for my wedding, since it was the only attractive garment in the bedroom cupboard. I possessed few clothes and the matter had never much concerned me, though the thought came that soon I would be able to have more. They could be the sort of dresses Thomas would enjoy seeing me in. And they would not have to be put together by the grumbling, dribbling Mrs Booth.

The practical matters that helped keep a certain calm during the walk home did not prove effective once I was back, and the door had closed behind me. The door to my *own home*, that had seemed such a liberating thing when my new husband had opened it on the night of our wedding.

Tom was likely to be back within the hour. I scurried to put his meal together, a process that brought with it a new concern. My cooking might be unexceptional – not a patch on Alice's – but at least it was *done*. When Tom arrived home each night, if a meal was not ready for him, then it was in the hurried throes of preparation. At worst it would have been left for him in a dish, to be eaten cold. Exhausted as he so often was, nothing was required of him other than to sit down and to devour it. I made sure also that there was always some beer, storing this in a stone jug on the cold floor of the tiny scullery.

My mind now began to conjure up an image of some pathos, in which the poor man returned to an empty house and sat alone all evening, trying to satisfy his hunger with days' old bread and a few bits of mouldering cheese. There would be no pudding, not even my indigestible suet. He would go up early to a cold bed, lonely and unsatisfied. And would remain unsatisfied, of course, in all respects.

I had not made time that day to light the fire, but it was a mild night and no hot water was needed for cooking. There were enough left-over scraps from the previous couple of days to make a good plateful for Tom and provide a small helping for me. Though I did not feel in the least able to eat, and did not expect to manage more than a few mouthfuls while these next few days were somehow being endured.

But it did occur to me, as I spooned out some rather unappetising pieces of cold potato and the remaining bits of what had been yesterday's treat of fatty bacon, that my husband had, in fact, lived alone before. And somehow he had managed to survive the ordeal. Many months had passed between his mother's death and my welcome arrival, during which time he must have obtained and eaten at least sufficient to sustain life. So perhaps it was foolish and needless to torture myself with such imaginings. Was I underestimating Tom, a grown man? He did, after all, appear to be in sound health, and was not impoverished. Those facts made him more fortunate than many.

Sometime – why should it not be so? – Tom would surely find someone else to share this home. A woman who would appreciate his hard work and steadiness, make it her business to keep him well fed and happy. One who might even give him children. I could not imagine others would condemn him for taking this woman into his home and into his bed. Not in the wake of my desertion.

It became tempting, even, to entertain the idea that however painful things might be for Tom in the immediate, in truth I was doing him a kindness. But honesty prevented me from playing such a trick with myself. I knew that thought to be a false comfort; nothing more than a cowardly way to deny the cruelty of what I was set to do.

'It's leftovers, Tom. I hope they're alright?'

'They're tasty, yes.' Tom was seated at the table, shovelling potato into his mouth like a half-starved man. 'Aren't you having any?'

'A little, I'll just have a little.'

I stopped trying to busy myself with pots, spooned a tiny amount onto the other plate and reluctantly sat down with him at the table. He gobbled on for a few moments, before raising his head and looking towards the food I had barely started.

'That's not enough, Mary! Won't keep a bird alive! Isn't there anymore left?'

'There's a bit, Tom, but you can have it. I'm not hungry.' His quizzical expression encouraged me to continue hurriedly. 'I ate a big crust of bread and jam with Alice. Some jam she's made to store away. She wanted us to try it.'

The personal detail made things sound more authentic, to my ears at least. And it was true, as it happened; though not true of today but of about two weeks ago. As hoped, the anecdote ridded Tom of his concern, and me of the need to force down a sickening amount.

'Ah, well. If you've had that, you won't be hungry.' He was easy to put at ease.

'No, I'm really not.' I attempted another mouthful and then pushed the plate towards him.

'You have this, Tom. I know you can eat it.'

'If you're sure.'

'I am. You need to eat up because there's no pudding today, I'm afraid.'

'That's alright.'

'But I'll make sure to do a suet tomorrow.'

My mind seemed unduly concerned, I realised, with *feeding him up*. Perhaps some foolish part of me thought the final blow would be less harsh if it came after several days of hearty eating. Did I imagine that more copious food than usual would provide a layer of fat that could insulate him from the sorrow to come? A vain hope, in any case. Tom's bones never had more than a thin covering of flesh, no matter how much he consumed. He was muscular but sinewy. Alice had remarked on the fact only recently.

'I don't think you can *feed* your husband, Mary!' she had declared, patting his flat belly playfully and shaking her head in wonder. 'He's like a stick.'

'Oh, she does, you know,' Tom had replied, loyally. 'It's just how I am.'

'Well, I bet *I* could put a bit more flesh on you. In no time at all!' Alice was proud of skills in both cooking and caring, and not above a touch of smugness. Nor did I miss the hint of criticism, for I was aware both of her affection for Tom and of her doubt that I looked after him as well as he deserved. As well as Alice believed any husband deserved.

She was right, in a way, though not quite as right as she imagined. I did not neglect to provide Tom with meals, to wash his clothes or keep our home in reasonable order. It was true these things were never done to a good standard. I admit that they were done only because they *needed* to be done, and not with the least pleasure or pride in fulfilling the task well. As far as domestic duties were concerned, I did what I had to do and no more. They were matters of necessity, not of devotion.

Perhaps that was what Alice saw and could not understand. It aroused a sympathy in her for Tom, whom she saw as a man who needed not just to be cared for, but to be *cosseted*. A man even more deserving of it, she may have thought, than her beloved Harry.

24

Wednesday came, and I knew I must tell Alice. For some reason there seemed a need to do this even before speaking to Tom. Perhaps this first ordeal had to be done with, before facing the more dreaded one with my husband.

I was well aware that Alice would be more deeply upset by the news than others in the family; that she would find it impossible to sympathise. It was likely to be at least as great a grief as when she learned I intended to marry and leave home in the first place. Alice felt things keenly and with passion – it had always been so, and indeed it is still, so many years later. In matters such as these, people do not change.

My other sisters, I thought, were not going to feel the same distress. Edwina might declare herself shocked, if being *shocked* was something life had not by now beaten out of her. But it would not be the shock of moral outrage. On the contrary, I expected the news to provide her with quite a thrill; she would be intrigued, desperate for detail of any and every kind. Though kind-hearted enough to feel some pity for Tom, she would assume that sooner or later he would be sensible enough to pick himself up and look about for someone else. 'Someone without all your fancy ideas!' I could hear her cheerfully declaring.

I could not see that anything would change much for Fanny, for I could try to make sure of seeing her as often as before. And least of all would it matter to my youngest sister. Though it did strike me that on occasions I might be able to slip dear Mrs Spence a little extra money.

Still less did I feel in any hurry to tell my brothers. A rotten thing, they would think, as far as *poor old Tom* was concerned, but a stroke of luck for me. 'Just make darned sure you look out for yourself, girl!' was the sort of remark I could expect of them. And soon enough they could be relied upon to seek Tom out, slap his back in hearty encouragement and cart him off somewhere for a large quantity of ale. That is the way they dealt with any misfortunes of their own. It is the way most men appeared to deal with misfortune, though I doubted it would cure the pain and disappointment soon to be inflicted on Tom.

Having decided that Alice must be the first to know, I nevertheless found myself putting off the moment. Whether this was the thought of causing her distress, or through some well justified sense of shame, I am not sure, but in the end the matter was not broached until the morning of the chosen Thursday itself.

Alice had not been expecting me. It was her *wash* day, as I well knew, and on my very early arrival I was greeted with the sight of grey bed sheets and dirty clothes piled in two separate heaps on the floor. She was in the process of heating water on the fire and the room was already heavy with dampness and steam.

'I'll give you a hand, if you like', I offered, ignoring her look of surprise and thankful to find at hand a basic and tiring task.

'Why not make us some tea first?'

'Alright, tea. That would be nice.'

I applied myself to this alternative chore. She continued with her own activity, but I sensed her looking towards me more than once.

'There's some bread and a jar of my jam too, if you like, Mary. I've eaten nothing yet this morning.'

'You haven't had porridge?'

'No – no, I haven't. Couldn't stomach it today, somehow. But I'm hungry now.'

I glanced at her, and attempted to banish a distracting thought from my mind.

'You ought to have porridge every morning, Alice. That's what Ma always said, remember?'

'Well I just didn't feel like it today.'

The tone was a little short, but at least we could mention Ma these days without immediate danger of tears. I busied myself with the spreading butter and jam – applying more than usual to Alice's portion – and with brewing tea. Nothing of importance would be mentioned, I decided, until she had eaten something.

We sat ourselves at the table, and within a couple of moments the bread had disappeared. Our mugs, though, remained full of strong tea and there was a slight tension in the air, or so it felt to me. I imagined something odd in my demeanour must have put it there. But this now seemed as good a moment as any and there was no point in delaying any longer.

I did not relate to Alice a tale of any great length. It seemed important to explain things simply, in as calm a way as possible, and for my words to be clear. She needed to grasp what had happened and what I was about to do. There must be no confusion for I did not want her left in any doubt as to my intentions, or imagining she might yet be able to dissuade me.

Not without awkwardness, and at times haltingly, I set about the task. Unusually for Alice, she did not once interrupt but listened intently, staring down at the mug, around which her hands were now clasped tightly. Her face seemed to tighten as I spoke, while a biting at the lower lip betrayed a state of increasing dismay. When I stopped, she did not look up at me and remained silent.

'Alice,' I said at last, feeling exhausted from my effort. 'I'm not asking you to *understand*. And I'm not asking you to approve. I know it's not possible for you to do either.'

'No, I can't. And I won't ever be able to, Mary.'

She stood up, holding to the edge of the table, and stared at me, her eyes tearful, bewildered.

'I can only think of poor Tom – the terrible way he's going to suffer. I mean… he's not even done anything *wrong*, has he? Nothing at all. You couldn't possibly be married to a kinder man, Mary. You have to admit it. All he's ever wanted is to make you happy. I think he's the nicest, most patient man I've come across in my whole life, and I don't mean to insult Harry by saying that because you know I love Harry very much. But, well – your Tom! He's just such a *good* person, isn't he? There's none better, and he… '

'Alice, I know all this!' She had found her voice and I sensed that if left uninterrupted the outpouring might continue forever. She stopped, with a sharp inward breath, raising a hand to where the lower lip was beginning to tremble out of control. I stood up and moved over to her, putting both my hands on her shoulders.

'I *know* what a good man Tom is. Believe me, I know. And I do wish with all my heart that I didn't have to hurt him in this way.'

She looked at me, and her voice became harder, more accusing.

'But you can't possibly wish it with *all your heart*, Mary! Because if you did, then you simply would never, ever do such a thing, would you?'

'No... no, I wouldn't.' I was shamed by her into honesty. 'You're right, Alice, I wouldn't. What I'm about to do is for me, I admit that. It's something I want to do for myself.'

She sniffed, then turned away from me and went to open the cupboard behind her. Picking out a small cloth from one of the neat piles inside, she wiped her eyes, before blowing her nose very hard.

'Oh God, I can't believe this. It's just so *sad*!' Her back was still towards me, her shoulders slightly hunched. The tone was turning to one of defeat.

'Yes, I know it is.'

'But Mary, I *knew* this could happen!' She turned round, and the voice was raised again. I had been mistaken in thinking her beaten into acceptance quite yet.

'Well – not *this*. I never really thought of this, but I knew well enough *something* would happen that wasn't good. I knew you'd never be happy. I *told* you, Mary, I *told* you –

and Pa did as well, didn't he?' I winced at the allusion to Pa.

'I could *see* you wouldn't be happy with Tom. That he wasn't the husband you needed. Anyone could see it. And *you* could see it too, I know you could. You should never have done such a thing, Mary!'

I sat down, feeling my own sense of defeat. 'No, I shouldn't. You're right. I admit it, Alice. But in all honesty I never thought that something would happen to make me leave Tom. Believe me, I never did.'

'Didn't you?'

'No, I didn't. But I knew what my reasons were for marrying Tom. I wasn't dishonest with myself – and I wasn't dishonest with you, Alice.'

'But you were with Tom! He thought you loved him.'

'I don't believe he did.' I realised, as I spoke, that this was true. 'Tom's not a clever man, but he's not a fool, either. I think he knew how things were. He saw just how it was. But he hoped that once we were married… well, that I'd be content with him, at least.'

'And you're not?'

I was silent for a moment. The fire had gone from both of us now.

'I thought I was content enough, at first. But no, I'm not now. I'm not content to be his wife anymore.'

She heaved a sigh, and the cloth went to her eyes and nose once again. A longer silence fell between us. She shook her head slowly, in the manner of one weary of life, with its endless miseries and betrayals.

'Thank goodness poor Ma doesn't have to know about this.'

'That's not fair. Leave Ma out of this.' I waited for a moment before adding, perhaps unkindly, 'You know as well as I do that if Ma was still alive I would never have needed to marry Tom in the first place.'

Alice sat down again heavily. She leaned forward on her elbows, staring down at the cloth that was now squashed into a tight ball inside her palm. Our mugs of tea sat on the table, cold and unappetising. I noticed her body had become a little rounder over the last couple of months. Contentment, perhaps, of the sort I did not have. Satisfaction with a life centred on caring for Pa, and most of all for her precious Harry. A state of mind I found simple, enviable, and beyond my reach.

The healthy roundness might also reveal that Harry's position within the family was now a certainty. If so, Alice's own contentment would be all the greater.

'You've always been different, Mary. Different from the rest of us, I mean.'

It sounded like an unhappy observation. I shrugged my shoulders.

'You're much cleverer than any of us. You want more. Simple things just aren't enough.'

It was my turn to sigh. 'If that's true, all I can say is that I'm not always glad of it, believe me.'

Alice stood up again. She seemed to hesitate, then came towards me and put out her arms. The gesture seemed to be an expression of sisterly distress, rather than one of camaraderie.

'When will you tell Tom?'

'This evening. I can't leave it longer.'

I felt her shoulders and arms tense, and withdrew myself from the embrace to meet her eyes.

'And then I shall have to go, Alice. I'll need to go straight away.'

A barely audible groan was all that emerged.

' But I shall come to see you, and Fanny too, just as soon as it's possible. And of course you'll come to me – to *us*.' My voice trailed off. The new *us* seemed a strange, unlikely concept. 'It can be done, you know. I shall only be in Bakewell, after all; it's really not far.'

'It *is* far.' She looked into my face with dark seriousness. 'And in any case, I'm so frightened for you, Mary, I truly am. Have you thought of what will happen… ' She hesitated. 'Have you thought *at all* what would happen – well, if this Thomas… '

'If he tires of me?' I raised my eyebrows in question. 'Well, he may do, I suppose, one day. He's almost bound to. But life will carry on, won't it, one way or another? I intend to survive, you see. Whatever happens.'

'I could never think like that.'

'I know you couldn't. And I'm glad of it.'

'What shall I tell Pa, Mary? I just can't imagine what he'll have to say.'

I could imagine only too well.

'No, please don't talk of this to Pa. I've no interest at all in what he might have to say. It's no business whatever of his.'

He would, of course, hear anyway; it could only be a matter of time, and probably a very little time. But he would not appreciate receiving the news from outside and it struck me I was putting Alice in an intolerable position.

'Tell him, then, if you feel you must,' I said, 'but there's no need to relate to me anything he says. I don't care and I don't need to know.'

There was a further blowing of the nose.

'Alright, I'll tell him. But not tonight, I just couldn't. I can't tell anyone tonight.' She thought for a moment. 'But *you* must tell Fanny. It wouldn't be right, not to. '

'I shall. And I'm sorry – I really am sorry, Alice – that I've upset you.'

I did hate to cause Alice hurt. Hated it even more, I realised, than the thought of causing pain to my husband.

25

I was tempted to pack my few clothes and possessions into a bag and simply walk out of the house. To put a note on the table telling Tom I had decided to leave and that nothing at all could be gained by searching for me. Telling him that I wished him well. Perhaps adding that I was deeply sorry. I tried hard to persuade myself that it would be easier and kinder for Tom in this way.

But it would be cowardly too, of course, and in any case Tom's reading was poor. He might well need help to be certain of even a very simply worded message, and humiliation would then be added to sorrow. Nevertheless I intended to keep things brief, as much for his sake as for mine.

Approaching the boat, tied up in its usual night-time place along the quayside, it struck me that this was the first time I had bothered to venture here since seeking Tom out just a few weeks before our wedding. Now, as on that occasion, it looked from a distance as if he were engaged in sorting out the ropes. This time the old mare stood just a few yards away, nibbling at some sparse grass and no doubt impatient for the better crop awaiting her in a nearby field. As I approached she raised her head, and a low, wet snort seemed to greet my arrival. Tom turned round and stared towards me.

'Hello Mary. What is it?' His face looked tired and pale. I realised he must also be hungry and that nothing had been cooked and left ready for him in the house. I was disconcerted too by a sudden sense that somehow he was expecting bad news and already bracing himself to receive it. Preparing for unhappiness. Perhaps patiently waiting for me to tell him his fate. There can be an ancient, animal sense of unease in us when such things are about to happen.

In that moment, taking in his worried, almost haggard appearance, I detested myself. Detested my selfishness, my lack of *goodness*. None of my sisters, I knew, would be capable of this. Ma would have been heart-broken at the thought of the injury I intended to inflict. I was looking at a man who had never in his life been guilty of a deliberate cruelty and did not deserve to receive it. He had tried his best to be a good husband, but ought to have been allowed to find himself the right sort of wife; not a woman like me. He should never have been *used* and it had been unforgivable of me to do what I had. I was aware that I deserved punishment, and wondered if I had set myself on a course that was, sooner or later, likely to bring it.

Nevertheless, I knew I was not about to change my mind now.

'What *is* it?' He repeated his question insistently, without a smile.

I stepped a little closer to him; tried to look up into his face. He was owed that much bravery, at least.

'Tom, I have to say something to you. And I'm so sorry, I truly am.'

His expression remained taut, the eyes wide, unblinking. I was reminded of my first visit to the boat, almost four years ago. But on this occasion his anxiety was not about to be put to rest with news of a joyful change of heart.

'I need to go away, Tom. You see – I have to tell you – that I'm going to leave you. I'm going to leave home… ' I hesitated, then took a breath and proceeded in a steadier voice. 'I'm afraid it's not possible, any more, for me to stay with you.'

He turned his gaze away from me to stare towards the boat. I saw his shoulders rise with a long, slow breath, and then fall more slowly still. He seemed to clear his throat as if to speak, but did not. There was a stillness; a thick silence hung over us, but I did nothing to break it. I became aware, suddenly, of feeling light-headed and nauseous, and remembered I had eaten nothing since the piece of bread and jam with Alice, early that morning. There was a need to swallow hard, to prevent a sour liquid from rising further into my throat.

In different circumstances, of course, I would have told Tom about feeling unwell and reached out to hold on to him. He would have placed his arm firmly round me while we made our way slowly back home, and had he sensed this was not enough, he would have lifted me into his arms and carried me. It had happened before, just once, after I had drowned my sadness at an old neighbour's funeral gathering with several mugs of ale and too little food.

'Yes, I know, Mary.'

The words came quietly, and took me by surprise. For a moment I struggled to respond to them.

'What do you mean, Tom?'

'I know, Mary… I know that you have to go, that's all. I know.'

'I'm so very sorry.'

There was no answer from him. What answer could I possibly have expected? He turned and took a couple of slow, reluctant steps to reach the horse, who lifted her head expectantly and nuzzled into his chest. I saw Tom's arm move and knew his hand was rubbing gently at her neck, under the long, tangled mane. His back was towards me.

'I'll go now then, Tom.'

'Yes.'

There was no more. I turned and walked quickly in the direction of our home, without glancing back. There was no shout, no heavy sound of feet running to catch me up, and I knew there would not be. Some way along I was forced to stop, for the feeling of nausea had increased and I stood still for a few moments and retched painfully. The bottom of my throat was burning and a nasty, bitter taste filled my mouth. But only a small amount of liquid was brought up, for my stomach must have been empty of all else. After a few moments, I wiped away a sweat that had broken out on my forehead and forced myself to walk on.

A canvas bag lay inside the small, dilapidated tool shed where I had left it, for I knew I would not want to go inside that house again.

Seizing the bag, I pulled the shed door to and headed off as quickly as I could manage in the direction of the quiet, out of the way establishment that Thomas had named. I knew now where it was, and how it could be approached using only quiet lanes and pathways across fields. I did not want to see or have to speak to anyone at all.

Even though dusk was falling, I could judge from outside that the place was almost deserted. Thomas must have been standing by the one small window on that side, waiting. Trees close to the rough path, in thick Autumn foliage, would have prevented him from spotting me from a distance, but as I approached the door in relief he was already pushing it open from inside. I was only too aware that I must look washed out and unkempt, and hoped this would not come as an unwanted shock. He was not used to seeing me in such a dishevelled state.

'My God, Mary, are you all right? You look ill!' The tone was urgent but he kept his voice low, though I could now see that the only other customer in the small room was an old man, huddled over his beer mug in a corner. The landlord was leaning across a half door on the other side, shouting at someone in the yard beyond against the noise of barking dogs.

'I'm all right, really I am.' I felt the need to reassure him, to return myself to the confident, self-possessed person he was familiar with. 'I'm just – you see – well, it's been such a difficult time.'

I heard my voice falter and feared for a moment that I might be about to weep, perhaps even with my head buried against his shoulder, in time honoured manner. By instinct I mustered the last bit of my strength to prevent it. I have always had a horror of dissolving into tears, fighting against it even as a young child being shouted at by Pa.

Other than Ma's death, nothing had ever succeeded in producing them. Dislike of Pa and my own pride to thank for it, of course; those ever reliable culprits.

'I think I just need to sit down for a minute.'

'Of course, forgive me.' Thomas seemed flustered, as if he had been found wanting. He took charge of my bag and I was guided to a small table near the fire.

'You're as pale as death.' He glanced over towards the little room at the back. 'Look, they must be able to provide some sort of soup, even in this God-forsaken place! I shall tell that fellow to get it warmed up for you.'

He was back to being decisive, in character. And there was no doubt at all that the *fellow* would jump to it in an instant, for even those who did not recognise Thomas knew at once they were dealing with someone of author-ity, a gentleman. I did not argue, for I felt faint with hunger and knew that a bowl of hot broth, however simple, was the very thing needed. Nothing else would deal as well with the weakness and nausea, the latter having now transformed itself into sharp, griping pains. And I would have struggled to tackle food that required any serious champing.

'His wife is going to see to it straight away.' Thomas had returned after just a few moments. He placed two small, thick glasses purposefully on the table and sat himself down to face me.

'Brandy. You need to drink it.'

'I don't think I could take anything so strong.'

'You can. And it's the best thing.'

I fingered the glass, uncertainly. 'I'm surprised you managed to get this here. In a simple alehouse.'

'He got it from the back of a cupboard. Only too pleased. I suspect the fellow likes a regular drop himself.'

There was a short silence, then Thomas reached out to touch my hand, smiling encouragement towards me.

'Come on, Mary – this is *it*, now. What we've been waiting for. Don't tell me that we shan't at least raise a glass together?'

He had lifted his own glass and was holding it ready to tilt against mine. There seemed a lighter look in his eyes now; a little less concerned, perhaps, knowing that nourishment was on its way. Already slightly mischievous.

I raised my glass to his and the two clicked together. A small gesture of triumph.

'To our new life, Mary!'

I saw a boyish grin. Behind that air of natural authority lurked a young man with a sense of adventure. Quite a bit younger, I reminded myself, than me.

The warmth and power of the first swallow was instant, strengthening. I looked across at him, and for the first time during that day felt I should perhaps allow myself a smile. The *deed*, unpleasant and reprehensible as it was, had been done. I might never quite be able to forgive myself, *ought* never to forgive myself, but it was over and would not have to be done again.

And now something more exhilarating beckoned. Something dangerous and unpredictable. Intoxicating.

Though not as immediately intoxicating as the brandy, which I had downed in two, rapid gulps. Perhaps it was fortunate for good behaviour that the *fellow*'s wife arrived very soon afterwards, bearing a large, steaming bowl of what she apologetically described as her *everyday broth*. 'But it tastes good, dear, or so he always tells me, and it's very feeding. Proper bone stock, you see.' It was as much as I could do to mutter a cursory thanks before attacking the unappetising, dark brown liquid with a ferocious enthusiasm. There was a loud chuckle, and for the second time in less than twenty minutes I had to hope that Thomas – the lover for whom I had trodden my respectable life underfoot – would not feel in any way repelled by the sight of me.

The good woman's everyday broth restored me. Bit by bit I sensed anxiety receding, to be replaced by a confused mix of relief and elation. I was even moved to suggest we indulge in a second brandy. Thomas, though, was more sensibly aware than me that we could hardly sit about in that place all night.

'We should get ourselves home, Mary.'

'Home?'

'Yes, *home*. Bakewell!' He was already rising to his feet.

It dawned on me that I had no idea how we were to get from the basic but comforting room we sat in to the house in Bakewell that Thomas and I were about to share. For the last day or two I had not thought beyond getting myself and my bag to this refuge, the place where I knew Thomas would be waiting for me. But no room, decent or otherwise, was likely be on offer here. The evening custom of a few farmhands probably helped to eke out an unreliable wage the landlord earned somewhere else.

Revived as I might be, however, I did not relish the thought of another walk; this time a distance of at least ten miles.

'And how are we to take ourselves *home*?'

'On foot, naturally. Don't tell me you're expecting luxuries already?'

He received one of my well-honed looks. I had already sensed the tease.

'Have no concern, Ma'am. A man and his humble carriage await us.' Thomas stood up and reached forward to take my hand, leaning forward to kiss it in a mock bow.

'Await us where?'

'In the yard, where else?'

'Goodness, and how long's the poor fellow been hanging around out there?'

'No longer than I've agreed to pay him for. He's happy enough with it. I suspect he'll have got himself an ale and a bite of something at the back door – which no doubt I've paid for also.'

The thought of paying people to be at one's beck and call was a strange one for me. I wondered if it would ever sit comfortably, but did not need to be convinced of its advantages.

'But it'll be dark quite soon.'

'It will, but there's a full moon, have you not noticed? We'll have no trouble at all.'

It was with a mixture of anticipation and weariness that I climbed inside the small carriage waiting in the yard, sinking into its well-worn but accommodating leather seat. The vehicle may have been simple enough of its type, but it was no common cart. Thomas stepped forward to discuss our impending journey with the driver, whose voice came dimly across in a low, inarticulate drawl. I strained without success to hear what was being said, but saw that Thomas was far from pleased as he returned to climb up the two steps to join me, pulling the door sharply in to secure it.

'Moon or no moon, it seems he's not happy doing the whole thing tonight. Some concern with one of the horses; he claims the damned thing was starting to go lame on the way here.' Thomas had now squashed himself into the seat beside me. I felt the whole thing judder as we clanked and jangled our way off.

'Oh, Lord – then what now?'

'It's a nuisance, that's all. He'll see how the thing goes. We're heading towards Rowsley, so if necessary we'll just have to stay overnight at The Peacock. It's not too far. And he'd be back there for us very early tomorrow morning.'

'Oh.' I felt in no position to question such an arrangement.

'He's promised to get hold of a fitter horse, too,' Thomas added. 'This one looks too knackered to be going the distance anyway, in my opinion, lame or otherwise. So he'd better see to it, if he wants his money.'

' But I'm not smartly dressed enough. Not for staying the night – somewhere respectable.'

'You're dressed perfectly well enough.' He sounded irritated, as if we were still discussing the coachman. But a few moments later he turned to look at me and his voice was softer. 'You do look a lot more *yourself*, now, Mary. And that's a wonderful thing!'

My expression must have suggested some doubt. He took my hand, which I could feel was a little clammy.

'From now on, we shall go where we choose. Stay where we decide to stay. That's what we wanted, isn't it? So why all the anxiety? It's not like you.'

It was not, and I knew I must quickly return to being *like me*. I needed to find my old courage, my old assurance. That was what Thomas had always admired, for he was not a man to be moved by the coy or the demure. I had a strong sense that the only way to live well with him was to take the part of an equal and to do so robustly. Anything less was likely to invite his indifference.

There was no hope, of course, of equalling Thomas in matters of his learning – study and listen as attentively as I might. There were few who would be able to keep pace, or even to trail behind within the distance of a shout. And my suspicion was that Thomas was comfortable with that. It was important to him to be in the forefront of his chosen work, to be seen as a leading light, an authority. As *the* authority, I had no doubt, before too long. The equality I sought needed to be of a different kind.

Most would think me mad for imagining there could be any kind at all, given the chasm of social difference that lay between us. They would claim that Thomas was a wealthy, successful young man, who happened to find me to his taste and had decided – for a while, at least – to take and to enjoy me. They would tell me the only way to hold his affection was to ensure that my beauty lasted as long as possible. They would advise me to be, at all times, agreeable and docile.

But I knew Thomas did not want docility. Nor did he see himself as someone beyond criticism, beyond argument. Holding his interest, I believed, would not be best achieved through humble compliance.

All in all, it seemed a good idea to walk into The Peacock Inn with my head held high, apologetic to no-one. And indeed, as we got down from the creaking coach and Thomas went forward to have another firm word with the driver, what finally swept over me was excitement and curiosity. The thought of sleeping anywhere other than *at home* was a strange one. I wondered about the room we would be shown to.

And I began to picture the night that lay ahead of us. The hours that would be spent together – unhindered, joyful. Here, there need be no fear. We would be able to take our time to undress one other, would see our naked bodies bathed in candlelight, exposed in their fullness for the first time. And later – much later – we would be able to fall asleep in the same bed, still close, touching.

Might it be all the more pleasurable, the more thrilling, for happening in a place that was unknown, in a room owned by someone else? A room to be paid for the following morning and never visited again? The thought seemed strangely tantalising.

26

I should have let all of this unfold. I should have allowed things to happen without the interference of words, and most of all of questions. But as we closed and bolted the door of the guestroom behind us, an awkwardness seemed to descend. Perhaps it was caused by those very circumstances, by the freedom, the sense of aloneness, so longed for. Now that we had them, naturalness seemed to desert us. The spontaneous, easy move towards one another, that would have happened at once and without thought under the trees, did not take place. Instead we hesitated, were not at ease.

The room we had been led to by a tired, bored-faced servant girl was small and low ceilinged, and even in fluttering candlelight it had a heavy air about it. It was also chilly, for no fire had been lit. Probably no-one had expected it to be occupied that night. The girl had mentioned that their better rooms were taken already. A small disappointment, surely, at most? For this was to be ours, we were to be alone here, private and secure. The bed, when I sat on it, felt even harder and lumpier than the one at home, but neither was that a care. It was a bed that Thomas and I could share.

I should have known how to dispel this strange edginess. Merely putting my arms around Thomas would have been enough to do so and that is the movement I should have made. Instead, it seemed to propel me into seeking information.

'Does your grandfather know anything yet, Thomas – about us?'

A foolish enquiry to make. Why did I ask it when all I wanted was to touch Thomas, to hold him? Why raise the matter at the very moment we found ourselves in a bedroom for the first time?

Thomas's face tightened and he sat down, not beside me on the bed but a good space away, on a small, armed chair that happened to be the only one in the room.

'No, not yet. Why do you ask?'

It would have been wise to brush the question aside; instead found myself ploughing forward.

'I don't know. Because you've told me so little about him, I suppose. Hardly anything at all. Beyond the fact that you find him difficult.'

'Well, I hardly wanted to spend the what little time – precious time – we've had together in tedious discussions about my grandfather.'

I should have left it at that, and put my arms out towards him. But some stupidity urged me on.

'Please tell me more about your home, Thomas. Your grandfather's home, I mean, not the house in Bakewell. I've so often tried to imagine it. I don't know whether you'll ever feel you can take me there? But I'd like at least to be able to picture it more clearly.'

He said nothing for a moment or two, but I noticed the fingers of one hand lightly drumming the rounded, wooden arm of the chair.

'Well, you can picture it as being *large*,' he announced at last, in a tone that suggested he was not pleased to have the information extracted. Or not just then. 'Which won't surprise you, I suspect, though it might be bigger than – well, perhaps you've imagined.' There was further hesitation. 'The place is called Middleton Hall.'

'*Hall*?'

'Yes, as I said, *Hall*. Grandfather had it built. It's on the site of an older – a very much older – place, that he decided he would have pulled down.'

'And that was also called Middleton Hall?'

'Yes. When he bought the estate ' – I think Thomas barely noticed my eyebrows rise at the word – 'that original mansion was very dilapidated. Barely weatherproof, so I understand. And not as spacious and comfortable as he believed he required.'

'My *Goodness*.' My exclamation was breathed out quietly. This enhanced image of Thomas's circumstances had taken me by surprise. Naturally I had pictured his grandfather's house as a smart and substantial one. Thomas was educated, he owned a horse, he possessed books. The family – if that's what the two of them could be called – had a carriage. Nor did it seem necessary for him to work; or not work as most would understand the word.

But a less striking level of wealth could have provided this; could have permitted a young man to follow his interests or pursue his studies – and enabled a daughter, of course, to do nothing requiring any effort whatsoever. A retired, comfortably placed businessman could still have been indulgent towards his grandson. And despite Thomas's antagonism towards his grandfather, I suspected the old man had always been indulgent.

'Are you a lord, then, Thomas? Should I call you *Sir*? Or Lord Bateman?'

Thomas snorted, whether in amusement or offence at the thought was not clear.

'No, you most definitely shouldn't!'

'Shouldn't I? Why not?'

'Because I'm not a lord, that's why not. There's no title whatever in the family, I'm thankful to say. Though I suspect Grandfather would love to have had one. I'm quite *ordinary*, I assure you. You can hardly accuse me, can you, of behaving like some pompous, puffed up aristocrat?'

I made as if to consider this for a moment. 'Well, perhaps not. But then, I've never met an aristocrat. I've very little idea of how one might behave.'

For some reason I felt peeved about not being told of Middleton Hall before that night, and oddly irked with myself for not asking. The annoyance was unreasonable, for what difference could it make? We two were a whole world apart in any case.

'Middleton Hall. That wouldn't sound like an *ordinary* house to most people, Thomas. So I don't think you can claim to be an ordinary person – can you?'

'Well, I am.' He stood up and walked to the shuttered window, then turned again towards me, his face a glare of indignation.

'I don't understand why you sound so very accusing. You've asked me a question and I've answered it. Nothing more. Are you expecting me to apologise for the nature of the house?'

I saw the need to be conciliatory and rose quickly to go across to him, placing a hand on his arm.

'No. Forgive me. It's just... well, I'd never imagined anything quite so *grand*. And it is so?'

'I suppose it is. Yes, undeniably. But I'm *not*, and nor was my father. Neither is my damned grandfather, for all his ambition. He did come from what you'd have to call a propertied family, I suppose. But here's no *noble* connection whatever, I can assure you, no bloodline. Though he was made the High Sheriff of Derbyshire a while ago, if you count that!' Thomas seemed to find this particular title amusing; there was some attempt at a grin, before his face became serious, and rather indignant, again. 'I happen to be the grandson of a rich cotton merchant, that's all, which most would consider a piece of good fortune, I suppose. And it is. I wouldn't claim to wish things otherwise. Or not most things.'

'But some?'

'Some. I've told you before that he and I are prone to disagreement. We've had a number of rows, of recent times. Harsh words. And I could explain that by saying he's a narrow-minded old bigot who has a hatred of not getting his own way.'

I nodded, familiar enough with those particular traits. It struck me as unlikely that presenting me to his grandfather would do anything at all to calm the situation. I stroked Thomas's arm, in reassurance, but his expression did not soften.

'So don't let's discuss him,' I suggested. 'Why don't you tell me something about your father, instead?' I seemed incapable of letting this conversation cease altogether, as if it had a will of its own beyond any power of mine. I imagined that the subject of his father would evoke from Thomas a more benign reaction, though an immediate frown suggested this might be yet another mistake.

'As I once said to you – or so I remember – my father was an *admirable* man!' The tone was emphatic but nothing followed that brief summary.

'Tell me something more of him, Thomas.'

There was a sigh, perhaps of resignation. Again I wondered what was driving me into this type of conversation. Why on earth did I want to discuss these things here? And why now? I was aware of my own folly, yet did nothing to override it.

'He was a very different person from Grandfather,' Thomas said at last. 'He had no interest at all in amassing money, or certainly not for the sake of being rich. That wasn't important to him. My father loved other things – art, the theatre, learning – and so it was books, not money, he chose to collect. There's a huge library at the Hall, a remarkable collection, in fact. Almost all of it down to him.'

'Then I would have found him admirable, too!' I smiled, sensing we were now on safer ground and also because the image struck me as so wonderful as to be almost absurd. A father who loved books and devoted himself to collecting them seemed a barely imaginable joy. Though it did occur to me, in the very next moment, that such a joy had been possible only through the hard work and ambition of the *old bigot*. Being rich, in fact, had been very important indeed, and I wondered at Thomas's naivety, or unfairness, in not recognising it.

'So many works of history,' he continued, for it seemed I no longer needed to extract the words through pained insistence. 'Especially the history of ancient times – he amassed just about everything ever written on the subject. I have him to thank, of course, for my own work. You see it wasn't that I was clever, believe me. I was no great scholar at all, at school. But these things have always fascinated me – because of him. And because of the way he would talk to me about them…'

My mind was thrown back to our very first encounter by the canal, to his enthusiasm, his intensity. I remembered the speed with which he had raised my own thoughts from the dismal clatter of the everyday. The sense of elation I had felt. And I saw also the tragedy that was dealt to him by this father's loss.

'It must have been very hard for you, when he died.'

'It was.'

The reply was clipped, and told me I should leave the matter there and press him no further. I waited for Thomas to say something else, or better still to finish with words and indulge in something of a quite different kind. What I wanted – had wanted since we came into the room – was for him to take hold of me. But he remained still, his back straight, his arms folded in a way that did not invite closeness. The sudden flow of words had ceased.

'He was a disappointment to my grandfather,' he stated dully, after a while.

'And why was that?' Though I did not need to ask.

'Oh, a predictable thing, I suppose. The ruthless businessman – single-minded, intolerant. My grandfather isn't wholly uneducated, you understand, but he isn't a learned man either. I wouldn't say he despises education as such – he was quite prepared to buy it for his children, and for me. What he's no time at all for is learning as an *end in itself*. For the life of him he can't see why anyone would want to pursue knowledge for its own sake. In his mind, it's only worthwhile if it enables you to succeed.'

I could say nothing to that, musing as I was on the luxury of being able to devote untold hours to reading, to learning. To the pursuit of these things for their own sake. A picture came to me of a household of servants attired in their dull, mended working clothes. While this loyal troop went about its duties, fascinating hours could be passed in the peacefulness of the library.

'You simply have no idea, Thomas,' I said quietly, 'what being *ordinary* means. And why on earth should you?'

He looked mystified by the statement, perhaps offended. Though I had not intended it as a reproach.

Shortly afterwards we undressed, without touching one another, and got into bed. I felt cold, as Thomas must have done also, but for a time we lay there silent, in darkness, the candle extinguished. I was reminded of my wedding night, and felt a sudden sadness that impelled me to reach out to him. He said nothing, but turned at once to the touch and moved his body against mine.

It was not the passionate, hungry encounter I had imagined this first night would bring. Nor did it last for long. But there was a warmth and a comfort in it, and for the first time I had the sense that it was comfort Thomas was seeking. It was not a need he had ever shown before.

Afterwards we slept. Battered and exhausted, perhaps, from all that had been endured in the course of that one, single day.

27

Thomas's house in Matlock Street did not disappoint. Standing outside the place in the late Autumn sunshine, I was aware – the more so after our exchange of the previous night – that it must seem run-of-the-mill enough to his eyes, but to mine it did not. Number eight was part of a high terrace, with a smart black door at its centre, large, square windows to either side and only slightly smaller ones on the level above. There was no garden or railing in the front, which gave straight onto the narrow pavement. The dwelling's mid-row position was not dissimilar to the house in which I had grown up, but this presented itself as something quite different. No-one could have mistaken the sort of people likely to inhabit either one.

This house, and the others like it that formed a row along the street, did not immediately suggest substantial wealth or high standing. What it did breathe was something safe, solid, promising; a home for the professional gentleman and his wife, perhaps, with their first child or two. A couple from good, respectable families – the sort that made provision, provided settlements.

'Well, are we going inside, then?' There was a playful grin on Thomas's face. A night's sleep and a hearty breakfast had restored his sense of well-being, and with it had returned a certain cockiness. 'Or are you going to stand and stare at the front door for an hour or two more?'

'I'm taking it *all* in,' I said, 'not just the front door.'

'Well, there's not too much of it to take in, it's really quite small. But allow me to show you.'

He took me by surprise, for in one deft movement my legs were swept from under me and I was borne swiftly from the roadside and up the two high steps in front of the door. At that point he bent his head and pressed his mouth fiercely against mine, before returning me to ground. One arm remained about my waist while his other hand searched a pocket for the key.

'Thought I'd lost the damn thing, for a moment.'

The hallway was narrow, as is almost always the case in terraced property, whatever its proportions. I noted various doors off and went straight to open the first of them, but Thomas put out an arm to waylay me.

'Downstairs can wait, can't it?'

Satisfying my curiosity would have to be postponed, it seemed, at least where the living areas were concerned. I felt a hand on my back guiding me towards the steep staircase and upwards. No carrying was feasible here and just as well, if we were to hold life and limb together, though I had a sense Thomas would have risked the manoeuvre if he thought it might make our ascent speedier.

For once, I would have preferred to delay. To put inquisitiveness before appetite and indulge in the more mundane pleasure of inspecting rooms, peering into cupboards, looking through windows. Thomas's needs, however, were not of the sort to be satisfied by cupboards. And he had, after all, seen the place already.

'This is the best bedroom!' He pushed open a door and ushered me inside. I took in the room as far as I could, given that heavy blinds made it dark and all that could be made out was a large bed occupying the centre of what appeared to be quite a generous space. Given, too, that within a couple of seconds I found myself lifted once again, and a moment later lay on my back upon the said large bed.

'Last night wasn't how I wanted it to be.' His face and breath felt hot against my ear, his hands were already pulling with impatience at my clothes. 'This time will be better. I promise you.'

Like the house, or at least what little of it I had managed to see, he did not disappoint. Afterwards we lay there a while, the ease between us restored. With my eyes now used to the dimness, I could make out an attractive, well-furnished room that offered far more substantial wardrobes than my miserable little collection of clothes required.

A while later and I was in the kitchen, putting hunks of bread and cheese on a couple of plates, along with hefty dollops of crab apple chutney that I had found in one of the otherwise empty kitchen cupboards. Thomas had ordered a few simple provisions to be delivered to the back door early the previous morning and the coolness of late October had not put them in danger. The bread was no longer newly fresh, but neither cheese nor milk had gone off and all were now stored in a small scullery at the back of the kitchen. Behind this lay a yard and beyond that a small patch of garden, from which a gate lead directly into a narrow street behind.

The delivery was a godsend, since once again I was feeling faint from hunger. Unlike Thomas I had managed very little at breakfast, for the start of the morning had brought with it a feeling of nervous anticipation which had quashed my usual appetite. And after breakfast had come a strangeness, a sense of discomfort even, in the new ways I would have to become accustomed to.

Naturally, Thomas had settled the bill for our overnight stay. Later he had also – after something of an argument – paid the driver. It had felt odd to me, standing to one side, the silent beneficiary. Tom had always been happy to hand his earnings over, to leave all dealings that concerned the spending of it to me, just as he once had to his mother. Even Pa, beyond the money he took for his drink, had relied on Ma, and now on Alice, for the same thing. This was not to be the case here, however, and despite my belief that Thomas was likely to be generous, I felt a stab of regret for the loss of that power.

The plates were heaped with more usual – since there was no longer cause to scrimp. I wondered if food, to say nothing of other chores, was to be my responsibility alone. I could not imagine it would be so.

'There's already a servant,' Thomas said, as if reading my thoughts. 'Or there could be. Ellie… somebody. She was here before, working for the people who moved out, which they did four or five weeks ago.'

'And where is she now?' I broke off a lump of cheese to eat, before even setting the plates on the table.

'I understand she's living back with her family. Probably not far. She knocked on the door a few days ago – caught me when I was here with the agent – I imagine she must have been keeping a lookout for someone moving in. Asked if I wanted her to come back.'

'And you said yes?'

'Not yet. I told her to call today, later this afternoon. She looked all right, I think, quite clean and tidy. Polite. But you can decide.'

I sat down and tried not to look taken aback at the thought of approving, or otherwise, a servant. It was gratifying that Thomas had left the decision to me.

'I expect she'll do fine.'

'Well, make sure you're happy with her. There's plenty of others around that need the work.' He spread a generous amount of chutney over his bread and cheese and bit off a large mouthful. 'There's an attic up there, with a bed. I don't know whether you noticed the staircase, at the other end of the landing?'

I would have smiled, had my mouth not been full. He carried on eating while I attempted to swallow. 'Well, I've noticed very little, up till now, Thomas. There hasn't been much of a chance, if you recall? As soon as we've had this I shall explore.'

28

As it turned out I was to be frustrated a while longer, for barely had the simple but satisfying meal been consumed than there came a tentative knock on the back door. The perpetrator was revealed to be an anxious, round-faced girl of fourteen or fifteen.

'I'll leave this to you,' I heard Thomas say, as he rose and his chair scraped on the floor. 'There's a letter I need to see to.'

I beckoned her to step in but she remained hovering nervously on the doorstep.

'I'm *so* sorry, Ma'am, if I'm here too soon.' The plump face was flushed bright pink and the words breathless. 'I couldn't remember, you see, Ma'am, just what time of day the gentleman said.'

'That's alright, no need to worry. Just come inside.' The sight and sound of Ellie had reassured me. Here was a simple girl, desperate to please. I imagined she might well have been reciting her opening apology throughout the walk here, however long or short that was.

'And it's Miss Ellie… ?'

'Oh – Watkinson, Ma'am. But just Ellie – on its own. That's what I'm always called. By everyone.'

'Well, Ellie – on its own – it is, then.' I smiled at her encouragingly. 'How long were you working here?'

'About a year and a half, I think it was, Ma'am. Or maybe a bit more. For Mr and Mrs Ranson. Till they went to… Nottingham, I think it was. Or Derby. Was it Derby? My mother will tell you where, and how long it was, if you like Ma'am. She remembers everything, my mother does. We live further down that lane, at the back.'

'But did you sleep here, in the house, when you worked for Mr and Mrs Ranson? Or did you live at home?'

'Oh *here*, Ma'am.' Her face became perturbed, as if she feared I might insist on a different arrangement.

'I did *like* to live here, Ma'am. In the attic. I can always be called on then, you see, day or night. And it's no trouble to me at all to make tea in the night, or make whatever it is that's wanted – no trouble to me at all. You'll only need say to me, Ma'am, what you need… ' She stopped, aware of presuming too much, perhaps. 'But that's of course if you take me on, Ma'am, I mean.' She took a breath, or more of a gulp, before confiding, 'there's ten of us at home, you see, Ma'am – I'm the third oldest.' I could see, and sympathise, all too well. What luxury is a cold and lonely attic!

'I'm always up very early, Ma'am. It never bothers me how early. You know, to light fires and get breakfasts, and all that.'

I had no doubts about taking Ellie. It was unlikely she would be able to cook an elegant dinner; I had not yet enquired whether she could cook at all but supposed she might, if only as well as me. But it was impossible not to warm to her. She presented the face of what she was; a plain, earnest, rather anxious girl, whom I could read at a glance and would be able to trust.

'Would you do me a favour, Ellie?' I said.

She looked surprised. 'Of course, Ma'am. Anything.'

'We arrived here just a short while ago, you see. I haven't had any time at all to take the place in. Perhaps you'd show me round the house? Tell me anything it might be useful for me to know?'

There was a broader smile. Ellie had a wide mouth and large, prominent teeth, giving the impression of smiling most of the time. 'Oh *yes*, Ma'am, course I will. Are we to do that now?'

'We are, yes.' I wondered if the 'Ma'am' title would come to grate on me, and whether anything else could be put in its place. It also struck me, as we went into the hall, that the bed Thomas and I had so recently tumbled out of had probably been left in an embarrassing state of disarray. I wondered whether to tell Ellie that Thomas was resting in that room and we should therefore not go in, but decided against it. Thomas might reappear behind us at any moment. In any case, the girl would be tidying our disarrayed bed often enough, and had no doubt tidied a great many such in her life before.

Ellie opened the door to each room and then stood back, allowing me to enter first. There were not many rooms; just three from the narrow hallway, one being the kitchen, with its small scullery and outside door to the back of the house. This, of course, I had seen already.

The next door revealed a dining room, a dark, highly polished table and heavy, double tiered sideboard making what might have been a generous space appear enclosed and cramped. The table was big enough to accommodate in comfort ten, even twelve people, though they would need to file in and out in strict order. I did not care for the room. Its bulky furniture and lack of light – perhaps it faced the wrong way, or the day happened to be dull – made it feel oppressive. Still, it was plainly a *dining* room, the first I had ever entered, let alone had at my disposal. I pictured eating in here with Thomas, just the two of us; it might be more appealing in late evening, candlelit. And candles would no longer need to be used sparingly, I reminded myself, or to be cheap. I imagined we would have nothing but beeswax.

'It's beautiful, Ma'am, isn't it? Mr and Mrs Ranson, they ate in here most days, when they didn't go out, that is. But they didn't go out too often, Ma'am. Mrs Ranson said she'd rather eat here. There was a cook, you see, Ma'am, as well. As well as me, is what I mean.'

'Ah, was there? And who was she?'

'Mrs Casey, Ma'am. She'd come in every day, you see, and do a light meal at mid-day and a dinner for the evening, that is if Mr and Mrs Ranson were eating here and not somewhere else. And she can make jam as well, and chutney, and things. I think she'd come back, Ma'am, if you asked her, I don't think she's gone anywhere else yet.' Ellie seemed anxious for the re-employment of Mrs Casey. Someone she was used to and – more important – would not need to share her precious attic.

'Can *you* cook, Ellie?'

'Oh, a bit, Ma'am, a bit I can, yes. Plain, everyday things. But nothing fancy, you see… especially not for when you invite.' I had given no thought at all to *inviting*; engaging in polite, interesting, mealtime conversation with people I did not know well lay beyond my experience. But it was likely to be something natural, even routine, to Thomas. Would he want to invite people to come here? There seemed so much we had not spoken of.

'Do you think you and your husband will like to live here, Ma'am? Might you stay a good while?'

She must have seen me start, and there followed a flood of anxious apology. 'Oh, I'm so sorry, Ma'am, I should never have asked that, it wasn't my place to ask it, I just...'

'Asking it was no crime,' I cut in. 'In truth I don't know how long we will be here, Ellie. But I'm hoping it might be a very good while.'

'Oh, I'd be so glad, Ma'am!' She realised she had presumed once again. 'If I was to work for you, I mean.'

It was not Ellie's question that had caused me to flinch, but the shock of hearing Thomas referred to as my *husband*. A quick glance at her told me there was no irony, no attempt to satisfy a curiosity by watching my reaction. She would be incapable of such ploys, in any case. The girl had simply made an assumption – a reasonable one – that we were man and wife. It dawned on me that anyone else who did not happen to live in Cromford or Middleton was likely to do the same. And I could see no advantage whatever in correcting the error.

The front room, or drawing room as I supposed I must get used to calling it, struck me as an altogether pleasanter place. There was good light and the feeling of space, and even a high, wide cupboard and several large leather armchairs did not seem to crowd or overpower. It boasted a substantial stone fireplace, more decorative than the one in the dining room, and I could picture sitting there in the

240

evening, while logs glowed and crackled. The heavy, green velvet curtains could be drawn across to hide us from any curious eyes in the street.

'I'd make this fire up early every morning, Ma'am,' Ellie assured me, as if seeing the picture in my mind. 'Make up a fire in any room you wanted.'

I smiled. 'This is a *nice* room,' I declared, 'I like it.'

'So do I, Ma'am, it's my favourite. And inside this cup-board' – she went forward to open it – 'there's shelves. Mr Ranson had a lot of books, you see, and he kept them in there. I don't know if you like to read at all, Ma'am?'

'I certainly do.' I could not help smiling again at the thought of the reading I intended to embark on in this house. New books, containing worlds and lives I knew nothing of. The cupboard with its shelves might not be adequate, but it was a something. Thomas had brought several tomes of archaeological works, and I thought I might try to read something from those also, however daunting. I wanted to be able to discuss the other object of his passion with something deeper than mere curiosity. I wanted to understand.

Upstairs there was less of interest. Once the blinds were pulled back, our bedroom – already made good use of – revealed itself as ample enough, and bright. As well as the wardrobes there was a low cupboard on which sat a large washing bowl and jug and in one corner a tall mirror on a stand. Like the drawing room, this room overlooked the busy Matlock Street.

'I took a nap in here, when we arrived,' I found myself saying, losing previous courage. The bed covers were revealed to be in a state of tangled chaos; Ellie would perhaps assume me to be a restless sleeper, prone to hectic dreams.

Next door was a slightly smaller, shadier room, containing a narrow bed and also a bureau with its upright chair. The bureau was open and Thomas's papers already littered it.

'Mr Ranson kept this as a study,' Ellie informed me. 'I think your husband will also, Ma'am?'

'He might well. And if not, then *I* shall,' I added playfully.

'*You*, Ma'am?' The thought was a puzzle to her.

'On second thoughts, I don't imagine I will. This room's too dark, and rather cold. I think I'll prefer to read and work in that nice room downstairs.'

'Are we to go up to the attic now, Ma'am?'

The attic, up a steep twist of stairs, revealed itself as a decent enough space, though offering full headroom only in a narrow strip along the centre. It was surprisingly bright – a liking of mine – on account of the fair sized window that formed part of an awning to the back of the roof. A small bed, stripped of covers, was tucked beneath the eave on one side and a low cupboard had been wedged below the one opposite. I could understand Ellie's affection for this den, her anxiety to be back inside it, and alone. It would be possible to squeeze in another small bed, but that would leave no fidgeting space and even getting dressed would be an awkward manoeuvre.

'I do *so* like this room, Ma'am,' she said, gauchely. There was a sigh.

'Where is all the bed linen kept?'

'Oh, I'm sorry, I should have shown you. It's on the landing, Ma'am. A big cupboard – big enough to walk inside. There's plenty of shelves in there for linens, for yours and your husband's, I mean. There's lots of very nice ones in there, Ma'am. And then, you see, there's another shelf for the... the older linens.'

'Well, perhaps you'd better go down and walk inside the cupboard. And get this bed made up. It won't be too comfortable for you like this, will it?'

It took a moment or two for the meaning to dawn. When it did, Ellie's relief was undisguised.

'Oh, *thank you*, Ma'am, *thank you*. I swear you won't regret it, Ma'am. Never. I like to work hard, you'll see I truly do.' She glanced round her attic in delight, as if taking in its tasteful colour and adornments, before looking back at me. 'Am I to start straightaway, Ma'am? I could run down and just tell my mother, you see. She'll be pleased... she'll be so pleased.'

'Won't she miss your help?'

'Oh no, Ma'am, not really. There's others, you see. We're all of us girls.'

'What, all ten of you?'

'That's right ,Ma'am, yes. All of us. No brothers.'

'Good Lord!' It was hard not to feel an amused pity for the father of this female brood. He had not been mentioned and I wondered if it had either killed him or driven him off.

'Go and tell your mother,' I said, 'and then I need you to go out and buy a few things, something we can make into a meal tonight, between the two of us.'

'I will, Ma'am.' She was already heading for the steps. 'It'll only take me a moment. I'll tell her, and I'll fetch my nightdress and my bits, and then I'll be straight back here, Ma'am.' I had no doubt at all that she would.

'There's a cook to be had as well, it seems. A Mrs Casey. She was coming in during the day, to do whatever meals were needed.'

We were in the drawing room and I nursed a brandy, the second such drink in two days. Thomas had produced the bottle and found what seemed absurdly large, bowl-like glasses. 'Much needed,' he had commented. 'You'll find it's a good digestive.' As at the inn, the first sip had proved a tongue burning surprise. I supposed it was a sensation one would get used to.

Just a while before, we had sat at the dining table to wade through an over-burdening meal of pork and vegetables, accompanied by some solid, unwieldy dumplings put together by Ellie. I felt full to the point of discomfort and noticed Thomas's hand was stroking his belly, as if to placate it.

'A cook? Well, that could perhaps be afforded. Might *have* to be.'

'Look, if there's some doubt – about the cost, I mean – then I can manage with Ellie. We can do things between us. I shall give the meals a bit more thought.'

'More thought and less dumpling. Feels as if there's a cannon ball inside me. Several. Should have eaten a bit less, but the things tasted rather good, at the time. Deadly in the aftermath.'

'She's good hearted. I can keep a closer eye on things.'

'Just as well we went upstairs when we did. I wouldn't be able to please you now, that's certain.'

I laughed. 'Perhaps this is the sort of stuff that Ellie's father is fed. To avoid the risk of more children.'

'Are there a lot of them?'

'Ten girls.'

'Dear God!'

He leaned back a little and then failed, to my amusement, to hold back a reverberating belch.

'It's no laughing matter, I'll tell you.' Though he was smiling himself. 'Get this cook, if you like, this Mrs Whatever she's called. I didn't want you with me in order to be spending most of your time in the kitchen.' He belched again, with an effort to be more discreet this time. 'But do make sure she understands the *as needed* aspect. Knows that she won't be paid when we're not here. And that it could be for several days at a time. On occasions.'

'Could it?' I looked up from my tentative brandy sipping in surprise. 'And where will we be?'

'Oh, *places*.' He smiled at me over the rim of his glass. 'Are you enjoying the brandy? It's a very good one, as it so happens.'

'Not really, but I shall persevere with it; it isn't going to defeat me. So where will we be?'

'Away – at times. There are meetings, here and there; *conferences* as they've started to be grandly named. There's one up in York in less than a month's time, in fact. I was imagining you might like to come? There's very interesting things to see in York.'

'Well, of course I would. I'd *love* to come!' He had taken me by surprise, and I felt at least as much delight as Ellie did, when instructed to make up her bed in the attic. I had never before visited a city, never travelled anywhere by stagecoach. 'If you think we can do that, Thomas. I mean – if you think it would be… ' It was unusual for me to be at a loss for words.

'If I think it would be what? Seemly? I don't greatly care. No-one is likely to know, in any case. And if it should happen that they do, I can't say it will trouble me.' He took a gulp of his brandy. 'Will it trouble you?'

'No. I'm sure it won't.' I threw back an amount larger than a sip myself, but managed not to cough. 'What's the difference, after all? I mean – whether we're together here or anywhere else?'

'Precisely.' He rose to retrieve the bottle from the top of the cupboard. 'We're living together. So, why shirk from anything? Why spoil things by being careful, or fearful?'

I wondered if he might be thinking aloud, establishing something as much in his own mind as in mine.

'I imagine it would shock your grandfather.'

Heaven knows why I said that. Perhaps because I knew how Thomas enjoyed going against whatever constraints the old man attempted to impose. But it was not the best judged thing to say.

'Why did you need to mention him? Why would he be more shocked by that than by knowing we're here?'

'*Does* he know we're here?'

Thomas made some sound of exasperation. He poured another measure into his glass and returned to sit down.

'Why must you always press things?' He put his head back and shut his eyes. 'He knows *I'm* here, naturally. And no, he does not know *we're* here, not yet. But he will, for I shall tell him very soon. Before he hears by some other mysterious means. Or even arrives at the door. In fact I intend to go across tomorrow and state the matter to him. So you'd better be ready to pour me a very large brandy when I get back.'

'I will be, Thomas.' My voice, I hoped, was reassuring. Thomas was brave, even if his bravery was in part a youthful rebellion, a wilful kicking over the traces. He had courage, perhaps, because he *was* still young. I saw I must learn to be careful when speaking of his grandfather, for the subject was a sensitive one that sharpened his nerves and could quickly turn a mood. Though I have to admit the image of this old man was one that intrigued me.

29

From the drawing room, plenty of vehicles could be seen and heard on Matlock Road, for carriages and carts passed by throughout the day. After going to the window on a number of occasions and hovering there a good while each time, I decided not to check any further, but settle down to some reading. Thomas would reappear at some stage, but as it had already passed evening meal time there could be no guarantee of it that day. After all, should things turn out to be amiable, his grandfather might well persuade him to eat at the Hall, and then he would stay the night. Though the likelihood seemed small.

If he was already on his way back to Bakewell, then the sound at the front door would soon be clear enough. In the meantime, I would read a fascinating account of treasures unearthed recently in York, mainly Viking but some even older. I had also found that morning – in a fusty little shop in the town – a small book about York itself, for I did not want to visit the famous city in a state of complete ignorance.

It was well into the evening when I heard the unmistakable sound of a carriage pulling up outside; the stamp of metal shoes and snorting of a horse, the banging of a door, the driver's raised voice as, having received payment, he shouted his thanks and goodnight.

Hoping to forestall Ellie, I went quickly to open the front door and smiled at him in welcome. Thomas's expression was an unhappy one, and there came no greeting in return.

I touched his arm, knowing better than to overwhelm him with an immediate quest for information. 'It's not too early for brandy, I think. Or are you hungry?'

'No, I'm not hungry.' He threw his cape at the chair in the hallway, as if that piece of furniture was guilty of insulting him. The kitchen door had opened as he did so and Ellie rushed forward to rescue the garment and to hang it in its rightful position on the stand.

'Can I get you some tea, Sir, or something to eat? Ma'am?' She looked expectantly from one of us to the other.

'No.' Thomas's reply was curt and he spoke without a glance at her. Ellie did not know what to do and stood there uncertainly. I put a hand to her elbow, guiding her back towards the room she had emerged from.

'Perhaps a beef sandwich, for Mr Bateman,' I said quietly. 'Just leave it on the kitchen table, covered, for later. He's very tired.'

I followed Thomas into the drawing room, where he threw himself into a chair with the same antagonism as had been used on the cloak. Experience had taught me it might still be too soon to put my arms around him. When angry or aggrieved, Thomas did not want to be engulfed in tenderness, and this I understood for it was a feeling I shared.

'Brandy?' I was already reaching for the bottle. He nodded in reply. I poured him a moderate measure, suspecting he had not eaten for a good while, and myself a smaller one still. I had barely picked at the light meal earlier on.

'You could have been a touch more generous.'

'There's more in the bottle, Thomas. Do try to be calm.' He grunted, before downing most of it in one, determined swallow. I remained silent, while he rested his head back against the chair and closed his eyes for a few moments.

'Was it very difficult?' I felt we did need to have this conversation; that it could be more awkward to delay it further.

'Exceptionally so.' He stood up to refill his own glass, remaining in front of the cupboard to stare at the wall, his back towards me. Anxiety crept inside my head, despite an effort to remain unruffled. I wondered how much Thomas's grandfather had managed to disconcert him. Plainly enough for the ill-humour to have lasted the duration of his journey home. I wondered whether he had succeeded – for he must surely have tried – in turning his grandson off course. My course.

'Do you want to tell me what happened, Thomas?'

'Not a great deal to tell. Let's just say he remained true to character. As judgemental and opinionated as ever. Pig-headed. Full of the most self-righteous, religious... *claptrap*.' He turned towards me, leaning back against the cupboard. 'He knows he can't do a thing about it, of course. And that makes him furious. He likes to be in complete control.'

'He tried hard, I would imagine... to dissuade you from having me live here?'

'*Dissuade* might be something of an understatement. I'd prefer not to discuss the particular line of argument he employed. Other than to say that they were hardly the words of a gentleman.'

'Well!' I could not help a little smile of wry amusement. 'They'll be words I suspect I'm very familiar with. You can be quite sure that nothing the dear old man said is likely to shock me in the least.'

Thomas, too, managed the flicker of a smile at last.

'Perhaps not, but I'm not about to repeat them, in any case. The fact is, there's nothing he can do. It's not *his* money, being used here, it's my father's – which of course means it's my own.'

He replaced his glass on the tray, before turning back to me with a look I did not immediately read. 'Do you know what I want to do, Mary – now, at this moment?' I did not, but he left no time for me to guess. 'I want us to go up to bed.'

'Are you exhausted?'

'No. I'm *not*!'

Once in the bedroom, there seemed an angry fierceness in his want of me. Had I not been able to respond to this with a hunger of my own, then his actions could have been judged rough, perhaps even violent. It did not last long though, as such things cannot. The appetite that occasioned it must have been pitched against exhaustion, for only moments afterwards he was asleep.

I edged my way from the bed and dressed again, in a simple, plain affair that was easy to pull on, and made my way quietly down the stairs. I took a candle that could then be used to light others in the drawing room, for it would be impossible, I knew, to sleep yet, though it was a respectable enough time to try. Our encounter had not given me the instant calm that it appeared to have given Thomas – men are more fortunate in that way, it seems. A further

251

time with my book seemed the best way to quieten an agitation that remained inside me.

I had no idea how much money had come to Thomas on his recent birthday, or how long it could be expected to last. It must seem odd that I had not asked him, but I had not. It was his business, after all, and I was aware it could be unwise to push Thomas about matters he was reluctant to speak of, though such awareness did not always stop me doing so. But in this instance, there was a part of me that did not even care. I had already traded my future safety for an exhilarating, uncertain present.

What was harder to judge was how much disquiet might lie in Thomas's mind. How strong would this stubborn will of his prove to be, now that the situation between him and his grandfather had shifted? For it seemed that *not getting on* had turned itself into a declared, hostile dispute between them. But would that exhilarating sense of flouting authority begin, at some time, to fade? Would he be *brought to his senses*? I presumed Thomas's grandfather must hope and believe so.

An hour or so later, having failed to get beyond the first page, I abandoned my reading. I collected the substantial plate of food left in the kitchen by Ellie and took it upstairs. If Thomas were to wake up later on, he would be hungry, and even if he did not then I would be, for I had eaten little that day. The sandwich, thickly cut from a large, robust loaf and filled with enough beef and mustard for four, could sit on a bedside table to await its fate.

Sometime during the night Thomas did waken, and roused me from my shallow doze by moving restlessly. I turned towards him.

'Are you hungry?'

'I think I am, as a matter of fact. Yes, very.'

'Then pull the curtain back a little, and we'll have this.'

'Have what?'

'*This.*'

There was a full moon, enough light to manage without a candle. I plumped the pillows higher, as Thomas heaved himself out of bed to push a curtain aside. A soft, grey light slid across the room.

'We'll have to share the plate – try not to drop too many crumbs. This is very decadent, don't you think?'

'Delightfully so.' His fingers touched my face briefly, and then we gave full effort to the food, tearing off hunks of it, indifferent to manners.

'You do know, don't you? ' He stopped for a moment to swallow, with some difficulty, 'You do know there's enough money? That you don't need to be concerned?'

'I'm not concerned.'

'That's what angers him so much, you see. Knowing he has no hold over me, and that he can't have, in the foreseeable future.'

I decided not to ask how far he could foresee. In fact in that moment I resolved not to dwell on the matter further at all. Thomas and I were together, in this house. We were devouring food in the middle of the night with the same greedy appetite we brought to everything, and spreading crumbs in careless fashion over the bed. My life was engaging, unpredictable. New sights, new experiences and new understandings beckoned. They were there to be seized, revelled in. Because once lived, none of these things could be taken away from me.

As soon as the sandwich had disappeared, I began to relish something else also. It might only be hours since we had last possessed one another; indeed my body still felt tender and bruised from it. Yet I was already desirous of more.

York was always to remain the special one, the visit I still recall most often and with most warmth. Though it was followed by many excursions to other places, all of them precious. Sometimes we would stay for a couple of days, at others for a week or more. There could be no danger whatever that these travels would start to become mundane events for me, or that the effort and discomfort involved might reduce their charm.

Over the months, the thrill of *setting off* did not lessen in any way. Nor that of preparing to set off, for I loved the sense of urgency, the decisions to be made about clothes and baggage and days of departure, my vain attempts to calm Thomas in his frantic determination to finish whatever piece of work he intended to take with him.

I relished the noise and speed of the stagecoach, the thought that it was taking me to a place I did not know but was about to discover. Even the crowded, cold discomfort of it all left me unworried, as did overnight stops and the uncertain hospitality we might receive. In this I was unlike Thomas, who once said he hated such public means of transport, adding that 'before too long, we shall use only a private coach!'

'What a spoilt creature you are, Thomas,' I had declared. He did not bother to mention the matter after that, perhaps not wanting a repeat of the accusation.

No discomfort or fatigue was too much for me; never had I known such anticipation, such excitement. They did not exist in life before Thomas.

But York was the first, and although we were later to return there, it is that visit which remains the most vivid. In my mind I can still watch as we stand outside the great cathedral, Thomas smiling as I stare up at its face in sheer disbelief. I see us inside, beneath the window of the Five Sisters, beneath the Rose, and later – perhaps the next day – as we walk together along the pathway of the ancient walls and through the narrow streets of the city. I hear us talking with people; those who have met Thomas in other places, and those who are pleased to be introduced to him.

'I haven't had the pleasure before of meeting your wife,' one gentleman declares.

'Oh, I'm so *sorry*!' Thomas does not even blink in embarrassment. 'So please let me introduce her now. This is *Mary*.'

I can still study us as we take tea, sitting by a window and staring at the city life that hurries or ambles past. And I see myself wandering alone into a dim, musty bookshop, one that contains more volumes on its sagging, wooden shelves than I once imagined could exist. I buy so many it is a struggle to carry them away.

Some of these turned out to be fascinating, others less so. It is not always possible to tell. But I still have them all.

30

'I think the time has come for you to meet my grandfather.'

The statement was unexpected, bald. Thomas had just appeared in the doorway of the drawing room, having spent the last couple of hours in the study, struggling to complete an article for publication. That, at least, had been the stated intention. From waking up he had struck me as being preoccupied, and his manner brusque. It was something I could always sense in an instant, for from childhood I have had an alertness to the demeanour of others. It was always wise to sniff out Pa's mood before opening one's mouth. Before doing anything at all.

I looked up from the book on my lap. When Thomas was occupied in the study, I could generally be found with a book on my lap. Thomas may not have liked to be disturbed himself, but he would often appear at the drawing room door, wanting to discuss some point or other, and even – to my satisfaction – seeking advice about the phrasing of an awkward sentence. So usually I would chose to remain in the house at such times.

'Why do you think that?'

Thomas sat down. I could see the effort to control a certain nervous agitation. 'He's getting old,' he said at last. 'And with that becoming... well, just a little more *benign*, perhaps. That's the feeling I've had – recently.' I had noticed his visits to Middleton had become more frequent of late. 'I'm not saying that he no longer disapproves of the situation,' he went on. 'He does disapprove, without any question. So there won't be any warmth of welcome, I'm afraid.'

'Then why do you want me to meet him?'

Thomas folded his arms and looked away, signs that he was finding a conversation uncomfortable.

'I feel it *ought* to happen. Because there's another matter, you see, that I need to discuss with you.' I stared at him expectantly, though with some apprehension. *Discussion* almost certainly meant that a decision of some kind had already been made.

'I want to build a house of my own – within the estate, at Middleton.'

This took me by surprise; I had not known what to expect, but certainly it was not that. I made no response, other than to raise my eyebrows in question.

'This place is just far too *small*,' he said, in a tone that implied the problem with Matlock Street was obvious. 'I don't mean too small for living in, as such. 'He turned his gaze towards me, and attempted to smile. 'However spoilt you think I am, I'm quite prepared to live in a modest house.'

I must have looked puzzled, or perhaps a little mocking. He looked away again. 'It's for the *work*, you see, because it's becoming more and more difficult. Impractical. The study here is minute – there's no proper space at all. I seem to be spreading things all over the house, and then having to move them. So nothing ever seems to be at hand. And of course nothing can be on display.'

He *was* spoilt, but I knew now was not the time to state it. In any case, he was destined to be spoilt for as long as he lived.

'So you're thinking of something larger?'

'Oh yes, much larger.' Now that the case had been stated, he started to speak with more confidence. 'A *proper* house, with bigger rooms and enough of them to set some aside for work. I want to display things, to set up... well, in fact set up something resembling a museum. I mean, the sort of place other archaeologists can visit, and where meetings can be held.'

It was clear that the house for which I had come to feel such affection in Matlock Street fell far short of what was required.

'But... ' I was still confused, 'you surely haven't enough money for something like that?'

There was a brief look of embarrassment. 'No, you're correct, of course. I do have some money still, though not enough to contemplate anything such as this.'

'So, you're saying that your grandfather's paying for the new house?'

'In large part, yes.'

My confusion was no less. 'But why would he do that – under the *circumstances*? Is he making the assumption that when you move in I won't be there?' I looked hard at him. 'Is that what's in your mind, Thomas? Have we just a few months left together, while this mansion of yours is being built?' I had no idea how long it would take to create such a place, but supposed it might require several months, at the least.

'No, that's not on my mind!' The tone was indignant. He rose and walked to the window, stared out into the street. 'I want you to be there with me, that's what I *intend*.' I waited for him to continue.

'*Look*, Grandfather wants me to live back in Middleton, he's wanted it from the moment I left. And he's getting old – not the man he was. Thank God! But he does seem to accept it can't be in the same house. Big as it is.' He smiled, a little self-consciously, suspecting I might find that impossibility laughable. 'And he also knows that I'm with you. Because with whatever ill-grace, he's had to come to terms with the fact.'

'So *he* manages to have you close by. And *you* get your very own big house, with space for this museum, and also keep me?' I could not help a wry smile. 'It strikes me you've got yourself a fine bargain.'

He turned from the window. 'Perhaps. And it shouldn't be too dreadful for you, Mary, either – should it?' I was unsure if there was a hint of sarcasm in the question. Or perhaps he was simply disappointed at the lack of excitement from me.

'We'll have a *proper* house,' he repeated. 'There'll be another two or three servants, at the very least. As well as a coachman to call on. *And*' – for my face still failed to show delight – 'a library. A good one.'

He smiled and put out his hands in an open-palmed gesture, a touch of pleading about it. Perhaps there had been no sarcasm, after all, simply a desire for me to share his delight at the prospect. It seemed churlish not to do so. I went across and put my arms round him, at the same time trying to picture myself in this wonderful library, with its shelves of books, its large table to work at. Perhaps it could even contain a pair of comfortable chairs.

It seemed wise to think only of the good things, for it was plain that this decision had been made, and very likely some time ago. I did not bother to ask if the building was in fact already underway, for I felt quite sure that it must be.

The thought of leaving Matlock Street was a sad one, though, for I was comfortable here. I liked the house, which in my own opinion was more than ample enough, but without pretention. And I was fond of Ellie, who was unlikely to come with us. Much as she adored her attic, she made sure to visit home every day, if only for a few minutes. Middleton may as well be the other side of England.

I also enjoyed our frequent ambles around Bakewell. The little town was pleasant enough, and even making efforts to enhance its looks, month on month. Many rotting and ramshackle buildings were being ripped down, with sturdier stone houses and shops replacing them along the winding and criss-crossing streets. The place was prettier than Cromford, the countryside that bordered it gentler, less demanding.

Though these days, of course, I did not walk alone in the countryside either as often or as far as before. If I did so it was during the day, when Thomas had left for a visit to Middleton, rather than in the evening. Evenings were spent together, much of them in leisurely dining, for food tasted far better now that I was no longer required to cook it myself. Between mouthfuls – for both of us had hearty appetites – Thomas and I would talk about his work, about other places, other people. Sometimes we spoke of political matters, for I was becoming more aware of such things now. We talked of education, of poverty. We discussed and argued.

I did not always see eye-to-eye with Thomas. Despite being all too aware that he was the provider of everything, I did not see it as my place to defer. Deference was not something he wanted, though there were occasions when he would walk out of the room in annoyance or exasperation. Occasions when I did, also.

It would be strange to live without the bustle and noise of our street, without the constant clatter of hooves, the creak and rattle all day long of coaches and carts. The new house would be quiet, isolated. I was aware that Middleton village was tiny; that it had nothing to it but its inn and a handful of cottages, and beyond these numerous small farms. Even Youlgreave, a larger village a few miles away, was unlikely to be as lively or congenial as Bakewell.

But we would have a carriage, or use of one from the Hall. There was also to be a lighter trap that I could learn to take out on my own. 'I'll teach you myself,' Thomas had announced with a grin, 'and you'd better do exactly as you're told and not try to race it!'

31

'Why did it take you so long to talk of this house?' I asked, as we walked out one morning. He had seemed in no mood for pouring over papers and journals in his study and suggested a bit of fresh air. The weather was chilly but bright, and we had just reached the ancient stone bridge. Shafts of sunlight from behind the small, scudding clouds sent shimmers of light across the water. I loved the river at that point; all the more beautiful for being unnavigable and left to its natural devices. There would be no such arresting sight in Middleton.

'I didn't want to unsettle you,' he replied. 'Not until things were firmer.'

'I think I can manage being *unsettled*. I'm not a child.'

' I'm sorry.' Our arms were linked. His other arm moved across to squeeze mine.

'I didn't mean to patronise you. Not at all.' He was only too aware it would be unwise to do that. 'I also delayed discussion because... well, I was worried it might cause you to believe I'm less than happy here. And that isn't so. I *am* happy.'

There was quiet, as we both stood still, staring down into the river.

'But it's become clear to me, recently, that I must start to take a greater role in the estate. Shoulder some responsibility. Grandfather can't do what he used to – much as it galls him to admit it. He has some good people there, but there needs to be someone else making decisions, taking *charge*.' He picked up a couple of loose pebbles from the wall and threw them into the water. I remained silent.

'It's going to be my task at some point, the whole damned lot of it – obviously. And even now I can't expect, I suppose, to receive income from it – and not take more interest.'

'*Income* from it?'

'A small amount, yes.'

'Since when?'

'For a while. I do, after all, discuss estate matters with him when I'm there.'

I sensed he did not want to be questioned any further. It seemed the headstrong, rebellious youth was beginning, at last, to see sense. Grandfather's sense. He was glimpsing where his long-term advantage lay, preparing to bow down to the inevitable. A growing up, perhaps, and a new wisdom. I could find no argument against it, but a painful sadness swept through me, nonetheless.

Times confuse me sometimes these days, though my memory for people and for events remains as clear as the proverbial bell. But I think the foundations for Thomas's house must have already been well underway when I was taken to meet his grandfather. Perhaps the building was growing above them, even. We did not stop by to look, however, the focus being on making our visit and getting it over with.

To avoid the awkward question of needing to take a meal there, we set off straight after an early lunch. A cup of tea – should it be offered – I felt was likely to be endurance enough on this occasion.

Our journey, in a hired coach, lasted around an hour, and would have been enjoyable had I not felt, if not quite a gnawing anxiety, then certainly something falling far short of hopeful anticipation. Thomas too, appeared strained and this did nothing to ease me. He answered my attempts at conversation with no more than the odd word, and we lapsed into a nervous, uneasy silence for much of the way.

Middleton Hall came into full view as the coach passed through a huge gateway and swept up the long, tree-lined drive. It was haughtily imposing, as I had expected. Not immense, in the manner of aristocratic houses I had seen in paintings, but substantial, and handsome. It also struck me as cold. Perhaps because this house was not an old one, its bright, unblemished walls lacked the warmth of stone that has been beaten by storm, faded by sun, over many generations. Perhaps they would all have once looked as severe as this one.

The coach drew to a halt close to the main door and we climbed down. Thomas directed the driver, one he had not used before, round the side of the Hall to the stables. He could water his two horses and be given tea in the kitchen, then stay ready to return us to Bakewell in due course. We had not planned on this visit being a long one.

A young servant received us into the hallway, with whom Thomas exchanged a cheerful greeting. Mr Bateman, she informed him, was in the morning room.

'We'll make our own way there, Sarah,' Thomas said, 'there's no need to come with us.'

'That's one of William's sisters,' he said, as she scuttled away. 'You remember, the William I was with that evening – the one who recognised you?' I could indeed recall the evening in question, in all its detail. Though it seemed distant now, for all that. Time belonging to a different life.

I was guided along the hallway and down a further short passageway off to one side, Thomas's hand lay gently on my back, as if in quiet reassurance. At the end of this passage he gave a couple of brief knocks on a high, heavily embossed oak door, then opened it without waiting for any invitation. The hand now propelled me inside the room, with more firmness.

A tall, slightly stooped man, with a full head of thick white hair, had risen from his chair with surprising swiftness and was already coming forward to meet us. I think Thomas must have introduced me, must have announced me by my name, for his grandfather was civil enough to put out a hand to shake mine, though there was no smile. His handshake was firm, without tremor. It was not that of an old or weakened man, and the skin did not feel dry and fragile, as some do.

He received a smile from me, for I knew some graciousness must be shown, even if the expression on his face could never have been interpreted as a friendly greeting. Thomas deserved an effort on my part; he must surely be relying on me for at least that. I sensed our future together depended in some measure on it, also.

'Did you ask Eileen – or was it Sarah – for tea?'

'Sarah. And I didn't, Grandfather, no. Won't she assume we'll want tea?'

'She might well. But perhaps you'd be good enough to go down and make sure? I'm afraid the bell in here isn't working efficiently at present.'

Thomas looked as reluctant to leave the room as I was to see him go, but he conceded. The old man had been wily, as I had been informed he so often was. He waited until his grandson had gone before turning to me.

'Well, sit down then, young woman. Not there – where I can see you, if you please, near the window. You're standing in shadow. My eyes are not good, these days.'

His sight might be failing, but his eyes were still a piercing blue, their look hard and direct. I did as I was bid and then looked straight back at him. I have a direct *look* of my own, which is capable of defending itself against anybody's, though I decided to soften it with the further suggestion of a smile. It was important to be cordial, though without the indignity of attempting to charm or ingratiate. Something told me he would recognise and despise such tactics. But neither did I intend to appear fearful.

It was some time before he spoke again. Perhaps the silence was intended to unnerve me. 'And do you find Bakewell to your *taste*?' he said at last.

'I do, yes… ' I hesitated a second, wondering if it would be correct to address him as *Sir*, but in the same instant decided against it. I was not a servant, after all. 'I think we both do.'

'No doubt. It's a pleasant enough little place. Though something of a building site these days, so I understand. Perhaps all will be to its improvement.' His gaze did not waver from my face. 'But Thomas now has, as I'm sure you will understand, responsibilities *here*. He's had them for some time, of course. But chosen to ignore the fact.'

'Yes. He's spoken, recently, of his responsibilities.'

'Which is why he now needs to *live* here, as I'm quite sure you can appreciate.' He seemed to be sure of quite a lot, where I was concerned. 'Though not in this particular house, as it turns out. It appears to be unsuitable for present purposes.' He raised his eyebrows. 'As I expect you've been given to understand?' I nodded, continuing to hold his steady gaze. 'Thomas is a grown man, now,' he continued, 'and he cannot expect to carry on behaving like some wild, self-indulgent youth.' The *look* at me seemed to intensify. 'Well as I understand the temptation to do so. And I do assure you that I can very easily understand it.'

I remained silent, wondering if the comments should be understood as some sort of compliment. 'But I'm afraid he needs to accept his position here. Start to set an appropriate example.'

'I believe he understands what's expected of him.'

'Does he, you think? Well, it's not before time.' Thomas's grandfather struggled to unleash a large handkerchief from one of his pockets, unfolded it with an impatient shake and blew his nose with what seemed unnecessary loudness. It was then squashed into a ball and pushed into a different, more accessible pocket.

'There are people here for whom he will be responsible, before long. People who are looking to him to ensure their futures – ensure the future of their families. They're expecting him to take a lead. To have some authority. And I don't *quite* see how that can be done under the present *circumstances*.' He paused for a moment and his face took on a quizzical expression. 'Do *you*?'

I heard Thomas's unmistakable footsteps returning at speed along the polished wood floor of the corridor. 'You can rely on me to convey your fears to him,' I could not resist saying, as the sound reached the door.

Taking tea was a strained, but manageable affair. Thomas spoke of the new house, mentioned altering the plans to provide an even larger library and museum, though it was plain his grandfather set little store by these features.

'You may not have the time that you imagine, for all that,' he interrupted, with clear impatience.' The estate needs to come first – I hardly need say, do I? Before your *pastimes*.'

I saw Thomas stiffen and gather his strength, and could imagine the nature of the numerous disagreements between them.

'I don't regard my work as a pastime, Grandfather. And nor do others who have an understanding of it... but I assure you there's no need for concern about the estate. The estate can be dealt with. And it will be dealt with.' He ought to have stayed content with that, but predictably could not. 'It's what enables me to do the things that are – when all's said and done – of a great deal more importance to me.'

The old man snorted in derision and shook his head. I suspected they had stumbled along this particular road many times.

'I'm not questioning its *interest*, what you do. Or even suggesting it's not worthwhile – as a *pastime*.' He seemed determined to employ the word that so infuriated Thomas. His attention then swung back towards me. 'Have *you* any interest in these things, young lady? These Stone Age carryings-on?' I presumed it was Thomas's presence that had transformed me from a young woman to a young lady.

'Very much so, yes.' My answer was true, as well as loyal. 'I've managed to read quite a lot on the subject, but I hope to learn much more. It's remarkable – all the new discoveries, the new knowledge.' I did not know how much he knew of my background, but was determined to dispel any idea he might have that I was ignorant, or even illiterate. That I had nothing to offer Thomas other than my willing body.

'And Thomas's work is at the forefront,' I added, 'as I'm sure you'll appreciate.'

He did not smile, but stared at me once again, nodding as if with a some slowly achieved understanding.

'Why don't you take Mary to see the gardens, Thomas, before you go?' He stood up, with unusual alacrity for a man of more than eighty years. A hand was offered to me once again. 'Forgive me if I don't accompany you; there's some important documents that I have to see to.'

'It could have been worse,' Thomas said, as soon as the coach door was shut.

'Could it?'

'Far worse. Believe me. I think he was quite *taken* with you.'

I laughed. 'I doubt it, Thomas, really I do. But if he was then I'm sure it won't influence him in any way.' I turned and leant to kiss him on the mouth, though briefly, for the ride at that point was a juddering and bumpy one. I felt light-hearted now, with the visit over. 'His message was clear enough, once you'd been dispatched downstairs. And it was that your life with me is *inappropriate*. Your duty lies elsewhere.'

Thomas leant across to kiss me in return. 'Well, he can just keep singing, can't he? Because his message doesn't interest me.'

32

'It's difficult to believe that we won't be here tomorrow.' It was late. Thomas may well have been asleep, or drifting towards it, but I was wakeful and less than at ease.

He turned over slowly to face me. 'We'll be somewhere better, Mary. And not too strange for you? You've been to the place now.'

It was true I had been inside, on two occasions. As on my arrival at Matlock Street, I had wandered along hallways, inspected rooms, taken in the views from the windows. At Lomberdale, of course, the investigation had taken considerably longer.

The rooms of the new house were spacious without being cavernous, and the décor had been kept simple – a point I had influenced, if from a distance, for I have never cared for the anything ornate. I find it can be oppressive. Several pieces of furniture had been brought across from the main Hall, which possessed far more than was currently needed by Thomas's grandfather, who now lived simply, made use only of a small number of rooms and rarely entertained. Unsurprisingly, I had not been invited to choose them, but urged Thomas to decline anything that looked heavy and overpowering.

'I don't know how far I can dictate things,' he had said. 'I'm afraid it might come down to what Grandfather decides to give – apart from my working rooms, of course, and the library. I've arranged for all the cupboards and shelving needed in those myself.'

'I'm sure you have.' I had felt irked, as did Thomas at my terse remark.

'The precise nature of furniture is hardly important, Mary, is it? We're very fortunate, you know, that it's there.'

'Yes, I *do* know.' I left the matter at that, sensing we were both on an edge of irritation. I did not need a reminder concerning my good fortune. Nor, when it boiled down to it, did I have any particular interest in furniture, beyond a desire for the rooms to remain bright and uncluttered. At least the curtains needed to be newly made, and as Thomas had not the least interest in fabrics, I had been free to select some favourite springtime shades of blue and primrose yellow.

Thomas's new home was charming, as well as handsome. I much preferred it to the larger and colder-feeling residence of his grandfather.

My second visit took place on a fresh Spring day. This time there was a bustle throughout the house, which was by then almost ready to be lived in. Servants moved about with an unusual energy, stowing utensils in the kitchen and scullery, carrying piles of bed linen up the back stairs, arranging and rearranging vases and glasses in their cabinets. They worked loudly and cheerfully, boosted by the newness of the place and the pleasure of a changed routine.

A group of gardeners laboured outside, forcing the meadow landscape into something more ordered and decorative. Already saplings had been placed to mark the garden's wide boundaries and in front of them large, oval flowerbeds were being dug and planted. By early Summer the place was destined to be a home, and a beautiful one.

But during that second visit, as I wandered about inside and out, as I stood still to stare, Lomberdale stubbornly refused to take on a feeling of being home. I perched for a while on a window seat in the larger drawing room, looked out towards the emerging gardens, and asked myself why. For this lovely building was to my taste, inside and out; I could find no fault with any part of it. It would provide us with a space and a comfort that was beyond most people's dreams or imagination. Nevertheless I felt a sadness, a disturbing, almost wretched pang, for the smaller, simpler house in Bakewell.

For a little over two years, Thomas and I had not only shared number eight, Matlock Street – we had lived there *together*. It was impossible to be far apart, for no room in the house was beyond calling distance from another, and for much of the time we occupied the same space. Its adjacent drawing room and dining room – tiny compared to what was here – were the spaces where we chattered and read, discussed and argued. It was hard not to be aware of the other's every passing thought.

At Lomberdale, life would not be confined. Here there were places where one could go to read or to think alone, or into which outsiders might be invited for private talk. There were rooms for the display of Thomas's precious objects, corners where he might choose to hide himself away in order to have quiet. And there were gardens big enough to wander in alone, unnoticed.

I could not deny to myself for a moment that all this was desirable and good, or that I was privileged beyond my own belief. But I knew, also, that had it been within my power, I would have chosen for us to remain in Bakewell.

It was not, of course, within my power; this was a matter over which I could exercise no choice whatever. Thomas desired a large house of his own, his grandfather had decided he must have him near, and they had accommodated each other in those wishes. Somehow – and I knew I should feel grateful for it – Thomas had managed to include me in that arrangement also. I chided myself that it was not within me to feel more delight.

'Just one more week,' he had exclaimed on the return journey home, 'and we'll be living there!'

'We will, yes.' My voice must have sounded more lacklustre than intended. He turned abruptly to look at me.

'What on earth's the matter?' The eyes seemed accusing. I gathered myself.

'Nothing. Nothing's the matter. I'm a little tired, that's all. It's going to be a beautiful house to live in.'

As indeed it was, and my appreciation of it, if reluctant, was encouraged by unusually lovely September weather. It would have been churlish, ridiculous even, not to enjoy living in such a place. The house was fresh, unspoiled, with no trace whatever of the damp mustiness that older buildings so often seem to have and which can never be entirely got rid of, no matter how thorough the cleaning or airing.

Even Middleton village – if its *Bateman Arms* ale house and cluster of cottages could be called a village – assumed a simple charm, and we took to meandering together after dinner, and at times earlier in the day.

Thomas was acknowledged, as often as not. Farm workers would even doff whatever headgear they wore over their unkempt hair and nod towards him, usually bidding *Sir* a good day.

'My very own *Lord of the Manor!*' I laughed, on first witnessing such charming deference.

'I'm no-one's lord of the manor. I dislike the term.'

'Yes, you are. Or will be. It may not be an official title, but that's what you are. No need to act humble.'

'Alright – as you will.' I sensed an embarrassment that conveyed itself as crossness, and learned to hear these things without comment.

I was looked at also, of course, often with a sort of unhidden curiosity that bordered on the insolent. At that time it did not seem likely that any villager would know who I was. Could I not be taken for a visiting relative? A cousin, perhaps. For it might have been common knowledge that Thomas had no sister.

As the weeks went on, though, the visiting cousin theory must have been thrown into doubt, even if no-one could know anything for certain. That, at least, is what I told myself, though in truth I did not much care if the truth had been discovered or not. Neither did Thomas seem concerned, which only strengthened my own indifference. Our arms would always be linked as we strolled along, and often we would be in earnest conversation.

I think we must have been living in the house for around four weeks when a note arrived for Thomas, delivered from the Hall.

He glanced at it and dismissed the servant without a reply. 'I can imagine what this damned thing's about.' He held it out for me to read.

There was no preamble to the message, no *Dear*. "An unfortunate matter has been brought to my attention," it stated, with stark formality, "and an immediate, private, discussion would be appreciated." The note was not signed.

'It could be about anything, surely?'

'No, I don't think so.' He screwed the paper up and put it in a pocket. 'Anything else he would have... elaborated. Given a hint, at least, of what the concern is. This is something to do with us.'

'Or *me*, more precisely?'

'What's the difference? But I've a mind to make him wait. Leave it a while and see how long it takes him to arrive here.'

That was an event I preferred to avoid. Thomas's grandfather, to my knowledge, had come through the door only once since we moved in. The morning after our arrival, a coach had been heard coming up the drive and he had been shown into the hall, where we both hurried to greet him. He had remained barely a yard inside the door, stiff, awkward and unsmiling. Following a brief, cursory nod in my direction, he had looked at and addressed only Thomas. After a while I had excused myself, and withdrawn. An offer of tea, Thomas later informed me, had been refused.

'I think you should go and talk to him now,' I said. 'Why risk making him any angrier? It's plain he expects you to go at once.'

'Which seems a good reason not to.' There was a silence. Thomas folded his arms and bit on his lower lip. 'But perhaps, if you think it best? I can understand you'd prefer that he doesn't come here.'

I thought a moment or two, while Thomas continued to battle the issue in his mind.

'If he should arrive here,' I said, 'Then I would be *resting* – upstairs. You'd have to say I was feeling unwell and apologise for me, because if I find myself in front of him, and he's as unpleasant and rude as before, then I really think I might... '

Thomas's doubts were resolved. 'Very well,' he interrupted, 'I'll go. I'll go now, and find out what the damned hell he wants.'

The language and tone were more vehement than usual, and within a moment he was through the door. Fortunately the late afternoon was warm, for he did not bother with a coat, although it was clear he intended to walk. I hoped the exercise would calm him and that this was not about to become yet another of their bitter and hard fought *disagreements*.

It was a good while before Thomas returned. Dinner had been delayed, rattling the nerves of Mrs Parsons, whose happiness and well-being relied on a strict routine. I had begun to wonder if Thomas had decided to eat at the Hall.

Dinner had been offered, I was told as he arrived, but he had declined.

'Tell Mrs Parsons we'll be at the table shortly. I'll just go and wash.'

'Thomas, it's very late. I'm going to tell her we'll be at the table directly. You look clean enough to sit and eat with. I've had to make my peace with Mrs P already.'

'Alright. I must admit I find the woman frightening myself. I can see why Grandfather decided to be rid of her.'

He did not seem to be in the state of anger I had sometimes seen. Nevertheless I sensed it better not to put questions to him until he had time to gather himself a little, and to eat. But patience is not something I am always blessed with; in this instance it did not stretch beyond the second mouthful.

'Is the problem what you feared?' I asked, without knowing just what he had feared.

There was no reply while he continued to chew on a piece of meat, which had become dry. It submitted at last, and was washed down with a hasty swig of wine. 'It's always as I feared,' he said. 'The old man doesn't surprise me much, these days. He's becoming predictable.'

'And so?'

He began to cut the meat into smaller pieces, then pushed them aside in favour of the potato. 'It's come to his attention that we've been *seen* together – outside. That there's rumblings of unpleasant gossip.'

'Come to his attention how?'

'Oh, it doesn't need much, you know that. A servant will have talked. Anyone could have talked. Set a few stories going.'

I laid my knife and fork down. 'Is he expecting me to remain in this house, night and day? Hidden away; your shameful little secret?'

I took a good mouthful of wine; it felt more necessary than food at that moment. As well as anger, a strong feeling of regret coursed through me; regret for our home in Bakewell, for the lively little town where we could be free and careless, could wander about unwatched and unremarked on. Where I did not need to be mindful of Thomas's grandfather.

He put a hand over mine. 'Look, he just needed to bellow and storm. Express a bit of his religious outrage. I know his views, they didn't come as any shock. And it doesn't change things between *us*.'

'Doesn't it?'

'No. Why should it?'

There was a faint knock on the door. Sarah came in and asked if we would like some apricot sponge pudding. I declined, but Thomas said he would take a small helping.

'Tell Mrs Parsons the rest can be taken as supper,' I said, 'if there's anyone who'd like some before bed.'

When she had left the room, Thomas ate another couple of morsels from his plate and then pushed it away. I sensed he was about to announce something, and waited.

'It might be better, though,' he said at length, 'for us to avoid the village – Middleton, I mean. Little places are all the same; people's lives are so narrow, they adore any-thing that comes as a bit of scandal.'

'I see.' My voice was quiet.

He turned to look me in the face. 'Mary, please don't start getting angry about this. Nothing will be different, it would merely be a matter of taking a little care. Of not fanning any flames. When we walk out, we can take ourselves in the other direction, towards Youlgrave. Not much further, but it's bigger, more people about.'

'He's used his power over you. So despite saying it makes no difference, it will, won't it?'

'No, it won't.' There was an edge of anger in the voice now. 'Why can you not see that it won't harm us – just to take a little care?' His fingers drummed against the table, as they often did if an argument rose between us. 'And you could perhaps remember the *battles* I've been prepared to fight – in order to live here with you!'

I was duly silenced, though left with the feeling that, despite his earlier bravado, a battle had been lost, somewhere. But it seemed wise to say no more on the matter. The pudding arrived and Thomas devoured what was rather more than a small helping. I began to feel a weariness and regretted not having a portion myself. Sweet things are best for restoring energy, and Mrs Parsons excelled when it came to puddings. It had often struck me how Tom would have adored them.

Afterwards Thomas stood and held out a hand to me. 'Let's go to bed, Mary.'

'So early?'

'Yes, so early. You told me a while ago it was late. So it's later now.'

I laughed, and we made our way from the room and towards the stairs. It seemed good, even a reason for joy, that we were able to soothe our distress in such a way. Though I was aware that it might not always be so.

33

For some time after that, his grandfather left us untroubled. Perhaps he accepted that manoeuvrings on his part were not going to change the situation, but likely to make his relationship with his grandson more difficult than it already was. Despite feeling suspicious of the quiet, I was glad of it. We made an effort to exercise care, as Thomas had suggested we should, and I bit my tongue and made no complaint.

If we walked out it was towards Youlgrave rather than Middleton. But more often now we chose to use the carriage and to go out a further distance. Thomas's grandfather possessed a comfortable barouche, and had John, an elderly coachman, still at his service. Since the calls on him these days were not many, John did other odd jobs around the Hall and grounds, and was there for Thomas to call upon. It would have been extravagant to keep a separate coachman at Lomberdale. I suspected the building itself had cost far more than anticipated.

I think John enjoyed his excursions with us. Thomas addressed him with a natural informality – he had known him, after all, since childhood.

'It was me first put Mr Bateman on a horse!' John informed me, with clear pleasure and pride at the memory. 'No more than three years old, he must've been, if that. Didn't want to be put on, though, he didn't. Shouting and screaming his young head off. Frightened the mare, even, and she was steady as they come. Mind you, he took to it, he did, no time at all – a duck to water.'

I chuckled, and Thomas looked suitably embarrassed, as anyone does when tales of childhood are dragged out.

We did keep at Lomberdale a light, open gig, that was in fact little more than a trap. It needed only one horse and was easy enough to manage. As promised, Thomas taught me to use this, though it was a while before I was allowed to take it out on my own.

'You must promise to take care,' he warned, as the time arrived. 'Keep the pace steady, and not go too far. I don't trust that wild streak in you.'

'It's what you like in me, I thought.'

'Not when a horse is involved – but mind you, I'm only giving you Sal.' Sal, a small, stocky cob had a patient temperament and no inclination for speed. She was a reliable puller of carts and had not shied or bolted in living memory.

I was thrilled with the trap, and perfectly content with Sal. Despite the self-professed *wildness*, I was nervous of the strength of horses and of their unpredictable ways. Sal had a respectable walk and trot but steadfastly refused, even with Thomas's encouragement, to progress to anything more. The stubbornness was reassuring, and I had started to develop an affection for her that quite surprised me. I found myself paying her regular visits in the stable or nearby pasture, seeking to strengthen our bond with the offer of a piece of carrot or some such thing from the kitchen.

It was a while before I ventured far, but it was agreed, one Sunday morning, that I would go and visit Fanny at the Big House – though the place no longer seemed so very *big* in my eyes. A little larger than Lomberdale, perhaps, but less grand than the Hall. An hour or so could be spent with my sister, while Sal was allowed to rest or graze. Tempting as it might be to take Fanny out for a ride, I had no intention of doing so. Thomas had not consented to it and I would not have demanded such a thing of Sal, who would deserve her breather.

I thought of sending a note to Fanny, who could read enough to make out a simple message, but decided against it. A surprise arrival on her free day – the first Sunday of each month – might be better, and if I set off early enough there should be no danger of missing her. She would have to attend church along with the rest before absenting her-self to visit Alice or to go anywhere else, though I could not think of where else she was likely to go. It was all too easy to imagine Fanny spending the day rather sulkily in her shared room.

Thomas checked the harness yet again, and prepared to wave me off.

'Make sure you're back in full daylight! No daring tricks, remember. Just a nice, easy pace.'

I smiled. 'I *do* remember, Thomas. You've mentioned it before – a time or two.' I took hold of the reins and arranged my fingers around them, then pulled the leather taut enough for Sal to sense. It felt quite natural to me now.

She lifted her head and Thomas stroked the soft, warm flesh of her nose.

'At least I know *you'll* behave.' He looked up at me. 'I hope you find your sister a bit more cheerful than you seem to expect.' He hesitated, and I delayed shaking the reins and shouting Sal forward. 'You know,' he continued, 'if you feel concerned about her, then she could come and live here... with us. We're hardly short of rooms, after all. And perhaps she would be good company for you, at the times I'm occupied.'

The idea was too much of a surprise for me to make a thoughtful reply. I must have uttered some sort of acknowledgement, then Thomas slapped Sal on her rear and we were on our way, clattering out of the yard and down the lane towards Middleton.

It was a good day, bright without being too sunny and with a light breeze. Once through the village and along the quiet road towards Elton, I started to relish the feel of fresh air on my face, the sound of birds, the sense of movement, of freedom. It had not changed for me, I realised. These were still sensations I loved, even if I did not hanker after or seize upon them quite as much as before. It was enough to enjoy them less often, for Thomas's company was also satisfying, also an intense pleasure. At least it was so on most occasions. And even when it was not, when our minds clashed or there was misunderstanding, the experience was still exhilarating. Being with Thomas absorbed my energies in a way nothing else ever had.

Nevertheless, I thrilled to being outside and already far from the house, in making my way to another place by myself. For Sal did not count, of course; she was a part of the freedom that could be breathed in. She enabled me to travel a greater distance on my own than ever before, though in spite of Thomas's fears, I had no intention of forcing the pace. This journey needed to be enjoyed, moment by moment. In any case, Sal was too good a friend to bully or overwork.

An hour or so on, and my mind turned to what Thomas had said. His words, his *offer*, had taken me by surprise – an ability he had never lost, even though I knew his opinions, feelings and tastes with regard to many things. The offer was sincere, for I knew he would not have voiced it otherwise. What was harder to decide upon were my own feelings. I was not at all sure that I wanted my sister to live with us at Lomberdale. I was not at all sure that I wished to share my life with Thomas in any way, even – perhaps especially – with a member of my own family.

Though Fanny would not be with us all the time. Perhaps not even much of the time, for she was not a girl who sought company. That, of course, posed the question of what on earth she *would* she do with herself. Since she enjoyed neither conversation nor reading, I struggled to think of what else there might be at Lomberdale to entertain her. But if she came to live with us, then it could not be to work. She was used to being a servant, but I could hardly act the part of lady of the house while my own sister served us at table, let alone slaved away in the scullery.

She might well appreciate the rest, the leisure of it all. At first. But in the absence of anything of interest to fill it, time would surely begin to hang heavy? Fanny could sew competently, but had never shown enthusiasm for the activity.

I could not imagine her hours filled with dressmaking or embroidery.

We could make occasional excursions together to see Alice and Edwina, though the truth was that my own visits there had become infrequent. I sensed they felt less of an ease with me these days. There was a certain awkwardness and, while sad at the change, I could understand. During these visits to Cromford, I would make a point of seeing Marguerite, who was healthy and growing, and as adored as ever. She was also, I could see, already sharper and cleverer than the rest of that family put together.

As for Fanny, there were the gardens, of course. Fanny did seem to like flowers. I could remember as a child she would stop and draw attention to wild flowers growing round the village, picking them sometimes to bring home and place inside an old jar.

Just for a moment, I pictured her standing amongst the well-kept, colourful beds of the gardens at Lomberdale. We had a young, apprentice gardener who could talk about plants and flowers; he would be happy to answer her questions, should she take the trouble to ask any. James was a pleasant, intelligent boy, not much older than Fanny. In fact… but I stopped my mind at that point from its idiotic wanderings. No decision needed be made today. It may not be necessary at all. I would find out how she was faring, and trust to my judgement and instincts.

She was not faring well, as it turned out. Before setting eyes on Fanny, I found myself quickly invited by Mrs Jenson into her housekeeper's room and offered a cup of tea, a refreshment I was grateful to accept, though the sourness of her expression was not encouraging.

'It's a piece of good fortune that you happen to be here,' she said, proffering a small plate with one biscuit, which I took also. 'Because I was thinking of getting a message to the family otherwise, and asking for someone to come and speak to me about your sister.'

I bit off half of the oat biscuit. The excitement of the ride across had left me hungry, and I suspected some energy could be required for this conversation.

'The girl is so very *listless*, from the moment she wakes till the moment she goes to bed!' Mrs Jenson took a bite of her own biscuit, continuing to talk while she crunched noisily. 'I'm at my wits' end with her, to be *frank* with you.' She brushed stray crumbs from her lap onto the plate, sweeping many to the floor in the process. 'At my wits' end.'

'Do you think she's ill, Mrs Jenson?'

'Well, she's a bit pallid, certainly, but I wouldn't know. I don't believe she is, frankly. But the thing is – the thing I have to point out to you – is that she's not pulling her weight, not doing the job she's paid to do. Or not doing it well enough. I'm quite used to pushing these young girls along a bit… '

'I'm sure you are.'

'But I'm needing to check on your sister all the time. Frankly, I'm sick to death of shouting at her, reminding her, pointing out what it is she's supposed to be doing.'

Not as sick as Fanny, was my suspicion.

'Perhaps you'd speak to her, since you're here. Because I have to say to you, if things don't change very quickly, I shall be sending her back home. I won't have any choice, quite *frankly*, it's as simple as that.' It was clear Mrs Jenson prided herself on frankness.

'Do you know?' she continued, putting her empty plate on the table with quite a bang, 'I was approached by our church minister last week. The Reverend *Hogarth*.' The name was emphasised; I did not know whether I was supposed to be impressed. 'He wished to give me the names of four girls. Four! All desperate for domestic work.' She sniffed, and squeezed her thin lips into an ugly sort of grimace. 'And all of them hardworking girls too, he took pains to assure me.' There followed a moment's pause. 'From *decent*, *God-fearing* homes.'

I wondered if the woman had learned, somehow, of my circumstances. I could imagine her having the sort of tight and self-righteous religious mind that would pounce on them. Not that any of that mattered, because all of a sudden my mind was made up.

'Please don't bother yourself any more, Mrs Jenson.' I lifted the cup to my mouth and drank the remains of the tea slowly, pausing a time or two, while she watched me with avidness, not knowing what to expect next. I replaced the cup and saucer carefully on the table and stood up. 'To be *frank* with you, I came here with the intention of taking my sister back home with me.' I smiled at her, enjoying the look of surprise and displeasure.

'She really has no need of work now, you see, none at all. Our circumstances have changed. So please do offer her position to one of the girls you mention. I'd suggest to the most *decent* of them. And now could you please arrange for Fanny to be called? Or perhaps call her yourself? I should prefer to drive us home well before dark.'

34

Fanny was too bemused to say much on the way to Lomberdale; perhaps I was, also. She sat clutching an old bag with her few bits of clothes in it – even fewer than she possessed, for some items, she had told me, were amongst piles of clothes in the laundry room. I had told her not to worry, and tried to concentrate my attention on the task of driving us with care. Sal was now hauling extra weight, though not a great deal of it for Fanny was shorter than me and quite thin.

Noticing this made me realise I had put on some weight over the last year or two. I was not plump, and Thomas was unlikely even to have noticed any change, but gradual adjustments to clothes made it plain that every part of me was just a little fleshier than before. In the early days with Thomas, I had been tempted to wonder if this could be a sign of pregnancy. These days I no longer imagined it could be that.

Fanny was coming with me to Lomberdale; in the end, the decision had seemed to make itself, though how it was likely to turn out was another thing. She looked wan and rather miserable – though no more so than when I had seen her last. I felt it would be nice to cosset her for a while, to put a flush in her cheeks and a little more meat on the bones. To see her smile, even, which could turn out to be the bigger challenge.

'We're not far, now,' I said at length. 'And just as well; it looks as if there could be a shower.'

'It wouldn't worry me,' she replied. 'I'd rather be out here getting wet than in *that* place, and dry.'

'Well it's never a good thing to be caught in the rain, without coats. We'd risk catching a chill.'

'What's it like, Mary? Your house?'

I chuckled. 'It's not *my* house. But I do live there, and it's... it's a lovely house, as you'll soon see.'

'Will you always live there, with Thomas?'

I did not rush to answer. 'I really don't know, Fanny,' I said at last. 'Perhaps so. But it isn't possible to be sure.' I turned to look at her. 'But I'm there now. And I don't worry too much about the future. Nobody knows what's going to happen, do they, in years to come?'

It seemed honest, up to a point. It was not true that I never *wondered* about the future, but I did not permit myself to dwell on it, and only on rare occasions did I wake up in the night feeling uneasy or fearful. An unwise state of mind, perhaps, but also a fortunate one. Concern about what life might or might not bring can destroy all pleasure in the present.

Thomas had never met Fanny. He was generous enough to welcome her warmly, despite what must have been a certain shock in seeing us arrive together. However genuine the offer of a home, he would not have been expecting it to be taken up with such haste.

'I'm sure you must be tired,' he said, looking at her drawn face as we all stood together, a little awkwardly, in the hallway. 'Why don't you take a little rest, and then join us for dinner later?'

Fanny seemed bemused. She was not used to being invited to *join* someone for dinner and stared at him without replying. Thomas turned to me. 'Do you think Fanny would like to have the blue room? It's a nice, sunny one.'

The blue room, as we referred to it, was a small but comfortable guest room. It lay at the opposite end of the house from our own and was therefore a good choice. Like Thomas, I did not want our sense of privacy and *aloneness* to be spoilt. The existence of a second, smaller staircase at the blue room end was a further advantage. Fanny's path would not always need to cross our own on the stairs.

'I think that would be perfect,' I said. I squeezed his arm in gratitude and then beckoned her to follow me upstairs.

'Do you need Sarah to help?'

'No, it's fine. I'll go up with her; settle her in.' The abrupt change from working as a servant to being assisted by one would have been too much for Fanny. Besides which, there was nothing much to help with; like me on my journey to Bakewell a few years ago, she had brought precious little with her.

'Thomas is handsome, isn't he?' We were sitting on the edge of her new bed, the empty bag in front of us on the floor. I smiled. 'Well, *I* think he is, certainly.'

I did, of course, consider Thomas attractive, though many people might have judged him to be unexceptional. He was not a tall man – with height only a little above my own – and his features were not striking in any particular way. Viewed in a group of men, and from a slight distance, I doubt if most women would have singled him out to remark upon.

But there was a power about Thomas, and once in conversation there was a palpable force and energy about him. Those who listened, who engaged with him, found themselves becoming animated also. Passionate, even. I had noticed it in others, and it had always been true of me, most of all.

I doubt if Fanny had felt any of this, or was likely to. She was simply impressed by his confident, easy air. Perhaps also by the well-spoken, courteous manner, to which she had no idea how to respond. So confused had she found herself, or overwhelmed, that I sensed her to be on the verge of tears.

'Why don't you have a lie down, Fanny? Close your eyes for a while.'

'How will I know when I have to come down?'

'I'll call you in good time. And meanwhile I'll find a dress for you – one of mine.'

She sniffed hard and wiped her nose with a hand. 'I don't want to come down tonight. I don't think I can eat anything.'

I sighed, knowing she had to be hungry. But the day had left me tired also, and I did not relish the thought of having her at the table that evening. I preferred to eat with Thomas alone, to explain things to him without her silent awkwardness.

'Not tonight, then. But *just* tonight. I'll bring a bit of something up to you, later on. And tomorrow – you must make an effort tomorrow, Fanny.'

'Alright.'

She looked a picture of misery, and I wondered if I had acted wisely today. Should I have placated the complaining Mrs Jenson and then given Fanny a firm talking to? Too late to think about it now. What she needed was to be left on her own a while.

'There's a pot under the bed,' I mentioned, rising to my feet. I smiled and touched her shoulder, hoping to lighten the mood. 'And it won't even be your job to empty it, Fanny!'

She looked taken aback. 'Oh… but I'd rather.'

I realised how accustomed I'd become, over the last few years, to a different sort of life. How I no longer questioned, or perhaps even appreciated it.

Over the next couple of weeks Fanny did make an effort, if at times a less than gracious one. She ate with us and became a little more used to conversation, or rather listening to it, for she said very little and needed much encouragement even for that. Thomas, I knew, found her hard work, but he was gallant in trying to find things to amuse her.

'I believe you like flowers, Fanny,' he ventured on one occasion.

'Yes.'

'Then I shall ask young James to show you round the gardens.'

'I walk round them already,' was her curt, unapprecia-tive reply.

'I'm sure you do. But he knows a great deal – which might make your own walks more of a pleasure.' I glared at her to smile. 'And he could show you the Hall gardens, also. They're bigger and better still.'

'Alright.' The expression did not change.

I have to admit it was a struggle to have patience with my sister. Thomas seemed to muster more of it than I could.

A price, however, was to be paid for his kindness. Within an hour of Fanny and the rather earnest young James returning from the grounds of the Hall, Thomas's grandfa-ther, whom I had not set eyes on for some time, arrived at the door. It was clear that he had not come to enquire after my health, but I invited him to come into the main draw-ing room and suggested tea.

'I'll wait here, thank-you. Perhaps you'd be good enough to ask my grandson to come and speak.'

Sarah had opened the door and was still hovering. I signalled to her to leave, for plainly we would have no need of tea. I was more likely to require it after he had gone.

'Thomas is in his study,' I said. 'I'll go and tell him you're here.'

I did not need to, as footsteps could be heard at that very moment. Thomas approached us, his face a little appre-hensive. I could have excused myself and left the two of them alone, but chose not to.

'Your young gardener – the son of one of mine, if I'm not mistaken – was walking around my grounds earlier this afternoon with a girl. A Miss Walton. *This* young woman's sister, I understand.' I noticed I was not a young lady on this occasion.

'She is, yes.' There was no sign of hesitation in Thomas's voice. 'I did mention her to you, Grandfather, some while ago.'

'Precisely. Some rather long while ago! I assumed she was staying here a day or two, a week at most. It appears, though, that this girl is *living* here.' He made it sound like an abominable discovery.

'For the time being, yes.'

His grandfather glared at him. 'Isn't *one* loose woman enough for you, Thomas? Have you any idea of the gossip this is going to stir up – yet again? The sort of things people will be saying? Two mistresses! Or do you think of them as *concubines*? Is that what *they* think they are, the pair of them? And are you man enough to keep two females well pleasured?'

'How dare you!' My shout cut in before Thomas was able to reply. 'What you've said is disgusting, repulsive! No gentleman would lower himself to say such things, but then – you're most certainly *not* a... '

'Mary, leave us. I shall deal with this.' Thomas's voice came low and insistent. I felt his hands on my arms, pushing me to go back up the hallway. '*Leave* us!' The tone became harder as he sensed my resistance. I glared at the old man then marched back to the drawing room and slammed the door behind me.

'He's gone.' Thomas was standing in the doorway. 'And I apologise. What he implied was unforgiveable.'

'He didn't imply, Thomas. He *said* it. And clearly.' I was still seething, pacing about in front of the window.

'*Said*, then. Mary, please do sit down. I've asked for tea to be sent up. Look – it was one of his outbursts. I've heard them before.'

'Not to do with Fanny, you haven't. How *dare* he!'

'He won't have said anything to Fanny, I promise you. It was all meant for me. Been boiling up again for a while. I'm used to it.'

'Well, *I'm* not prepared to get used to it. I didn't get myself away from a foul-mouthed father in order to put up with coarseness and filth from your grandfather!'

'Oh come *on*.' Thomas began to sound less appeasing and more irritated. 'He's been quiet for weeks. Months! It was an outburst.'

'So you've said. Does that excuse it in some way? He's very fortunate I didn't slap his arrogant face. I wish I had.'

'For Heaven's sake, calm down.' He went towards one of the cupboards. 'I suggest a brandy. It might work better than tea.'

'I don't want anything more to do with the man,' I announced, reluctant to let go of my outrage.

'You have precious little to do with him already.' Thomas sounded impatient; I sensed he intended to draw this to a close. 'It's *me*,' he added, removing the glass stopper from the decanter, 'that has to *do* with him, for my sins. But for all his moralising, he hasn't stopped me taking an income from the estate – an income that keeps both of us here and your sister as well. To say nothing of the servants. So let's just leave it at that, shall we?'

It was not put to me as a question, and I did not bother to answer it. By the time Sarah arrived with the tea I had swallowed half of a large measure of brandy, and there was peace, of a bristly sort, between us.

35

For a good part of the following months, Thomas and I were away from Lomberdale. My love of being *on the move* had not diminished in any way; if anything it seemed to have become stronger still. Was this, at least in part, because a return to Lomberdale never brought me the same sense of pleasure and light-heartedness as the returns to Matlock Street? A stupid thing, no doubt, and not a feeling shared by Thomas, who had delighted in the house from the start and was already discussing plans to enlarge his beloved museum.

In fairness to him, what had appeared a more than generous space appeared now to be filling, at breath-taking speed, with burial treasures of all kinds. Sculls and whole skeletons already occupied a large section. Pots, ornaments and jewellery had taken over another, bookshelves and document drawers a third. The area left contained a large working table and chairs, for it was not unusual for his associates to visit us, sometimes several at a time.

Few ancient burial grounds of Derbyshire had now escaped his spade. Or more often the spade of others, for Thomas had acquired a band of faithful helpers almost as ardent in the task as himself. On a good few occasions I was among their number. The loyalty shown by the others came as no surprise to me, for Thomas had an easy, natural ability to inspire it. Our old friend Will, though, remained the closest and most valued member of the band.

It did not surprise me either, some five or six months after her arrival at Lomberdale, that Fanny decided to leave it. She had never settled, never found her ease in the house, had always seemed out of place. In Thomas's company she managed to talk a little, provided that I was there also to aid and prod and to finish her sentences for her. If guests were present she would take stubbornly to her room and insist on eating alone.

Offers to accompany us on our trips were declined, leaving me anxious about her loneliness during those periods as well as – it must be admitted – frustrated and vexed. I longed to shake her out of the narrow world she insisted on remaining in; wanted to show her the remarkable life, the breath-taking sights, of distant cities. It was beyond my understanding that some-one could be offered such a chance and not want to seize it. Though perhaps it should not have surprised me. In my previous world, I was the oddity, the freakish one; the plant that had somehow been seeded and grown in the wrong garden.

On our return from one such trip, an anxious faced Sarah met us at the door.

'Miss Walton, Sir, she's asked me to thank you – to thank you so very much indeed – for your kindness and hospitality.' Those, I knew, were Sarah's words; she was far better with them than Fanny. 'But she's decided it's best if she goes to live with her sister.' She looked at me.

'You do mean *Alice*?' I could not imagine it being Edwina.

'Yes, that was the name. She insisted, you see, that she wanted to go. So Eileen and I walked to the Hall – I do hope that was alright? We asked if she could be driven to Cromford in the carriage, and one of the servants went to ask Mr Bateman Senior. He agreed and… '

'I'll bet he did!' I cut in.

''That's alright, Sarah.' Thomas cut in on me just as quickly. 'You did the right thing, there's no problem at all. Could you ask Eileen to bring us tea?' Sarah was a couple of years older than Eileen and did less, these days, of the fetching and carrying. She was an intelligent, presentable girl, able to see to the smooth running of the house and to assist the guests who quite frequently appeared.

'Well, that's that,' he said when we were alone. I hope you're not too upset. It's perhaps for the best.'

'Perhaps.'

We did not discuss the matter further; there seemed little point. I would see her on my next visit there, whenever it might be.

I recall that event – Fanny's departure from Lomberdale – as being in the late Autumn. For it was just a few months later, during April, that Thomas's grandfather became ill.

It is a surprising thing that we found ourselves so shocked. The man was eighty-six years old, after all; surely some illness was to be expected? Most people would be in their graves by that time. The amazement was that he had not fallen ill before, had never in anyone's memory had to take to bed and to be nursed. His health had always been as rude and robust as his nature.

302

Overnight, Thomas seemed to become anxious and agitated. He could not settle to anything, and least of all to his work. A proposed visit to Nottingham – not too great a travelling distance – was immediately cancelled, and as days went by and there was no improvement, more and more of his time was spent at the Hall. After a week or so he took to sleeping there.

'I need to be at hand,' he said, on a brief, rushed visit back to Lomberdale. ' I need to be able to talk to him – when he's able – and of course talk to the doctor.' The doctor had started to visit several times in a day, but proved as ignorant as anyone else regarding the cause of the old man's fever and weakness, of his heavy, painful breathing.

'It's *old age*, Thomas,' I pointed out; gently enough, so I thought, though the statement turned out to be ill-advised.

'I'm aware of how old he is!' came the snapped reply.

He kept a sharp watch on the nurse who had been appointed to stay at the Hall, making sure she carried out the doctor's advice to the letter. Five of his prescribed drops had to be put in hot water and given by teaspoon hourly. Hot flannels were to be placed on the belly, mustard poultices administered to the calves. I doubted these things would do any good, though I did not put it past the old man to recover, despite them. But Thomas was insistent that all instructions must be followed, day and night, and I accepted what he said without argument, for his distress and anxiety were plain. Indeed, they were becoming a worry to me in their own right.

Considering that for some weeks he had barely left his grandfather's side, it was a cruel twist of fate that Thomas just happened to be in Lomberdale House at the moment the old man chose to die. A scrawled note, hastily written by the nurse, was rushed across in the hands of a young servant and brought to us in the library. We can only have been in there a matter of fifteen or twenty minutes; Thomas had already been gathering himself to make a return. On receiving the note he leapt to his feet with a gasp and was straight through the door and on his way, without explanation and without stopping for a coat or cloak.

'Let me come with you!' I called after him, rushing after him from the room and along the hallway.

'No, no. I'll go alone. It's best.'

I considered ignoring these words. Thought for a moment about following him after getting our cloaks, for although the May afternoon was a sunny one it was bound to turn much chillier later on. It seemed foolish to put our own health and lives at risk. But I did not, for something told me that Thomas did not want me to follow him, that he did not feel it wise for me to enter the Hall.

It was difficult to know whether I was offended or relieved. I decided to go out into the gardens, to walk about, take fresh air. Whether his grandfather was worsening, or had already died, I had no idea, for the note had disappeared. Thomas must have left with it still in his hand.

As it turned out, he had died during that brief time that his grandson was away from his bedside, an unfortunate thing for which Thomas – quite unjustly, as I attempted to point out – blamed himself.

'Thomas, you could *not* have known,' I insisted, on more than one occasion. Two or three days had passed, during which he alternated between criticising himself for his neglect and sinking into a deep, silent gloom. He ate very little during that time.

'When you came here, you said he seemed a little better,' I said. 'This situation could have carried on for many more weeks – for *months*! How could you sit at a bedside for months at a time? You really must stop this; you're going to make yourself ill.'

'I'm sure it's what he wanted, for me to be there. I feel as if I've failed him, disappointed him – yet again.'

I did not ask what *yet again* referred to. A slight chill seemed to go through me, but I ignored it and went to put my arms around him, something he had not seemed to want during these last few days. This time his own came around me in return; he sighed heavily into my neck.

'Why don't we go to bed for a while?' I found myself saying, then feared at once that he might find the suggestion clumsy. Even offensive.

'Won't it look bad, if people don't know where on earth we are?'

'No, it won't. I'll let some-one know you're going to be resting, and mustn't be disturbed. You look exhausted anyway. It'll seem a perfectly natural thing to do. And not odd for me to be with you!'

My confidence in the suggestion was restored; he had not taken it amiss. How foolish to imagine he might – I must have forgotten for a moment the forces that exist in men's minds and bodies. Even grief and exhaustion struggle to subdue them.

Once in the bedroom, Thomas became as passionate as I had ever known him; more fiercely so than he had seemed for some time. I savoured it, was thankful to give him pleasure and release. There was a satisfaction in knowing he had cast off care, if only for a while; that he was wanting and breathing only *us*. Though throughout, a part of me stayed alert, remained anxious for him.

The funeral was planned for just a few days later, on the first day of June. It was to take place at Hartington, where the Bateman family had owned property and land long before Thomas's grandfather managed to earn his own fortune and buy himself the Middleton estate. Interment would take place there also, in the family vault. It crossed my mind that Thomas must be destined, one day, to be interred there also. The thought of it sent a slight shiver through me.

Thomas spent the greater part of those days, between his grandfather's death and the funeral, at the Hall. There were relatives to receive, some of them elderly and from considerable distances. Servants needed to be organised, rooms prepared and meals arranged. There were discussions with church ministers and with lawyers, arrangements to be made for carriage hire. I offered to help in all or any part of this time consuming effort, but he seemed intent on coping with it unaided, fulfilling some need to spend every waking moment in energetic, almost frantic, activity.

'Why don't you at least let me write some of the letters for you?' I asked. 'Surely that would help?'

'What *would* help,' Thomas replied, ignoring the offer, 'would be for me to take a couple of servants over to the Hall for the next few days. Including Mrs Parsons's new kitchen girl – Jane, is it? If you don't mind? You did say she was good. The old cook over there won't be able to cope with all this, she's not used to it any more. Oh, and Sarah perhaps. She's good with visitors – better than Eileen.'

'Of course.' Mrs Parsons would not be pleased, but then, she rarely was.

'Am I to come to the funeral, Thomas?'

He looked shaken and flustered, as if the thought had not yet struck him.

'Perhaps... not, Mary. I think it might be better not. It could – you see – be *difficult*.'

I shrugged my shoulders. 'Very well.'

Thomas seized both my hands and put them to his lips, held them there for some time without speaking, his eyes closed, his forehead creased into a heavy frown.

'Forgive me, this is a difficult time. Forgive me.' I said nothing, in forgiveness or otherwise, but leant forward to kiss his neck.

'After the funeral,' Thomas said, 'when we get back to the Hall, there'll be food, and then the formal reading of the will. Anyone who happens to be present can be there for that, if they choose to be. Grandfather discussed the thing with me a while back – I know he's made a good few family bequests. And he always said he wouldn't forget any of the old, retired servants. That's as well as the local chapel, of course, and goodness knows what else. It could all take a fair while.'

'And then?'

'Then I'll be back here for dinner, even if it's a late one. Anyone still at the Hall will be looked after, and they'll be leaving in the next couple of days. What I shall want is a bit of peace and quiet. With you.'

'Isn't that a contradiction?' We both managed a smile at last, though Thomas's seemed an unconvincing one.

I did not expect to find the day of the funeral an easy thing, and it was not. I felt edgy and unsettled, aware that there were many hours to fill, for Thomas was unlikely to return to Lomberdale before nightfall. For once, reading held no appeal. Neither did I have any desire to go for a walk, other than a few pointless meanders around the garden. There was an odd sense of loneliness; unusual and disturbing for it was not something I was familiar with. Normally I found no problem whatever in spending time alone.

In fact it was early evening, and therefore sooner than expected, when Thomas arrived. I noted with disappointment, even with a certain irritation, that he was accompanied by a man who had visited him once before at Lomberdale, to whom I had taken an instant, if unfair, dislike.

'I think you've met Mr Hodgson, Mary. My grandfather's executor?' They were just inside the main door. Thomas's face, I saw, was drawn with tiredness.

'I have, yes.'

'Indeed, yes!' Mr Hodgson beamed, and in the absence of a servant stepping forward, started to remove his coat. It seemed he intended to stay.

'We'll be in the library, for just a little while,' Thomas said. It was clear that this was another occasion to which I could not be invited, and I hoped for both our sakes it would be brief.

Perhaps the bulbous-faced Mr Hodgson needed to be shown hospitality; no doubt his throat was dry and sore after a long and loud reading of the will. I suspected the courtesies would include a glass – or several – of Thomas's brandy.

Such an occasion could hardly be hurried, and it was not. Now the official duties were done, I could imagine Mr Hodgson warming to the subject of his cantankerous old client. It was doubtful he would have found him other than testy and difficult, but as a looser mood emerged with the second or third brandy, he would do what is expected under the circumstances and start to reminisce with new-ly-found affection. All the more so on remembering the substantial bill he would be sending – just as soon as decency allowed. The rewards for dealing with an estate of this importance were unlikely to be small.

36

It seemed a long while later that I heard Thomas emerge from the library with his guest. He called out to Eileen, who must have appeared along the corridor. Perhaps she was on her way to ask if he wanted tea or food brought to the library.

'Please tell Mr Hodgson's coachman that he's ready to leave!' The coachman was probably in the kitchen, drinking his own tea. I was thankful for the long, Summer evening – at least there was no need for rooms to be offered for the night.

For the moment I remained in the drawing room, not anxious to engage in any form of polite conversation with Mr Hodgson, who had seemed, on first acquaintance, pompous and self-important. But perhaps men of law are always so; I imagine it must be part of their training and those who cannot achieve it are advised to find some other employment.

Thomas accompanied him outside and several more minutes elapsed before I heard the carriage arrive in front of the door. At length, the wretched man must have heaved his considerable bulk into it and the main door of the house closed again. I heard Thomas clear his throat as he returned towards the library. Once again he closed the door behind him; a sign, perhaps, that he needed a little private time for recovery. But I considered I had remained in discreet isolation for long enough, and that the moment had come to intrude. If he had decided to pour himself another drink, then he could pour one for me also.

'Alright, Thomas?' Standing in the doorway of the library, I was disconcerted. There was no pouring of anything; Thomas was already slouched in one of the comfortable chairs, head resting back and eyes closed. Something about him suggested more than exhaustion. The fire had almost gone out but it was still very warm in that room, stuffy even, the heaviness of cigar smoke not quite disguising the lingering, unpleasant whiff of Mr Hodgson.

He opened his eyes, with what seemed like pained reluctance.

'I didn't wake you, did I?'

'Of course not. I could hardly be asleep, could I? I've only this moment come back in.' The tone was one of distinct irritation.

'Well, do you want anything? Perhaps some tea?'

'No, thank you.' There followed an exaggerated sigh. 'Thought the damned fellow was never going to leave – I couldn't face inviting him to stay for dinner. Discourteous of me, no doubt, but there we are. Can't say I've ever cared for him very much.'

'Quite understandable. But – everything *is* as you expected, Thomas, is it? I mean, your dear grandfather didn't take it into his head to bequeath the whole estate to the church, perhaps? Or else to some bastard child you've never heard of?'

I joked, of course, if awkwardly. The old man could be pig-headed but he was never likely to disinherit his beloved grandson. At least the suggestion produced an amused snort.

'Oh *no*. All predictable. One's expectations fulfilled.'

'Well then?'

He made no reply, merely closed his eyes again. I am not sure just what I expected him to say, but clearly the recent fulfilment of *expectations* was not occasioning any glee as yet. On the contrary, it appeared to be weighing heavy. Perhaps there loomed in his mind the unwelcome transition from carefree young man to landowner with serious responsibilities.

' I wouldn't mind a brandy,' I ventured, in part to deal with the taut absence of conversation. 'Just a small one.'

'Oh, of course.' He dragged himself up and walked across to the shelf where a large decanter and several glasses stood on a silver tray. The decanter, which had been topped up that morning, was almost half empty.

'You don't want another yourself?'

'Oh God, no. I've had enough of the stuff. Not as much as *he* had, mind you.'

I was handed the glass, a modest measure poured into it. Seating myself, I began to sip at the strong, dark liquid with appreciation. Over the past five years, I had developed quite a taste for the soothing warmth it could be relied upon to provide.

'So, Thomas?'

'So, it's been a damned exhausting day. And I've a raging headache.'

'I'm not surprised. You should let me ask for tea'.

'I don't *want* tea!'

Irritation was bordering on bad temper. When suffering from severe tiredness, Thomas tended to be ill-humoured. Neither of us spoke for a minute or two, but before I had finished my drink he was rising again to his feet.

'Look, I'm going to take a bit of air before dinner. Can you ask Mrs Parsons to hold it a while? Half an hour, perhaps? It might help to cure this head.'

'If you like.'

I suspect my tone, like his, sounded terse. I took a large swallow of brandy, replaced my glass on the tray and we left the room together. Without a further word, Thomas headed off along the hallway towards a side door while I made my own way down to the kitchen, knowing I was about to annoy Mrs Parsons, who resented any change of timing. Fortunately the meal turned out to be simple enough for it not to cause too much fuss.

'Well, it's to be hoped the air gives him an appetite!' was all she declared, albeit with a hint of exasperation. 'I've baked his favourite almond tart – it'll have to be eaten cold, of course.'

'Cold will be fine, Mrs Parsons. Thank-you.'

Returning to the library, I added a little more brandy to my not quite empty glass, then decided to take both it and myself back to the drawing room Much as I loved to sit within the dense, leathery smell of books, the library, just then, felt oppressive.

Thomas ate little at dinner and complained that his headache had not improved. I tried to take his mind off whatever heavy thoughts were in it by not alluding to the will, to Mr Hodgson or to any other aspect of that day, but speaking of the next visit we were to make to London, in just a few weeks' time. But Thomas added little to the conversation and eventually I gave up, feeling less sympathy than perhaps I should have done.

'Too much brandy on an empty stomach!' I declared, with some impatience. 'you plainly need a good sleep.'

'Yes, I plainly do,' came the crisp reply.

Shortly afterwards, he pushed the remains of his meal almost roughly to one side of the plate and laid his knife and fork down.

'I won't have any pudding.'

'What, not even Mrs Parson's almond tart?'

'No. It's taken me all my time to manage this, and I'm exhausted, frankly.' He was already getting slowly to his feet. 'I'm going to take myself off to bed – I'll sleep on the small bed in the dressing room, so don't feel you need to worry about coming up late or having to be quiet.' He squeezed my shoulder as he passed, as if in some sort of vague apology. 'No doubt I'll snore long and loudly all night. Either that or I'll wake in the small hours and be very restless. Kinder not to inflict either on you.'

'Well, if it's what you prefer… '

'It is. For tonight. I'll see you at breakfast'.

Thomas cannot have fallen asleep as readily as he expected, for when I hovered briefly outside the dressing room around an hour later, there was no sound of the rhythmic snoring which often followed a good quantity of drink. I did not open the door, for he had made it clear enough that he wanted to lie alone and remain undisturbed.

There had been occasions before when he had taken himself off to sleep alone, after some sort of heated disagreement between us. Sometimes I had chosen, late into the night, to disturb him; at other times Thomas had disturbed me. Vexed or not, we wanted one another. Only stubbornness and pride ever stood in the way.

This time was not the same; I knew it was not. Irritation had hovered but there was no quarrel; no angry passion had been aroused. What I sensed was that Thomas felt troubled in a way that lay mysteriously beyond my reach. There was a coolness, a withdrawal, and I sensed that if I should enter that room, he would ask me to leave. This was a new, disturbing thing and I had no strategy to deal with it other than by remaining, like Thomas himself, aloof. Passion, be it angry or otherwise, could not be brought to the rescue.

My night was a lonely, dispiriting one. Far more restless than Thomas feared his own might be, for in fact he slept long and soundly, and would have slept longer still had I not opened the door to the dressing room and suggested we ought to delay breakfast no further. There were still guests at the Hall, and I imagined courtesy would require him to show his face there before they left.

'I shall be down directly,' he muttered, 'as soon I've woken my face up with cold water.'

I thought I could sense a lighter mood, though of course it is possible to be mistaken in these matters.

37

To this day I admire Thomas for being prepared to face up to things. He did not think up reasons to delay, or not beyond the time that was needed for sleep. And he did need to sleep, as well as to spend some hours alone and unharried. I see that now. Perhaps he cannot be thought of as a wholly honourable man, but he was not a dishonest one, and he did not lack courage.

'I need to speak to you about something, Mary.'

We had barely spoken until that point. Not until Eileen had left the room and both of us had swallowed our first dose of hot, strong tea. I replaced my cup on its saucer and waited expectantly. Thomas's eyes were downwards as he reached across the table to pick up the large, breakfast teapot. He appeared to take longer than necessary to sieve more liquid into his cup and add a little milk.

'I'm listening. What is it?'

He took another gulp and winced slightly. Perhaps it had become more bitter. I imagine he must have been tempted to get to his feet and pace about the room, for that was always Thomas's habit when speaking of difficult matters. To his credit he managed to remain still, facing me across used plates and cups, his hands now laid on the table, right hand uneasily fingering at the left. For some reason his knuckles appeared to me to be bony and white, almost resembling those of a much older man.

Long and uncomfortable as the silence seemed, I sensed it was better not to put my question again.

'Mary, I have to tell you something.' The fingers of each hand were now interlaced, their fidgeting had ceased.

'And what's that, Thomas?'

'I have to tell you... I need to explain to you... that we cannot continue to live here, in this house, together. I'm afraid it will no longer be possible.'

'No longer *possible*?'

'That's so, yes. No longer possible.'

'I see.'

There was another pause. Thomas stared down at his hands. I sat still, looking towards his face, determined to say nothing else until he had raised it and his eyes were on mine. This took another while.

'I take it that what you've just said has something to do with yesterday? Something to do with the will?'

'Yes. Unfortunately it has.'

'And what, precisely?'

He hesitated, looked away once again, as if searching the wall for some crucial part of that document's writing.

'The terms of the will. There are certain matters.'

'I see.' I found myself stuck in that pointless phrase. What could I see? Not a great deal. But enough.

'Why don't you just tell me, Thomas? Tell me what's happened.'

A further silence. Again I waited, with an outward patience that I did not feel, for it to end. I sensed that the exact nature of what had *happened* was not important.

Whatever it turned out to be, Thomas had stated what must now happen as a consequence. I knew him too well to imagine he had spoken carelessly, without intent.

In those strained, quiet moments Thomas managed to muster something stronger. He turned his face to look at me straight, and his eyes seemed a little harder. The words, when they came, were firm, unfaltering.

'I'm afraid it's been made a condition of my inheritance that we part.'

So there it was. How simple.

'And that you leave this house,' he added needlessly, as if concerned I might have failed, in my shock, to grasp the point.

I think I may well have said 'I see' for a third time. Blankly, without emphasis.

'I'm so very, very sorry, Mary.'

The expression had become gentler. Did he feel he could now relax a little, the unpleasant deed having been done, the words of sorrow spoken?

But it did not require any further moments of silence for me to find a response.

'Oh, in the name of *God*, Thomas! Please don't bother with polite apologies.'

Anger cloaked the shock of what I had just heard. His doleful expressions of regret struck me as an insult.

'At least speak as if you hold me in some respect. I believe I'm capable of understanding things quite clearly. So keep to the facts, if you would, and save the rest!'

'Forgive me.' He opened out the palms of his hands towards me in what seemed a gesture of peace, or perhaps a plea for it.

'Let me help you,' I continued, in a tone that must have suggested anything but a desire to help. 'Am I right in thinking that your grandfather has left the whole of his estate to you, apart from a few minor bequests?'

'That's so, yes.' His face looked a picture of injured misery.

'But if I continue to live with you, then it's clear there's some sort of problem. Do you perhaps lose total control of the estate? Would responsibility be shared with some other relative?'

He looked at me solemnly. 'I would lose all responsibility. I would lose *all* of the estate. I would – in fact – lose *everything*.'

There must have passed another silence, for I noticed that my words had stopped, that my mind was retreating into a chilly calm.

'Do you understand, Mary?'

I nodded, then looked past him to gaze through the window behind. 'Yes. I do understand, Thomas.'

There came a sudden, melodramatic thump of his fist on the table. Perhaps emotion could no longer be contained, or perhaps he decided it must now be appropriate to show some anger.

'I can't find the words to tell you how furious I am!' He forced his chair back savagely from the table and scraped it along the tiled floor, creating a noise that would normally make me cover my ears in discomfort. 'How dare he – *dare* he – dictate this!' Reaching the window, he stood there rigid, his arms folded and his back resolutely towards me.

'And I know I can never ask you to forgive me. It would indeed be an insult to expect that.'

I ignored these breast-beating statements, rose quickly from my chair and left the room. It happened to be a dry, pleasant morning and I made my way towards a door that would take me directly into the part of the garden I had always liked best – a side area of rose beds and winding, grassy pathways, invisible from all the main windows of the house. I trusted that Thomas would have the kindness and good sense not to follow me.

I must have been loitering in that small piece of garden for around half an hour when I heard Thomas depart. Or at least heard sounds from the other side of the house that announced a carriage was being wheeled out into the yard. This was followed by low whinnying from the pair of horses and the clatter of metal shoes on a cobble-stoned surface. Moments later came the unmistakable noise of carriage and horses disappearing down the gravel-stoned driveway. I stood still, deliberately not moving in order to glimpse the departure, but waiting for all echoes of it to fade.

The real surprise was that we had not predicted this. The old man had kept it as a trick up his sleeve and I saw now, with sour clarity, why his manner towards me had shifted a little during the last few months. Within that vague period of time he had managed to be a little more civil; never pleasant, but at least less prone than before to open rudeness. I had begun to imagine that time and habit were finally warming him towards me.

I saw now that this was a mistake, a stupid misjudgement. He had not warmed. The barely perceptible change of attitude had come because his final plan was in place. He knew he had me trounced. How relieved he must have been that I had not managed to produce a child! A bastard child could have made things so very much more difficult. But after a while the confidence must have grown that no such child was ever likely to arrive. And he could also, of course, predict the behaviour of his grandson.

Was Thomas about to give up his position, his privileged state of affairs? Of course he was not. Was he minded to sacrifice everything that would, with one single, simple condition, become his? How ridiculous to think it, even for a moment! Only a woman with absurd romantic notions could waste her time imagining such a thing, and I have never been given to notions of that kind.

Though I refused to tell myself that Thomas had no choice. He *could* have sacrificed his precious inheritance. He could have shrugged his shoulders at the grand properties, and at the wealth he had had no hand whatever in creating, any more than his father did before him. That achievement belonged to his grandfather – to him alone. Much as I disliked the man, he had always had my admiration.

Thomas, by contrast, saw wealth as his birthright. He had been brought up in the expectation and the certainty of it. And it was – quite clearly – what he *wanted*. He wanted his wealth and position more than he wanted me. Needed them more than he needed me. Those were simplicities that I could understand.

38

'You've been out a long time. I was beginning to wonder whether to expect you back at all today.'

'I needed some time alone, Mary. I imagined you might need time also.'

'No doubt I did.'

For the moment neither of us proceeded beyond these crisply delivered statements. Thomas sat himself down on a chair in the hallway and began to wrench off his boots, which were covered in mud.

'Where on earth did you go?'

He did not reply, but looked thoughtful while placing each boot on the small mat to one side and then brushing off what looked like a large, dead insect that had attached itself to the bottom of his breeches. These too, I saw, were mud bespattered.

'They need to be properly cleaned, or else they'll be ruined. And all your clothes look damp. Why don't you go up and change?'

Heaven knows why I felt the least concern about cleaning or changing. Perhaps it was simply a means of remaining calm. Alice came to mind suddenly. When anxious or distressed she would turn instinctively to practical things; the greater the worry, the more demanding the chosen task. Scrubbing the hearth until it was free of every last speck of grime, until it was so pristine that a dinner could be eaten from it, could be taken as the measure of her deep disquiet.

'Very well, I'll change'. He rose and started to head towards the staircase, quite likely relieved that I had provided him with an easy excuse to disappear. But I had no desire to pass further hours fretting alone, while he buried himself in his dressing room or avoided further conversation by taking to his bed at some ridiculously early time.

'I don't know if you've eaten, Thomas?' I called after him. 'But Mrs Parsons has left out some cold meats and potatoes.'

'I don't want any food, thank-you.' He went up several steps before stopping to turn his head a little. 'But perhaps you should eat? If you haven't had something already, that is.'

'I'm not in the least hungry,' I replied, with some emphasis. 'What I could better do with is a drink, so I'm going into the library to pour one for both of us... and when you've changed, Thomas, I think we should at least talk a little – don't *you*?' His head dipped into a barely perceptible nod, though without turning any further towards me. No doubt he felt dogged by a sense of wary resignation.

He was brave enough to appear at the library door within just a few minutes. Though perhaps it was not bravery, nor even kindness, but simply a desire to have this *talk* of mine over and done with. During the endless hours of that day – and I had no interest in knowing how he had spent them and did not intend to ask – Thomas must have wondered what to expect of me on his return.

Would he find me in a state of well-stoked fury and out-rage, or was I more likely to have turned to ice, ready to ignore him until he could negotiate some humble means of approach? He would have known better than to picture me reduced to tears and pleading, though in such sudden and drastic circumstances, perhaps even these might have loomed as a dreadful possibility.

Tears would be difficult for him to cope with. Not because they would move him to pity, and therefore to guilt, but simply because he would have no idea at all what to do. Female distress did not lie within Thomas's experience; his mother had died long before he ever had chance to witness her crying, and he had grown up with-out sisters, under the control of a man who was tough and unyielding. Perhaps it was for these reasons he did not care for the sort of woman prone to dripping outbursts.

As it was, he must have felt some relief that these awful possibilities did not seem to be materialising. The two of us were simply to spend some time in the library, our conversation soothed by a generous measure of brandy. Uncertainty, though, must have remained. Just *what* was I planning to say to him?

In truth, despite the painful passing of many hours, I had very little in mind to say. It was the thoughts that lurked in Thomas's head I felt determined to know, for it would be intolerable for things to remain as they had been left that morning. Surely he could not assume that his state-ments across the breakfast table meant this unpleasant matter was concluded? Did he really see it, now, as over and done with? I wondered if he had even hoped, on returning to the house, that I would already have gone.

'I know I owe you an explanation, Mary.' I looked at him calmly, but without response. I was not willing to make this easier for him.

'I need to be honest with you – about what my situation is.'

He appeared to take thought for a moment, then picked up the glass and took a quick mouthful of brandy.

'So I'm going to be truthful. Completely truthful. Because there's no other way to deal with this.' Thomas replaced the glass and cleared his throat. 'The facts of the matter are these... ' He looked straight at me. I noticed the whites of his eyes were slightly bloodshot, his cheeks redder than usual and the skin dry. It was a less than healthy look but I recalled there had been a sharp wind throughout the day, and he had perhaps spent many hours walking in some wild, unsheltered part of the countryside. Like me, Thomas often chose to deal with difficulties in that way. I could see no signs that he had hidden himself in some inn, drowning the problems or summoning up false courage.

'You *must* believe me, Mary' – his insistence came across as a plea – 'when I tell you I have no wish, no wish whatever, for us to be parted. On the contrary... ' He cleared his throat. 'I would much prefer for us to remain living here as we are – in this house – together. I'm sure you must know that?'

I made no comment, just took my own sip of drink. His eyes turned away; he appeared to be staring at one of the book-laden oak shelves behind me. 'But I wish also to claim my inheritance.'

We were seated in the library's comfortable, red velvet chairs. Though they were not providing the usual comfort now, for neither of us was sitting back in a relaxed way, but stiffly and straight. I could feel a deep and unaccustomed ache down the full length of my back. At length, Thomas's face turned again and his eyes met mine. They were solemn, unsmiling.

'I've been informed that there's no legal method by which both these things can be achieved.' The eyes still did not flinch. I had to admire his calm in delivering this. Whatever turmoil he might have felt during the day, there was no sign of it now. 'And so, I have to tell you, that my intention is to lay claim to what has been bequeathed to me in my grandfather's will.'

Why did I feel a jolt, hearing something that I knew already? He added nothing else and we sat, opposite one another, in silence.

'And in order to do that,' I suggested after a while, finding the words oddly difficult to pronounce, 'I take it you've decided to... dispense with *me*?' My mouth felt dry, my tongue sticky and immobile.

'If you insist on thinking of it in such a way – then yes.'

'How are you thinking of it, Thomas?'

He drained the last of his brandy and rose to fetch the decanter, replenishing the glass and then doing the same, unbidden, to mine. He sat down heavily and leant back his head against the chair.

'Mary, what I'm trying to be is honest. If there was a means – any legal means at all –to keep us as we are, then I would use it.'

'But you're not prepared to sacrifice your inheritance, in order to keep us *as we are?*' It was a pointless question; some cruelty in me wanted to force him to state it.

He raised a hand to his face and rubbed a knuckle slowly against his cheek, as if in reflection. Though of course there was none.

'I have to say *no*. Because in truth I must tell you that I'm not prepared to do that.'

The hand came down. He stared into the remains of the liquid and swirled it round the glass. I could not judge whether the downcast look implied shame, or simple melancholy. If either of those. We were cast into a further bout of awkward silence, and I began to bend my own glass this way and that, watching the brandy swirl in obedience. The movements became more vigorous; I did not care if it spilt onto my clothes.

'The estate means too much to me, Mary,' Thomas announced at length.

'That's plain.'

'My work means a great deal, also. And I can hardly pursue it, can I, if I'm cast out of here penniless? Can I ask you to understand that?'

It was a relief to me, and perhaps wise on Thomas's part, that he did not suggest clinging to his possessions was some form of *duty*. The honest, straightforward acknowledgement that one thing is wanted more than another, and that it will therefore be chosen above another, is something I can accept. It is something I understand.

Perhaps it seems strange that neither of us mentioned the word *love*. Though looking back, it is not a surprise to me, for the word had never been passed between us. Not even at times of greatest passion or deepest intimacy. It was not something I yearned to hear, and I resisted any temptation to ask. Nor did I use the word myself. I think it is something better done without; it can create an unwanted burden.

'We always knew, didn't we,' Thomas added, 'that there might be a time when we would not be able to continue – in this way?'

He was sounding less nervous now. As at the breakfast table, perhaps he felt the worst of it was over. His intentions, even if a part of him recognised them as shameful, had been made clear to me and I had not created a terrible scene, had not screamed or shouted insults. He may have begun to feel a cautious sense of gratitude.

It passed through my mind, once again, that there could have been circumstances where deciding not to continue *in this way* would have caused him a weightier problem. Nature had been kind in not inflicting motherhood on me. Kind to Thomas, also, as it happened. But at that moment I would have gladly exchanged a few years of my life for the satisfaction of creating a little havoc. To announce 'But I need to tell *you* something, Thomas. I need to tell you that I'm carrying your child. I haven't mentioned it before, not until I was quite sure. But it *is* so! What an amazing thing, don't you think, after all this time?'

Nothing but a fantasy, of course. It was tempting to say it nonetheless, just to see how he would deal with such news. But I did not.

'What is it you want me to do then, Thomas? Or to be more precise – when am I expected to leave?'

What could Thomas say now that would not sound callous? His hand reached out for the decanter yet again.

'Do you think it's wise to drink any more of that? You'll have a very painful head tomorrow.'

'I'm sure I'll have a painful head anyway.' He poured himself a smaller measure than before. I shook my head as he held the container out towards my own glass, eyebrows raised in question. Draining it in one swift, head-back swallow, he replaced the glass on the side-table.

'We've had five joyful years. Carefree years. I know I owe you so much, Mary, such a very great deal... ' The voice trailed off. We were both aware that his carefree, joyful years were over. They were over the moment his grandfather drew a final breath even though, like the corpse, they were not formally dispatched until a week or so later; the day of the will .

'I do intend, of course, to settle some money on you,' he continued, 'though it can't be a vast amount, for the estate requires... '

'Don't trouble yourself! I fared well enough before I met you Thomas, and rest assured I shall fare well enough again. So keep your grandfather's hard-earned money! You and the precious estate will need it.'

I was aware that my tone had become hard, scornful; this was the only weapon in reach. The feel and sound of it was welcome; it offered protection against helplessness and tears. I shrank from the thought of appearing pitiable in Thomas's eyes.

'Please, I'm not trying to insult you. There's no need to drag pride into this. You have every right to receive something.'

'I have no right. No *legal* right. None whatever. I'm not your wife and you have no responsibility for me. In fact I've no more *right* to anything than a street woman would have. Or some little kitchen maid who's made herself available in your bed for a while.'

'Oh please, don't talk like that!' He stood up with abruptness. 'We need to end this conversation *now*.'

The unwelcome tears threatened and I blinked them back, rising a little unsteadily to my feet.

'No, Thomas, please. Do sit down again. Just for a moment. Please do.'

He did not seat himself again but hovered uncertainly in front of me, his face wretched. I had a sense that he might not be wholly safe from giving way to tears himself. With some hesitation, he reached out and took my hand but the hold felt nothing like his usual, warm grasp. We stood still, silent, and I was aware he was desperate for this encounter to end.

'Look, there's no need for any haste,' he managed at last, his voice slow, weary. 'We can talk about *when* in due course. And there can be no question of not – of there not being – some provision.'

I could not find it in me to form a reply. It seemed pointless. I felt an overwhelming tiredness and longed, suddenly, to be in bed.

'It's late,' Thomas said, as if he had noticed this. I felt a slight squeeze of my hand before he let it go.

He made once again towards the door and would not, I knew, be deterred from making an exit this time. But having pushed it open, he hesitated a moment further, half turning towards me.

'I will of course respect your privacy, Mary… from now on.'

'Thomas, please go! To hell with your *respect*. How sanctimonious you sound.'

He closed the door behind him, more firmly than necessary. I supposed he was now angry. His footsteps along the oak floor of the hallway towards the staircase suggested haste and intent. I sat down again, for some perverse reason choosing the chair normally occupied by Thomas. It was still warm, and I leant my head back into the cushioned hollow that his own head had made.

A silence settled heavily in the room. I felt a need to cross my arms and wrap them tightly around my body, digging my finger nails hard into the flesh down my sides.

39

Unsurprisingly, I lay on my own that night. Thomas must have decided even against using his dressing room, for I noticed on my eventual way to bed that the door of that room was ajar and a brief glance inside confirmed it to be empty, the coverlet untouched. Did he fear I might disturb him there? Perhaps he thought I might attempt to continue our conversation or invade his *privacy* in a way he would find difficult to deal with. Was that why he must have taken himself off to one of the guest rooms? He need not have been concerned, for I had no such will or desire. By that time my only thought was to lie down in quietness.

I must have gone to sleep quickly enough, for there was no later recollection of lying miserably awake beforehand. The brandy to thank for that, no doubt. It can be a good friend. My sleep was restless and dream filled, but at least it held me until morning, when I woke from the last of these unpleasant dreams with a sharp headache. I felt unkind enough to hope that Thomas had woken with an even worse one.

Headache or not, I had no intention of languishing. Nor did I intend to wait around the house, brooding and fretting the entire day, for I suspected that if Thomas had not already left then he would do so soon, and might well be absent for the best part of it. If yesterday had given him enough of rambling about in the wilds, then the business of the estate could be used as an excuse to be going here or there, visiting this person or another.

Sitting for a few moments on the side of the bed, hands pressed to the sides of my head in an attempt to reduce the pain, I decided to wash and dress quickly, without bothering to call on Sarah to help, and ask for porridge and tea to be served to me in the little sun room. That should at least wake me up and help push back the heavy feeling of inertia. And then I would set out – on foot – to visit Alice. My sister was the person I most needed at that particular moment; the only one I needed.

Normally I would have chosen to ride the distance. Sal and the trap were always at my disposal and I adored the freedom of taking myself out with them, especially on such a pleasant, sunny day. But this morning I felt the need to walk, to stretch my limbs and take deep breaths, to force my whole body into exertion. It might complain or rebel, but it would be given no option. And at a brisk pace the journey should take a little less than two hours.

My sudden arrival would be a surprise for Alice, of course. Rather to my shame, we had not set eyes on each other for many weeks. Probably for as long as four months, if not nearer five. But I knew she would be happy to see me. Her pleasure and relief could be relied upon as much as that of a faithful, if slightly neglected, dog.

Unpleasant as that comparison must sound, I mean no offence by it. Quite the contrary. What I needed was the certainty of feeling her arms around me in warm greeting, then for the two of us to sit down at her well-scrubbed table to have tea and cheese and bread. The pair of equally well-scrubbed children would be there as well, of course, vying for her attention. But whatever the surrounding irritations, there would be the comfort of being close to some-one who so cared about me.

As often, things were not quite as expected; Alice was too distracted to give me more than the briefest of welcomes. Fanny, I was told, was in some house down the street, caring for the child of a woman in the throes of labour. But little Martha and Luke had been feverish and full of misery throughout the night. They lay curled up together on a blanket near the fire, lit even on this warm day, and I saw at once they were covered in pink spots and angry blotches Although in a shallow, restless sort of sleep, the two of them were scratching as if they had fleas.

'They're too hot,' I said. 'Look, they're both sweating, Alice. Surely there's no need for them to be so near the fire?'

'But they do need to be kept warm.' I was reminded of Marguerite and her awful fever; of how close she had come to death. Alice knelt down to feel foreheads, to soothe and reassure, as I knew she would have done a dozen or more times that morning.

'Perhaps you're right. Help me to pull the whole thing a bit further away, will you?'

'I just hope *I* don't end up with whatever they've got!' I announced, though not with seriousness. Childhood fevers, illnesses and rashes must have rampaged through our house as we grew up, as they did through everyone else's. Not that I had any clear recollection of them; from the age of four or five we had seemed an unusually healthy, robust lot.

We began to drag the blanket, with its over-heated load, further away from the fire. Startled, the children opened their eyes, but while Martha's face seemed to grimace with some dismay at spotting me, Luke's mouth broke into a gummy grin. Strangely, Alice's rather odd looking little boy, with his untameable ginger hair and sharp, slightly rodent-like features, had taken to me from the start, failing to notice that I had very little interest in young children.

For the first time, his expectant, smiling recognition touched something in me. Though perhaps touched is not the correct word. It would be more truthful to say that it *stabbed*, for without warning I experienced a sharp feeling, a sense of something that was painful. I could not, in that instant, recognise what it was, but looking back I wonder if it was regret. Regret that I had no child, and was well-nigh certain never to have one.

'I'm going to try them again with bread and milk dip,' Alice said, before adding, a mite slyly, 'will you go and see if Pa's alright for me, Mary?'

'If you say I must.'

'I do say. Get yourself upstairs!' There was a teasing tone to her command and she appeared a little less anxious than before. Perhaps when young children are ill it is comforting to have another woman in the house, however ignorant or incompetent. At least I had got them away from the fire.

I did as I was told and climbed the stairs, knocking once on the bedroom door but opening it without waiting for a response.

He sat in his old wicker chair, shoulders and neck slumped forward, his mouth slightly open and the lower lip drooping. Watery eyes were slowly raised. They looked towards me without any sign of recognition.

'It's *me*, Pa,' I announced, before being thoughtful enough to add 'it's *Mary*.'

'Mary.' He repeated the word, without expression.

I approached, pulling across a three-legged stool, and sat down close, or as close as I could bring myself to be, for despite Alice's care, the smell that came from him was unpleasant.

'I've come to see Alice, Pa – and the children. They're ill, you know.'

'Ill.' Perhaps only repetition was possible today. I wondered if he knew who was speaking to him.

'I've walked here,' I continued, 'from Middleton.' There was no response. Did he remember there was such a place? Was he still aware, these days, that he lived in Cromford, or had once worked for the old mill? It was impossible to tell. Alice had said they came and went, the things he knew, what he remembered. I wondered if he realised it was Harry who had to put food on their table, these days. That Alice eked things out by selling her vegetable and fruit pies.

We sat in silence for a while, the only sound in the room being his regular sniffing. Despite it, some mucus was seeping from his nostrils. I took the small piece of clean rag that had been tucked into the sleeve of his shirt and made some effort to wipe it away. Replacing it in the sleeve, I wondered what to say next. Nothing came to mind and we continued to sit together, though not too uncomfortably, without words. My thoughts began to wander away, back to Lomberdale House. I wondered what time Thomas would be back; whether he would come back at all that day. And I wondered, when he did, what we would say to each other.

'*Tea*!' The word was loud and came out of the blue, causing me to start. 'Cup o' tea!'

'Alright.' At least there was a reason to get up and leave, even if it did entail carrying out an order from Pa. He could have his cup of tea, and I would make it with my own hands. A few years ago I might have had to fight a temptation to spit into the cup, but the venom in me seemed to have lost its strength. There was no possibility that I would ever love my father, no matter what his state, no matter what his suffering. When he died, I did not intend to make any pretence at mourning him. But my feelings were no longer brittle with hate. Hate seemed pointless. He was a pathetic figure now, a helpless, spent old dog with neither bite nor bark.

'He wants tea. I'll make it for him.' Alice smiled approvingly. 'And some for us, too, while I'm about it.'

'Oh Mary, I'm sorry, I've given you nothing, have I? And you look so tired. You *must* be tired, after that walk.' She peered at me more closely, feeling freer to do so, perhaps, now that she no longer feared her children were about to be carried off by a fever. I noticed an empty bowl beside the blanket, and presumed some bread and milk had been consumed. Both of them were now awake and fiddling with a few bits of wood-carved toys that had been put within their reach. One was a three-legged horse, which perhaps had once had a fourth leg. Harry went to more trouble for his children than many fathers did.

'In fact you really don't look well, I can't think how I didn't notice it before. Why don't you sit down and I'll see to the tea?'

'No, I'll do it. And then let's both sit down for a while – you look tired enough yourself – and I could eat a bit of something, if you've got enough to spare.' I was aware of light-headedness. The small helping of porridge was all I had eaten for the best part of two days.

'I'll get something. Mary, *please* sit down, you look very much as if you could faint.'

I gave in, allowing Alice to prepare Pa's tea, as well as our own. Sitting down, I placed my head on the table, wrapped by both arms. There was an urge to weep, but this time it was fought back; I had no intention of giving in twice to tears.

I said nothing to Alice while she hurried to make the brew, then listened to the heavy creak of the stairs as she made her way carefully up, to the lighter one as she came almost at once back down. Pa was not to be given any unnecessary care this morning; he had been elbowed along the queue by her children, and even by me.

40

'What?!' Alice whipped round from the fireplace to face me. She had got up from the table to poke the embers into more life.

'Exactly what I've said. He loses everything if I stay. And so he's told me that I must go.'

'Like that? As simple as that?'

'Well, it's a simple thing really, I suppose.'

And indeed it had never struck me quite so simply as at that moment, in voicing it. Poor Alice had no idea what to do or to say; there was something close to panic in her face and I was touched by the distress so plainly felt on my behalf.

'But after so long – that's cruel. It's wicked!'

'What else is he supposed to do? Give up his entire wealth?'

Knowing her romantic turn of mind, I imagined Alice would shout 'Yes, of course he must!' to that suggestion, but instead she frowned in puzzlement. Perhaps it seemed to her that I was trying to justify Thomas. Maybe I was. We sat in silence for a few moments, while she stared vacantly towards her children. They appeared to have a bit more life about them now, even struggling for possession of the three-legged horse. As Martha pushed her fist into Luke's face and he squawked in pain, Alice was woken from her thoughts and rushed across in an attempt to restore peace. This could only be achieved by lifting him up and sitting him on her knee at the table. The object of desire was seized by his more determined twin sister, who would have got it in any case, one way or another.

'You should have called her *Mary*,' I observed wryly, but Alice's thoughts were again elsewhere and she made no chuckle in response. Luke stretched a hand towards me and I reached out to tickle his fingers. Pink spots vied with ginger freckles on his hot, flushed face.

'Thomas must want to get himself married!' Alice announced.

I raised my eyes from Luke to look at her. 'Why do you say that?'

'If he didn't, he'd find a way round this, wouldn't he? A way of some sort. There's *got* to be a way for a man like that – who's so rich. Hasn't there? So that's what he wants to do.'

I fell silent. As so often before, she had cut through my confused meanderings with one simple statement. Despite the tea, my mouth seemed to go dry. Luke began to wriggle on Alice's lap, struggling to get down. She let him do so and he tottered unsteadily towards me, arms held out in anticipation. I scooped him up and sat him on my own knee, bending my face down into the fluffy, carrot hair. Had Alice been taking notice she would have been surprised; it was not the sort of thing I would normally do.

'I suppose he *would* want to marry, wouldn't he?' Alice spoke slowly, in the manner of someone thinking aloud, her forehead wrinkled again into a frown. 'You know, for the sake of the estate. So that he can pass it on – to a son.'

She stopped gazing into space and looked at me. 'Do you think that's why he's doing this to you, Mary?'

'I don't know. I suppose it could be… yes, might well be. I imagine that it could.'

My thoughts were floundering and my use of words along with them. What Alice had said struck me as a clear bit of common sense. I wondered how I could possibly have failed to think of the situation in those simple, stark and obvious terms, myself.

'I need more tea, Alice.'

I felt even less capable of providing us with this than before, and remained stolidly seated while she got on with the task. I became aware of Luke, who remained on my knee, and also recall thinking that brandy would have been a great deal more useful than tea at that moment. There would not, of course, be any in the house, and in any case Alice would not approve; would be horrified to know how much of the stuff I drank. She would inform me I was looking weak and peaky enough without taking strong drink, and that a cup of sweetened tea would do me far more good.

While she prepared this, I nuzzled into Luke's warm curls once again, and – almost in that instant it seemed – made two decisions. The first was that I would stay with Alice for the night. It would mean sleeping on the kitchen floor, wrapped in a rug or old blanket, for there was nowhere else. Pa occupied the smaller room above and nothing would persuade me to share it with him. The rest of the family made do with the other upstairs room, while Fanny used the tiny landing.

If Thomas returned home, he could spend the hours of darkness wondering where I was and feeling, I hoped, more and more anxious for my safety. The thought was a satisfying one. He might presume I had come to Alice but he could not be sure, and I suspected he would be reluctant to arrive at the door in order to find out.

The second decision was that I would rise very early (an inevitable thing anyway, as the hardness of the floor was unlikely to encourage sleep), fortify myself with a bowl of porridge and then walk home. To the place I still considered to be home. I hoped Thomas would be impatiently awaiting my return, if only to be assured I was safe and well. As soon as the two of us stood face to face I would insist on being told the straight, hard truth. Any expressions of misery or regret would be brushed aside.

Alice, too, must have been thinking. She did not turn round to me but her voice was firm as it broke into my own thoughts.

'I don't suppose you'd ever go back to *Tom*, would you, Mary? I mean, not even if he wanted you to?'

'Of course I wouldn't go back to Tom! How could you think of it?' I felt aggrieved that the thought had crossed her mind. 'Even if he begged me on his knees I wouldn't do it. And you do know, Alice, that he has some-one else there now?'

'Yes, I do, of course. Daisy.' She brought the pot over and put it on the table. 'But he so... adored you.'

'Daisy is far better for Tom.' I felt unreasonably annoyed with Alice for raising the subject of my husband. 'Don't *ever* say anything like that again.'

She shrugged her shoulders and poured the tea.

'Well then – more than ever – Thomas needs to see you right.'

' He doesn't need to do anything, Alice.'

'Yes he does. If he's a decent man. *Is* he a decent man?'

She was doing nothing to ease my irritation. Perhaps it was beyond ease. 'Of course he's *decent* – whatever you mean by that.' I fell silent for a moment or two before adding, in a resentful tone, 'I know very well you don't approve of him, Alice. Or of me.'

She made no denial of it. There was another shrug of the shoulders.

'What I feel about how it's been, well, it doesn't matter, does it? Thomas needs to do the decent thing. He needs to see you right.'

'Well perhaps he will, won't he? Or try to. But maybe I don't want to be *seen right*, as you put it. Don't you think I might rather walk away with my head up, and with a bit of pride?'

'Oh Mary, don't talk like a complete, damned fool!'

I was taken aback. The insult was uncharacteristic.

'*Look*,' she said, facing me with an expression as hard as she could muster, 'you're not too far off thirty years old. And you'll never want to be with anyone... well, in the village, will you? Not Tom or anyone else. No-one'– she searched for a suitable word – 'no-one who's just *ordinary*. Even if another man, well... '

I helped her out. 'Even if another man would want me after I've left my husband and then whored for five years.'

'Oh, *don't*.' She started to look upset, and I felt ashamed of allowing bad feeling to rise between us. 'What I'm saying,' she went on, with brave determination, 'is that

343

you're going to be on your own, very likely, aren't you? So you must be sensible, Mary. Being proud isn't going to keep you, is it? It'll be no good to you when you're old, and can't work. When you're ill, or if you've got noth… '

'Alright, alright, I understand.'

There was a sniff and a rapid blinking that suggested her own tears could be on their way.

'You've always got a home with us, Mary, you know that. But I can't see you being happy living back here, cooped up all the time with… '

'No, you're right, I wouldn't be,' I interrupted, then tried to smile at her. I knew it was wrong to be angry with Alice. 'But I'll stay here for tonight, if that's alright. And don't let's talk about this anymore. Not today. Not tomorrow. And no word to Harry.'

I gave Luke, who despite the loudness had managed to go to sleep in my arms, a gentle rock. 'For Heaven's sake, let's get this tea drunk. I'll bet it's already cold!'

The return walk seemed far more demanding than on the previous day, when I had walked the same distance in the other direction. For the last mile or two I found it a trial to put one foot in front of the other and there was a sense of relief when the familiar buildings of Middleton, and finally the house itself, loomed into view. Why exhaustion dogged me I do not know, for usually I had no lack of energy and stamina. Even spending the night on Alice's floor could not be blamed, for she had managed to unearth not only a couple of warm, serviceable blankets but also a thick piece of straw matting. This provided good protection against the stone floor and I had surprised myself by sleeping rather more soundly than usual. There was an early awakening, of course, for both Harry and Alice were up and about not long after daybreak, and Harry left the house soon after. I realised how very lazy I had allowed myself to become over the course of the last few years.

But perhaps exhaustion lay in the mind rather than in the body, for the closer I got to Lomberdale House, the more strongly I was dogged by a heavy sense of finality. It was a lonely, unsettling sensation, and I understood that I had made an error, five years ago. Not an error in agreeing to live with Thomas – I could feel no regret about that and never expected to feel it. The mistake I had made was a far graver one. It was imagining that such an experience could end without the most severe, crippling pain.

41

I decided not to enter by the front door, which would entail one of the servants coming down the hallway to let me in. Instead I would walk round to the back of the house, where by this time one or other of the doors should already have been opened and were likely to remain unlocked.

Though being seen by a servant was no great concern, I reminded myself, since all I had done was spend a night with my sister. What was remarkable about that? It might be thought odd, even eccentric, that I had chosen to go on foot and without a bag of any sort, but even this was unlikely to attract much comment. It was known that I was inclined towards unusual behaviour, including a liking for walks even when a carriage was on hand.

In any case, why on earth did it matter? This place was unlikely to be my home for very much longer; possibly not beyond that very day.

The scullery door was open, as predicted. This area led into a side kitchen, itself leading, via a short passageway, through to our breakfast room. I entered quietly and saw that Thomas was seated at the table in his usual place, facing the doorway. He appeared to have taken breakfast, for a bowl had been pushed towards the middle of the table, along with cup, saucer and jug. His hands lay on a still folded newspaper in front of him.

He looked up quickly as I entered the room and rose to his feet.

'My God, I was *worried* about you, Mary!' The tone suggested a mixture of relief and anger, like the mother who has just found a strayed child.

'Were you?' I sat myself down, with some relief, at the opposite side of the table and stared up towards him. 'There was no need, Thomas, I've been quite safe. But I'm exhausted, and parched as well. Could you ask Jane to bring in more tea? A very *large* pot of tea?'

He moved obediently across the room to ring the bell, then changed his mind and turned towards the door. 'I'll go and tell her,' he announced.

Perhaps he needed a few moments out of the room, a chance to settle his thoughts again after my sudden and bristly entrance. 'And some bread and jam also!' I called out after him. Alice's porridge had got me back home but there was a distinct need for more sustenance now. And at that particular moment, I sensed some inner strength would need to be summoned.

At first I chose to say nothing, not until a full cup of tea had been gulped down – still too hot – and I had devoured a large slice of bread, thickly spread with butter and straw-berry jam. Throughout this operation, Thomas sipped thoughtfully at his own drink, and avoided looking up and having to meet me in the eye. It was difficult to judge his state of mind. I sensed discomfort, certainly, and sus-pected he would love to have been anywhere other than in that room, sitting at a table opposite me. But there was also a tightness in his face, a certain set of the mouth and jaw, that suggested he would be immune from persuasion, should I decide to attempt it.

I poured myself a second cup and sat back a little.

'I was worried about you,' he stated again, more flatly this time.

'Well there was no need to be. Didn't you imagine I might have gone to Alice?'

'Of course, yes. That came to mind. But I wasn't sure. You could have told some-one, perhaps? Or at least left a note. It wasn't easy, waiting here, knowing nothing. I felt very concerned.'

His insistence on worry and concern was becoming an irritation.

'But not so worried as to come and find out.' I reached again for the milk, as the tea seemed a little bitter. 'But no matter, I'm here now. Perfectly safe, and also very hungry, as you'll have noticed. I'd forgotten what it's like to walk so far.'

'And how is everyone over there?'

'They're well, thank you.' My brief reassurance did not invite further discussion, for I did not want to sidestep into conversation about Alice, or her children's recent fever. The two of them had seemed well along the road to recovery that morning, if shouting and demands were anything to go by. Pa's wellness or otherwise I rarely mentioned to anyone and certainly was not going to discuss with Thomas just then.

An edgy silence ensued. Thomas stared into space, his face a picture of discomfort, while I continued to sip at my now cooling tea. After replacing the cup carefully in its saucer, I picked up a teaspoon and began to stir the remaining liquid slowly, studying the raised circles that formed and moved on the surface.

'Are you intending to get married, Thomas?'

The question took him by surprise, as it was meant to. He looked at me sharply.

'Why do you ask that?'

'Because I haven't asked it before, I suppose. And because, well – it strikes me as a rather likely explanation of things.'

'But… I've already tried to *explain* to you, Mary. I've asked you to see the difficult position I'm in – to understand how things are for me.' The voice sounded woebegone. 'And none of this is what I *want*!' he added, more emphatically. 'You do *believe* that, don't you? Because I've been happy, these years we've been together, Mary. Very happy. More so, even, than I imagined could be possible – at the start.'

'And so have I, Thomas.' It seemed only right to state the truth. I put down the teaspoon and looked at him. 'It hasn't been peaceful, always, has it? But then, I didn't want peace. I'm wouldn't have known what to do with it. We've never shirked from battle, have we, you and I?'

'We haven't, no.'

He forced a smile, but added nothing else. Clearly the important question was not going to be answered without insistence.

'And what is it that you want, Thomas – that you intend – regarding marriage?'

He sighed and I saw a slight rolling of the eyes; it was hard to tell whether from resignation or impatience. He leaned back as far as he could in the upright chair and folded his arms.

'Alright. I'd really hoped to spare you – to spare us – any further discussion of this, but I see you're intent on it.' There was a briefly thoughtful look, then his expression seemed to set itself into something more determined. 'So – since you insist on knowing – then yes. I do have to admit to you that I expect to marry at some time. Perhaps before too long, in fact. I believe it's *incumbent* on me, in honesty. And I don't think that's too strong a word.' He paused and looked at me. 'And I sincerely wish that I could marry you, Mary. But – quite aside from the will – we both know that's impossible. And there's no reason to imagine it won't remain so.'

I could not contradict him. Tom was not only alive but, as people seemed to take occasional pleasure in letting me know, in excellent health. In better health, very likely, than when I had care of him, for it seemed Daisy was everything I was not – a capable cook and housekeeper, a devoted mate who saw Tom's wellbeing as her principal task in life.

He did not discover this jewel himself, I later learned. Daisy, it turned out, was cook and general maid for dear cousin Abe of Matlock Bath, who was kind enough to find a means of throwing the two of them together. He had needed to find the means several times, for Tom was too shy a man to take such bait at once. But the good Abe persevered; he must have seen her suitability for Tom as clearly as he had seen the opposite in me.

All I felt was a vague sense of gratitude. Hearing she had moved into the cottage several months ago came as a relief, for it suggested my cruelty to Tom had not blighted his life for ever. And there was a chance she would give him the child that I had not; perhaps several children. Tom, for all his diffidence, was not without enthusiasm in bed. Nor would Daisy be, I suspected, for a sighting of them in Cromford had suggested a simple, plump and hearty earthiness which he might find reassuring, as well as enjoyable. She was the sort he should have picked in the first place, had he not been so foolish as to be misled by me.

And the two of them seemed cheeringly undeterred by the fact that they would never be able to marry, or not unless I was thoughtful enough to expire myself.

'*Incumbent on me*. Now there's a heavy phrase, Thomas. I don't think you've felt anything to be *incumbent* on you, before now, have you?'

His right hand made a small, dismissive gesture, perhaps acknowledging the pomposity of the claim. He had the grace to look a touch embarrassed.

'I'm sorry. But if a sense of duty sounds more acceptable, then I suppose that's what I have, and what I feel obliged to act upon – at this time.'

'I'm sure it amounts to much the same. But please don't worry. I shan't attempt to stand – or perhaps it would be truer to say *lie*? – between you and your *incumbent duty*. God forbid!'

Thomas closed his eyes and remained silent. I paused only to draw breath, for a miserable anger was rising in me and I could hear my voice becoming harsher. 'It seems I can only wish you success in your desire to marry, Thomas. You might be advised to seek out someone virtuous. A devout, religious woman, perhaps, with a strong sense of duty to match your own. No matter at all if she's numbingly dull.'

I let the thought of such a woman hover in my mind for a moment, and hoped it might be hovering in his.

'She may never feel desire for you,' I continued relentlessly, 'or do something so crude as to *seduce* you, but perhaps that won't matter, will it? Not if it's something you don't need any more. You can of course expect her to *submit* herself – dutifully – whenever you wish it. Or often enough, at least, to provide you with a son to leave your precious estate to… '

'Oh, do stop this!' Thomas's own voice was as loud as I had ever heard it. Having spat out my ugly little speech, I heard myself make a foolish sound, somewhere between a snort and a choke. Tears rose and began to spill down my cheeks before I could check them, a state of affairs that must have appalled both of us equally. I was aware that my face must look raw, even ugly, in its distress.

To his credit, Thomas did not retaliate with harsh words of his own. Nor did he do what he must have longed to and walk from the room – or not at once. He stood up and moved nearer to me. I had the sense that he wanted to touch me, even to take me into his arms, but he did not. Perhaps he feared worse emotion from me should he do so. Something wilder.

It was wise of him to refrain, for much as I longed for his arms to be around me, I suspect I was not open to being comforted. The tears, sudden as they had been and almost as quickly brushed away, had left a sensation that was humiliating. I felt naked, exposed, and now wished to be left alone. But Thomas continued to hover.

'I suspect, at the moment, anything I say is likely to make you angry,' he said.

'You're right, Thomas. It is.'

He cleared his throat as if preparing to continue, then changed his mind. 'I've caused you enough distress, I shall leave you in peace,' he announced before going – no doubt with relief – from the breakfast room.

'In the light of day,' I can remember Ma saying, 'things that've troubled you in the night, things you've lain awake worrying and fretting yourself over – well, they never seem quite so bad.'

This piece of wisdom has never been true for me. It was always in the daytime that I found a simmering annoyance could bubble into anger, that it was all too easy for me to push a simple disagreement towards a row. In the silence and darkness of night, my mind could calm itself, begin to discover peace and reasonableness again.

Sometime during the sleeplessness beyond dawn, I saw that the situation Thomas found himself in was a wretched one. What was he expected to do? What did *I* expect him to do? He was heir to an estate, heir to wealth. His life and upbringing had been lived in the promise of it. Under the immovable threat of it. There had always been an inevitability. Never had he suggested to me that this would not, at some moment, be the situation. He had made me no promises. On the contrary…

I was aware of the part of him that did not want this future, and had never wanted it. It was the part of Thomas that longed only to learn, to discover, to revel in the company of the like-minded. It was the Thomas who had no real idea of capital, of costs, of property investments, and little interest in knowing. It was the young man who had caused his grandfather constant vexation; driven him at times to open fury.

There must have been a few short periods of restless, unsatisfying sleep. It was still dark, though, when I got up. I put on my silk dressing gown, used the bowl and jug of water to wash, then opened wide the doors of any cupboard in the room that contained my clothes. None had been laid out for me the previous evening, for I had told a puzzled Sarah there was no need.

I chose around half a dozen dresses and put them on the bed, selecting only the plainer ones. I did not expect to have need of many dresses, and certainly of nothing that could be considered fancy. Most of the clothes in these cupboards would be left; Thomas could do what he liked with them. There were likely to be plenty of grateful recipients around, or if he chose he could simply have them heaved onto one of the regular fires that disposed of debris and foliage from around the grounds. I did not much care.

To these were added a few slips, petticoats and stockings. I had come into Thomas's life with very few garments, I recalled grimly, and there was a pride in me that was prepared to walk out of his house with only a very few more. Though after a moment's hesitation I did pick up a hairbrush and added it to the modest pile; a handsome thing, the back and handle in plated silver with my initials embossed. Thomas had bought it for me in London some months before, as a birthday present. I still have it.

None of this could yet be packed, for our bags – there were a good number of these, in various sizes – lay in another cupboard, in a different bedroom. It was a corridor length away from this one, and possibly where Thomas had decided to spend his night.

Getting back into bed, I closed my eyes, aware of the small extra weight over my legs. For some reason, I now felt more relaxed, more at peace, though sleep did not return. I lay in stillness, aware of my deep, steady breathing, allowing my mind to float away at its own will.

42

Thomas did not avoid coming into the breakfast room. He entered – if with slight diffidence – at the usual time, as I had known he would. I had already asked Jane for tea and porridge for both of us and she was in the process of laying these things on the table as he sat himself down.

'Would you pour the tea for us, Jane?' My tone was light, cheerful. I saw Thomas glance towards me in surprise.

'We're both feeling tired this morning. Tired and very lazy!'

'*Course* I will, Madam.' Her voice, too, was cheerful, as it always was. I was going to miss her. I would miss them all. I wondered what Thomas would decide to say to them, for I did not intend to give anyone an explanation myself.

'Are you alright, Mary?' He had waited for Jane to go. His face, as I had already noticed, was wan; there was a tired greyness about it that did not look healthy. It struck me that he had not looked healthy for some time.

'I shall be leaving Lomberdale soon,' I said. 'Shortly after this breakfast, in fact. That's if you could arrange for the carriage?'

Thomas had barely tasted his porridge. He put down the spoon.

'Well I can, of course. But you know, Mary, you don't have to leave so quickly. There really is no need.'

'There is need, Thomas. We both know there is.' He stared down at his dish, making no move to pick up the spoon.

'Let's eat,' I suggested, scooping up a good mouthful myself. It was rich and creamy, a different concoction from the one that had helped keep me alive until five years ago. I nodded towards Thomas's dish. 'Put some honey in it. It'll make you feel better.' He did as he was bid, and I finished my own helping without further words, then pushed the bowl to one side. While Thomas ate a little more, I reached across for the teapot and shared what remained in it between the two cups.

'I'll need somewhere to live, Thomas,' I said, replacing the pot on its cork mat. His spoon stopped in mid-air. He looked at me. 'A small house,' I continued, 'a cottage, even. But a respectable one.' I stopped for a second. 'One that *I* will choose.'

There was an almost imperceptible nod. He laid the spoon on the table again.

'It would need to be done properly,' I went on. 'Something – legal. A document drawn up by Mr Hodgson, and signed. I want a promise that the estate will pay the rent on it for my life. That it will carry on paying, even if… ' I looked straight at him. 'Even if *you* die first.'

Thomas stared back at me, his eyes wide, then looked down, frowning. There was a silence while he seemed to pull his thoughts together.

'That's not unreasonable,' he said at last, without looking up. But at length he raised his face to me again. 'I never intended that you should go with nothing.'

357

'But that's not quite all, Thomas.' Unsure if I could hold my nerve, I delayed a moment and stirred the tea. 'I shall need an allowance to live on. A modest one – but liveable.'

He winced a little, I thought. There was no reply for a while. Both of us remained very still.

'Of how much?'

'I don't know. Not precisely. Enough to eat, to live decently. I'm not talking of greed, Thomas.'

There was a sigh, but he had the goodness to remain seated, to keep looking at me. Not, I thought, with a face of unkindness.

'I know you're not,' was what he said, at last.

Just a short while later, Thomas set off for the Hall. He would, he said, arrange for John to come across for me in the carriage.

'I shall stay at the Hall,' he told me. 'I do *not* want to watch… as you leave.' It was difficult to tell whether he was close to tears. Perhaps it was sheer tiredness that caused his eyes to look rheumy. 'And nor could I bear to come straight back here. I've decided to set off for London, tomorrow morning – from the Hall. And to stay there for a time.'

There did not seem anything for me to say. I nodded, resisting the temptation to touch him. I had a keen sense that luring him to the bedroom would be an easy thing at that moment. As easy as it had ever been. But that it would be without purpose.

He swallowed. 'If you could write to Mr Hodgson soon, Mary – tell him where you are? Then he'll know to… to *deal* with things.' I noticed Thomas did not ask me where I would be.

Thomas may have decided not to witness my departure, but I watched his. I was standing at an open, upstairs window in the front of the house. I heard the main door open and close, saw him appear from beneath the wide, stone porch, heard the sound of gravel under his feet as he strode down the driveway without looking back. He carried no bag, but a servant could always be sent over to collect whatever was needed. I wondered which of the two houses he would choose to live in, on his return from London. It was hard to imagine it would not be the beloved Lomberdale.

I watched until Thomas had disappeared from sight and sound, and indeed for many minutes after both of those were gone. I knew there was little chance I would ever set eyes on him again.

It cannot have been too much later when Sarah tapped on the door of the small drawing room, just before opening it. Hard to say, though. I had been sitting there for a while, certainly, half a dozen or so books on the table beside me and thirty or more in two piles at my feet.

'Mr John's arrived, Madam, with the carriage. He says it's for you.' I had heard it, of course. Sarah looked puzzled and uneasy. I wondered if she had seen the chunky bag I had already put to one side of the front door. She was used to seeing us go away, but normally there would be instructions, bustle, arrangements being talked of. And there would be Thomas at the centre of it all.

'That's right.' I got to my feet. 'I'll need something for these books, Sarah. Could you find me a couple of boxes? And then go and get James to carry them to the carriage for me – they'll be heavy.' I could see James in the garden from where I sat.

'Of course.' She looked unhappier still. It was tempting to say something, to explain, but I held my resolve not to do so. It was a task that would be left to Thomas.

John put out his arm to guide me up into the carriage. His look of gentle concern threw me, for a moment. It must have been a fatherly look, I think – that of an affectionate and worried father. The sort of look I had never experienced.

He was still holding my elbow as I bent to take a seat inside. 'Now, I'm to drive you to wherever you tell me,' he said. 'But Mr Bateman – well, he did say that you might like it to be the inn. The Greyhound Inn, was where he said – in Cromford. If you'd perhaps want to stay there for a while? Until things are… you know, a bit more settled for you.'

I fought the temptation to fling my arms around the neck of this gentle, elderly man in an outburst of relief and gratitude.

'I *would* like that, John. Very much. Thank you.'

I had not wanted to arrive at Alice's door. Dreaded it. My sister loved me and I would have been welcomed; she would have wanted to listen, would have tried to comfort. But I felt no desire to talk, and could not bear the thought of sympathy. Least of all did I want to live within the noise of the place, to be squeezed around the old table with

Harry and Alice and Fanny and the children. To edge twenty times a day past Pa, now so often asleep in the room downstairs, bent over in something halfway between a chair and a bed. That household was crowded and busy, and I shrank from the thought of having to be part of it, even for a few weeks. The simplest of rooms at the Greyhound seemed like a gift from Heaven.

43

A little over a month later, I was installed in my home – a small, terraced house in Wirksworth. I chose the town because it is not too far from Cromford but separate, distinct. It is a bustling little place that reminds me, in some ways, of Bakewell, though it is plainer. My house is in a quiet street not far from the town's market place centre.

It is not *my* house, of course, but I have now lived in it so long – for more years than anywhere else – that I think of it as mine. The whole terrace belongs to a wealthy family, none of whom I have ever met. A Mr Turner, tucked away in a tiny office above one of the shops in town, acts as the family's agent. He was a young man when I moved in, but is now quite old; a similar age to me, I imagine. The rent, he once told me, is paid to him twice a year, and each month I visit him to receive my allowance. I understand everything is made over to Mr Turner from a trust, set up by the Middleton estate. Nothing to do with Mr Hodgson, of course, these days. He died years ago.

The sum I receive, which rises by a very small amount every two or three years, is enough. I am able to eat, and also to save a little each month for my regular visits to bigger, more interesting places. Places that teem with real life, with restless energy. Streets and squares that offer libraries and bookshops and museums and theatres. The railways, of course, have now become a thrilling prospect! So much quicker, so much easier; they will make even more distant places possible. I fail to understand those who say they do not want them.

I took to this house at once. It consists only of a front room, with a small kitchen at the back, and just one room upstairs, which is bright, with windows to both front and back. The downstairs room, too, has good light and when I walked into it a large chair had been pulled into the sunny, bay window, inviting me, it seemed, to sit and read. There was a blank wall that I decided would soon be bookshelves, top to bottom and edge to edge. They probably make the room look crowded and even smaller, but no matter. It is *my* room, for I do not intend to share my life with anyone else.

It took me a little while to find the house; there were others I was shown that did not feel right. Though it was a rightness that had little to do with comfort, for some of them offered more space and better furnishings than the one I chose. Mr Hodgson did not try to hurry me, and I assumed that Thomas had told him not to do so.

Thomas, in any case, was probably in London for much of that time. He had friends there and plenty to occupy himself; I could not imagine he would be in any hurry to return. Though the estate and its new responsibilities might have started to weigh on him. It may be that they pulled him back earlier than he intended to the Hall. And to Lomberdale.

It was impossible not to wonder what his feelings would be on arrival, to ponder on his state of mind. I did not try to force myself not to, for I found it easier, just then, to let the mind go wherever it chose. The possibility occurred to me that Thomas might feel sadder, lonelier, in the luxury of those mansions than I felt in my simple space in Wirksworth. But it was impossible to know.

What I do know is that the funeral of Thomas's grandfather took place on the first day of June, in the year eighteen forty-seven. That within days of it I had left Lomberdale House. I remain clear – crystal clear – about those times.

Barely two months later, on the fifth day of August, I was seated in the young Mr Turner's poky little office. In his careful, laborious style, he had counted my money aloud, placing notes and coins in separate little piles on the table between us, before asking me to sign for receipt. Once he saw the money was tucked safely into my small, leather bag, Mr Turner picked up a newspaper that was lying on a heap of documents to one side of us. I noticed, as he held it towards me, that it had already been folded to an inside page.

'I don't know if this might perhaps be of interest to you? It's a bit of news that came to my attention – about Mr Thomas Bateman, at Middleton.' He would know I had some connection with the estate, of course. I am quite sure he was unaware of what it was.

'Yes. Thank you.'

He had drawn a circle around a few lines of print that made up just one of a long column of announcements. It looked shorter than any of the others, above or below. The announcement inside the circle, I saw, was a brief, simple one.

"Register Office, Bakewell. Monday the second of August. Thomas Bateman of Middleton-by-Youlgreave to Miss Parker of the same place."

Sarah. For some reason her Christian name did not appear, but there could be no doubt. There was only one Miss Parker known to Thomas; only one Miss Parker *of the same place*. Our servant; the sister of old friend Will. I sat for what must have seemed a strangely long while and stared at it.

'May I take this?'

'Of course you may, Mrs Mason.'

I do not know why I wanted to take it. Perhaps to reassure myself, later, that I could not possibly have misread the words.

I had not misread them, of course. Just three days before, Thomas had married Sarah; it was as simple and clear as that.

There had never been anything but a respectful fondness between the two them; of that I was quite sure. Had there been anything else, I would not have missed it. Sarah was as guileless and straightforward a girl as Ellie, if a calmer, more thoughtful one. And I knew she had become as fond of me as she was of Thomas, that her distress on seeing me leave the house was heartfelt. She was intelligent enough to know I would not be back.

Thomas had decided to marry. He had decided to marry without delay.

He may have judged it the only way to prove – to who-ever might demand the evidence – that I was gone. That I was gone and would not be returning. To show the world, or at least the part of it that resided around the small-minded and gossipy Middleton, that he was now a respectable man, worthy of taking charge of the estate. I could almost hear Mr Hodgson's voice: 'It could well be wise, sir, if I might be bold enough to suggest it, for you to consider the benefits of bringing... well, a *lady* into the home. People will see a wife – and a family too, in due course – as a very *reassuring* thing.'

He had chosen some-one well beneath him, which was likely to be the cause of a good few snide remarks. But they would not last forever and he had, after all, dealt with worse. At least Sarah was a spinster – an available, conven-iently placed one. She was a good organiser; his house would be well managed. She would fulfil all her duties and allow Thomas to get on with his work.

Sarah was also a perfect twenty-two years old to Tho-mas's almost twenty-six. Her face might be unremarkable, if not a little on the plain side, but she appeared to be a fit and healthy young woman, who had every chance of providing him with an heir.

The thought of that, of all that was implied in it, felt like a sudden gash to the flesh; a profound, injuring one. It dawned on me that Sarah must now have shared a bed with Thomas for the last three nights. How many times had he already possessed her?

I wondered if she aroused in him the strength of passion and need that I had; whether he would even want her to. I wondered if he had seen her naked, standing in front of him. Whether she would pull him down on top of her as she lay on the bed, while each of them ripped clothes from the other with burning impatience.

I could not imagine any of this being so. The truth must be that these were not the things that Thomas was seeking. He was seeking now to be respectable, to be accepted. To be seen as *the* Mr Thomas Bateman of Middleton Hall. Looking to pursue his work without undue distraction. Perhaps he had even decided to be undisputed master of his own house, and to be that person without the danger of dissent or argument. There would be no risk of rows with Sarah. Or not for a very long while.

And with regard to *pleasure*... well, he would not be without it, of course. But he would need to content himself with something milder, more placid, than he had enjoyed with me. Of that I felt certain.

Milder or not, it was enough to result in a child less than a year later – a daughter, christened Sarah. I did not miss the newspaper announcement this time. And nor did I miss the others, over the next several years. I made a point of perusing that column, which always lurked on the same inside page. No issue of the regional newspaper was ever missed.

Eleven years after their wedding at Bakewell Register Office, Thomas and Sarah had four daughters and a son. How different must Lomberdale have been from when I was there! Surely so much noisier, more bustling? There would be nurses and tutors about the place, there would be more servants than we had needed, there would be activity inside and out. If Thomas wanted quiet, undisturbed study then he had not, I thought wryly, gone about things in the right way to ensure it. I wondered how he felt about this buzzing family life; how much he chose to be a part of it, how often he was away.

Perhaps my attention to this suggests I did not manage to *live*, in any real sense, during those years; that I existed, in some strange and sad way, only through Thomas. This was not so; it has never, at any time, been so. I have always lived in the way I chose, and I choose it still.

My house is in constant danger of being submerged in a sea of books – a quite ridiculous number of them quickly spread beyond the shelves and are now to be found on top of cupboards, under chairs, piled up in corners. Occasionally I am forced, reluctantly, to give a few away, but they are soon replaced by others. Thank God, my eyesight is still very good, despite what it has had to cope with over the years.

And I still live, as ever, through my visits, my *travels*. That thrill of being on the move, of going somewhere unknown, has never faded. My great love is for cities, and next year I intend to leave these shores for the first time and to visit Paris.

It is well worth making do with old clothes, or having a week or two without meat, in order to make sure these things are possible. Here and there I come across interesting people, of like mind. Or as *like* as is possible, for I recognise myself, now, as an oddity. I see that I have always been one, but have very likely become more so, over the years. With a few of these people I manage to stay in touch – I have become quite a letter writer.

Marguerite, too, writes to me, now and then. She is the only one of my brothers and sisters who has enough skill to do so with any ease, but she was lucky. By the time Marguerite was a few years old, a school had opened in the village. A school that merited the name, not the paltry, two hours of a Sunday affair that was what the rest of us had to make do with.

She is also the only one of us to marry someone from another place and to move away. Occasionally I make the trip to Manchester to visit her. Marguerite, I think, understands my life a little better than the others are able to.

There is no doubt the rest of my family view me as an eccentric, even though that might not be a word they would know. They are content to see me just now and then, to assure themselves I am not ill. Even Alice, I think, is happy enough with that, surrounded as she is with offspring of various ages, and with grandchildren. She has Fanny to provide her with womanly company, for Fanny has never left that house, never married. She has become the helpmate, and the spinster aunt of many. Not a talkative or a warm one, I think, but always there, always on hand. Part of the general clutter of the place.

I am an aunt too, of course, but not a close one. There are so many children – it would be hard for me to keep in touch with the ups and downs of the family broods from here, even if I should choose to. Though I do not choose to. I lead the life I want to lead, and I leave them to theirs.

369

Fourteen years after his marriage – and ten years ago, almost to the day – I caught sight of another announcement. It was in a different column and could easily have been missed, so used had I become to perusing the births. But this notice stood out at the top, and had its own heading. It was written in larger print than others, and at greater length. It told me that Thomas was dead.

He was thirty-nine years old, the notice said. The words spoke of his failing health, of a period of incapacity, of a sudden and terrible haemorrhage during the early hours of a morning. They spoke of great sadness, of a painful loss to the community. Of the debt owed to him by Archaeology. Of his stricken and grieving family.

It was not possible to read it all, just then. The words became a blur, for my own grief was instant and overwhelming. I was taken unawares by the bitter tears, by the raw and awful sounds of my acute distress. The tears I shed were of the sort Thomas would once have found impossible to deal with, that would have driven him from the room.

It took me a while to read the whole notice of his death. He was not, it turned out, to be buried with his grandfather in the vault at Hartington. I can only think he recoiled from that idea as much as I did. He had chosen to be laid to rest in the ground at Middleton, at a quiet spot close to the chapel but a little further up the hillside.

I go to his grave, on occasions. Not often, admittedly, but I do go. A stone urn has been placed on the monument, a replica of something pre-historic. He would never have chosen to risk a real one there; I imagine all those are still safe and secure in his museum. Though who looks at them, I wonder, these days?

I go to his grave because I know Thomas saved me. He took me from a world that would have brought frustration to the point of madness, eventually. He held out to me the life that I wanted, the learning I craved, and I have these still. Things are simpler, these days, than before, and poorer. Compromised, in certain ways, and without the finer touches. But I have them.

I am content in this life of mine, in which new experience and new knowledge always beckon. Content, also, in leading it on my own. There could never have been a satisfactory replacement. Nor will there be.

Does that mean it was love, I had for him, of a sort? And have still?

Perhaps so.